NEVER BE THE SAME

What Reviewers Say About MA Binfield's Work

Not This Time

"I have to say, MA Binfield knows how to write yearning. Sofi and Maddie circle around their feelings for each other throughout the book, and the tension is delicious. I was definitely kept up past my bedtime because I couldn't wait to read the next angsty chapter."—*Lesbian Review*

One Small Step

"I really loved this book and the gradual way Iris and Cameron's relationship builds. It feels very authentic as they both gain confidence from their genuine care for one another. The author takes time to carefully build something real between the two of these women. This book kept me intrigued."—*Bookvark*

"I lost myself in Iris and Cam's growing feelings and doubts in a very enjoyable way. They're both endearing characters, and the web of friends and teammates around them is full of interesting people." —*Jude in the Stars*

"The author crafts a deeply emotional romance that is as grounded in stark reality as it is elevated by the ethereal nature of love. …*One Small Step* is a tremendous romance début. MA Binfield's portrayal of a couple in search of the courage to fight for the love that they deserve is written with sheer honesty, humor, and heart."—*All About Romance*

Visit us at www.boldstrokesbooks.com

By the Author

One Small Step

Not This Time

Never Be the Same

NEVER BE THE SAME

by

MA Binfield

2021

NEVER BE THE SAME

ISBN 13: 978-1-63555-938-5

This Trade Paperback Original Is Published By
Bold Strokes Books, Inc.
P.O. Box 249
Valley Falls, NY 12185

First Edition: August 2021

CREDITS
Editor: Cindy Cresap
Production Design: Susan Ramundo
Cover Design By Tammy Seidick

Acknowledgments

Huge thanks to my editor, Cindy Cresap, who improved this book immeasurably, and is still helping me with my Britishisms and comma splice with a good deal of patience.

A socially distanced hug to all the wonderful people at Bold Strokes Books, who make this whole thing a lot easier for us authors, and who make me feel proud to be part of the BSB family.

I miss London and I miss Brighton—in fact, I miss everywhere that isn't my house right now—so I'm grateful for the opportunity to revisit some favorite haunts with this book. Watching the sunset on the beach next to the crumbling West Pier is highly recommended, as are the seafront fish and chips! And although Café Brunest is long gone, I still hanker after Estelle's pies.

Finally, to EVERYONE on the frontline during this dreadful pandemic—whether you're a part of our wonderful NHS, working in retail, keeping the trains and tubes running, or caring for the vulnerable—I thank you from the bottom of my heart. Every one of you has my admiration.

Dedication

For Helen Lewis, with love

CHAPTER ONE

.

C asey felt grimy and more than a little grouchy. Her clothes looked like she'd slept in them—which she had, sort of, if you added up the various catnaps she'd managed during the flight—and being back in London meant not just dealing with her mom's latest mess, but facing everything she'd up and walked away from a year ago.

She loaded her suitcases onto a trolley. At least she'd arrived in time for Pride and she would get to see David. She resolved to fix her mood and try to count her blessings. She pushed the trolley toward the arrivals hall.

"Ow." Casey felt a sharp pain across the back of her calves as something hit her from behind. She turned, ready to let off a stream of expletives, and found herself face-to-face with a blond-haired woman gripping a trolley laden with a huge pile of suitcases. Casey had enough good manners to swallow the curse words she'd been ready to offer.

"I'm sorry, I lost control. It's too heavy to steer properly. I hope I didn't hurt you." The voice was breathy, the accent American, somewhere southern.

"It's okay." Casey fought the urge to lean down and rub her legs where the low metal bar at the front of the trolley had hit her. "It does look pretty heavy." Casey pointed at it. "Here for the weekend?" She tried for a joke.

The woman—perfectly turned out in a blue summer dress with accessories fully coordinated—was now looking at Casey with a seductive smile. She was attractive and she knew it.

"I'm running away." She lifted a sculpted eyebrow. "Want to come? I surely could do with a handsome stranger to make the adventure a little more exciting."

Casey blinked.

It'd taken a while, but she'd eventually gotten used to the forwardness of women in the States, and she'd gotten very good at deflecting. But she hadn't been expecting a come-on like this in London. And not at the airport. So now she was gawping at the woman rather than coming back with some witty flirtatious banter of her own. Not that witty flirtatious banter had ever been her thing.

"It was worth a try." The woman spoke into the silence, moving her trolley backward and forward to illustrate what she meant. She smiled. "Hope it didn't hurt too much, but sometimes a gal's gotta try. I saw you from across the hall and couldn't resist introducing myself."

"It hurt." Casey found words finally. There was a compliment somewhere amongst the woman's madness. "Next time just ask for a phone number before that whole assault-a-stranger-with-a-trolley move."

"Can I have your number?" The woman winked.

This time Casey laughed.

"You're something else." Casey guessed the woman was looking for a bit of no-strings-attached fun. But she had also just rammed Casey with her trolley in the hope of an introduction. She shook her head. "Sorry. My girlfriend wouldn't appreciate that." It was a lie. Casey was as single as the Pope, but right then, it seemed like the safest response.

"Okay." The woman U-turned her trolley with surprising ease. "But you're a honey. Tell her she's a very lucky woman." She moved away, leaving Casey bemused. She ran a hand down her wrinkled shirt. She wasn't feeling much like a honey.

She tried to let herself be flattered by the attention, but Casey wasn't one of those women who felt comfortable with a big come-on like that. She was a meaningful glances, hidden feelings, and long courtship kind of woman. She shook her head. Maybe things would be easier if she wasn't.

Casey made her way toward the exit, ready for the shock to her system that the chaos behind the doors would provide. She glanced at her watch with a yawn. It was still on Portland time and told her that it was three a.m. She willed herself awake and pushed her trolley out into the hall, blinking as she took in the scene in front of her. Families festooned with balloons and welcome signs. Rows of vigilantly bored drivers standing along the edge of the exit walkway holding up names hopefully. And ahead of her, dozens of café tables overflowing with people, reminding her that a strong black coffee was just what her body needed.

Heathrow wasn't that much different from any other airport of course—just big and busy, like the rest of London. She'd had no choice but to leave all this behind a year ago, and while she'd missed some of her friends—and even her mom—there wasn't all that much of this noisy, congested, snake pit of a city that she missed. But London was where she was, and she was going to get done what she needed to get done and leave as quickly as she could.

Casey made herself scan the signs properly and caught her name in large red letters on the screen of a tablet held by a tall man in a smart gray uniform wearing a chauffeur's cap. She approached him and he smiled warmly. Jeez, he was handsome. David had obviously started to recruit Abercrombie & Fitch models as his drivers now. Nice.

"David sent me for you. He's waiting in the car upstairs." Handsome model guy smiled again. "He said to make sure we bring him a coffee."

"Sounds like David." She laughed. The idea of seeing him lifted her mood.

This trip to London hadn't been planned. Her mom had had another crisis, and according to her brother—who lived a lot closer than the fourteen bloody hours it had so far taken her to get here—needed help. Help he was seemingly unwilling to give her. Casey had vacation days in the bank, and Gina had happily agreed to some extra leave, giving her a month to sort things out and get back home to Portland.

In fact, Gina had been a little too happy to agree to the time off, suggesting Casey needed "some proper rest and recreation." The last two words said with the kind of smirk that only Gina—a serial womanizer—could get away with. But Casey needed a clear head to deal with what being back in London was going to throw at her. And she wasn't sure that the kind of "recreation" Gina had in mind would help with that. She picked up the coffees and followed her driver and her trolley into the elevators to the parking garages.

"Hey, handsome." Casey could see David scrolling through his phone while leaning against the side of a shiny black Bentley. He looked up at the sound of her voice and then moved quickly toward her, arms outstretched to wrap her into a big hug.

Casey was tall—five eleven in her socks—but David was a big bear of a man and one of the few people capable of making her feel petite. She let herself enjoy the feel of him. She missed sex—though she'd never admit it to Gina—but she missed being held like this almost as much.

He pulled away and put his hands on her shoulders.

"You look well. You've lost some weight but somehow kept all those muscles." He squeezed her arm. "I thought you'd be as big as me by now eating all that mac 'n' cheese." He patted his round stomach. "Got any weight loss tips?"

Casey laughed. "I have, but none you'd thank me for. Gina's persuaded me to go vegan. No butter, no cream, definitely no mac 'n' cheese."

"Gina's a great boss, but she is the roommate from hell. I figured that out when she tried to make me eat kale salad as if it was an actual meal." He raised an eyebrow, the picture of camp. "But since you're not sleeping with her, you don't need to try to impress her with all that healthy living crap."

"She's the only one of us that can cook. Her food is better than anything I'd ruin, vegan or not. I'm letting her feel like she's improving me, while also getting her to cook all my meals." Casey smiled. "And I can always grab a burger when I'm out if I'm feeling the need for something meaty."

"Oh, Casey, I'm trying so hard not to tell you just how often I feel the need for something meaty."

"Ew. I might have missed you, but I have not missed your penis-related double entendres."

He took a bow before opening the car door.

"Come on, the traffic on the M4 is crazy today. We'll have plenty of time to catch up on the way. Mikey." David pointed at the trolley. "Help the lady with her luggage." He winked at Casey. She bristled as David expected her to.

"I can manage, Mikey, thanks." He popped the trunk, and she hauled her suitcases inside with ease. She could handle her own luggage.

Casey settled into the back seat with David as Mikey pulled out of the parking space and headed for the exit.

"Thanks for meeting me. It feels very weird to be back."

"I bet, but it's good to see you. I might be too much of a Brit to say it as often as I should, but I miss you."

"I miss you too. And thanks for finding me some work too. Mom's in a crazy mess and I really need the extra cash. There's a chance she might lose the house." Casey had told him most of the sorry saga a couple of weeks before.

"I'm happy to have you back. You were always one of my most popular drivers. And it's brilliant to have another woman on the team because some customers actively ask for one."

"You sound like a pimp."

He laughed. "I am. Of sorts. I'm serious though. I've only got two women drivers, and one of them only wants to work daytimes. The number of times we've had to turn down some Chinese billionaire because he won't trust a male driver to take his daughters to Harry Potter World." He grinned. "Okay, so it's only happened once, but it still upset me. And what with you fluent in all those languages, you're a real asset."

"Yeah, that's right. I can do Cockney, three sentences of French, and a lot of bad language." For different reasons, neither of them had done well at school. It was a standing joke between them. And a small miracle they'd both done okay for themselves.

"You'll need the bad language. London drivers haven't got any better while you've been gone." He nudged her. "But I've got the best job for you, starting tomorrow, for two weeks." He bounced a little in his seat and Casey couldn't help but smile. "You're going to love it."

"Cool." She doubted she would, but she wasn't in a position to be turning down work. She'd never enjoyed driving. It was what she'd done when her chosen career was no longer possible. And somehow driving always reminded her of that—of the loss, of having the job she'd loved taken away from her.

"Actors, actresses. In London for some promotional work and filming an episode of their hottest-thing-in-town queer TV show. *The West Side.* Even you must have heard of that one. They need a hottest-thing-in-town queer driver, and I thought you'd be perfect."

"Actors? A TV show?" Casey frowned. "I mean, I'll do it obviously, but I don't even own a TV. I hope they're not going to expect me to sound interested."

"There'll be lesbians. Attractive ones. And they're going to love you in that chauffeur's cap. It's the best welcome home job I could have given you. You could try to look a bit more grateful." He smiled as he said it.

"I'm not wearing the cap." Casey had had this conversation with him already. "I'll wear the suit—minus the tie—but not the cap. And since it seems I'm the only queer woman driver you have for this very important job, I think I'm in the 'driving seat' when it comes to dictating terms." She took as much of a seated bow as her seat belt would allow.

David groaned at her. "Okay, okay, you win. No cap." His phone rang. "But it's your loss." He put the phone to his ear, and Casey listened in briefly as he began to curse at whoever was displeasing him.

She sighed. The last thing she wanted was to be driving around a bunch of status-obsessed airheads pretending to hate their privacy being invaded, while ringing ahead to make sure the paparazzi caught their every move. She stifled a yawn. She was tired, but now she was cranky too. *The West Side*? She'd never heard of it.

David ended the call.

"Oh yeah, something else I meant to tell you. The schedule for the TV people is really full on, so I've asked Tania to help you out."

He had a sheepish look on his face, and Casey waited, knowing there was more.

"And they decided they wanted one of the drivers to live in so they were available for short notice work and early starts. Tania can't do it because of her kids, so..."

"A live-in driver?"

"Yeah, you'll be staying at the hotel with them for the next two weeks, not at my place. I should have said. It's much more lucrative for you. And for me. They're paying a lot just to have you on call. The hotel is super swanky. Spa, sauna, gym, pool. You'll love it. Better than my spare room with its saggy mattress."

"With them? I'm staying where they're all staying? And I need to be available to drive them any time of day or night?"

"Not any time day or night. But unsocial hours definitely. I hope that's okay. It's super well paid, Casey."

Casey couldn't think of anything worse than being at the beck and call of a bunch of bratty actors, but she needed the money, and right then, the idea of taking advantage of the sauna to steam the tension from her muscles after the long flight sounded like heaven.

"Okay."

She heard the sigh of relief he let out.

"It's just the first two weeks." David threw an arm around her shoulders. "And I'll make sure you get the night off for my Pride party. You're here just in time. It's going to be fab-u-lous."

Casey let her head rest on his arm, enjoying the contact. His Pride parties were legendary, and she knew damn well he'd been planning cocktails, playlists, and house decorations for weeks. Last year, Casey missed it. She'd already run away to Portland.

"When is it?"

"Saturday after next."

She nodded. But she wasn't sure she wanted to go. It would mean seeing Hannah—with Zoey. And facing up to all their friends. It had been a year, but the humiliation and the hurt sometimes felt as intense as if it was yesterday.

David took another call. So she sank back and let herself doze as they passed Hammersmith tube station. She realized she hadn't even asked David where the hotel was, but the truth was, she didn't care. She needed to shower and then go and see her mom. The sooner she could get things sorted with her, the sooner she could leave this place. She'd loved the city for a very long time, but now it just reminded her of every bad thing that had happened before she left and she couldn't wait to leave again.

Chapter Two

I can't believe this schedule." Louise lay on the couch in their trailer, her bare feet up on the dressing table and her phone held up in front of her face. "The only full day we have off is the day after we arrive in London, when we'll be too jet-lagged to do anything anyway." Louise put down her phone and turned to face Olivia, propping herself up on an elbow. "Are you even listening to me?"

"Of course, I am," Olivia replied. "You're complaining about the studio working us too hard while we're in Europe and I'm trying to get my makeup done and not listen to you, because if I do, I'm going to forget my lines." Olivia had the script on her knee as Evan, their makeup artist, worked the foundation into her face.

"Yeah, sorry." Louise sat up, stretching. "Want me to prep the lines with you?"

"That would be great." Olivia passed the papers to Louise.

"The scene that's highlighted?" Louise asked.

"Please." Olivia spoke as she watched Evan's fingers in the mirror applying a little color to her cheeks. Olivia found the sensation enjoyable. Too enjoyable. A faint blush spread across her face almost rendering the coloring redundant. She really needed to have someone who wasn't their makeup artist pay her some attention.

"*I can't keep doing this.*" Louise managed to sound just like the actress Olivia was playing the scene with. "*I'm not letting you turn up here whenever you're bored or horny and use me as some kind of stress reliever.*"

"*C'mon honey, you know it's not like that,*" Olivia replied as Susie, sounding like a much more seductive version of herself. "*I'm here because

I miss you and I wanted to see you, that's all. Can I not come in and at least talk to you?"

"There is a moment's hesitation before Ellie stands back from the door and lets Susie in." Louise read the stage directions. "Susie goes to her and takes her hands. They are standing close together."

"Just seeing you is all I want. I don't need to do anything but look at you." Olivia made it sound like Susie meant it, but her TV alter ego rarely did. She was a heartbreaker and Ellie was simply the latest in a long line of women she would love and leave. "Then I move in for the kiss."

"And another one falls into Susie's arms for a lengthy sex scene." Louise stood. "Shame it's not real life, babe."

"Funny. We can't all have your luck…or stamina." Olivia muttered.

"You could. You get enough offers. You just choose not to take advantage."

Olivia tensed. This was a familiar conversation between them.

"It's Susie who gets all the offers, not me. I don't get time to meet women who aren't already in love with Susie and dating them feels kind of weird. I always think the real me would be a disappointment." Olivia wasn't looking for reassurance. It was a simple truth. She didn't have any of Susie's moves, or her confidence. "And the last time I tried, it didn't exactly end well."

"I know, I know. I'm sorry. Look at you though." Louise was standing next to Evan to look at Olivia's reflection. "You're gorgeous, Liv. It's a damn waste. If you weren't my best friend…" She pivoted and dropped back onto the couch with a deep sigh. "And I can't believe they've got you doing a reshoot the day we travel. It's ridiculous. We never get any time off. As soon as we finish shooting, we're promoting, as soon as we finish promoting, we're shooting."

"Don't, Lou. Not now, please. I'll lose my lines."

"Yeah, okay, sorry." Louise held up a hand. "It just gets to me sometimes."

"Me too."

Evan removed the tissue paper protecting Olivia's shirt before stepping away and tidying her supplies into a large vanity case. Olivia considered herself in the mirror. She had been transformed into Susie, the unorthodox political fixer whose superpower was making women fall at her feet. The eye shadow and eyeliner were much heavier than Olivia would wear, but they certainly made her eyes stand out, their hazel color looking more intense. And the foundation—thick and dark enough to stand up to the lights on set—made Susie look more like a resident of West Hollywood than the Brooklynite that Olivia was. The splash of color across her mouth was a deep red. Olivia smiled. Susie was not subtle. She was irresistible though, and mostly, she was a lot of fun to play.

"You're just getting cranky because we're not getting enough time off for you to bag yourself a minor royal while we're over there. I knew I shouldn't have made you watch *The Crown*," Olivia teased her, wanting Louise out of her bad mood.

"Yeah, maybe. Or maybe I just imagined being able to get a bit of a vacation vibe going with you and Liam. Fat chance. According to the schedule, we're doing seven fan events. Can you believe it? How can there even be that many people in England who want to see us? That country is tiny."

"Maybe it has a high percentage of queers, or maybe we're just more appealing than we realize. I'm just grateful we're in one place for two weeks. After that it's six countries in twenty days." Olivia sat on the couch, the script on her knee, waiting for the knock that told her she was needed on set.

"I'm grateful too. And I know I shouldn't complain, because this is a much better gig than a lot of people have." Louise's tone grew serious.

They didn't often say it out loud, but they both understood how lucky they were. They were working on a great show, they were earning very good money, and they got to travel—maybe a little too much.

Olivia had been playing Susie in the show since episode one. She hadn't expected to still be playing her three years later. But the part was a good one. Susie led a group of badass outcasts who made it their business to right wrongs, and the show positively represented people who were often outside the television mainstream. Olivia felt good about that and held on to it tightly on the days when the BS that went with it got to be too much for her.

"Well, I'm going to enjoy being in Europe," Louise said. "And not just because of all the sexy accents. I'm going to enjoy meeting the fans and try to have some fun. And you should do the same. Maybe you should let Olivia off the leash while you're over there. Let her have some Susie-type fun." She winked.

"You're not exactly helping me remember my lines." Olivia pointed at the paper. She was pretty sure she had the lines down but wanted to change the subject. She didn't need another pep talk from Louise about finding a woman.

"Sorry, sorry," Louise said. "I know you got this, but let's go again. Starting after they stop fucking."

They ran through the end of the scene together with no mistakes.

"See. You're good to go."

Louise smiled at her encouragingly, and Olivia was reminded of the Louise she got to know back in Brooklyn. It'd been hard sometimes, but they'd stayed in touch, and when Louise got the part of Jessie, she encouraged Olivia to try out for Susie and she was more than amazed to land the part. She remembered her first day on set like it was yesterday. It had been nerve-wracking, and she'd flubbed more than a few lines that day. But she'd shared a trailer with Louise, and Louise had been helping her learn her lines ever since.

"Do you ever get tired of it?"

"What?" Louise asked.

"All of it. The show and everything that goes with it. Maybe it's LA, maybe it's just the living in a trailer for half the year thing, but…" Olivia paused, not sure what the problem was. "I sometimes want other things."

"Like what?"

"I don't even know, Lou. Cold weather, a dog, the chance to do some theater, some acting with my clothes on. Maybe even someone to walk the dog with." She laughed an embarrassed laugh. "I'm being ungrateful, I know. I've got a great life. I think I'm just having a bad case of the grass is greener."

The door flew open and Liam climbed into the trailer. He was wearing shorts and a tank and holding a magazine.

"Seen this? It's got an interview and photospread with Billie in it." He sounded out of breath.

"Did you run here?" Louise asked.

"Not the whole way. I got them to drop me halfway." He dropped the magazine in Olivia's lap as he sat on the armchair opposite them and checked his watch. "I ran the last seven and a half miles."

"You're gonna get that chair all sweaty." Louise made him get up. He grouched but stood obediently, waiting while she fetched a towel. After laying it across the seat, Louise pushed him backward until he toppled into it, causing him to complain loudly.

Olivia smiled. Liam was the youngest member of the "holy trinity," Louise's name for the three of them, and Olivia was the oldest. Sometimes Liam and Louise bickered like siblings and she felt like a long-suffering babysitter. She picked up the magazine and put it on the table.

"Thanks, but why would I wanna read about Billie? I have more than enough of her when we're on set." Olivia tried not to sound too bitchy, but Billie had a habit of rubbing her the wrong way.

"Seven and a half miles?" Louise said. "I can't even do seven and a half minutes on the treadmill." She shook her head at Liam and then picked up the magazine.

"You'll both get annoyed, so don't shoot the messenger, okay?" Liam stood and began to stretch out his muscles. Olivia saw Louise staring, looking at him a lot like she hadn't eaten that day. She supposed that Liam had a good body—and Louise was definitely all about equality when it came to sex—but still, it was unexpected. Olivia shook her head. No, Liam was like family. Louise wasn't looking at him like that. She probably was just hungry.

"She," Louise indicated Olivia with her thumb, "has a reshoot and doesn't need any distractions right now, so I'll read it and decide whether to shoot you." She opened the magazine. "I guess you running in here all dramatic means that Billie's done or said something bad, so sit your sweaty ass back down while I find out."

The words sounded cruel, but Louise's tone was light. She loved Liam as much as Olivia did. The three of them were a team, and she wouldn't have survived LA without them. It was sometimes cruel and often shallow, and in four years, they were the only real friends she had here.

"She said that she's coming back in season four as a regular and that part of the reason she couldn't say no 'when the producers begged her,'" he wrapped the words in speech marks with his voice, "was because of Liv and how close the two of you have become." He spoke directly to her. "Apparently, she's excited that season four will see you take your amazing off-screen chemistry onscreen for everyone to enjoy."

"You're kidding?"

He shook his head.

"What the hell." Olivia grabbed the magazine from Louise.

Billie's photos were splashed across three pages. She looked good. She had been a model and knew how to make the most of what she had—and what she had was a fine pair of breasts, great legs, and a mouth that could pout to an Olympic standard. In the corner of one page was a picture of Olivia with Billie, side by side at some studio event a few weeks before. The text in the box was almost exactly as Liam had reported, and the magazine designer had encased the picture of the two of them in a big red heart.

"Great." Olivia's mood crashed. She and Billie had no chemistry and she had zero interest in them developing any. And the idea of Billie staying for season four as a regular was not a fun one if this was the PR game she was going to play.

Louise took the magazine. "She's a real piece of work, even by LA standards. She'll do anything for publicity."

"I was grabbing a drink and I heard some of the crew talking. They were saying that Liv must have asked the producers to keep Billie on and that it wasn't fair because Billie can't even act." Liam ran a hand through his hair—the dark strands across his forehead looking wet from his run. "At least that part was true."

"You're not helping, Liam." Louise shot him a glare.

"Not my fault. I told you, don't shoot the messenger."

There was a knock at the door, and one of the production assistants shouted for Olivia.

"Try not to kill each other while I'm gone, and if you get bored, feel free to go and tell everyone on set how, if anyone asked for Billie to stay on the show, it's that writer she's rumored to be fucking. I bet that's why she's got a regular spot." Olivia turned back as she reached the door. "And you," she pointed at Liam, "shouldn't go anywhere near the fridge. I have plans for every bit of that food. I don't care how many miles you've run."

She took in a breath and as she climbed down the steps of the trailer, let Susie take over. She would nail this scene, go to Europe, and try to keep as far away from Billie and her PR games as possible.

CHAPTER THREE

"Hello," Casey called out as she knocked before stepping through the open back door. The kitchen was empty, but her mom was definitely home because the smell of bleach was overpowering and the contents of one of the kitchen cabinets were spread across the dining table. The kitchen was in the midst of a deep clean. And Casey understood this meant her mom would be sober but stressed. She always cleaned to keep the demons at bay.

Casey picked her way across the floor, not wanting to make a mess, but not willing to remove her shoes. Depending on her mom's mood, she might not be staying long.

"Casey," her mom said from the opposite doorway. She sounded happy to see her. "You're earlier than I thought you'd be." She touched a hand to her hair and then patted her dressing gown. "I'm not ready. I was going to get dressed, but then I realized what a mess the kitchen was, and I thought I'd do a bit of cleaning first." She waved a hand across the room.

"Yeah, I can see. Smells pretty clean now." Casey wrinkled her nose.

She looked properly at her mom. She was only fifty-eight and often looked a lot younger, but today, she could have passed for ten years older. Her hair needed to be washed, and her dressing gown was stained and grubby. Her eyes looked heavy, not with drink, but Casey guessed some kind of medication to help keep the craving at bay. Her skin, though barely lined, was gray-white in color. It was hard to see her like this again, but there also wasn't much she could do about it. Casey had tried and failed with her emotional rescue missions so many times and eventually had to accept that her mom had to want things to be different before she'd do a thing about changing.

"Want some tea, love?" her mom asked, seeming confused, like she might not be able to manage it if Casey said yes. She hadn't moved from her position in the doorway between the kitchen and the hall.

"Yeah, but I'll do it, eh? Maybe we could have a bit of toast too?"

Her mom looked even thinner than usual, and Casey imagined that she hadn't been eating properly. She crossed to the kettle, sitting in its usual place and switched it on. "I'm hungry even though I already had lunch." She'd grabbed a sandwich and eaten it on the tube, but it hardly counted as lunch.

Her mom spoke from the doorway. "You need to be careful about having two lunches. At your age, all that muscle could easily turn to fat."

Her mom—the snarky, unhappy mom she had expected to see today—was back. Just like that.

"And being fat won't help you get a girlfriend. You're not like me and Jack. We can both eat whatever we want and never put on weight. You were always such a chubby kid, it's still in there somewhere." She watched as, without waiting for a response, her mom disappeared down the hallway and into the living room.

Casey counted to ten and found some bread to toast. She opened the fridge. Apart from a pint of milk and some margarine, it was empty. She sighed, not understanding if the emptiness was lack of energy or lack of money on her mom's part. It didn't matter. She'd do some shopping while she was here. And then she needed to get to the bottom of just how bad things were. She was pretty sure she hadn't been told everything on the phone.

Her mom was sitting at the dining table looking a bit spaced out, but she'd obviously been busy while Casey was out shopping. The stuff had all been put back in the cabinet and she'd gotten dressed. Her hair had been combed and she'd even tried to color her cheeks. But the way she carried herself suggested she was suffering more than she was going to admit. It wasn't the first time she'd seen her mom defeated by a scumbag of a man, but it was still heartbreaking.

She put the fresh food in the fridge and began putting the cans away.

"He's not answering my calls. I even rang his sister's house to try to talk to him, to see if he was there, but she said she hadn't seen him." She waited and Casey knew she was leaving space for her to react.

"Why the hell would you do that?" Casey didn't disappoint. She gripped a can in her hand tightly and felt it dent under the pressure. "She's just as bad as he is. You know that, Mom. Half the time he took money off you, you said it was because she needed it, that she was the one putting him up to it. Can't you just be glad he's gone?"

Her mom seemed sad for a second, but then it was gone and was replaced by a stubborn blankness that was familiar.

"He's sorry, I know he is. He just doesn't know how to say it. I know him a lot better than you do. And, yeah, she's responsible. I'm pretty sure that's where he's moved to. But it's just because she needs him to help with the kids. They're his nephews, what's he supposed to do? What kind of man would turn his back on his own family when they need help?"

"The kind of man who spent your savings, maxed your credit card, and pretended to pay your rent for a year while stealing the actual money. And he's left you so fucking destitute that you can't even afford to eat properly, let alone pay your bills." Casey made herself slow down and lower her voice. Shouting wasn't going to get them anywhere. "I know you don't want to admit that I was right about him, but this isn't about saving face, Mom, it's about saving this house and your sanity. Let's not pretend him coming back is gonna help you in the slightest, and I don't wanna be hard-faced about it, but I'm not helping you get everything sorted just to see him waltz in here and sit right back down next to you again."

Casey knelt in front of her mom. She could hear her sniffling, trying to hold back the tears. She was stubborn and frustrating, and she had terrible taste in men, but her mom was hurting. Of course she was. She'd been betrayed and left looking a fool. And Casey knew from bitter experience just how much that hurt. She put out a hand and tentatively stroked her mom's knee. They were not a family that showed each other affection.

"It's all right, Mom. We'll sort out the house. And I'll stay around for a bit till you get back on your feet. The council will probably be sympathetic about him stealing the rent. They might even help." She stood and went back to unpack the rest of the shopping. "What did the police say about the chances of him being charged and you getting things back from him?"

Her mom shifted in her seat. It was a slight movement, but it told Casey everything she needed to know.

"You didn't call them." It was a statement, not a question.

Her mom lowered her eyes. The shake of her head barely discernible.

Casey couldn't muster surprise, never mind anger. She could probably even script her mom's excuses. She took a deep, slow breath. "How about we have some more tea and try to figure out what other bills need to be paid?"

She switched on the kettle and sat opposite her mom, opening the overflowing folder of bills and letters that her mom used to keep so organized. Casey was a realist. She had to be with her upbringing. Her mom had made bad decisions before, and she'd make them again. Casey adding her own disappointment to the mix had never helped, and it certainly wouldn't help either of them now.

She scanned the room. The microwave was gone, and the small TV that used to sit on top of the fridge was missing. He'd even taken the coffeemaker. What a bastard he was.

Casey would earn as much as she could while she was here. She'd find a way to pay off her mom's arrears and then go home. To Portland. To a place that had never treated her as badly as London had. If it went well, she might even be back home for the end of basketball season. And she wasn't going to feel guilty about not being here. Her mom had Jack, her beloved son. He was useless in a crisis, but he was a lot closer to home than she was. And since he now had a regular job and a girlfriend her mom was always praising, he had no excuse for not helping out more. Her mom might need her, but she had never much acted like she missed her.

After getting back from her mom's, Casey couldn't decide whether to nap or work out. The soft, deep mattress had lured her in, but she was far too agitated to sleep, so after tossing and turning for half an hour, Casey hit the gym hard, working out all the frustration about her mom's situation that she hadn't been able to express while they were together. Every lift, every stretch, she imagined getting her hands on Neil—a guy who almost made her stepdad seem decent—and somehow making him pay her mom every penny back. But of course, it was impossible, so Casey pounded the treadmill until she was ready to drop.

And then, later, still unable to manage more than a fretful nap, she decided to try the sauna. It was electric and not that large, but it was wonderfully hot. She wasn't the only occupant. On the middle bench opposite the door was a woman stretched out in a towel. They nodded a hello to each other as Casey took her place on the adjacent set of benches. She had a British person's fear of small talk and relaxed only when it was clear that the woman wasn't going to try to make conversation.

Casey had put on a sports bra and shorts, not knowing if the dress code would allow her to be naked, and as she lay on her back, she opened her towel, wanting to feel the heat more directly on her skin. She closed her eyes and let it permeate deeply, melting away the tension in her muscles. The feeling was blissful.

There was movement opposite, and Casey opened her eyes and turned her head, wondering if the heat was chasing away her companion. But the woman had simply changed position and was now sitting—legs stretched out in front of her—showing no sign of going anywhere. For a second, their gazes locked, and Casey felt herself captivated by the woman's hazel eyes until she closed them and tilted her head back, leaving Casey feeling oddly dismissed.

She took a moment to consider the woman. She had pretty fair hair, more auburn than blond, tied up in a messy bun. Beneath it, her beautiful face carried a frown, even in rest. And Casey found herself wanting to know why, to know what it was that was troubling her. She shook her head at her momentary insanity and made herself look away. It wasn't cool to admire other women in the sauna, and Casey felt bad that she'd even noticed that the skin on the woman's neck and shoulders looked so soft and kissable.

She closed her eyes and willed herself to concentrate on the feeling of the heat on her skin, on the tension draining from her body. She wasn't Gina and she wasn't the kind of person who got all worked up about being close to an attractive woman—a very attractive woman—in a skimpy towel.

"It's a little too hot for me," the woman said, and Casey opened her eyes, avoiding proper eye contact by staring at the ceiling.

"Want to turn it down?" Casey sounded a little raspy. She reached for the water bottle she had grabbed on the way in.

"No, no, I'm good. I think I'm done anyway." There was a pause. "And you look like you're enjoying it."

The accent was American, and Casey could detect a smile as she spoke.

"I am. I like it hot. But honestly, feel free to turn it down a little if you want to stay." This time she turned her head. And caught the woman staring at her with interest.

"Like I say, I'm good." She nodded at Casey, leaned down to pick up her own water bottle, and got up off the bench. At the door, as Casey did the unthinkable and blatantly checked out her legs, the woman turned.

"Don't fall asleep though, it's dangerous. You look like you might." She gave Casey a shy smile. "Maybe I should come back and check on you later."

"See if I'm cooked?"

"Something like that." Again, the smile was adorably shy. And every kind of beautiful.

As the woman left, Casey let out a breath. *See if I'm cooked.* She muttered the words, mimicking herself. *Great banter, Casey. I'm not surprised she didn't stick around.* She closed her eyes and willed herself to relax, to let the heat take over again. The woman's shy smile came into her mind's eye. So. Damn. Cute. Maybe they could become sauna buddies and eventually, if the woman's hotel stay ran into several years, Casey would pluck up the courage to ask for her name.

She made herself take some slow, deep breaths, wanting to empty her mind, but knowing it was impossible. It'd been quite a day. She'd arrived, got herself a job that allowed her to stay in this swanky hotel, and found her mom in an even worse state than expected. And now she could add getting all hot and bothered about a beautiful stranger to the list.

Yeah, quite a first day.

CHAPTER FOUR

Casey rubbed her neck and stretched out with a groan. She looked at her phone and realized she'd been reading for an hour and a half. It was a quarter to ten and no one had called on her to drive anyone anywhere, despite her getting up early and being down in the lobby in her driver's uniform since eight. If there were going to be long periods of downtime like this—coupled with the hotel's deluxe facilities—she might start to like this job.

It was surprisingly quiet in the cavernous lobby. A handful of people were hanging around the reception desk looking like they were checking out, and a few others were sitting in the leather armchairs that formed a lounge area opposite reception. Like her, most looked as if they were waiting for someone.

She guessed that most of the guests had already headed out for the day and would come back later with tired feet, lighter wallets, and piles of shopping. London was big, overwhelming, and expensive.

"Hey." David answered her call on the first ring. "Everything okay?"

"I think so. Just checking the arrangements. Did you say they've got my number and they're gonna call if they need me for anything?"

"Yeah, why?"

"No calls at all so far. I'm staked out in the lobby, and there's no sign of anyone remotely resembling a TV star."

"Like you'd know." David scoffed.

"I'd know. Suntanned, Botoxed to the point of no return, and taking worshipful selfies of themselves for their adoring fans to like on Instagram."

On the other end of the line, David laughed. "Judgmental, much?"

"Completely."

Across the lobby, the elevator doors opened, and the woman from the sauna wandered out. She looked every bit as alluring with her clothes on. She had sunglasses on her head, a small pile of books in one hand, and a phone in the other. Her legs—the very same ones that Casey hadn't been able to take her eyes off last night—were now encased in a pair of pale green Capri pants, and her outfit was topped by a sleeveless white summer top. She had a purse hanging off her shoulder that matched the color of the pants perfectly. Casey sat up straighter and ran a hand through her hair, surprising herself by caring what she looked like to the gorgeous stranger.

She tore her gaze away from the woman and tuned back in to what David was saying.

"I mean, I'll check I gave them the right number for you, but maybe they're just having a lie-in. And maybe you should get off the phone with me in case they're trying to call you right now."

"Okay, boss."

"Funny. Get off the phone." David paused. "You wearing the cap?"

"What do you think?"

"Just make sure you wear the jacket."

Casey looked at it, draped across the arm of the chair she was sitting in. "It's going to be eighty-five today."

"And that beautiful SUV I've given you has top of the range air conditioning. Wear the jacket."

"David?"

"What?"

"I should get off the phone in case they're calling."

"You're insubordinate."

"And inscrutable."

"And incorrigible." He laughed first.

They had once constructed a dating profile for her that consisted only of words beginning with I. It was a happy memory, now clouded by the fact that it was the dating profile that had attracted Hannah. For a while, she and Hannah had been happy together and David claimed his "I" words were responsible, but then there was absolutely nothing about the relationship for her to be happy about and David had ceased claiming credit.

"I'd better go." Casey couldn't help but sound flat.

"Sorry, babe."

"Don't be. Not your fault. Being back here is all the reminder I need anyway." Casey shrugged even though she knew he couldn't see her. "I'm putting the jacket on."

"We both know you're not." His voice contained a smile.

"See you later."

"Yeah."

He hung up and Casey realized that her sauna woman had chosen the seat that was at a right angle to hers and was now leafing through the books she had been carrying. She was so close that their seats touched at the corner. This seating choice was despite the lobby having about six other empty armchairs that didn't in any way touch hers. Great. Now she was gonna have to make small talk with a woman so poised and beautiful that it made Casey anxious just to look at her. Not for the first time in her life, she regretted her complete absence of "game" when it came to women.

She gave herself a minute, steeling herself to say hello and to point out that she had survived falling asleep in the sauna, but the woman's phone rang and Casey breathed out a sigh of relief.

"Hey, where are you guys? I'm downstairs and ready to go. I've gone through all the guidebooks and the tickets they gave us and planned the perfect day."

It was rude to eavesdrop, but their chairs were very close together and, short of getting up and moving to another chair, Casey had no choice but to listen to beautiful sauna woman's end of the conversation, while acting like she wasn't listening to her end of the conversation.

A long pause and a sigh followed. "Oh, c'mon, Lou, don't do this. We're not gonna get much more free time after today, y'know?"

Casey watched as the woman began gently kicking the leg of the table in front of her with the toe of her bright pink—and obviously brand new—Converse trainers.

"Yeah, I know. If he's sick, he's sick, but I don't know why you need to blow me off to play nursemaid. Maybe he can just go back to bed for a few hours and we can catch up with him later."

The response must have been negative because the woman sank back into her chair.

"I get it. No problem. Of course, it's miserable for him and you're a sweetheart for staying behind. I was just being selfish and wanting some company. No, I'll be fine. I'll go and see some stuff and see you later. Maybe we can grab some dinner before tonight's thing. Okay. Bye, babe. Give Liam a kiss from me."

After disconnecting the call, the woman cursed softly.

Casey didn't know what to say. She felt uncomfortable at having listened in but also felt a hard-to-explain wish to say something to make the woman feel better.

"Forgive me for overhearing, but it sounds like your sightseeing day has hit the buffers. I'm sorry about that."

The woman turned to her in surprise, and the heat Casey felt in her cheeks told her she'd embarrassed herself by speaking up, effectively admitting she'd been listening to a stranger's phone call. She tried telling herself it was okay because they weren't technically strangers, they had met in the sauna, they'd exchanged actual sentences. She wasn't weird. Honest.

The woman looked at Casey appraisingly and then surprised her by yawning deeply and raising both arms above her head in a long stretch. "I don't know what the hell buffers are, but I do know I'm not going to waste the only free day I'll get on this trip. I'm going to go out and see London without my sick friends."

Casey felt warm. It had nothing to do with the weather and everything to do with the glimpse of midriff she had seen in the gap between her top and the waistband of her pants as the woman stretched. She willed herself to stop behaving like a hormonal teenager. It wasn't as if she hadn't talked to a beautiful woman before. Okay, so it had been a while since one had her feeling all flustered like this, but it was all in there somewhere. She made herself concentrate.

"Why've you got so little free time while you're here?"

"It's a working visit. We got in last night and this is pretty much the only free day we've got, but," the woman sighed, "jet lag had me sleeping in, and now my friends are too busy being ill to come out with me." She smiled. "Buffers have been hit, apparently."

"I can't even explain it to you," Casey replied. "I don't know what they are either. I just know they get hit when things go wrong. Sorry."

"You apologize a lot for someone who hasn't done anything wrong."

"British," Casey said. "We're sorry for everything that ever happened to anyone."

They looked at each other for a beat. Casey could get lost in those eyes.

"Are you sorry enough to come sightseeing with me today?"

❖

Olivia wanted to swallow the words as soon as she'd said them. The dark-haired woman now staring at her—in what looked a lot like horror—was gorgeous. The kind of gorgeous that had stayed with Olivia long after she left the sauna last night. She had fallen asleep thinking of how great the woman looked stretched out, all sweaty and muscular in her hot boi-shorts. It had been so much better than counting sheep.

But asking the woman to go out with her for the day, when they'd barely exchanged a few words, was the kind of move Susie would make. And it was completely out of character for Olivia. She fought the urge to run away.

"Me?" The woman pointed a finger at her own chest. It drew Olivia's attention to her dark gray shirt—tight in all the right places.

Olivia shook her head, shaking Susie away. She was Olivia Lang and she did not ogle, proposition, or flirt with total strangers, however hot they were.

"I'm sure you have plans. You're waiting for friends, family, partner, whatever. My turn to apologize. Turns out I'm more eager for company than I realized."

The woman hadn't stopped staring at her. Olivia was pretty sure that last comment could be construed as an insult. She really was bad at this.

"I'm afraid I'm busy working, or I'd probably—"

"Sure you are." Olivia cut her off, not wanting to hear the excuses, not wanting to feel the embarrassment. The woman was in a hotel lobby, mid-morning, with a book on her knee. None of it suggesting she was working. Even Olivia could recognize when she was getting the brush-off.

"I've got a very specific itinerary anyway. It probably wouldn't be your bag. And I'm very busy, like I said." Olivia picked up her books, wanting the ground to swallow her up.

The woman's dark brown eyes would have been the standout feature on anyone else, but Olivia couldn't see past her mouth, past those perfect lips. A few minutes ago, they were oh-so-kissable, but they were pursed now, seeming to judge Olivia as someone crazy. And to be fair, she was kind of acting that way.

She picked up her phone, her face hot with shame. "I have to call my driver, excuse me. He should be here waiting for me. They said he would be." Olivia scanned the lobby. "If he's late, then that's going to make a bad day even worse. I don't have the time to waste hanging around." She couldn't stop herself from sounding like a prima donna.

Olivia turned away, found the number they'd given her, and pressed the *call* button, sensing rather than seeing that the gorgeous but disapproving woman was still looking at her.

As the call connected, Olivia heard the ringing tone in the ear she had pressed close to the phone. At the same time, she heard a phone ringing in real life and saw, from the corner of her eye, her lobby companion leaning back to fish it from the pocket of her pants.

"Hello." They spoke at the same time and Olivia turned back to see the woman shrug before taking the phone away from her ear.

"Your driver." The woman gave her a small smile. "Here waiting for you like they said I would be. And like I said, most definitely working. I'm Casey." She stood and held out a hand for Olivia to shake.

Olivia had already pegged her as dark and handsome, but the fact that she was also tall made her want to roll her eyes. They'd really sent her a driver who looked like her every fantasy? Not fair. She felt a surprising amount of desire and from somewhere else, an anger that this woman had been playing with her all along.

"Olivia Lang." She shook the woman's hand reluctantly. "But then you knew that."

The woman—Casey—shook her head.

"I didn't actually. I thought you were just the woman from the sauna who was worried about me falling asleep and dying in there."

"I'm pretty sure you must know who I am. Unless you're telling me you're unprofessional enough not to have bothered to find out which set of TV stars you're driving around for the next two weeks?"

Olivia didn't understand why she was being so snarky. She didn't believe her, but so what. It wasn't Casey's fault that Olivia had embarrassed herself by accidentally inviting her driver to go out with her for the day for no good reason.

"I figured the people I was driving would call me," Casey held up her phone, "and then I'd know who I was driving. Driving doesn't require much preparation." A wry smile spread across her face.

Olivia found even that annoying. Charming definitely, but also annoying. She'd been to England before. She knew all about the diffidence, the sarcasm, the micro-gestures that suggested they thought that everyone from "across the pond" was a little stupid.

"Perhaps if you were wearing a uniform, I'd have realized who you were and I—" Olivia was going to say "wouldn't have made a fool of myself," but she wasn't going to admit it out loud. Casey didn't look like the type she could have laughed it off with. "I wasn't expecting a woman."

It was true, but she immediately wished she hadn't said it out loud.

"We're allowed to fly airplanes too. Not me, though. I just drive cars. But I am definitely your driver, and I am certainly female. I'm also parked right outside and ready to go." She picked up a jacket from the chair and put it on. It transformed her instantly into a uniformed driver, rather than just the hot butch woman in pants and a fitted shirt that Olivia had thought she was, and Olivia felt even more stupid.

"Okay." The word came out a little croaky. Olivia tried again, tried to sound more in charge than she felt. "Okay, then. I want to go to the Tower of London first and then the British Museum, then Shakespeare's Globe Theatre after that, and if there's time, I want to drop into Harrods." Olivia was determined to rescue as much of this disaster of a day as she could.

In front of her, Casey hadn't moved. She was looking at the guidebooks that Olivia had picked up and had her bottom lip trapped between her teeth. She was frowning and looked a lot like someone who had something disapproving to say.

"Can we please get going?" Olivia was determined to maintain the upper hand.

"Sure." Casey said the word, but still wasn't moving toward the door.

Olivia really needed Casey to stop staring at her and get a move on.

"But doing all that today is going to be a challenge. The queues will be long, and the traffic is going to be horrendous. You're gonna hit the afternoon rush hour at some point. And, given everywhere you've chosen is going to be really busy..." She paused, and Olivia couldn't help but feel her choices were being judged and found lacking. "It might be better to go by public transport."

Olivia felt the last of her patience drain away. "You're my driver and you're telling me to go by public transportation. Are you even serious?" Olivia was a big TV star, even if she didn't always feel like it. She wasn't going to let herself get told what to do by her uppity English driver.

"I'm not 'telling' you anything. I'm happy to drive you. I'm your driver, as you helpfully point out." The sarcasm wasn't hidden. "I'm just advising you. I know the city, I know the traffic, and I know sitting in the car all day isn't going to be much fun for you."

"I'll decide what's fun for me, thank you. And I would very much like it if you'd drive me like you're paid to?"

There was a flash of something in Casey's beautiful eyes and Olivia felt tension in the air between them. And then it was gone.

"Whatever you say, Ms. Lang." Casey nodded, turned, and walked slowly to the revolving doors. Rather than walk through them, as Olivia had expected, she waited to one side for Olivia to go ahead of her. Her good manners shamed Olivia slightly. She had behaved like the entitled diva that she definitely wasn't. Something about Casey knowing better—and judging her—was getting under her skin.

But there was something else about Casey too. Olivia was madly attracted to her. And she wanted her approval, not her disapproval.

She passed through the doors and waited for Casey to join her outside. Casey pointed to a black luxury SUV parked across the forecourt and set off to open the doors. As Casey was standing, back door open, waiting for Olivia to climb inside, she wanted to stop and apologize, to ask if they could start over, to tell Casey that she wasn't normally like this. But Casey was now avoiding her eyes and there was something about her, about the combination of being so hot and buttoned up, that made Olivia feel like she shouldn't say a word. She climbed into the car and watched as Casey walked around to the driver's side, cast off her jacket, and got inside.

"The air conditioning is set at seventy, but let me know if you want me to change the temperature at any point. There's a remote control in the seat pocket in front of you that controls the stereo if you'd like to listen to some music." She sounded completely professional, but also like someone who had absolutely no interest in talking to her, and Olivia couldn't help but feel sorry. It was her own fault for being such a bitch, but it was going to be a long day with no conversation.

"Thanks." Olivia couldn't think of anything else. She leaned her head back against the headrest, gave in to a huge yawn, and hoped that Casey wasn't right about the day she was about to have.

"This is ridiculous." Olivia said it for the third time. It was as if saying it out loud would make the traffic move quicker. "We've been in the car for an hour and my phone says it should only have taken fifteen minutes."

"It's summer. The tourists are out in force. As well as the Tower of London, you've got HMS *Belfast*, Tower Bridge, and the river boats. And this road is the main arterial route crossing the river. It's also the only road we could have taken to get from the Tower to the museum." Casey's reply was even in tone and contained not a hint of the I-told-you-so that Olivia was waiting for.

They got to the Tower of London in reasonable time and she'd felt a little smug, like Casey had been exaggerating how bad it would be, out of, she supposed, sheer laziness. But then Olivia had had to line up for what felt like hours to get in—her prepaid ticket not making much difference in the wait time—and then she'd waited again to be shuffled past display cabinets containing the Crown Jewels with hundreds of other tourists who oohed and aahed as much as she would have if she'd had someone to enjoy them with. She picked up the glossy brochure she'd bought—yes, she'd lined up for that too—and opened it out again on her lap with a sigh. The jewels were beautiful—literally jaw-dropping—and almost worth the headache that she was beginning to develop.

She looked at her watch. It was a quarter after two, and while she'd snagged a coffee and a muffin from a street vendor enterprisingly parked next to the line at the Tower, she hadn't had lunch. It wouldn't have mattered, but she'd skipped breakfast too.

"Is there nothing we can do?" She wanted Casey to simultaneously cure her headache, satisfy her hunger, and make the traffic disappear. She had a Q&A later. It was at the hotel, mercifully, but she still needed time to shower, dress, and hopefully eat something with Louise and Liam. But she hadn't even gotten to stop two on her planned itinerary. This day was driving her crazy.

"You might do better if you—" Casey stopped speaking and Olivia waited a beat.

"What?"

"You could walk. We're really not very far away. It might be quicker on foot for you. I could give you directions. Then I could wait out this traffic and meet you in the square behind the museum in an hour or two. I know you want to be driven everywhere, but honestly, we're crawling along and the museum is just up there. You can practically see it." Casey pointed out the front window. "You'd get there in no time if you walked."

"I can't walk. No way. I'll get lost." Olivia felt a rising panic. She didn't know this neighborhood at all and she'd heard a lot of stories about London. "Why don't you come with me? You know the way. You could park somewhere here and take me there. You're being paid either way, so it shouldn't matter to you if you're sitting in traffic or walking me to a museum. And even you must want to see the British Museum."

The tension in Casey's shoulders wasn't hard to miss. She took a long time to respond, and Olivia figured she hadn't quite worded her request as well as she could have.

"I'm getting paid to drive you." Casey's tone was brusque. "Not to play chaperone. Walk there yourself, or sit in traffic, it's all the same to me."

She deserved that response. Objectively, Olivia knew that. But it didn't help.

"Maybe you're forgetting that I'm a TV star, that people will recognize me, will stop me, harass me. Why do you think they gave me a driver in the first place? A driver who doesn't seem to want to drive, a driver who seems to have driven all the busiest roads, probably just to prove a point." Olivia couldn't stop her frustration from bubbling up.

"You think that I'm trying to get us stuck in this traffic?" Casey didn't wait for an answer. "You couldn't be more wrong. I don't want to spend a minute more in this car than I have to. If I could get you there quicker, trust me, I bloody well would."

"Take me back to the hotel. This day is a total bust and your attitude stinks."

Olivia couldn't help raising her voice. The jet lag was making her tired, and her head was thumping. She was annoyed that Louise and Liam had bailed on her and forced her to spend the only day she was going to get off this trip with a driver who obviously thought she was some kind of idiot. She slumped back in her seat and willed herself not to cry. She knew Casey was watching—and no doubt judging—and she didn't want to give her the satisfaction.

"I said take me home."

They moved forward the length of a few cars in silence and Olivia couldn't believe that Casey was going to ignore her. But then Casey held up a hand out the driver's window to ask for the oncoming traffic to wait for her while she U-turned. She accelerated down the road they had just crawled along, the traffic in that direction being a little lighter.

Olivia considered apologizing for her temper, but she couldn't imagine Casey doing the same, and anyway, her tiredness now felt overwhelming.

"I'm not scared of the city, if that's what you're thinking." She said the words through the sleep she was trying to keep at bay. "I'm from Brooklyn. I might not sound like it anymore, but I am. Born and bred. And I walked every inch of that city, even the neighborhoods I was told to avoid. I'm not as useless at this as you seem to think I am." She didn't know why she cared, why she needed Casey to know.

They sat in silence for a few minutes, the humming of the engine, the warmth of the car, making Olivia drowsier and drowsier.

"Well, I probably know every inch of the British Museum. I'm not the uncultured heathen you obviously think I am." The muttered words and Casey's dark eyes staring back at her in the mirror in the dim light of the car, were the last things Olivia remembered as sleep overtook her.

CHAPTER FIVE

Casey got back into the car, closing her door gently, trying not to make a noise. She put the coffees on the seat beside her and looked over her shoulder. Olivia was still sleeping like the proverbial baby. Her face relaxed enough to suggest she was in a deep slumber. The occasional twitch suggesting she might have been dreaming.

Casey had pulled into the hotel parking lot, expecting Olivia to wake up as they parked and storm off into the hotel to raise hell about what a terrible day she'd had and how it was all Casey's fault. She almost called David to get her side of the story in first, but that would have meant admitting to a disastrous first day on the job and she didn't want to do that. David was one of her oldest friends, but that didn't mean he wouldn't be mad as hell.

And blaming Olivia for being a bitch would get her nowhere. A lot of the people she'd driven for had treated her like crap. It came with the job, and there was never any point getting mad about it.

She decided instead to simply let Olivia have a nap. Maybe it was what she needed and maybe, just maybe, she'd wake up acting a little more like the sweet, kind of shy woman she'd met in the sauna and a lot less like the entitled obnoxious TV star who had climbed into the back of her car.

She took the lid from the coffee and blew on it before turning and considering Olivia again. Her face looked almost cherubic as she slept, her head poking out from underneath the jacket Casey had draped over her after it had become clear that she wasn't going to wake up without a firm shake to the shoulders. Casey had done enough to upset her today and she wasn't going to add an assault charge to her list of misdemeanors.

She sipped the coffee. It was hot and black and just what she needed. But mostly what she needed was food—lots of it—and for Olivia Lang, TV star worried about being accosted by her fans walking through the not-very-mean streets of Bloomsbury, to wake up in a much better mood than she took with her into sleep.

She picked up her book vowing to make the most of the downtime this ridiculous situation afforded her, trying—and failing—not to steal glances at Olivia in the rearview mirror. She really was beautiful. It was a shame she didn't have the attitude to match.

"Where are we?" The voice from the back of the car sounded sleepy, and Casey couldn't fight the urge to see if Olivia looked as gorgeous waking up from sleep as she did when she was sleeping. She looked over her shoulder.

"The hotel. Specifically, the parking lot out front."

Olivia sat forward to look out the window, the jacket falling from her shoulders as she moved, her face a picture of adorable confusion. She turned back to Casey, and Casey waited for the telling off that was about to come forth.

"Why are we parked out here?" She yawned. "Is that coffee?" Olivia's eyes widened.

"I got one for you." Casey passed the extra coffee back to Olivia, who removed the lid without hesitation. "I didn't know if you took milk, so I got it black. But I grabbed some creamer and sugar if you want it."

Casey watched as Olivia's lips caressed the side of the Styrofoam cup, testing the liquid for temperature before taking a long, slow sip.

"That's good." Olivia sank back into the seat, pulling the jacket back around her shoulders. "How long have we been out here? Why didn't you wake me? I could have gone inside. It's not your job to babysit me while I nap in a parking lot."

"We've only been here half an hour. We made good time back, but you were fast asleep when we got here, and I figured you needed some sleep. I think the jet lag was making you…" She hesitated ever so slightly.

"A bitch?" Olivia lifted an eyebrow.

"I was going to say cranky." Casey could have said worse. "I didn't want to wake you, and I wasn't sure you'd thank me if I left you here alone." She had been tempted. Olivia had behaved exactly as she'd expected, and she wasn't impressed. "But I wouldn't have let you sleep too much longer. I know you have things you wanna do."

"Why are you being so nice to me? I've been horrible."

"I'm a professional. It's my job to be nice to clients, however they behave." Casey saw Olivia react to the words with something that looked a lot like hurt.

She was a mystery. Hard-faced one minute, super sensitive the next. Casey relented. She could be nicer than this, and it was gonna be a long couple of weeks if they couldn't find a way to get on.

"And I know what jet lag feels like. I just got in from the States myself. I guessed you just needed a nap. Plus, your friends bailed on you and this is your only free day. I'm not surprised your mood was a little off." Casey held Olivia's gaze, willing her not to react badly to her honesty. It wasn't just that she didn't want her to complain to David. Something about Olivia intrigued her, despite her behavior today.

"Yeah, and buffers were hit. Let's not forget that. And I haven't even managed to have any proper food. I mean, anyone would be cranky about that, right?" Olivia sipped her coffee and sighed. For a second, neither of them said anything.

"They're like shock absorbers. Buffers. Those big round metal things on the front of a train, in case it hits something. I googled it while you were sleeping."

"Huh. Who knew?"

"We do, now."

If nobody needed her to drive this afternoon, Casey had things she could be doing. She should encourage Olivia back into the hotel and get on sorting through her mom's bills. But she had a strange yearning to keep Olivia talking.

"And you presumably got to admire the world's oldest jeweled anointing spoon on your visit to the Crown Jewels, so the day hasn't been a total disaster."

"I did. It was a very cool spoon." Olivia rewarded her with a small smile, and Casey couldn't help but think that if she responded that well to sleep and coffee, maybe the job wouldn't be so bad. "But it doesn't seem like much to show for my only day off this trip."

"What time is your evening thing?"

"Eight. But I want to try to get dinner with my friends before it starts." Casey looked at her watch.

"Want to go for a walk with your driver who hates driving?" She was taking a chance that Olivia had a sense of humor hidden in there somewhere. "There's this cool museum about fifteen minutes' walk from here. It's a bit off the beaten track, and I can almost guarantee that at this time of day there won't be a line."

Olivia was looking at her with wide eyes, and Casey waited for the lecture about being far too keen on walking for a driver. She was ready for it this time. Of course, she was keen on walking, most professional drivers hated driving. Obviously. What was less obvious was why she was offering to spend more time with Olivia when she'd spent the last four hours wanting to be as far away from her as possible.

"I just feel bad that you didn't get to see even half of what you'd planned." Olivia's plans had been crazily optimistic, but that didn't mean Casey was being insincere. "And this museum happens to have the advantage of being right next door to one of London's oldest and finest pie and mash shops. I'm hungry, and if sampling pie and mash isn't on that list of touristy must-dos of yours, then it should be."

Casey told herself that she was trying to get back into Olivia's good books, to try to avoid her complaining to David. It was half true, but there was something else, something about Olivia that made her feel protective. It was something that Casey didn't want to acknowledge.

"You're offering to take me to a museum?"

"I am."

"And to eat pie?" Olivia sounded confused.

"Especially that."

"But you already made it super clear that you're not my chaperone."

"I'm not. But you're the one who reminded me that I'm getting paid regardless of whether I'm driving, eating pie, or watching you sleep." She blanched at the fact she'd said that last part out loud. Clearly, Olivia wasn't the only one in need of sleep. "And I like visiting museums and eating pie, so…"

"I'm sorry, I'm usually not that much of a bitch."

Casey didn't reply. She had no idea whether or not that was true. She didn't know Olivia at all. And she did seem like someone very used to getting her own way.

"Well, if you're serious. I would really like that. And not just because I'm starving."

"I'm serious."

Olivia pushed herself up in the seat, took a long pull of her coffee, and opened the door. "I'll just go to the bathroom. I'll meet you back here in three minutes." She climbed out and then leaned back in. "Thank you."

Casey watched as Olivia disappeared into the hotel, hoping she wasn't going to regret her offer.

❖

"What the hell is this place?"

Olivia's horrified expression made Casey tense. Olivia was reacting in just the way she imagined Hannah would have, if she'd ever tried to bring her to Estelle's. She looked around and took in the interior as if she were coming here for the first time. The cafe had white tiled walls, chipped Formica tables, and a chest-high counter running along one side of the room. It was made of dark wood and cracked glass and looked a hundred years old. The overall ambience wasn't great, but she loved the place. It reminded her of her childhood, of the cafés her mom would take them to. And Estelle's homemade pies were awesome.

"It looks like it's closed. It doesn't have any menus—or any other customers. And the tables..." Olivia ran the tip of her finger across the corner of their table where the wood chip was visible. "Did you bring me here just to laugh at the spoiled LA rich girl?"

"Not at all. It's a bit of a hidden gem." Casey felt a little defensive. "I used to work at a place a few minutes from here, so I came here a lot." She tried not to let the memories overtake her, wondering why the hell she thought bringing Olivia here was a good idea. "And this place has been here forever. Usually has free tables, always has the same menu. I couldn't resist coming back. I'm sorry. I know it's not very Hollywood. It's not very Portland either, but the food is a thousand times better than the decor. And you're the one who said you enjoyed exploring new neighborhoods." There was a challenge for Olivia in her words. "Consider it an authentic London experience. And you'll love the pie and mash, trust me."

"Like I trusted you to choose a museum, and you took me to see a two-hundred-year-old operating theater, with three rooms full of gruesome old surgical instruments that are gonna give me nightmares." Casey was relieved to hear teasing underneath Olivia's reply.

"You loved it. It was fascinating, admit it."

Olivia had enjoyed it. She had been full of questions, taken a hundred photos, and Casey practically had to force her to leave so she didn't faint with hunger. It surprised her. The museum had been a risky choice, but Olivia's curiosity was appealing.

"I loved it until you explained what some of the instruments were for."

"Yeah, you did go a little green."

"How did you know all that super-specific surgical information anyway?"

"I made most of it up." Olivia rewarded her honesty with a groan.

"Yet you expect me to believe you when you tell me this," Olivia waved a hand around the interior, "is the best café in London?"

"Not the best café, the best pie and mash."

Olivia seemed to relent and leaned back in her seat, no longer looking like she was about to bolt for the door. Again, Casey was surprised by her. She wanted to eat Estelle's pie, so bringing Olivia here hadn't been about testing her, but for a famous and presumably very rich actress who probably fine-dined most of the time, Olivia didn't seem completely out of place.

"So you just got back from the States. Where'd you go? Was it a vacation?"

"Being in London is my vacation actually."

Olivia looked confused.

"I live in Portland. I'm just here for a few weeks sorting some stuff out."

"You're working as a driver during your vacation?"

"I am." Casey didn't imagine that Olivia would understand, so she didn't try to explain. She didn't want Olivia looking down on her any more than she already did. She waited for the question Olivia looked like she wanted to ask.

"Well, I guess I lucked out coinciding my visit with yours. I'm not sure about your driving, but you're a very good tour guide. And you're very easy to talk to. I don't usually find it this easy to talk to people I don't know." Olivia's voice was low and confiding, and Casey felt her attraction to Olivia all over again, but she chased it away, annoyed that she was letting herself be affected by Olivia's compliments. She was an actress and probably a real player.

"I'm sure it's just the excitement of a day off in a new city," Casey said.

"Hey." Olivia put a hand on Casey's arm. "Take the compliment. You're just good to talk to." She smiled and Casey was pretty sure her cheeks flushed red. She forced herself to remember that this was the same Olivia who had shouted at her three hours ago.

"Are you sure I'll get back to the hotel on time? I have no idea how close to home we are. I've given up even trying to figure out which part of London we're in."

"We're in London Bridge." Casey looked at her watch. "And don't worry. It'll only take about half an hour to get back to the hotel from here. I'm not going to make you late."

"Thanks. Though I'm tempted to stay here and see how many of those wonderful sounding British desserts I can stomach." She pointed at the chalk board on top of the counter. "Spotted dick with custard, jam roly-poly with custard, treacle sponge with custard. I don't know what they are, but the 'and custard' is all I need to know. Maybe I'll just stay and eat custard—and make myself late—and tell the studio that it was your fault. That you kidnapped me and then tortured me with ancient surgical instruments and British puddings."

Olivia's eyes sparkled, and Casey couldn't help but enjoy being teased by her. If Olivia was practicing for the part of a charming stranger, she was nailing it.

"Are you very famous?" Casey wasn't sure if the question would be considered rude, but she was curious.

"You really don't know?"

Casey shook her head. "I don't watch TV. Sorry."

"Don't be," Olivia said with a smile. "It depends what you mean by famous—and how you measure it. Instagram followers, magazine covers, times I get stopped in the street, how many stalkers I have—"

"You have stalkers?"

"No, thank God. I just mean it's hard for me to say. Right now, I'm on a popular show. And they promote it heavily—you've seen our schedule—so we get a lot of attention. But maybe a better question is whether I feel famous."

"And do you?"

Casey liked this. They were chatting happily, easily and it was nice getting to know this Olivia. She was much more like the sweet woman she'd met in the sauna.

"Not at all. I mean, some of it I've gotten used to, but inside—where it counts—I'm an imposter. Just some shop worker from Brooklyn who accidentally ended up in LA on this hit show and who's going to get found out soon."

Olivia's expression got very serious, and Casey wanted to say something meaningful or reassuring. But she couldn't think of anything.

"Well, maybe I'll check out the show. If I get time—"

"Please don't." Olivia's response was emphatic. "You don't even watch TV and I'm pretty sure you wouldn't like it."

Casey wasn't sure what she'd said wrong, but Olivia now seemed tense.

The colorful strips of plastic ribbon hanging over the doorway to the kitchen parted and Estelle's shuffling figure came into view. She headed toward them. She was wearing slippers, as usual. Casey assumed Bruno—her long-suffering husband—was in the kitchen doing the cooking. On Sundays, when the nearby market filled even Café Brunest with hungry diners, Estelle's niece would help out, but on every other day, the café was quiet enough that it could be managed by just the two of them.

"Hey, Estelle, how's it going?" Casey wasn't sure Estelle would remember her. It'd been over a year since her last visit.

"Honey, nice to see you." Her voice carried enthusiasm, but it didn't mean that Estelle remembered her. She was like that with almost everyone. "How's America treating you? Did you come home because you missed my pies?"

Casey couldn't help but smile. She'd been a regular, and they'd chatted often, but that didn't mean that Estelle had to remember her. She had a lot of regulars.

"I'm just visiting, not back for good. But yes, I definitely missed your pies."

Estelle waved a hand in Olivia's direction. "You finally persuaded your girlfriend to come in and try the food. Well, it's about time I met her."

"No, no, it's not Hannah." Casey's response was quick. "This is Olivia. She's in town for a visit and I'm showing her around. She's never had one of your pies, and I want her to."

Casey felt Estelle's mistake like a small, shameful stab. Hannah wasn't ever willing to eat Estelle's kind of food, but Casey had talked about her often with Estelle. She'd been proud of her once—of her growing success on YouTube and even of her healthy non-pie-eating lifestyle. She'd been such a fool.

"This one looks too skinny to want to eat pies." Estelle peered over her glasses at Olivia. "I bet she wants an omelet or salad or something." She made the word *salad* sound distasteful.

Casey held Olivia's gaze, a dare in her eyes, wanting Olivia to be game enough to try one of the pies. They were obviously unhealthy, and the mash was usually loaded with butter. She was an actress, she probably had to watch her weight.

"What kind do you have?" There was a reluctance in Olivia's voice. A reluctance to offend, coupled with a probable reluctance to eat the pie.

"Steak pudding."

Olivia looked confused.

"It's a pie but it has a steamed suet pastry instead of short crust. It's very English and it'll be good, I promise." Casey couldn't help but explain, wanting to reassure. "Trust me."

Olivia gazed back at her. The connection, for a moment, was intense, and Casey felt something shift slightly in her core. It wasn't just that Olivia was beautiful. Sometimes she looked so lost and vulnerable that Casey had this odd urge to protect her. It was ridiculous in the circumstances. She made herself pull her gaze away and back to Estelle.

"I'll have that." Olivia's voice sounded a little husky. She cleared her throat. "The pudding thing. The steak pudding." The way her mouth formed the words was delightful to Casey.

"Me too." She nodded at Estelle. "And tea."

"Water for me," Olivia said.

Estelle shuffled away.

Casey rubbed her temples. She was tired and she was ravenously hungry, but it wasn't just that. Being here reminded her of her job, of the career she had worked hard for and then lost. And of every horrible thing that had led up to it. She was surprised that her primary emotion about it wasn't sadness or even anger. It was shame. It had all been her own fault.

"How long are you here for?" Olivia leaned forward as she asked the question.

"A month. Maybe less. I have some things I need to do, but I don't want it to be a long trip. I'd like to get back as soon as I can."

"I guess your girlfriend doesn't want you to stay away too long."

"She's not my girlfriend. I mean, she was when I lived here, but not anymore. And she's not the reason I'm here, not at all. I have other stuff I need to be doing." Casey didn't know why she was explaining. She didn't owe Olivia any information about her personal life. It was like she was reminding herself somehow.

Neither of them said anything for a minute.

"Well, our schedule seems so full, I'm pretty sure we're going to be keeping you very busy. I can't imagine you'll get much time off to do your own things. You're going to need a vacation to recover from your vacation." Olivia smiled, seeming pleased with her joke.

Casey didn't like being reminded of the fact that she needed to work two jobs, or that she was at Olivia's beck and call. She wasn't stupid. She hadn't imagined them having this afternoon had changed the dynamic between them in any way, but she'd wanted to enjoy their meal without having her serfdom thrown in her face again. Clearly, Olivia had a need to keep reminding her of who was in charge.

"I'll find time. There's two of us working the job, and I assume you'll need to sleep and eat. Even you can't need a chaperone the whole time." Casey chose her words carefully, sounding as chippy as she felt. And just like that, the tension was back between them.

"I didn't mean that."

Casey was pretty sure she did.

"I just meant they have us doing three or four events a day, and even with another driver to share the work, it's going to be pretty full on for you. We can't be late for things and we can't have missed appointments. The schedule is worked out to the minute." Olivia looked at her with an expression Casey simply couldn't read. Was she sitting there and suggesting Casey would be unprofessional enough to miss appointments?

"I'll manage. I'll do my job and I'll be available when I'm supposed to be. Don't worry about being kept waiting. I know your time is very precious." It was a low blow, but Olivia had gotten under her skin.

Casey wanted the food to arrive and she wanted to eat and leave. She assumed that when they got back to the hotel, Olivia would find her friends and do her event and Casey would get the evening to herself. She was expecting to get a proper two-week schedule from David tonight, and starting tomorrow, she would do only what was absolutely necessary. No impromptu museum trips and no more feeling sorry for Olivia—the TV star she had simply been hired to drive for. If nothing else, Olivia had helpfully just reminded her that this afternoon was valuable time wasted as far as her own objectives for this trip were concerned.

"I'm sorry if I said the wrong thing."

"You didn't."

"Then why has the temperature in here just dropped ten degrees?"

"It hasn't."

Casey needed to get a grip. Olivia wasn't trying to offend her. She was just stating the obvious. Casey was her driver and she was pretty sure that being driven around by some nobody she expected to be able to boss around was as ordinary to Olivia as taking a shower.

Estelle headed toward them with their drinks balanced on a plastic tray. She put them down in front of them and stayed to ask Olivia some questions about her trip. Casey was happy to be relieved of the responsibility of making awkward small talk.

Her stomach growled softly. If she was going to enjoy anything about this strange day, it was going to be the steak pudding and mash. Then she would get some badly needed sleep and wake up tomorrow determined not to do anything that would give Olivia the slightest reason to doubt her professionalism. Olivia was clear what she expected from Casey—be on time, wear a uniform, and do what you're told. It was disappointing, but it wasn't difficult. And it was only disappointing because she had let her attraction cloud her judgment. Olivia had the fame and celebrity that Hannah had always craved and which Casey couldn't understand ever wanting. If that wasn't reason enough to give her a wide berth, Casey didn't know what was.

Chapter Six

Casey flopped down onto the bed and groaned. She wasn't just stuffed after the huge meal they'd eaten, she was tired and stupidly full of regrets about the day. She shuffled into a more comfortable position on the bed, cast several of the pointless brocaded cushions onto the floor, and closed her eyes.

Her brain was whirring. She couldn't help but wish things had gone better, that the cherubic, slightly mussed up Olivia who had woken from sleep in her car had been with her the whole day. The wondrous expression on Olivia's beautiful face as she sipped the coffee had been as close to perfect as Casey had seen in a long while. Sadly, Olivia was also someone who seemed to enjoy putting Casey in her place, and she was annoyed with her own naivety in trying to help Olivia rescue something from her day. She took her annoyance with her into sleep.

Startled by the sound of her phone ringing, Casey sat up and looked around, confused by where she was. She picked up her phone and offered a groggy hello.

"Babe, did I wake you? Did I get my timing wrong? I thought it was evening over there." It was Gina.

"It is. I fell asleep."

Gina laughed. "You're napping in the middle of the day. That's not gonna get you laid. Get up, go outside, meet women. London is your oyster and you, Casey Byrne, are a pearl."

Casey rubbed her head as she leaned across to look at the bedside clock. It was almost six and she'd only been asleep for twenty minutes, but she couldn't blame Gina for that. Her brain was sluggish, but she did the math while reaching across for the bottle of water next to her bed.

"You sound a bit perky for a Sunday morning."

"Some things are worth getting up early for. And the sweetheart next door fixing me breakfast is definitely one of them."

"And the 'sweetheart next door' doesn't mind you calling me when you should be giving her all your attention?"

"Nope. She is putty in my hands right now, and I know I don't have to tell you why."

"That's right, Gina, please don't tell me why. I know the TMI concept is hard for you to grasp, but some things are best left unsaid." Casey couldn't keep the smile out of her voice. "Anyway, what's up? You're not calling to cancel my vacation, are you? I mean, if you've discovered some kind of travel website emergency that requires me to come home immediately, I wouldn't mind. Not even two days under my belt and I've already had enough."

"Really? How bad is she? Worse than you thought?"

"Mom's doing okay, I suppose. She's trying to stay off the drink." She looked at the stuffed folder of unpaid bills that she'd brought back from her mom's yesterday. "But she's in a pretty monumental mess. I don't know how long it's been going on, but I suspect she's been hiding how bad it is from Jack."

Casey didn't want to lay all of her gloom at Gina's feet, not when it seemed like her own day had started so well. She made herself sound brighter.

"But David already found me work. And it's the best, and worst, driving job in London."

"Explain."

"Well, the good news is that I'm speaking to you from a very expensive hotel where the clients have 'insisted' I stay so that I'm available as needed. I've already hit the gym, the sauna, and enjoyed the depth of this mattress more than I should. Bad news, I'm on call to a bunch of overindulged actors and actresses in from LA on some kind of promotional tour for their shit-hot TV show. And—"

What could she say? I already have a crush on this gorgeous woman I saw through the fog of a sauna who turned out to be kind of spoiled, and I just wish I didn't feel quite so disappointed.

She decided to spare Gina that version.

"Do you know Olivia Lang?"

"Are you kidding? Everybody knows Olivia Lang. At least in my gay-ass world they do. She's the best thing in that show by a long mile. I mean, it's a great show, but she is fire. I've never missed a single episode. I mean, where else do we see our queer selves represented so positively?"

"That good, huh? I've never seen it."

"I tried to get you to. Remember me raving about how well they handled that storyline about that trans guy getting assaulted by his friend when he came out to him. That was that show. Susie—Olivia Lang's character—is a boss. She ruined the guy who did it. He was some bigot senator's son. It was so satisfying. And not just because of how good she looks in business suits." Gina whistled softly.

"A boss," Casey said. "Yeah, that makes sense. She's keen to keep letting me know who's in charge."

"Wait. You're driving Olivia Lang around London? No fucking way."

"Not just her. Four of them. It's just that today, the rest of them didn't turn up." Casey looked at the schedule David had finally managed to get from the production company. She scrolled down to the bottom of the email on her phone. "Liam Morris, Louise Garland, Billie Carpenter. I think they all act on the show too."

"They surely do." Gina squealed as she spoke. "The first two are part of the original cast from season one. Liam plays Michael—that trans character I just told you about. He's awesome. Louise plays Jessie. She's like the show's comic relief and beating heart all wrapped into one amazing character. And Billie Carpenter is one of those ambitious as hell models who's made a move into acting. Surely even you've heard of her. She was voted, like, sexiest newcomer in Hollywood last year, or something. She turned up at the end of season three as some senator's wife with an eye for the ladies."

Casey was in awe of how Gina managed a social life, a busy job, and still kept track of every single item of queer popular culture.

"That is every kind of incredible. I think I'd combust at the idea of having Olivia Lang in the back of my car. Sorry, babe, couldn't resist. I know it's objectionable, objectifying, whatever, but she's damn hot. How did you concentrate on the driving?"

Casey felt herself flush at Gina's words. There had been moments when she'd sneaked a glance at Olivia and lost concentration before feeling instantly guilty for her passing feelings of lustfulness, and—yes—at her objectification of an actress who probably got pretty sick of people looking at her that way.

"It wasn't hard. She slept half the time and grouched at me when she was awake. Needs a babysitter as much as a driver." Casey felt disloyal bitching about Olivia. She hadn't been that bad. They had different lives, but it didn't make her a monster. "I'm not being fair. She's okay when she wants to be. We had food, went to a museum. I guess I forgot what it's like to be a driver, to be treated like the hired help. I'm probably just being sensitive."

"She took you to a museum and to eat and you're complaining she's treating you like the hired help?"

"I took her. Not that it matters. It won't happen again. I'm a driver, not a tour guide. We both kind of agreed it was better that way."

There were muffled voices on the other end of the call, and Casey guessed that Gina's breakfast was ready.

"Babe, I have to go."

"Sure."

"We will definitely continue this conversation later though." Gina lowered her voice. "Just tell me she's every bit as hot in real life as she is on the show."

"I couldn't say, I've never seen it."

"Casey." Gina sounded exasperated at her refusal to play the game.

"What do you want me to say? She's beautiful. I mean, eye-wideningly, skin-pricklingly, muscle-tighteningly, jaw-droppingly beautiful. Enough?"

"Good to know you noticed." Gina laughed and then said her good-byes and Casey was left feeling like that last sentence was the most honest she'd been with herself all day.

Olivia was standing in the doorway at the back of the room. She was late. Only a few minutes, but enough that her costars were already seated and Max—their emcee for the evening—was on her phone, obviously asking someone where Olivia was. The room was packed, and some of the studio people had been left standing along the wall on one side. She could see their relief as they caught sight of her in the doorway.

"They're going to knock on her door." Max put her hand across her phone and spoke to the audience. "She's probably gonna have to peel herself off some woman she met in the elevator." There were laughs and whistles and the odd "wish it was me" comment. It was Olivia's job—as the actress who played Susie—to play along with the innuendos. It wasn't always her favorite part of the job, but it was fun, mostly, and the adoration she got as Susie contrasted spectacularly with the lack of attention she got as Olivia.

She took in a breath and got into role.

"Sorry I'm late, bathroom break, and don't get excited, it was just little old me in there today. Sorry to disappoint y'all."

Every head in the large conference room turned to look at Olivia as she made her way down the central aisle, the crowd bursting into applause and cheers. At the end of season three, Susie had enjoyed a threesome in a hotel bathroom with a woman and her wife, while they'd been on their honeymoon. Even by Susie's standards, the scene had been pretty risqué.

As she approached the table, Olivia noticed that the chair that had been left for her was between the emcee and Billie. As the crowd settled down, she remembered the article that Liam had shown them and wondered whose idea it had been to seat her next to Billie.

Olivia climbed a little awkwardly up the steps at the back of the raised platform and squeezed past Louise and Liam on her way to her seat. She put a hand on Louise's shoulder as she passed. "You couldn't have saved me a better seat." She muttered the words without moving her mouth.

"We don't believe you. We just hope she—or they—were worth keeping us waiting for." The emcee played to the crowd, making the joke at Olivia's expense.

Olivia took her seat as Billie put a hand on her arm and leaned into the microphone. "I'm gonna get mighty jealous if it's true. I've got high hopes for us next season."

The crowd cheered as Billie turned to smile at her. It was, she supposed, a nice smile. But everything about Billie made her wary, and she'd learned the hard way to listen to her instincts when they told her someone wasn't to be trusted.

Olivia moved her arm away, breaking the contact between them.

"We've all got high hopes for next season." She spoke directly to the audience. To the people who loved the show and loved the characters. To the people she felt needed them to represent them in the best way possible. "And we're beyond happy that we get to shoot even a little part of it here in London town. I'm not sure we have room for all of you as extras, but I definitely think we should try." The crowd laughed and Olivia felt herself relax for what felt like the first time that day.

Except it wasn't. She'd felt relaxed waking up under Casey's jacket and under her watchful gaze. Her dark eyes making Olivia feel safe and secure. She shook the thought away. Casey was her driver. They had nothing in common. And she was pretty sure Casey didn't even like her.

"What's your favorite thing about London so far?" A woman with spiky blond hair sitting at the end of the front row was called on by Max to ask the first question. Liam got everyone's sympathy when he explained he'd been ill in bed all day and hadn't ventured outside of the hotel.

Billie responded next.

"Well, I already fell in love with your accent. And if I hadn't promised this one I'd be on my best behavior," she made Olivia cringe by casting a thumb in her direction, "I'd be trying to get myself an English girlfriend for sure."

The implication was that Olivia wouldn't approve of Billie chasing other girls. And she could tell from the audience's reaction they'd taken Billie's meaning that way too.

Max invited Olivia to speak next. She guessed she was supposed to flirt back with Billie and act a little jealous, but she didn't want to play that game. She looked out at the crowd and decided to ignore Billie's bait in favor of being more honest.

"Definitely not the traffic. I saw a little too much of that today." The audience murmured in agreement. "But I was taken to this fantastic little old pie and mash place near London Bridge." She leaned into her microphone. "The portions were huge, and I'm pretty sure I'll be digesting the food till Tuesday, but I recommend the steak pudding highly."

Olivia caught the quizzical look Louise gave her. She had left the café visit out of the highlight reel she had given Louise and Liam. She didn't have to tell them everything. And for now, her afternoon with Casey was something she wanted to keep for herself.

CHAPTER SEVEN

Olivia was sitting in the same armchair in the lobby she had occupied two days ago. When she had made a fool of herself with Casey. Except it was four hours earlier and this time, she had Liam and Louise for company. The ridiculously early start was because they were doing a live appearance on one of the UK's most popular breakfast shows.

"What's the point of us all getting up at stupid o'clock if we're just sitting here waiting for Billie and end up being late anyway." Louise was not at her best in the morning.

"She likes keeping us waiting. It makes her feel important," Liam replied without looking up. He was bent over his phone. "She did the same yesterday, but you weren't so beat up about it because it wasn't six a.m."

Olivia was half listening to them and half watching the elevators. Like them, she was waiting for Billie, but more than that, she was waiting for Casey. Yesterday, they'd spent most of the day together but hardly exchanged a word and it hadn't felt good. Casey had driven them to three different radio stations and then to a fabulously ornate hotel near King's Cross station where they were going to be shooting next week.

Every time they'd finished what they'd been doing, Casey had been parked outside waiting for them, and Olivia had watched as she carefully put her book on the seat next to her and got out to open the doors for them. She wanted to ask if it was boring following them around. She wanted to know what Casey was reading and whether she was enjoying it. Anything that wasn't the awkward silence that seemed to sit between them.

She'd only tried to make conversation once—asking Casey if she'd been back to the sauna—but the shake of her head didn't offer much opportunity for any kind of a follow-up and Olivia felt stupid for even trying. Casey wasn't interested in her and Olivia shouldn't give a damn about what her unfriendly driver thought of her. But the trouble was that she did and she couldn't help wanting to try for a better connection. She didn't understand where the yearning came from, but it was there and it was surprisingly strong.

The elevator doors opened and Roger hustled over to them. "She's not coming. She's not feeling well."

"She just realized that." Louise was the first to respond. "Fucking awesome."

"I think she thought if she got up, had a shower and some breakfast, she'd feel better, but she doesn't so…" He shrugged. "You should probably go on without her."

"She had breakfast?" Olivia asked. "We've been waiting for her for the best part of thirty minutes—time when we could all have been having breakfast—and now we're just being told to 'go on' without her. I don't know why she thinks she can pull stunts like this…and I don't know why you guys pander to her so fucking much. It's not even like she's the star of the show." Olivia's frustration got the better of her and her voice was louder than she intended. She spun around, wanting to just get the hell out of there, and found herself face-to-face with Casey, standing a few yards away. She looked down as Olivia tried to meet her gaze, a dead giveaway that she'd heard the whole thing, heard Olivia, yet again, being a bitch.

She moved closer to Casey. "Sorry if we kept you waiting. I didn't realize you were already outside."

"I'm always waiting. It's what I'm paid to do. You don't need to apologize." Casey turned and walked ahead of Olivia toward the doors. As ever, her tone was infuriatingly reasonable. Olivia watched her go.

She hated herself for caring about Casey's opinion of her almost as much as she hated herself for noticing just how good Casey's ass and thighs looked in the tight gray uniform pants.

"How is it that I didn't notice how hot she was yesterday?" Louise appeared at Olivia's right shoulder as Liam joined her on the other side. "Was she even wearing that uniform yesterday?"

"The pants and fancy shirt but not the jacket," Liam replied, sounding a little sullen.

"Well, I'm surprised I didn't notice."

"She spent most of yesterday in the car, Lou. Not even you can develop a crush on the back of someone's head." Olivia felt her temper spark again. She did not need Louise to start "noticing" Casey.

They reached the car, where Casey was standing at attention with the back door open, waiting for them to climb inside. Olivia followed Liam into the back of the car and then watched with surprise as Louise slammed the door shut and climbed into the front passenger seat. They all waited for Casey to get inside.

"I was thinking I might travel up front with you if that's okay. I'll get to see a lot more this way." She looked back at Olivia with a wink before buckling her seat belt, not leaving room for Casey to object. Not that Olivia expected her to. She was nothing if not accommodating.

Olivia was annoyed she hadn't had the nerve to think of sitting up front herself. It would have been the perfect way to try to engage Casey in some conversation that didn't make her seem like a bad tempered bundle of privilege.

"It's about a forty-minute drive, but we're late setting off so there'll be more traffic. I'll try to get you there on time, but I can't promise." Casey pulled the SUV out of the hotel parking lot.

"If we're late, I'm just going to tell them it's because we waited for Billie to decide whether she could be bothered to join us." Louise seemed to get annoyed all over again. "I'm pretty sick of the way she's allowed to pick and choose what she joins in with. It's not fair—"

"People get sick, Lou. Look at Liam. You guys bailed on me that first day and I just made the best of a bad situation. And I had a pretty good day in the end." Olivia was talking to Louise, of course, but she was also talking to Casey.

"Why don't we just change the subject. I'm pretty sure Casey doesn't want to hear all about our office politics," Liam cut in.

"I bet Casey's pretty good at not-listening." Louise turned to Casey as she spoke, and Olivia could almost hear her eyelashes fluttering. "You must hear a lot of stuff said in the back of cars that you're not supposed to. Maybe you're like a priest and can't tell anyone what happens in the black leather seats that act as your very own confessional chamber." Her tone was flirty. No one had ever said "black leather seats" with as much innuendo as Louise managed in that moment, and Olivia was irritated to see Casey react with a smile.

"This is my first driving job for about a year, so I'd forgotten what it's like, but yeah, people can get pretty relaxed and forget where they are. Forget that there's this thing too. We see everything." Casey reached up and tapped the rearview mirror, and for a second, she locked eyes with Olivia. "Some things you wish you could unsee, but some things are utterly charming." Olivia felt heat prickling across her skin as Casey held her gaze a moment longer before looking back at the road.

"Ooh, do tell. You can leave out the names—"

"What's the horsepower on this thing?" Liam leaned into the space between the front seats, interrupting Louise mid-flirt. The inside of the car was silent for a beat, and Olivia wanted to hug him for throwing Louise off her stride.

"Three hundred and six," Casey replied.

Liam nodded as if it mattered. Though Olivia knew damn well he had about as much interest as she did in cars. They were all acting like other people today. Except maybe Casey. Olivia didn't know enough about her to know what she was normally like, but she was responding to Louise's friendliness—for want of a better word—much better than Olivia had expected.

"Zero to sixty in five point two seconds. Top speed of one hundred and fifty-five miles per hour. It's Mercedes's fastest SUV," Casey added, interrupting the silence.

"You like fast cars?" Louise made it sound like she was asking Casey something else entirely. It had been a long time since Olivia had seen her flirt this hard. Casey waited a second before answering, and—in the eyes that she could see in the mirror—Olivia detected amusement. Surely, she didn't think Louise being like this was appealing?

"Not at all. But I know people are always going to ask me so I try to make sure I've got something convincing to say. Truth be told, I hate cars and I hate driving. I'm much happier when I'm on foot." This time Olivia was pretty sure that Casey was talking to her. She wasn't sure whether to smile or be offended.

"Was I convincing?" Casey addressed her question to Liam.

"I don't know. I don't know anything about cars either. I was just making conversation." He sat back in his seat. "Conversation that's more appropriate to the circumstances anyway."

Louise turned around to look at him, a frown on her face. The tension in the car had notched up a few degrees. And there was only another thirty minutes of this to endure. Olivia leaned across and lifted the remote control from the pocket in the seat in front of her.

"I'm going to find a news channel to listen to if that's okay. I feel out of touch since we got here. Be good to find out what's happening in the world." Olivia began to flick through the channels, not knowing what she was looking for. Casey pressed a button on the console in front of her and the sounds of a newscaster filled the car.

"News channel."

"Thank you."

The slight lift of Casey's shoulders was all the response she got.

"The London Eye!"

Olivia had been dozing, and Louise's shriek of recognition made her jump.

"Stop the car. Let's take some pictures. That's an Instagram moment for sure."

Olivia looked out the window to see that they were crawling along a wide bridge and London's famous giant wheel was on the opposite riverbank up ahead of them.

"You're shrieking at that, but you just let Big Ben go by without a mention." Liam pointed out the famous tower through the rear window.

"No way." Louise swiveled in her seat before placing a palm on Casey's thigh. "Please, can you pull over so we can take some pictures?"

"I can't, I'm sorry. Double red lines. It means no stopping…under any circumstances." Casey hadn't pushed the hand away and Louise hadn't moved it. Olivia couldn't help but feel jealous. Louise had all the moves, and Casey seemed as receptive as every other one of her targets.

"Please, Casey."

"She already said she can't, Lou. Stop whining. No one's going to change England's traffic rules just because you want a selfie." Liam spoke through gritted teeth. His mood didn't seem any better than Olivia's.

"Okay, jeez, someone's a party pooper today." Olivia could hear the pout in Louise's voice. "We're in London and these are London landmarks. It's good publicity for the show. Shame I'm the only one who cares about the importance of maintaining an Instagram profile."

She finally withdrew her hand from Casey's thigh and pushed the button that lowered the window. They were on the left-hand side of the bridge—the best side for Louise to at least get a photo from her seat. She tried a couple of selfies, but as the traffic slowed to a halt, she handed her phone to Casey. "Can you try?"

Olivia waited for Casey to say no. She was their driver, she was in charge of the car, on a busy road, and Louise was being a pain in the ass.

"Sure." Casey surprised Olivia by taking the phone, and after a quick glance at the traffic around them, took a handful of photos. She looked at the screen before handing the phone back to Louise and putting her hands back on the wheel just as the traffic started to inch forward.

"Fantastic. Thanks, Casey." The smile Louise gave Casey was returned. It was a smile Olivia hadn't seen since the steak pudding.

"I don't think we should do that again." Olivia found herself speaking, unable not to react. "I mean, it's dangerous and Casey should be concentrating on the road. She's our driver, Lou, not our tour guide."

"Exactly," Liam muttered.

Before Louise could respond, Casey spoke. "You're right, Ms. Lang, that was irresponsible of me. I'm sorry. Won't happen again." This time her eyes didn't search for Olivia's in the mirror.

"Tight-ass." Louise kept her voice low, but the response was clearly audible to all of them.

"I just—" Olivia started to respond but realized there was nothing she could say to defend herself. She was being snippy because she was stupidly jealous that Casey seemed to be finding Louise every bit as charming as she found Olivia annoying. She sat back in her seat and took in a breath, willing the embarrassment to fade.

"You're right, Lou. Liv has a nice tight ass. In fact, if I'm not mistaken, it was voted best ass on TV in 2019. I think you placed eleventh." Liam put his hand over Olivia's and squeezed. She appreciated the solidarity.

"Get it right, I was tenth," Louise replied. She waited for a beat. "Out of ten."

They all laughed and the tension was gone. It was impossible for them to stay mad at each other for long.

So what if Louise wanted to flirt with Casey. And so what if Casey seemed to enjoy it. Olivia had no claim on either of them. Her absurd jealousy was something she was just going to have to swallow.

Casey was standing near the exit for the bridge at Embankment tube station as arranged, watching people teeming through the automatic barriers. David was late, like always, but Casey didn't care. She was enjoying the people watching. Occasionally, someone would approach the barriers with no clue of how to navigate them, holding their ticket against the wrong part of the reader so that the gates wouldn't open. Casey watched and winced, as even a moment's hesitation caused a line of impatient travelers to build up.

This had been her life for so long. In fact, that could easily have been Casey tutting and sighing behind some hapless tourist, rushing to some stressful home visit or other. Her job as a youth worker had seen her hurrying across east London from one broken home to another, from one school to another, to meet with the kids she had a responsibility to keep an eye on. It might have been stressful—and at times it was downright heartbreaking—but she had loved every minute of it. Every day, she'd felt like she was doing something righteous, something that mattered in the world. And it had mattered—until it was gone. Until it was taken from her. There was a tightness in her chest whenever she thought about it.

Standing there waiting for David, she couldn't imagine ever needing to be in such a hurry again, and she wasn't sure whether to be happy or sad about it. Working with Gina was a lot of fun and it was a thousand times better than being a driver, but it didn't fire her soul the way working with young people had. When she'd lost that job, Casey had felt the loss like a bereavement. It had hurt almost as much as Hannah's betrayal. Being unable to follow through on the promises she'd made to some of the kids she'd worked with and not even having the chance to explain why had been the most painful thing of all.

Casey caught sight of David coming through the barriers. Her mood lifted at the sight of him.

"David." Casey waved and shouted at the same time. He turned toward her and smiled, opening his arms for a hug.

"I can't believe they gave you an evening off. What are the lesbians doing without their driver?"

"They're not all lesbians."

"I know, but I feel like they're the ones that are probably missing you the most." He smiled.

"They're doing some interviews at the hotel and then one of those events with the fans. Nobody needs me or the car."

"Do the fans throw their underwear at them and ask them to sign their breasts?"

"I have no idea. But I'm intrigued now about what kind of fan events you've been attending."

Casey tried to imagine Olivia being bombarded with panties and presented with breasts to sign. She couldn't. She just seemed so buttoned up. Louise, on the other hand, probably had a special signature she used just for breasts. She couldn't help but smile at the difference between them.

The day they'd spent together had been fascinating. Olivia had such a disapproving older sister vibe. And Liam had been mad as hell with Louise for flirting with her. She wondered if Louise knew he had a thing for her. If she did, the blatant flirting was pretty cruel.

"I've got us return tickets for the boat to Greenwich." She pulled David toward the riverside exit.

"Great." He rolled his eyes.

"Hey, I've been away a year and that qualifies me as a visitor, so I definitely get to do touristy things. You'll enjoy it, and if you don't, I'll buy you fish and chips when we get to Greenwich."

"You just said the magic words." David patted his stomach.

The boat was not as full as Casey had expected it to be, and she and David easily snagged a seat on the outside deck. Casey wanted to watch the bridges disappearing behind them one by one as they traveled eastward along the Thames. It was early evening but still pretty warm. As the boat pulled away from the pier and began to chug its way along to Waterloo Bridge, David turned in his seat to face her.

"How's it been going? Has it been manageable?"

"Yeah, completely. A couple of early starts but nothing too bad. I thought I might find the driving a bit stressful after so long away from London, but it's been fine. Wish I could say the same for the clients."

"What do you mean?"

"Nothing, not really. Some of them are nice, some of them are…" Casey was silent for a moment, watching the beautiful building that housed the Courtauld Gallery slide by. "I guess some of them are just living up to how I expected big shot TV actresses to behave." She badly wanted to talk about Olivia, about how she was so hit-and-miss in the way she related to Casey and about how Casey got so foolishly tongue-tied in her presence. But she was far too embarrassed.

"One of them—Olivia—seems like the biggest star. She certainly acts like she is, anyway. But the others are pretty friendly. A little too friendly perhaps." She smiled, not able to take Louise's advances seriously.

"Don't tell me they're getting frisky with you. I knew you in that uniform would be hard to resist." He lifted an eyebrow. "Just be careful, I don't want any complaints about you breaking hearts."

"I'm not going to mess with the clients, and I'm not going to let them mess with me. I'm only here for a few weeks and I'm hoping to cut and run as soon as I can. And you know me, I'm not exactly the type to be interested in actresses from LA, even ones voted as having the best ass on TV."

There had been a moment, after she'd dropped them all off, when Casey was tempted to google it—to actually google Olivia's award-winning ass—but she hadn't. Louise had invited her to wait for them in the green room while they did the interview, but as hungry as she was, she said no. She had calls to make—to Jack, to her mom's landlord, to the police—and she had read Olivia's and Liam's moods well enough to understand that whatever Louise was saying, neither of them were keen on her tagging along. She'd waited outside, making her calls, reading her book and trying not to think about why Olivia Lang intrigued her so much.

"Well, I think you should enjoy the attention while it's on offer. You've been single for longer than I have."

Casey didn't bother responding. She'd had the odd date in Portland—usually when she got tired of saying no to Gina's efforts to set her up—but she didn't see why she had to say that. She could be single for as long as she wanted. She had plenty of reasons to be.

"I wasn't sure whether to tell you and I don't suppose it matters to you after all this time, but Hannah and Zoey got engaged." David looked at Casey with eyes that were full of concern. Casey wondered if he thought the news would upset her. It was weird, but she couldn't even decide if she cared.

"Good for them. They deserve each other."

She obviously cared enough to still feel annoyed about it.

"And of course, they've got some wedding video deal. A sponsor. A fat check. Hannah was all excited about it when they came over for dinner last week. You know what she's like."

"I do."

There was a lot more Casey could have said, but she didn't want to. It was awkward enough for David trying to maintain a friendship with them both.

"I'm just telling you so you're prepared. They'll be at the party. I can't believe she won't flaunt it. She knows you're here and that you're coming. She was asking a lot of questions, talking about how good it would be to see you, how she hadn't wanted things between you to end as badly as they had. If she wasn't Hannah, you might even have imagined some actual regret in there."

"She cheated on me, got me arrested, cost me my job, and then told everyone it was my fault because I was a nightmare of a girlfriend who'd tried to ruin her career. I'm not sure there's a way back from that." Even now, being reminded of it was hard. "I know I did some stuff I shouldn't have when I found out about her cheating, but I didn't deserve what she did to me."

"She behaved badly. I think deep down she knows that. It's been hard for me to forgive her too, but it was a long time ago. You've both moved on."

Casey looked up at the massive bulk of Blackfriars Bridge as they passed underneath it. Seeing Hannah again was not something she had prepared herself for. She tried to figure out how she felt about it, about her being engaged and happy. But she couldn't. After it all happened, she cut off her emotions, got on a plane, and left. And she forced herself to forget all about it. She wasn't Casey who'd been horribly wronged and then callously blamed, she was Casey the woman who was ready for a fresh start. It was moving on, kind of.

"I do like one of the actresses." Casey was surprised she said it and felt instantly foolish.

"Which one?" David's eyes widened.

"It's ridiculous." Casey's doubts about talking about it—about acknowledging it at all—were reasonable. They'd only had a couple of days together and she knew next to nothing about Olivia.

"Why?"

"It's a cliché. She's a superstar and I'm her driver—the hired help who gets on her nerves by not being obedient enough." Casey couldn't help but feel sheepish. "We spent a few hours together having a great time on her first day, but we've mostly just given each other a wide berth ever since."

"Sounds like someone has a little crush developing. So cute." He poked her in the cheek playfully. He was just about the only person she knew who could get away with that.

"She's gorgeous and she's interesting—and also everything I'd normally run a mile from. But somehow I can't stop myself wanting to know her better. I can't explain it, and yeah, I know its laughable."

"Well, I'm not laughing. You know me, I'm always falling in love with someone—the bus driver, the guy who delivered my groceries last night. I'm the last person to laugh at you for falling for someone—"

"I'm not falling for her," Casey cut in, wishing she hadn't said anything. "I'm just saying I had a good time when we spent time together and now I'm curious about her. She's all ice queen one minute and super sweet the next. It's just something I need to get out of my system." Casey was not "a little crush" kind of person. It was annoying she couldn't seem to shake it off.

"You know the best way of getting something out of your system?" David grinned back at her. "Go for it. You're only going to know each other for two weeks. No strings. And no reason not to make use of the fact that you're staying in the same hotel. It would be a great holiday romance story to tell everyone at the party."

"I don't work that way, you know that. And Olivia's far too famous to be interested in someone like me." Casey paused. "I don't want someone who lives to be adored and whose main worry is whether their ass is in award-winning shape. It's not my vibe."

Being with Hannah had taught her that. She could never understand the way some people chased after celebrity, and she definitely wasn't a happy-in-the-limelight kind of person.

"What do you know about her? Is she single?"

"I'm not interested in whether she's single or not." Casey told the white lie. "All I know is she's from Brooklyn. She blows hot and cold, has a smile that could heat a room, and she looks great in a towel."

"Huh?"

"We shared a sauna."

"You are a weirdo. You're literally the only person I know who wouldn't have googled the hell out of that woman." He pulled out his phone and tapped at the screen.

"Olivia Lang. Has played Susie Collins on *The West Side* for three years. Most popular character, resident heartbreaker. Blah blah blah. Aged thirty-four, born in Brooklyn. Came to acting late."

"Don't." Casey put her hands over her ears. "I don't want to know. If she ever wants me to know any of that stuff, she'll tell me. I don't need to spy on her."

"Okay, okay." David put his phone away and looked at her. "She's a Gemini by the way. Might explain the hot and cold."

"Stop." She punched his arm playfully.

"Was single, but recent rumors suggest something might be going on with her costar, Billie something or other."

"David." She said his name loud enough that several people turned around to look at them. "I said I don't want to know."

"Sorry." He looked contrite, but Casey knew he wasn't.

They sat for a moment watching the riverside. Casey hated the feeling in the pit of her stomach that the news that Olivia and Billie might be dating had caused. She didn't like Billie at all. She seemed hard and her friendliness seemed inauthentic, but she was poised and very beautiful. And of course that was exactly what someone like Olivia would be looking for.

"Mercy was asking me if she should get in touch. She and Naomi want to see you, but they're not sure you want to see them. I said it might be hard for you to find time. I was trying to buy you some cover if you didn't want to see them."

"Thanks. I know I should see them, and it'd be good to see Mercy. I've missed her. I've been meaning to set something up. It's just been busy with my mom and the job."

Casey felt a tension in her chest. She was usually much more honest than this with David. She had been busy, but the job had given her more free time than she'd expected. She had the time to catch up with friends, she just felt nervous about doing it. She hadn't exactly left things in the best place with everyone.

"I still can't help feeling like I don't know who to trust. I don't know what Hannah told people, and I don't know how much of it they believed. And I know I'm making myself lonely by staying away from people, but I'd rather be lonely than a fool."

"I get that, babe. Take your time."

"Being back here is strange, that's all. Too many not good memories."

As they passed under the Millennium Bridge and St. Paul's came into view, Casey suddenly felt tired. A year ago, she had lost her job, her girlfriend and her sense of self. Running away had let her avoid thinking about it. Coming back made it impossible not to. No wonder she was happy to have an Olivia Lang-shaped distraction.

Chapter Eight

The bar was slowly filling up with guests, and the noise had Casey wondering if she might be better off taking her drink up to her room. She had her mom's folder of bills open on the small table in front of her and was slowly working through it, trying to figure out what had been paid and what hadn't. It had to be done, but it wasn't the best way to spend an evening. She took a long pull on her beer before standing and stretching, feeling an ache in her lower back. The hours she was spending in the driver's seat weren't doing her body much good.

Another cheer erupted from the conference room along the corridor from where she was sitting. It wasn't helping her concentration to know that Olivia and the others were just fifty yards away being questioned by a roomful of adoring fans. Judging by the cheers and applause, it was going well. She thought about David's comment about the fans throwing underwear and the cast being asked to sign breasts and wondered how close that was to the truth. It sounded raucous—but not that raucous.

She lifted a hand to the waiter in a gesture that signified she was stepping out for a minute. He gave her a matching wave. A wave that Casey understood meant that he would half-watch her stuff, but if anything went missing while she was gone it wasn't his fault.

She headed down the corridor to the room where all the noise was coming from. The large sign outside made it very clear it was a VIP, ticket only event, but no one was guarding the door. She slipped inside and lined up against the back wall with several others who had presumably arrived too late to secure a seat.

Olivia was sitting with the rest of the cast behind a long table that was set on a raised platform. She looked incredible. A midnight blue shirt, buttons open at the neck showing off the soft, smooth skin that Casey couldn't help but remember from the sauna. Her hair was in a messy bun. She looked relaxed as she laughed along with the audience at an answer Louise had given to a question Casey hadn't heard. Rows and rows of velvet-covered chairs sat facing them—probably about a hundred or more. Every chair was occupied and every head was facing the stage, where Billie, Liam, Louise, and Olivia were sitting alongside a short-haired woman in glasses who seemed to be directing proceedings.

"Is it true that you're filming some scenes here in London?"

The question came from a woman on the front row who sounded a little breathless.

"And is it true that Susie and Phoebe are gonna get together? Because I'd totally love that." She laughed and the audience broke into claps and cheers.

"Speaking as Phoebe, I think she'd be down for kissing Susie slash Olivia in whatever storyline the writers can dream up." Billie stepped in to answer before any of the rest of them could speak. "I mean, look at her." She fanned herself with her hand. "I think our chemistry would make that storyline sizzle." She gave Olivia a long look and a big smile before sitting back in her chair looking satisfied as the audience sounded their approval.

Casey couldn't help the pang of jealousy she felt watching Billie compliment Olivia so confidently. Olivia seemed to take in a breath before leaning forward.

"We're excited about shooting here. All we've been told is that Susie has some business to deal with in London." She smiled. "I mean, of course she does, she's always up to something exciting. We're filming at the St. Pancras hotel—which is gorgeous by the way—and the Eurostar terminal. But none of us know what's in store for season four. We haven't even seen the scripts yet, so any speculating about who's sleeping with who is just gossip. And Phoebe is married so that wouldn't be at all appropriate of Susie." She flashed a smile at the fans, along with a well-timed shrug as the audience laughed along with her. Casey wasn't in on the joke, but she assumed that Olivia's character wasn't someone who cared what was "appropriate," and would happily sleep with a married Phoebe.

Seeing Olivia there next to Billie and among the fans who adored her—flirting, chatting, and finding characters cheating on each other funny—reinforced Casey's feeling that she needed to bury her crush on Olivia. And then pour concrete over it. Olivia lived a life that was a million miles away from her own. And Casey was glad to be reminded that any spark of interest she might have imagined Olivia showing her these past few days, was just like this—her being charming because she was an actress and she was expected to be nice to people.

Her mom's debts were what needed her attention. She was here because of that, not to torment herself with thoughts of how much she might have liked to get to know Olivia better. She slipped out of the room and back to her table in the bar. She picked up her beer. A couple of gulps and it was gone. She signaled the waiter for another before opening the binder to take out the next bill.

Olivia had sat signing autographs and posing for selfies for as long as it took to make sure everyone had what they came for. The line of fans for the others had dwindled a little quicker than hers, and Louise and Liam had just taken the chance to slip away, giving her a small guilty wave as they left. For some reason, Billie had hung around, moving to the chair next to hers and joining in with photos and conversations as if she had a right to. Olivia was in no position to tell her to leave, but it annoyed the hell out of her.

As the last of the fans said their good-byes and were ushered out of the room by the studio people, Billie turned to her.

"Let's get a drink. I think we deserve one after the day we've had. We could hit the bar upstairs, or we could go out somewhere. I noticed a couple of cute old pubs not too far away. Could be cozy. And we could make sure we got seen, call some paparazzi. Good publicity for the show." Billie angled her head as she spoke. When she ran the tip of her tongue across her upper lip, Olivia understood that she was flirting rather than just being friendly.

The drink part sounded good, just not with Billie—and definitely not with a bunch of paparazzi watching them. It wasn't that Billie was overly ambitious, indiscreet, and surgically enhanced—or at least that wasn't the entire problem—it was that everything about her seemed calculated somehow. And Olivia thrived on straightforwardness. She was from Brooklyn after all.

She smiled inside at the memory of Casey being very straightforward with her, and how it had pushed her buttons precisely because she'd forgotten what it was like. Her business, her life in LA, was all about pretending.

"I'm pretty tired—"

"But isn't it your solemn duty to take the new girl under your wing and show her the ropes? We could develop our characters over cocktails," Billie interrupted, putting a hand on her arm as she spoke. Her eyes were wide and expectant.

"I'm sorry, Billie, I'm not in the mood. I want a long bath and time to relax. We have another early start tomorrow. I think I'm just gonna get something sent up to my room."

"I'm not used to people saying no to me. I'm kind of irresistible, or so I'm told." It was a joke and also absolutely not a joke. Olivia didn't doubt that Billie believed it.

"I'm sure that's the case, but I have this really boring rule about not mixing work and pleasure so it might be easier for us both to just stay friendly." Olivia kept her tone even.

"I was being friendly. I was suggesting a friendly drink between friendly colleagues who are probably going to get pretty friendly on screen this coming season. It kind of makes sense for us to get a little closer, no?"

It was the second time Billie had hinted about their upcoming storyline and it made Olivia's heart sink.

"I know you're single, Olivia, or I wouldn't suggest it. And I know you care as much as I do about the show doing well." Billie smiled a confident smile. "So I'm gonna keep asking. I think we'd be good together and I'm pretty persistent when I have a good idea." She picked up her jacket and moved off toward the door, her hips swaying as she walked. At the door, she looked back and winked, expecting that Olivia would be watching her leave.

Olivia waited a minute, wanting to be sure that Billie had gone before making her way along the corridor to the small, open-plan bar next to the reception area. It wasn't as nice as the one upstairs, but she wasn't going to stay. All she wanted was a glass of wine to take upstairs to drink while taking that bath.

As Olivia headed to the counter, she spotted Casey sitting alone at a table in the corner. She had her head down, reading something, and the table in front of her was strewn with papers. She hated the fact that her heart began beating a little faster. Ever since that morning—when Casey had responded far too well to Louise's flirting—Olivia had tried not to think of Casey, tried not to want to talk to her, tried not to respond to the sight of her in exactly the way her body was now doing.

She needed to make good on her intentions, take her wine upstairs and leave Casey be. Especially since Casey hadn't shown a scintilla of interest in talking to Olivia for almost two days and Olivia's continued interest was becoming embarrassing. She had never been one of those women attracted by someone who seemed out of reach.

"Hey." She spoke softly, but Casey still jumped a little in surprise. Olivia raised a hand. "Just saying hi, not trying to disturb your night off. And you look kind of busy anyway." Olivia already wished she hadn't come to the table. Her nervousness around Casey was not something she enjoyed.

Casey looked up at her. Her face carried a hesitant expression, but her dark eyes held Olivia's gaze steadily. They were captivating. Olivia meant to walk away, but found she was still standing there.

"Yeah. Some paperwork I have to deal with. I figured if I did it with a beer, it wouldn't feel like such an awful way to spend the night."

Olivia wanted to say something in response, but no words came.

"You looked like you were having fun in there." Casey angled her head toward the corridor containing the conference rooms.

"You were there?"

"I snuck inside for a little while. I could hear the cheers. I was curious. A friend told me the fans throw their underwear and ask you to sign their breasts. I wanted to see if it was true, but it was all very sedate and civilized." Casey smiled and Olivia liked the way it made her feel.

"Were you disappointed?"

"More like relieved." Casey smiled again. Just a small one, but it encouraged Olivia somehow.

"Do you want another drink? I was going to get one…" Olivia pointed at the bar.

Casey lifted her beer bottle. It was almost empty. For a beat, there was silence between them.

"Sure." Casey leaned forward and tidied the loose papers into a single pile before closing the ring binder and moving it to the floor. She closed a paperback book that had been spread open and placed it on the papers. Olivia watched Casey's hands move. She had beautiful long fingers, like a pianist. Olivia blushed and prayed it wasn't obvious.

She sat in the chair next to the space Casey had cleared for her and signaled the waiter. She ordered the large glass of Malbec she'd been craving and a beer for Casey.

"Is it a lot of fun for you?" Casey asked.

"The meet and greet?"

Casey nodded.

"Usually. I mean, it all depends on the crowd, the questions, the energy, the emcee. But most of the time, I enjoy them. The fans are passionate and funny and they have a good sense of what works well on the show—and what doesn't—and that keeps us on our toes. This last season we had a few writing issues and you hope that no one notices, but they always do. And the fans say what the studio needs to hear, what we—as the actors who have to say the lines—would never dare to say." Olivia stopped herself. She didn't want to be unprofessional and more than that, she didn't want to bore Casey. "I'm sorry. I know you don't watch it. And I shouldn't complain. It's a great show. It's been good for me."

"How's it been good for you?"

Casey was blunt. Like a New Yorker, but with an English accent that was all soft edges—and a lot more alluring.

"I was struggling. Louise had persuaded me to move to LA—said it'd be great for my career—but I just couldn't get a break. Even though I auditioned for everything." She emphasized the last word. "The low point was probably not getting picked to advertise this new hemorrhoid cream, because 'I didn't look like the kind of person' who would suffer from hemorrhoids. I was on the point of scuttling back to Brooklyn, feeling like a complete failure, when this show came up and Louise encouraged me to go for it."

"I guess sometimes things work out when you least expect them to." Casey sat back a little in her chair. "And missing the hemorrhoid gig seems like a good thing."

Olivia couldn't tell if Casey was being nice or mocking her somehow. She decided to give her the benefit of the doubt.

"I was so happy to get the part of Susie…and then I panicked. I'd come to acting late and I'd only ever done theater before. It was a small miracle I got cast, and I felt so out of my depth when I got on set. If it wasn't for Louise, I'd have sunk without a trace that first season I think."

Olivia no longer felt the butterflies—performing for TV had become a routine part of her life—but she never ceased thinking that doing this for a living was somehow miraculous.

"Well, you must be doing something right. There was a lot of love for you in that room."

Olivia liked hearing Casey say it.

"What about you? How long have you been a driver?"

"Four days." Casey took a swig of her beer. Olivia enjoyed the rippling of her throat as she swallowed. Her shirt was open at the neck, the sleeves rolled up, showing beautifully muscled forearms. She felt the attraction more than she wanted to.

"Four days?" Olivia responded a beat too late.

"I don't drive as a job. Not usually. It's…" Casey waved a hand dismissively. "It's too boring to explain."

"Except I want to know."

"I live in Portland. I work for a travel company there. We specialize in LGBTQ travel. City guides, safe destinations, organized tours. It's all web based. It's my roommate's business. I like it even though it's just something I fell into when I left London and needed a job."

"Would Café Brunest and that scary old operating theater be on one of your London tours?"

"No way. Things that special, I keep to myself." She held Olivia's gaze as she spoke. "But I'm back here because I have some stuff to do for my mom." She indicated the pile of papers. "And I need to be earning while I'm here, so my friend got me this driving job."

"But it seems like you've done this before. Driving, being a driver. It doesn't feel like your first job."

"It isn't. I did it for a while before I moved to Portland last year." She shrugged. "And I've lived here my whole life, so I obviously know the city well."

"Why the move to Portland?"

Casey reacted to the question, and Olivia got the feeling it was something she shouldn't have asked.

"I'm sorry. I didn't mean to interrogate you. I was just curious."

"It's okay." Casey took a drink of her beer and kept hold of the bottle, picking at the label. "I needed a break. I had a friend there who offered me a place to stay. And then she offered me a job. So I decided to stay." She lifted her eyes from the bottle and Olivia saw a sadness in them.

"You said you came to acting late. What did you do before?"

Olivia let Casey change the subject. She had the feeling there was more to the Portland story, but it wasn't her business to pry.

She told Casey about her mom and dad's dry-cleaning store, about her dad getting sick and putting her hopes of acting on hold to help her mom run the store. She was happy to talk about her parents. She loved them. They had given her everything they could.

"When my dad was well enough to go back to work, he surprised me with acting lessons at the theater school across the road. It was a good school and I worked my ass off to be good enough to eventually get theater work. Small parts, small theaters, but it was what I'd dreamed of. And my parents were so proud of me. It was amazing the first time they came to see me perform in a proper theater. My dad gave me a standing ovation at the intermission. He didn't know any better, but I was nothing but proud of him."

It felt so good for them to be talking without tension, without misunderstandings. And it felt even better for Olivia to be able to tell Casey she'd had this ordinary upbringing in Brooklyn, to show that she wasn't the privileged LA type that Casey obviously thought she was—at least not in her heart anyway. Olivia wasn't sure if it was the beer or the fact they were both "off-duty," but Casey seemed much more relaxed and it was nice.

"So there's just you?"

"Yeah. My mom wanted more kids, but she couldn't, so they got stuck with me."

"Don't say that. It sounds to me like the three of you make a pretty good team."

"Do you have siblings?"

"Just one brother. Jack. He lives here. We're not that close." Casey seemed to hesitate. "Not just because I don't live here. We were never that close when I did. He's younger. And still my mom's baby boy—even at twenty-five. We're just very different."

"I get the feeling you hate driving. Am I wrong?" Olivia saw the tension return to Casey's face and shoulders. She'd said the wrong thing. "I'm not saying you're not good at it, and I'm not talking about the fact you wanted me to walk—"

"It's okay." Casey cut her off, saving her embarrassment. "It's a job I do when I need money, but it's not a passion of mine, no."

Again, Olivia waited. Casey was talking to her, but it seemed like she might clam up at any moment and Olivia didn't want that, didn't want that at all.

"I was a youth worker before I was a driver. You know, helping kids who were struggling at home, mediating with the families, helping them find somewhere to live if it didn't work out at home. It was..." Casey looked like she was searching for a word. "It was hard sometimes. Hard, but always important. I could never understand how people could treat their kids that way. Some suffered because they were gay and couldn't tell anyone, or they'd told someone who hadn't taken it well. Some were being bullied, neglected, harmed."

Casey stopped, seeming lost in her thoughts. Olivia wanted to ask Casey what it was like, how she had coped with the heartache, but talking about it seemed to have put Casey on edge.

"Do you miss your parents? Do you get back to see them a lot?" Casey again moved the conversation back to Olivia. But her gaze was serious and interested, and it made Olivia feel like they were the only two people in the room.

"Not as much as I'd like. It's a pretty demanding schedule. I miss my mom. She's always been so supportive about everything. I can't even begin to tell you the number of times she's helped me out. I'm so lucky compared to some of those kids you worked with."

Olivia remembered every single time her mom had been there for her, every one. The care packages she'd lovingly sent when Olivia wasn't working. The time she'd called home crying when the producer had put his hands on her shoulders and told her she'd have to undress for him if she wanted the part. Even the time she'd got the part of Susie and then got freaked out because she had to have sex on camera.

And when Kristin had cruelly dumped her, and then been disgusting enough to cash in by leaking a recording of them having sex, despite her mom being as embarrassed as hell, she was the one who had convinced Olivia to stop hiding and start fighting back.

"Maybe that's why you give off that vibe."

"What 'vibe'?" Olivia made speech marks around the word with her fingers. "I'm not sure I like the sound of that."

Casey smiled. Her expression was often thoughtful, sometimes stern, but when she smiled, it was like the sun peeking out from behind a cloud. And being smiled at like that warmed Olivia. Warmed her in places it probably shouldn't.

"You just seem like someone who has been loved. Who knows her own value."

Olivia couldn't stop a bitter laugh from escaping.

"What?" Casey frowned. "Did I say the wrong thing?"

Olivia shook her head. "No. Sorry. Not about that. They loved me. I'm grateful for that. I just think..." What did she think? Hadn't she stopped thinking? Wasn't that the point? "I just think that, apart from them, I don't feel very loved, or very lovable. Lately, Susie seems like everything everyone wants and everything everyone likes about me. I don't feel like

Olivia gets much of a look in." She leaned forward. "But you know what, I hate myself for saying that out loud. Please forget that I did. I know how privileged I am to have this life, this career. A lot of people don't get to work at jobs they love. And I love acting. I wouldn't swap this life for anything."

It wasn't true. Lately, she had felt more and more like she was losing herself and found herself fantasizing about just getting on a plane back to New York and trying to live an ordinary life again. She could act there for fun and leave Susie behind in LA.

"Doing a job you love is important. You have a right to want it. We all do. And you have a right to complain about not having it."

Olivia agreed. But she had the feeling that Casey was talking about her own situation.

"If you liked being a youth worker so much, why did you give it up? Don't you miss it?"

It felt like an obvious question, but as soon as she'd said it, Casey's expression closed and Olivia felt the change. She had somehow asked the wrong question.

"I just couldn't…I wasn't able to do it anymore, and…" Casey faltered.

"Hey." Louise's voice rang out across the bar. She headed in their direction. "I've been calling, but you," she pointed at Olivia, "are not answering your phone. I assumed you got caught up with some fans and was gonna come and rescue you. But I see it's Casey you got caught up with." She gave Olivia a sly smile.

"I just came by to say hello. We got to talking. I haven't been here long." She was annoyed with herself for feeling the need to explain things to Louise. She hadn't done anything wrong. But she was more annoyed that Louise was interrupting them.

"Hi, Casey." Louise sat down.

"Casey has stuff she needs to get on with. I was just leaving." Olivia pushed her chair back a little as if to show Louise she was about to leave. She didn't want to watch Louise flirting with Casey again.

"That's good because I was going to see if you wanted to come out for a drink. I'm sure Liam will come too, but he's another one who isn't taking my calls."

Olivia wanted to say no. It wasn't just that she was tired. She had half a hope that she might be able to stay here and keep Casey talking.

"There's Liam." Louise jumped up.

Olivia looked through the etched glass panels that served to screen the bar from the rest of the reception area. Liam was crossing the reception area, toward the exit. He was dressed up. Fitted dark green shirt, faded black jeans, and shiny black shoes. He looked handsome. Louise waved at him from the entrance of the bar and he headed over.

"Hey." He lifted a hand in greeting as he got closer to their table.

"Where are you going?" Louise asked.

"Out for something to eat."

"Without us?" Louise sounded edgy.

"Yeah. Just meeting someone—from this morning. Remember that showrunner who looked after us? The cute Scottish one with those weird square glasses? We started talking while I was waiting for you to finish and she said there's this bar near their studio that does these amazing cheeseburgers. I mean, I'm not saying the food here isn't good, but I'm definitely missing good burgers." He shuffled from one foot to the other, seeming awkward.

"You're going on—"

"You got yourself a date—" Olivia half-squealed, speaking over Louise without meaning to. "Scottish, cute, burgers. Sounds like that could be fun."

"I guess." Liam looked sheepish.

"We're going out too. I thought you'd come, but we obviously can't compete with the promise of great burgers and a Scottish accent." Louise sounded a little snarky.

Olivia realized that Liam abandoning Louise for his date meant she now had no choice but to leave Casey and go out with her. If she had Louise's confidence, she'd have asked Casey to go with them so they could keep talking, but she didn't dare.

"Uber waiting. Wish me luck." Liam gave them a little wave and headed off. They all watched him till he passed through the revolving exit doors. They were silent for a long beat.

Olivia spoke first. "Okay, Lou. Let me grab a quick shower and change and I'll come and explore some cozy pubs with you."

"I've changed my mind. I think I'll just have a soak in the bath and an early night." Louise sounded glum all of a sudden.

"If you're sure." Olivia's heart lifted at the idea of more time getting to know Casey.

"I think I'll head up too." Casey picked up her ring binder before draining her beer. "If I stay here, I'll drink too much and be hungover. And

I've got these demanding clients who seem to specialize in early starts." The wry smile she offered Olivia wasn't enough, but it was something.

"Well, my original plan had been a soak in the bath and an early night. But then I saw you here and I couldn't resist—" Olivia stopped speaking, giving herself room for a mental face palm. "I mean I couldn't resist having a drink." Great. Now she was making it sound like Casey's presence was irrelevant. She made herself slow her brain down and stood up.

"It was nice chatting with you, anyway. I hope you get done what you need to get done, and I'm sorry for disturbing you." Her embarrassed formality was almost British.

"Same," Casey replied. "And I didn't mind the disturbance." She held Olivia's gaze and Olivia felt the pull of her attraction. She wondered what Casey would say if she knew the effect she had on her.

"Maybe I'll get a bottle to take upstairs and drink in the bath," Louise said.

"Good idea. Why don't you go up? I'll get one and we can split it." Olivia put a hand on her shoulder. She wanted Louise to leave first because there was no way she was going upstairs and leaving Louise alone with Casey. Louise was a tour de force when she decided she liked someone, and Olivia wasn't yet convinced she didn't have Casey in her sights.

Olivia was relieved when Louise finally said her good-byes and left them.

"They'd be cute together, but one of them needs to make the first move, or it's never going to happen." Casey gathered up her papers and tucked her book under her arm.

"Louise and Liam?" Olivia looked at Casey. She didn't seem to be joking. "It's not like that. They're just friends. I mean, they're close—we all are—but it's a friendship, nothing more."

Casey frowned. "She got all down in the mouth about him having a date tonight and he got annoyed when Louise was flirting with me in the car. That's a lot of jealousy for two people who are just friends."

Olivia waited as Casey stepped around the table.

"No, you're wrong. I'd know if that was the case. They just like spending time together. Liam was probably annoyed because Louise was being annoying. I'm sorry you had to put up with that by the way." She felt a sliver of disloyalty calling Louise out, but it had been hard to watch her flirt with Casey with such ease.

"Oh, I didn't mind at all." Casey's reply was not what Olivia wanted to hear.

They were standing looking at each other for a long moment.

"I'm going to pay my bill." Casey pointed at the bar. "So I'll see you in the morning."

Olivia nodded. She felt a little like she was being dismissed. But when Casey waited there a beat longer without moving, chewing her bottom lip and fidgeting with her papers, it felt like maybe they both wanted to say something else.

"See you tomorrow." Olivia was the first to blink. She gave Casey a small wave before heading over to the elevators. When she looked back, she saw Casey at the bar, wallet in hand, talking to the bartender about something. She took in a breath. Casey was a surprise, full of heart and soul she hadn't expected. If Olivia wasn't such a spectacularly slow mover and so horribly suspicious of everyone she ever met, her full-blown crush on Casey could get her into a lot of trouble.

"Excuse me." The voice was close, in her ear. She spun around and found herself face-to-face with two middle-aged men.

"Are you Olivia Lang?" the taller man asked.

"That Olivia Lang." His friend smirked as he said her name. He slurred her name slightly, sounding a little drunk.

"I'm sorry." Olivia wasn't sure how they knew her. They definitely didn't seem like fans of the show. "Do I know you?"

"Nope."

"Though we know you very well."

They were quite the double act, but something about the way they were looking at her made her nervous. Most people who stopped her simply wanted a selfie and the chance to say hello, but this had a different feel. She didn't like it.

"I was just going up to my room so maybe you could catch me tomorrow." Olivia wanted to be far away from them.

"That's not very friendly." He smirked. "But there's always Pornhub, so we can catch you before tomorrow if we want to. And Pornhub Olivia Lang seems a lot friendlier than this one." He smirked again. And Olivia felt nauseous. She knew exactly what they meant. They had seen her video, seen her having sex with Kristin. She almost doubled over as the realization hit. Of course they'd seen it. According to her lawyers it had been viewed hundreds of thousands of times before the website took it down. She had tried to make herself believe that they'd managed to take down all copies of it, but she knew very well that it was still out there. And that people like the assholes in front of her still had access to it. Kristin hadn't just betrayed her, she'd ruined her ability to trust in anyone's interest in her.

The bell dinged and the elevator doors opened.

"After you." The words were accompanied by a gesture that suggested the men had every intention of getting into the elevator with her. There was no way she was going to let that happen.

"I've just remembered I need to get something from reception." She made to move away, but one of the men grabbed her arm. "Don't be like that." She tried to shake him free, but his grip was strong. "We just want a selfie. To show our friends. They're also big fans of yours." He pulled her toward him. His friend had a phone in his hand.

Just as Olivia was about to scream for help, someone shoved two hands into the man's chest, knocking him backward and forcing him to release his grip on her.

"Take your hands off her." Casey spat out the words. "And get the fuck out of here before I get you arrested."

The men looked at Casey. One of them—the one who hadn't been shoved—stepped forward. Olivia could tell they were weighing the situation. Casey was taller than both of them, and—to Olivia—her anger made her seem like someone you wouldn't mess with. It seemed like the men agreed with her because, muttering words like "bitch" and "dyke," they moved off toward the bar.

Casey slipped an arm around her waist and shepherded her into the elevator. Olivia started to shake, and Casey held her closer, her arm wrapped tightly around her waist, seeming to understand—even better than Olivia did—that she needed the support as her legs turned to jelly.

"Are you okay?" Casey's voice was gentle.

"I guess."

"I'm sorry I didn't get there sooner. I saw them—saw you talking—but I thought you knew them." Casey's dark eyes flashed. "I can't believe he put his hands on you."

"You got there just in time." Olivia put her hand on Casey's arm. "Thank you."

The feel of Casey next to her was soothing. She started to feel more solid, less panicky. But then she realized, with a flush of shame, that Casey probably heard them talking about the video. It wasn't any kind of secret, but for some reason, she hated the idea of Casey hearing them talk about it.

"Do you get bothered like that a lot?"

"Never. Not like that. I mean, sometimes fans come up to you for a selfie, or they slip you a phone number." She couldn't help shuddering as she remembered the man's sweaty hand gripping her arm. Casey responded by pulling Olivia closer. It was exactly what she needed. "But nothing like that."

The doors opened and they stepped out into the corridor.

"Which way?" When Olivia pointed, Casey steered them in the direction of her room. When they reached her door, Casey finally let her go. Olivia felt the loss of her more than she had a right to.

"Which room is Louise's?"

Olivia pointed across the hallway.

"Want me to knock? I think you should probably have some company."

"I didn't bring her wine."

"I think she'll understand." Casey smiled at her. It was a beautiful smile, soft and full of concern.

"This is Louise and wine we're talking about. She might forgive me, but she won't understand." Olivia reached into her pocket for her keycard and opened her door. "I could use room service to order some."

"Good plan," Casey said. "I have to go back down and get my stuff. And if those guys are in the bar, I'm going to report them and get them booted out of here."

"Casey, be careful. Don't get into anything with them. They seemed pretty nasty."

"Don't worry. I'm a lover not a fighter." Casey waggled her eyebrows and Olivia laughed. Without thinking, she moved the short distance between them and wrapped Casey in a huge grateful hug. Casey took a second to respond, but when she did, the feel of Casey's arms around her was wonderful. Olivia pulled away before she wanted to and for a few seconds they just looked at each other.

Olivia felt a little warm. Casey's heroics tonight had escalated her crush into a full-blown swoon. It was fine. Understandable even. The trouble was, if Casey didn't stop gazing at her like that, she was going to faint at her feet.

"Well, good night. I hope you can sleep." Casey hesitated. "This is my room." She pointed at a door three rooms away from Olivia's. "If you need anything, just knock." She turned away before Olivia could respond and headed toward the elevators.

"Casey," Olivia called after her and Casey turned, a concerned expression on her face. "Thank you." She had more she could have said. "Thank you so much."

Casey looked at her for an instant before nodding and moving off.

Olivia went into her room, kicked off her shoes, and sat on her bed. She willed herself not to cry, not to let those Neanderthals get to her. Before they had spoiled her evening, Olivia had enjoyed getting to know a little more about Casey. It sounded like she had given up her job and London because she'd needed to get away. She wondered if it was woman trouble and whether, if it was, that meant that she was single. It shouldn't have cheered her as much as it did.

She set the bath to run, determined not to give in to the shame and embarrassment that the incident had unleashed. She had a lot of other Casey-shaped things she could think about.

Her phone dinged.

They aren't guests. They were just using the bar. It was VERY satisfying to see them get kicked out. I hope you're settling down. See you tomorrow.

Olivia felt the relief in her body. She hadn't realized how tense she'd been.

Thanks again. I owe you.

Casey's response was simply the hug emoji. It made Olivia smile. She didn't seem like a hug emoji kind of woman.

She called room service and ordered up a bottle of white wine and then she called Louise. Casey was right. She needed company. Trouble was, if she was honest, she'd rather it was Casey than Louise. Tonight they'd made a connection and she wanted more of it.

CHAPTER NINE

It doesn't make sense that Jessie and Michael would get it on. They're too good as friends and they don't have any kind of spark like that." Liam had the script in his hand and was pacing across the carpet in Olivia's hotel room. "And I definitely don't think Michael would be the first to confess his feelings. He's too careful, too uptight. Listen to this." He looked for his place on the page.

"This is my line. '*I have been avoiding you, you're not wrong about that. But you're wrong about why. The truth is I've fallen for you. And finally admitting to myself that I want you has made it hard to see you.*' I mean, he would never admit to it, it's just not his way." Liam stopped pacing. He was standing next to Olivia's chair, looking at her in the large mirror. She was midway through applying her mascara but knew that him stopping meant she had to pay more attention.

"He just wouldn't tell her he wanted her like that. He'd be too worried about ruining a beautiful friendship."

"What happens after he tells her?" Olivia had skimmed through the scripts last night, but she had only focused on Susie's scenes.

"He kisses her and they end up back in his hotel room. He…I mean… he undresses her, they make love." He swallowed, looking terrified. "I've never done a sex scene before. And it's beyond scary."

Olivia tried not to smile. She'd had exactly the same kind of feelings before her first sex scene. It was a long time ago now. She had taken her clothes off and had her hands and mouth on other actresses more times than she cared to remember. It had almost become routine, and Olivia had gotten very good at disassociating.

"And it's Louise…" Liam let his voice trail off. "I can't undress Louise. I can't kiss her. And I certainly can't do it with a film crew watching.

It's going to be super fucking awkward." He pushed his glasses back up his nose. It was a nervous tic.

"It's not Louise, it's Jessie. You have to remember that. It's awkward, I know. It always is the first time, especially when it's someone you know, but Louise is a pro. She'll help you. She'll laugh at you, sure, but then she'll help you." Olivia smiled. "And if you're feeling too sorry for yourself, check my scenes." Olivia pointed at the papers on the edge of her dressing table as she applied her makeup. "Two episodes in, Susie and Phoebe get together, just like Billie wanted. And their first sex scene is in the front seat of a car outside the St. Pancras hotel while Phoebe's oblivious husband is inside. And we're shooting that scene in five days, assuming I haven't pushed her under a double-decker bus by then."

The scripts were dropped off late last night. She was already in bed. Trying to sleep, but unable to push the horrible experience with those men out of her mind. She had no intention of reading them until today. But at midnight, a text from Billie arrived that said *Finally* with a flame emoji and an annoying red heart. Olivia had guessed what it meant. It was obvious that the writers had been toying with the idea of Susie getting together with Phoebe, and given Billie's constant comments, she had the feeling that Billie had been pushing hard for it.

When Olivia gave in and finally picked up the script, she found out what was going to happen. She normally didn't care what Susie got up to, but there was something about getting naked with Billie that bugged her. She sighed and turned her attention back to Liam.

"At least you and Louise were both smart enough to insist on 'no nudity' clauses, so they'll have to make it tasteful."

"It's Louise, though. She'll eat me for breakfast." He sat on the arm of the couch, kicking his feet together like a toddler. He was quiet for a while and Olivia put the finishing touches to her makeup.

"I just wanted our first kiss to be special."

"What?" Olivia turned and gave him a quizzical look.

"I just mean, hell, I don't even know. I always kind of hoped I could wear her down over time, persuade her to like me like that. I had this idea of what it'd be like the first time our lips touched, and in my version, there was never anyone watching." He stared off into the distance. "But now this is going to ruin it."

"You like Louise?" Olivia widened her eyes. "You like Louise like that?"

Liam held her gaze. "Yeah, I do."

Olivia was amazed. Casey had picked up there was something going on and she barely knew them. How on earth had Olivia missed it?

"When did this happen?"

"I guess it's always been there somewhere. But I kept it buried. I'm not stupid. I know she's not into guys, trans guys, whatever, but sometimes I let myself hope. It sounds weird probably, but sometimes the way she looks at me, the way she is around me, I just thought…" He pushed his hands together in his lap. "We get on so well, we laugh so much. I guess I was holding out some stupid hope about the two of us. We've been having a good time together here, but then she was flirting with Casey, so I decided to go on that date. But all the time I was there I just kept thinking that I was wasting an evening I would have rather spent with her."

Liam had it bad. Olivia felt for him.

"What makes you think she's not into guys?"

"I've only ever known her to date women—and I saw that tattoo, the one that says 'Girls Do Girls Like Boys Do.' It doesn't exactly take a rocket scientist."

Olivia laughed. "Don't mistake a drunken Hayley Kiyoko tattoo for a life philosophy. Louise has dated lots of guys. And she's definitely not the type to limit herself to a type. Your problem isn't that she wouldn't like you as a guy, it's that you're a friend. A good friend. If you've got any chance of anything with her, you've got to get out of that friend zone."

"Do you think?"

"I do."

Olivia looked from Liam's earnest face to her watch. It was one minute to eight.

"I'm about to go, but we are definitely continuing this conversation later. And don't think that me giving you advice means that I approve in any way of the two of you getting together. I do not want to be third wheeling you guys all through season four. And I definitely don't want to be picking up the pieces if you try and it doesn't work out. Sometimes friendship is worth a whole lot more than a shot at love."

As she finished speaking, there was a knock at the door. She knew it was Casey. She was always on time. Last night, she'd sent Olivia a text suggesting that she call for her rather than them waiting for each other in the lobby, and Olivia liked it a lot that Casey was thinking about her safety. When she replied to agree it was a good idea, she hadn't been able to stop herself from adding a sentence—a sentence that didn't need to be added—about how grateful she was for Casey's help and how nice it had been to spend some time getting to know her.

This morning, when she read it back, she cringed. She'd inserted herself into Casey's quiet time with her book and her paperwork and then got her embroiled in something dangerous. The fact that Casey had been so sweet about all of it didn't mean a thing. This morning she resolved to be a lot cooler, but knowing Casey was just outside her door, Olivia felt her heartbeat speed up a little.

She quickly checked her reflection in the mirror. She was going to do a photoshoot and an interview with a queer lifestyle magazine. They would redo her makeup completely when she got there, but for reasons she was acutely aware of, she didn't want to be picked up and driven there by Casey with her face completely bare.

"I'll get it." Liam crossed to the door.

"Liam?" He turned back to her. "This might be a good thing, you know. She's gonna taste those lips of yours, put her hands on that super toned body of yours. Give her your best moves and maybe it'll be just what you need to get you out of the friend zone." She smiled at him and he smiled back, but the tension in his face told her that he wasn't convinced.

As he opened the door wide, Olivia saw Casey standing there. She was wearing pressed pants, her gray shirt fully buttoned up, but her sleeves were rolled up over her forearms. Olivia remembered—with a sense of arousal and a strong feeling of gratitude—the feel of Casey's arm as she'd wrapped it around Olivia's waist and gently shepherded her into the elevator the night before.

"Hi, how are you doing this morning?" Casey's eyes showed concern and her voice was soft. It was like a caress.

"I'm fine, thank you." Olivia picked up her bag. "And I'm ready when you are."

Casey stepped away from the door, and Olivia followed Liam out into the corridor, letting her room door close behind them.

"How was the burger?" Casey addressed Liam.

"It was amazing. The date not so much."

"It happens," Casey said. "I think I'm supposed to say something reassuring about fish, sea, and plenty at this point. But it might be better if you hear it from someone who believes it."

Olivia had offered exactly that platitude to Liam when he told her the date was a bust, but she wasn't sure she believed it either. He headed into the room next door to hers, just as Billie emerged from the room on the other side.

"I thought I heard your voice. Good morning." She looked Olivia up and down. "Well, someone looks ready to slay." She took a few steps forward and put her hand on Olivia's arm. "I enjoyed our chat last night. I'm glad that you're as excited as I am by us getting to be together on screen finally."

Sometimes Olivia wondered if Billie was a little crazy. She had said no such thing. She had been polite in responding to Billie's texts, but done her very best to close down Billie's flirting. And she distinctly remembered saying that she would wrestle a grizzly bear if they paid her to. It wasn't kind, but she wanted Billie to get the message and leave her alone. And it worked—last night. But here she was again acting like they had something special going on.

Olivia instinctively moved a little closer to where Casey was standing. "We're just heading out to a magazine shoot."

"I know. I know your schedule."

Billie's eyes drifted from Casey to Olivia and back again, and she gazed at Casey with a curious expression. It was like she had just noticed Casey's presence. "And our tall, dark, and handsome driver does house visits now? I hadn't realized the service was that good. I'll be sure to ask for that for next time."

The look Billie gave Casey suggested she wasn't happy to see her.

"I just asked her to knock for me on her way down. She's staying on our floor. It avoids hanging around the lobby and being bothered by fans." Olivia couldn't help but feel defensive of Casey and of her own interest in her.

"Well, have fun." Billie didn't sound like she meant it. "And I'll see you later for the run-through. I can't wait to get Phoebe and Susie started."

Olivia almost cursed. She had forgotten they were doing that this afternoon. Sitting around a table and running through the script was one of the things she'd always liked doing. Before Billie. And her gigantic ego and her appetite for making Olivia feel uncomfortable. Last time, nearly all the suggested rewrites had been Billie's, and they had mostly been intended to give her more to say. Running through Susie and Phoebe getting together wasn't going to be a lot of fun.

Olivia walked off down the corridor, knowing Casey would follow. As they were standing together in the elevator, Olivia wanted to thank Casey all over again for stepping into that situation for her last night, but something about Casey's demeanor stopped her. She seemed gloomy and uninterested—the opposite of how she'd been in the bar. As they reached the ground floor, Casey headed back to the bar without speaking, and Olivia watched as the bartender immediately placed two takeaway coffee cups on the counter.

As she rejoined Olivia, she held one out. "Thought you might need one."

"Thanks." Olivia smiled. It was a sweet gesture. But Casey's face was impassive.

"I thought maybe you might not have slept well. And maybe I was right."

Olivia couldn't read what was underneath the words, but there was definitely something. They headed out to the car in silence. Things were weird between them again, but she didn't know why. She opened the front passenger side door before Casey could open the back door for her.

"Do you mind if I sit up here? I mean, it's just me and I thought we could..." She wanted to say they could chat. But Casey's blank expression was a little off-putting

"Sure." Casey moved to the driver's side and got in. "It's a fifty-minute drive." She flipped a switch and a little tray table slid out. Olivia slotted her cup into the cup-shaped hole and sat back. Whether Casey wanted her company or not, she wasn't going to spend the journey in silence. Last night, they got on well. And she was pretty sure that Casey could have made an excuse and escaped at any time. But she hadn't. So Olivia was going to take heart from that and hope this strange mood of Casey's was just her being grouchy because they were heading out into rush hour traffic once more.

The traffic had been moving well, but as they reached Holborn, the congestion slowed them to a crawl. Casey rolled her shoulders and rotated her neck to ease the stiffness. If she didn't have to drive Olivia to this appointment, she'd have gone to the gym and tried to work off the stress she was feeling on the treadmill. Instead, she was sitting in traffic—Olivia beside her—trying not to let her stinking mood show.

Casey had finally managed to persuade her mom to speak to the police, but the officer in charge had called her bright and early to tell her that, while her mom acknowledged that Neil had taken the rent money, she said that he sometimes paid other bills, so it shouldn't be considered theft. Her mom's choices in life were often mystifying to Casey, and she had no idea why her mom would want to protect Neil that way. But she did, and there wasn't a damn thing she could do about it.

On top of that, this morning's encounter in the corridor suggested that maybe Olivia and Billie did have something going on. She had no right, but she couldn't help but feel disappointed. She had spent the last fifteen minutes telling herself it was for the best. Having feelings for Olivia was ridiculous, and knowing she was interested in someone else, someone like Billie, should help her close those feelings down. Of course, it would help if Olivia didn't turn up every day looking fucking gorgeous, but it seemed that was Casey's cross to bear.

"Do you think you'd like to have children?"

Casey turned to Olivia. "That's a strange question."

"I'm sorry. It's just that last night you were talking about your youth work, and I wondered if that meant you like kids. And I'm assuming you don't already have any because you've come over here for a long trip." Olivia faltered. "But, if you do…I mean, I'm not saying you shouldn't leave them in Portland. I'm sure they're being looked after by someone."

Casey couldn't help but smile to herself. Olivia was digging a hole. She held out a metaphorical hand.

"I don't have kids, no." She made herself carry on, made herself push through her bad mood. "But I'd like to have them one day."

"Same here," Olivia replied. "But I haven't ever been in a situation where it seemed even halfway possible. Work, this job, life—just seems to always get in the way. And I haven't really—" She stopped and Casey glanced at her. She was chewing the inside of her mouth, looking like she was trying to figure out whether to say something.

"Go on." Casey spoke gently. Olivia made her want to be gentle.

"I just haven't ever met the right person. It's a cliché, but it's true. Louise would say I haven't tried very hard, but dating in LA is scary. I'm not saying everyone's on the make, or trying to use you somehow, but I fear I seem to be able to pick the ones that are."

Olivia sounded like she'd had some bad experiences. She wanted to know but didn't think it was right to ask.

"My last girlfriend and I talked about kids a lot. If I was honest, I should say we fought about them a lot. I wanted them, she didn't. I would have been happy to foster or adopt—there's so many kids already in the world who need a good home—but she wouldn't even consider that. Like you, she had a career that was more important to her." Casey stopped, realizing that it might seem as if she was judging Olivia. She was, but only a little bit. "I just mean that I had the kind of job where I could have taken time off, but Hannah was an 'influencer.' She was building an online following. She didn't think kids would fit with her brand."

It was hard for Casey not to sound bitter about it. It was how she felt. She'd wasted time with Hannah, imagining they were building a life together. But Hannah hadn't been thinking the same way. Her career always came first.

She beeped her horn at a black cab that cut in front of them, coming perilously close to scraping their car. Olivia was startled and grabbed for her arm, gripping it tightly. For a few seconds, she left her hand there and it was enough to get Casey flustered.

"I'm sorry." Olivia withdrew her hand. "I got scared."

"Cab drivers, they think they own the road."

Casey wanted them to keep talking. The way they were before, but the interruption seemed to have silenced them both.

"You and Louise never dated back in the day?" Casey already knew the answer was no—Olivia and Louise just didn't have that kind of vibe when they were together—but she was hoping that it might prompt Olivia to tell her about Billie.

"God, no." Olivia laughed. "I can't imagine that. She's wonderful and all of that, but she's like a sister to me. A really annoying younger sister, but still a sister. But, oh my God, I forgot to tell you." Olivia turned to Casey excitedly. "Liam and Louise. You were right. Liam told me. I feel bad gossiping, but you already spotted it so it's not news. Liam confessed he has feelings for Louise."

Casey couldn't help but smile. She wasn't a gossip—and she didn't even know these people—but somehow Olivia's excitement made her happy. "Does Louise feel the same way?"

"I don't know. I can't ask her obviously, and I don't know if Liam ever will. He's convinced she would never want him that way. It might end up being one of those things that could have been something but wasn't— because he isn't brave enough to make the leap and say something about how he feels."

For an instant, Olivia's words stirred something in Casey, but then she felt embarrassed. Olivia wasn't giving her a hint; she needed to calm down.

"And if I'm honest," Olivia said, "I don't want them to. I don't mind them falling in love, but when they fall out of love, I don't want to have to pick up the pieces. Or worse, choose sides."

"Maybe they won't fall out of love."

"Maybe. But people do and the aftermath can be awful."

"Sounds like you're talking from experience." Casey didn't want to pry, but she was curious.

"Maybe I am. Maybe I learned that when you fall for someone, there's always a heavy landing waiting for you somewhere along the way. And the faster you fall, the more it hurts."

Casey felt saddened by Olivia's words. For some reason, she hated to think that Olivia had been as badly bruised by love as she had.

"You're right to be worried. Dividing up friends after a breakup is harder than just dividing up the books and cats—" Casey's phone interrupted her. She looked at the screen, sitting in its holder on the dashboard. Her mom. She cut off the call. A moment later, it rang again. This time—after a quick sorry to Olivia—she answered it, using her earpiece so only she could hear her mom.

"*You know you said you were coming this morning?*" Her mom sounded oddly cheerful. "*Could you bring some tea bags? I'm out and Neil doesn't drink coffee.*"

The hairs on Casey's neck stood up.

"Is he there? Are you okay? Do you want me to call the police?" Casey willed her mind to remain clear. "I swear, Mom, if he steals another penny from you, I'll—" She couldn't finish the sentence.

"*No, no, don't go to that much trouble. PG Tips is just fine. Nothing else.*" Her mom stressed the last two words. "*Oh and guess what? Neil's sister is pregnant. Great news, yes. Just bring tea bags. Like I said. You're on your way? Great. See you then, love.*"

The call disconnected without Casey needing to respond to any of it. Her mom was telling her he was there and that she wanted Casey to come, but not call the police. Her mind was racing.

"What was that?" Olivia sounded concerned. "Is everything okay?"

"I have to go and see my mom. It's an emergency." Casey faltered, not wanting to tell Olivia the grubby details but needing her to understand that she wouldn't just bail on her without a good reason. "She's going through some bad stuff. It sounds like she needs me."

Casey let out a sigh. Maybe Olivia would be pissed off with her, but she had to hope she'd also understand.

"It's partly why I came back. My brother's here, but he's useless. He never steps up, and anyway, she thinks it's not his job, that daughters have to be the ones to deal with all the shitty stuff." Casey screwed up her face willing herself to stop speaking, to stop spewing out all this family drama. Olivia didn't need to hear it.

"I'll drop you off at the magazine and get Tania or another driver to pick you up after. I'm pretty sure you won't have to wait. David has a lot of drivers, I'm sure someone will be free. I'm sorry, but I have to go and see her, y'know?"

Despite her effort to remain calm, Casey couldn't stop her voice from cracking. She wanted to cry, wanted to scream with frustration. She wanted to tell her mom that this was on her—she could have had him arrested, but she chose not to. But of course, she did none of these things. She just gripped the wheel even harder, and her chest felt tight with the effort of maintaining her composure.

"Are you okay?" Olivia put a hand on Casey's arm. Casey welcomed the touch, could hear the concern in Olivia's voice. It helped and yet it didn't. Casey tried to slow her breathing, to say words that sounded professional, that would alleviate Olivia's concern.

"My mom is—" She took in a breath. "My mom is in an emotionally abusive situation. The guy has turned up. My mom has let him in. She doesn't know how to say no, how to make good choices for herself. She never has." Casey wanted to be mad at her, but she couldn't. "She's too vulnerable."

Somehow, putting it like that, for Olivia's benefit, made her understand, helped her see. Her mom was vulnerable. She didn't love or respect herself enough to say no to him. And he was taking advantage of that.

"And you're going to do what? Drop me off and go driving over there to confront him? Don't you think you should call the police?"

When Casey didn't reply, Olivia put her hand back on Casey's arm. "Casey?" Her voice was low, sure and soft. "Pull over here please." She pointed at a store to their left that had a huge empty parking lot outside. The store looked derelict. Casey pulled down on the indicator lever and turned into the lot, parking right outside the double doors chained together at the front of the store.

"You can't go into a situation like that on your own. It could be dangerous. Call the police, or call your brother and ask him to go."

"She called me. She expects me to go. And she doesn't want the police. She made that clear. He's not dangerous, not really. She just can't ever say no to him. He's probably come looking for money again." She sighed with frustration and began to clench and unclench her jaw. It was an anxious habit—one she'd forgotten.

"How far is it from here?" Olivia looked at her watch and Casey felt terrible.

"I should get you to the studios. None of this is your problem and you're going to be late. I don't want to be the reason for a missed appointment." Casey switched the engine back on before Olivia reached across her to turn it off again.

"How far away is your mom's?"

"Fifteen, twenty minutes. But we're going in the opposite direction."

"Not anymore we're not."

Olivia fished her phone out of her bag and called someone.

"Hey. We're going to be a couple of hours later than we said. Might even be three. No, it's fine, I just need to do something. Can you call them, apologize, and rearrange it for noonish?" Olivia's fingers played with the clasp on her bag as she listened to someone on the other end. "I'm aware of that, obviously. I wouldn't ask if it wasn't important."

Casey tried to focus on the call, on Olivia. But her mind kept drifting back to the brittle cheerfulness of her mom's voice. And to the idea of Neil feeling so sure of himself—so sure of her mom's weakness—that he would call in to see her just a few weeks after stealing half of the contents of her house.

"Let's go."

When Casey didn't respond, Olivia turned to her.

"Come on. Let's go and see your mom."

"We can't do that." Casey lifted her eyes. Olivia gazed back at her, kindness written across her beautiful face. It was almost too much for her.

"We can. I understand that you're worried about me meeting her because you know your mom is going to love me. Moms always love me. Louise's mom loves me more than she loves Louise. But you're going to have to put up with that because," her voice grew more serious, "your mom is in a situation and she needs you. Kind of like I was in a situation last night. You didn't hesitate to help me, so consider this payback."

Casey couldn't find any words. She stared back at Olivia gratefully, with all the tenderness she felt for her in that moment.

"Okay, if you're sure."

"I'm sure."

Casey put the car into gear and started the engine before turning to Olivia.

"Thank you."

Chapter Ten

Her mom's driveway was empty. It didn't mean he wasn't inside. Casey didn't even know if Neil still had a car. But it was wise of him not to bring it if he did, because she didn't trust herself not to cause it some damage. The memory of knocking over Hannah's beloved camera and it crashing to the floor poked to the front of her mind unhelpfully. Casey hadn't always had a good grip on her temper.

She pulled up in front of the house.

"You can wait here. I won't be long." Casey wasn't worried for Olivia's safety—Neil wasn't that kind of guy—but she didn't want Olivia to see the way her mom was living, or to hear the things she had come to say to Neil. She didn't want Olivia anywhere near the whole damn mess.

"I'm coming in." Olivia had a determined look on her face as she unbuckled her seat belt. "You have your plan and I have the tea bags." She held up the box—the box Casey had bought from the shop on the corner. "And I'll be a useful distraction."

They got out and looked at each other over the top of the car. "I'm sorry about this." Casey couldn't think of anything else to say.

"Don't be. Your mom needs you. Let's see what we can do."

"Mom," Casey called out as she entered the house through the back door. The kitchen was empty, but she heard voices in the living room. She tracked along the corridor, wanting and not wanting Neil to still be there. Olivia was at her elbow. As she reached the door, the deep voice of a man was loud and clear inside the room. She heard her mom laugh—a little too loud, a little too eager.

"Damn." She pointed toward the living room. "He's still here. And I think she's been drinking. I'm sorry."

Olivia placed the palm of her hand on Casey's back. "Don't be. It's okay." Her hand moved up and down stroking gently. It gave Casey the encouragement she needed. She pushed the door open.

"Hey, Mom, we bought the tea bags. Shall I make us a brew?"

Her mom stared at her with a slightly glassy expression. They had spoken half an hour ago and she sounded sober. On the coffee table sat a half empty bottle of vodka. It didn't need Hercule Poirot to figure out the way things had gone. He had brought drink, knowing her mom wouldn't—couldn't—say no.

Neil stood. She was gratified to see that he seemed nervous.

"Casey. Long time no see. How's America treating you?" He held out a hand. She ignored it.

"Not long enough. Why are you here?"

"Casey." Her mom said her name like a warning. Casey knew how this would go. Her mom—so keen for her help in getting rid of him—would now take his side. "Don't talk to Neil like that. It's rude."

"Is it rude to rob you? Or to pretend to pay the rent, steal the money, and leave you homeless?" She turned back to Neil. "What is it? Run out of spending money, or maybe your sister's sent you here to get some money for the new baby. You're not welcome here, and there's nothing left to steal, so I suggest you leave before I call the police." Casey could feel her temper rising, the burning heat in her cheeks. She willed herself to calm down.

"We haven't met. I'm Olivia. A friend of Casey's from America." Olivia walked over to her mom, gave her a huge smile and a kiss on both cheeks. Her mom actually blushed.

"I haven't tried these tea bags before." She held out the box like an offering. "But Casey tells me that they're awesome. We don't have them in the States. Would you be so kind as to show me how the British make a nice strong cup of tea?" Olivia had a hand on her mom's back, guiding her toward the kitchen as she spoke. Her voice low and confiding. "The traffic was lousy, I'm desperate for a cup. And Casey has told me so much about you. I'm so happy to meet you." Olivia was an actress, so Casey shouldn't have been so impressed by her ability to improvise, but somehow she was.

"I saw a video where some American woman showed everyone how to make tea in a microwave. I nearly died," Casey's mom replied as she retreated down the corridor with Olivia. As hard to resist as Olivia was, she couldn't quite believe her mom had gone so quietly.

Casey turned back to Neil, still standing five feet away. He looked at her with a sneer now, seeming like he'd regained his composure.

"Nice uniform. Or is that what you lesbians wear for fun these days?"

"I want the money back." Casey ignored his attempt to rile her. "And whatever you've still got of her stuff, or I'll get the police involved."

Casey was experiencing a strong sense of déjà vu. She had stood toe-to-toe with her stepdad, just like this, asking for him to return her mom's jewelry. She had threatened the police then too. It hadn't worked.

"We both know your mom's not going to press charges." He leaned down and picked up his cigarettes, slowly putting them in his back pocket. "And everything I stole, every penny I took, I deserved for putting up with her. We both know what a pain in the arse she is."

Casey balled her fists, breathing deeply to keep her composure. Neil screwed the cap back onto the vodka bottle and picked it up.

"And the rent money?" Casey tried to keep her tone calm. "I suppose you stole that to spend on drink?"

"Nah." He headed for the front door, then turned back. "I took that to give to my sister, for the kids. She needed it."

"My mom needed it. You were supposed to be paying her rent. She might lose this house because of you, because of what you stole."

"Maybe." He hesitated at the door, an unpleasant smile on his face. "But I'm sure you'll help her out. You always do. Tell your mom, I'll see her another time—when she hasn't got company." He made it sound like the threat it was.

He slammed the door shut as he left, and it took all the control Casey had not to march after him and punch him squarely in his nasty, smug face. He didn't give a fuck about her mom, maybe he never had. She was just a soft touch, and he knew it. Her stepdad had lasted a lot longer than Neil, but in the end he had treated her just as badly. Her mom had a way of attracting the worst kind of men.

She took in a couple of deep breaths. Her mom's debts were manageable. She could pay off the most urgent ones and—hopefully— come to an agreement with the landlord to slowly pay off the arrears. But Olivia was right, the number one priority had to be making sure that Neil stayed away so her mom could rebuild—with Casey's help—and not have him hanging around like a bad smell, waiting to prey on her.

She hadn't wanted to tell Olivia any of it, but she insisted. So, sitting in the car outside the corner shop, Casey had told her everything. Hannah had always made her feel embarrassed about her mom and Casey couldn't help but think that hearing it would be enough to make Olivia back off and put an end to whatever closeness Casey had felt developing between them. But Olivia had listened quietly, and together they had come up with a plan.

Casey walked slowly to the kitchen. Her mom and Olivia were at the table, eating biscuits and drinking the tea that Olivia had told her mom she was desperate for, the tea she admitted on the drive over that she didn't like all that much.

When Olivia looked in her direction—her face a picture of concern and care—Casey held up her phone and gave Olivia the thumbs-up. The recording she'd made—on Olivia's advice—might not be enough to get Neil arrested, but she had to hope the threat of it would be enough to persuade him to stay well away from her mom in the future.

She sighed as she sat at the table.

"Olivia was telling me about the time she was on the red carpet at the Emmys and she stumbled and nearly knocked Gerard Butler over. I said I wouldn't have minded falling on top of him. But of course Olivia wouldn't have enjoyed that as much as me." She laughed, but Casey could tell she was still upset. "I can't believe you didn't tell me you'd met someone while you were in America and that your girlfriend's a beautiful actress." Her mom sipped at her tea. She seemed a lot more sober now.

"Olivia's not my—"

"Your mom showed me how to 'mash' the tea to make it stronger." Olivia interrupted her. As she spoke, she inclined her head toward her mom and shook it ever so slightly. The message was clear. Olivia didn't want Casey to correct her mom.

"I like her a lot more than your last one." Her mom looked in her direction as she said it, before returning her attention to Olivia. "I'm sorry to say it, but she was a bit stuck up. I could always tell she thought she was too good for us, too good for Casey. I didn't say it, but I was glad when they broke up. Casey deserved better,"

Her mom was almost saying something nice about her. Almost.

Olivia sat quietly, just listening, letting her mom speak. She seemed oddly at home.

"She was cut up about it of course. She might look tough, but she's got a soft heart and I know it was hard—"

Casey felt herself tense.

"Mom, Olivia doesn't have time for all this. We only came because Neil was here. We need to get back to—"

"I drive her crazy always getting into these kind of situations. I don't know how to make it up to her, but even if I did, I couldn't, because she just left—went to America and left me." For an instant, her mom looked upset, but then she brightened. "And she met you. A famous actress who doesn't think she's too good to eat my custard creams." Her mom looked from Casey to Olivia. "I'm glad. I'm really glad."

"I have to go and have my photos taken for a magazine article." Olivia glanced at Casey, a mischievous smile spreading slowly across her beautiful face. "But I've definitely got time to look at any photos of Casey you might have from when she was a baby. You must have some for us to look at while we finish off this pot of tea."

Casey had never seen her mom move so fast. In the blink of an eye, she had the lid off a square metal biscuit tin she extracted from the sideboard against the far wall and was riffling through the photos.

"This is when she had her First Communion." She held out a photo for Olivia to take.

"That's a very pretty dress." Olivia smirked in her direction. "Why is she scowling?"

"Because of the dress." Her mom laughed. "She was never happy in a dress."

She handed another photo to Olivia.

"That broken tooth happened after she fell off a chair in a café. She was trying to pet a dog that didn't want to be petted. I'd gone to get a napkin or something and when I came back she was on the floor. She was crying, but not because of the pain. She was just mad at the dog."

Casey poured herself some tea and sat back in her chair. She was going to spend the next however many minutes watching her mom show Olivia old photos of her, while Olivia pretended to be her famous American actress girlfriend, having potentially just been helped to see off the man who had been exploiting her mom. It was turning out to be a strange but unexpectedly good morning.

"That's great. Could you put both hands on the umbrella and stick your ass out a little more…yeah, like that, like you're a really sexy Gene Kelly or something." The photographer snapped away as she spoke. "Maybe lift it to your shoulder like a rifle? That's it. Keep looking at the camera like that. It's perfect."

Olivia did everything she was told without a murmur of complaint. The photographer had dressed her up in a pinstripe suit and bowler hat and just handed her a long umbrella with a wooden handle to play with.

Casey was sitting at the back of the room—in semidarkness—watching with rapt attention. Olivia looked amazing. She was wearing the suit without a shirt underneath. It was all very tastefully done, but it was impossible for Casey's blood not to feel hot at the sight of Olivia dressed like that.

When they arrived an hour ago, Casey expected to wait in the car. But Olivia had insisted she come inside and keep her company during the shoot and she couldn't say no. Not after what Olivia had just done for her.

And if she was honest, she didn't want to be away from Olivia either. The experience with her mom, with Neil—seeing how well Olivia handled it all, how solid she was—made Casey feel all kinds of other feelings on top of the attraction she normally felt whenever Olivia was anywhere near her.

"Okay. That's fantastic." The photographer lowered her camera. "Let's do the cocktail party scene and then we'll call it done."

"Not done—then we need to do the actual interview." The interviewer—Alice—was sitting in a chair on the other side of the room. Casey didn't like her. She'd been asking questions of Olivia the whole time they'd been there, and it seemed to Casey as if she was trying to catch Olivia off guard.

She had the feeling Olivia didn't like her either. She kept her answers short, and when Alice asked whether Olivia ever had trust issues when it came to relationships, "for obvious reasons," Olivia gave her a withering "Really?" and shook her head wearily.

Casey had no idea what Alice meant, but it was clearly something that made Olivia unhappy and annoyed. The temptation to google Olivia—to find out things about her—rose up again, but she resisted. She wasn't going to do that to Olivia. She was going to let her decide what she wanted Casey to know.

When Alice asked Olivia about Billie, about what it was like for them to work together, about whether their off-screen chemistry was as strong as it seemed, Casey again felt something she recognized as jealousy. Olivia closed down the line of questioning, but it left Casey wondering if her refusal to believe Olivia and Billie had something going on was because she wanted Olivia to have better taste in women, or because she wanted Olivia's friendliness toward her to mean something.

Olivia tipped her hat off, left it on the chair, and walked toward her. The sight of Olivia approaching her in that low-cut suit sent her libido into overdrive, and Casey felt a little ashamed of the reaction. The outfit was a thirst trap and she'd fallen in headfirst.

"Still awake back there?" Olivia's tone was light and teasing.

"Very awake. I'm a big fan of musicals. I was waiting for you to give us a chorus or two of 'Singin' in the Rain.' I'm assuming you sing and dance, as well as act. I have a lot more faith in your talent after this morning." Casey hadn't been able to stop thanking her for what she'd done, but she knew it was making Olivia uncomfortable, so she made herself not say it again.

"You wouldn't have that faith if you heard me sing. Small children have been known to cry and animals hide."

"That bad, huh?"

Olivia nodded. Casey started to smile.

"What?"

"I'm just thinking about how much it rains here and how cold the winters are. You'd catch a definite chill walking from the Underground to your swanky office in the city in that outfit."

The suit artfully covered Olivia's breasts, but the creamy skin of her chest and the curves of her cleavage were visible. And the effect was disgracefully sexy.

"You're sitting back here worrying that I might catch a cold?" Olivia said the words slowly, sexily. "That was not the impact I was hoping to have."

"What can I say? I'm a very caring sort of 'girlfriend.'" She accented the word with speech marks. It was the first time either of them had acknowledged her mom mistaking them for lovers. "The kind that would make you put on a warm scarf and send you off to the office with a healthy packed lunch and a kiss on the forehead." She was flirting. Kind of.

Olivia looked at her for a beat without saying anything and Casey felt the best kind of tension between them.

"Well, you're definitely going to be worried about me catching a chill when you see this next outfit." She moved into the curtained off changing area at the back of the room with a swagger and Casey couldn't help but grin.

Being around Olivia had stopped being a trial and started to feel good—probably a little too good. And because of that, she needed to guard herself better. She had another ten days of Olivia's company and that was that. Olivia was off to the next city on their European tour and would forget all about the driver she'd had in London. Casey was pretty sure Olivia left a trail of people who had fallen for her charms behind her at every stop.

While she waited, Casey distracted herself with tasks. She emailed the audio file of Neil confessing his crimes to the officer in charge of her mom's case. She didn't expect it to make any difference to their willingness to charge him, but if there was the tiniest chance it would help them do something to scare him away, she wanted to take it. She made an arrangement to go to dinner with David and her mom, and she sent a gloating message to Gina about the fact she was watching Olivia Lang do a photoshoot.

The curtain was pulled back and Olivia stepped into the room wearing a short, blood-red dress that looked like it had been painted on. Casey wasn't proud of the up-and-down look she gave Olivia, but her legs, her curves, the heels she was wearing to match the dress, caused a throb of arousal low down in Casey's center and not staring seemed impossible. When she returned her gaze to Olivia's face, she saw that Olivia was blushing.

"You look amazing." Casey couldn't help but say it. "Positively sinful, but also amazing."

"It's all Susie." Olivia smoothed a hand down the dress. "I'd never have the confidence to wear this as Olivia." She hesitated, seeming nervous.

"I can't imagine anyone, including Susie, could wear that dress and look as good as you do right now." Casey meant it; it wasn't a line.

"Well then, I guess we're both glad you like it." Olivia smiled, her gaze holding Casey's for an instant before heading back to the brightly lit area at the front of the room.

Damn. Casey let out a breath. The pulsing between her legs was letting her know that her attraction for Olivia was not, despite her best intentions, going anywhere.

The photographer handed Olivia what looked like a margarita and she moved to settle herself on a barstool. The dress was so tight that it wasn't an easy maneuver, and as she shuffled herself onto the seat, the wedge of lime perched on the side of her glass fell to the floor. Olivia hadn't noticed, and neither had the photographer. Casey moved to pick it up from the floor and handed it back to her. As Olivia took it from her, their fingers brushed and Casey felt the contact like a small electric shock.

"Thank you." Olivia's eyes were wide. "You're very gallant."

"I try. It's all in here somewhere. I just need a little practice."

They stared at each other for a moment. There was something between them. Casey didn't understand it, but it felt good. It was something she hadn't felt for a very long time.

"Hey, do you think you might want—" The photographer spoke to her.

"Yeah, sorry. I'll get out of the way. I was just picking up the…" Casey pointed at the glass as she backed out of the space.

"No, I didn't mean that. I mean, do you want to stay? Maybe I could take a couple of shots of you with Olivia. I mean, you look great together. Why not?" The photographer looked over her shoulder at Alice, who was now standing in front of her chair, looking interested.

"That is a great idea. It would totally suit the vibe for Susie to be getting her hooks into someone at the party and you," she pointed at Casey, "are gorgeous." She turned back to the photographer. "Could she be a guest at the party? Or maybe she could be a hot bartender. Do we have a tux or something back there she could wear?"

The photographer headed to the changing room. Casey felt panic rising from her feet. She didn't want to be photographed with Olivia. She wasn't here for that. She looked at Olivia, willing her to tell them it was a terrible idea, so that she wouldn't have to.

"It's good your girlfriend is so game for this." Alice spoke to Olivia. "It's gonna be great. I was wishing we had brought Billie to the shoot to spice things up, but this is even better."

"I'm not game for this—" Casey finally found some words.

"She's not my girlfriend—" Olivia spoke at the same time. "She's just my driver." Her tone was crisp. It was true, of course, but there was something about the way she said it that made Casey feel small. However close to Olivia the events of the last couple of days had made her feel, to Olivia she was still "just" the driver.

Alice peered across at Casey, who had retreated slowly into the semidarkness at the back of the room.

"Oh, I didn't realize," Alice replied, "but that's even better. Susie would totally be banging her driver—especially if she looked as good as her. Maybe we could play with that trope a little. It would look great on the cover, and it'd do wonders for circulation of the print edition."

"I'm not doing that." Casey spoke louder than she intended. "I'm not playing with any fucking tropes, thank you." She made herself calm down. "I'll wait for you in the car." She spoke as she turned for the door, not looking at Olivia.

None of this was Olivia's fault. They weren't girlfriends and she was the driver, so Olivia had every right to clarify that. But for some reason, Olivia's rapid denial of her had hurt. And she felt stupid for hurting.

"Casey." Olivia said her name as she was half out of the door. She turned back to her.

"I'm sorry about all of this. I shouldn't be long."

"Doesn't matter to me. I'm paid to wait." She couldn't miss the disappointed look in Olivia's eyes, but she didn't know why. Was she supposed to have said yes? To have let them dress her up, in the absence of who they'd really wanted and play the oh-so-bangable driver with Olivia—with "Susie'"—in her clinging red dress. She couldn't believe that was what Olivia wanted. She might be "just" her driver, but she wasn't a bloody prop.

Casey stalked back to the car. She didn't know how Olivia could bear it. The intrusive questions, the being on display, the empty obviousness of it all. Olivia seemed like a great person, but at the same time, this was the life she had willingly chosen for herself. It was hard for her to square that circle. And something about it reminded her of Hannah, of Hannah's relentless pursuit of fame, money and "influence." Whatever that meant.

Her mom was right, Hannah had never thought Casey was good enough—joking that Casey was her "bit of rough." She'd been offended by it then. But she should have embraced it, because it was true. No wonder Olivia had felt the need to make it so clear that Casey wasn't her girlfriend. And she didn't even know the rest of it. If she did, she'd have plenty more to disapprove of. Casey let out a curse as she got into the car and slammed the door. She had to care less. Olivia's opinion of her didn't matter.

Except it did and that was the problem.

Olivia had her script on her knee. She'd missed the read-through because of delaying the photoshoot, and missing it made it even less likely she'd get her lines nailed before they started filming. She was reading the words, but the movement of the car—coupled with Casey's brooding presence next to her—meant nothing was sinking in.

She couldn't even make herself feel sorry about it. The scene she was prepping had Susie and Phoebe confessing feelings for each other, sitting in a car outside the St. Pancras hotel. Except Susie was not someone who found "feelings" easy, so she was mostly confessing a desire to get Phoebe upstairs and into a hotel room, so she could do what Susie did best.

Olivia was an actress. She'd told Liam to be a pro about kissing Louise, to put all his own feelings on hold, because that's what acting was. But as she read the script, she felt a real dread at the idea of having to kiss Billie. And the script suggested Phoebe and Susie were going to be doing a lot more than kissing.

Olivia sighed deeply and looked out the window as they passed a small theater. *The Ovalhouse.* The sign above the main entrance advertised a play she knew well. She had the impulse to go and see it. To ask Casey to go with her so she could pretend they were on a date, pretend she was back in Brooklyn at that cozy little theater she loved that was two blocks from her apartment. The one where she'd made her debut. And maybe she'd take Casey home to meet her parents and they'd fall for her accent and love just how real she was. She shook her head, shook the silliness away. She was a dreamer once, but not anymore.

Next to her, Casey was tapping her fingers against the steering wheel in time to the music Olivia had put on to try to fill the silence. They hadn't said much at all since leaving the magazine, and Olivia didn't know what to say to get things back to the way they were before Alice had mistaken Casey for her girlfriend and tried to force her into participating in the shoot. They had been getting on well. Talking easily—flirting even—and it felt good. Really good. She put the script back in her bag with a sigh.

"Have I done something to upset you?" Olivia decided to just ask.

"No, not at all." Casey turned to her briefly before returning her eyes to the road.

"Are you sure? It seems kind of chilly in here."

"I can turn down the air conditioning."

"You know that's not what I meant."

Olivia waited. Casey had a stick up her ass about something. She wanted to know what. She wanted them to get along. Badly wanted them to get along. Wanted Casey to go back to being sweet to her, not to be like this. In fact, she hadn't wanted someone to like her this much in a very long time. And she couldn't deny that three minutes ago, she'd been mentally introducing Casey to her parents.

"You've done nothing." The words were defiant, but Olivia noticed the slump in Casey's shoulders as she relaxed them slightly. She waited a beat longer.

"Look, I'm sorry my mom was stupid enough to think you were my girlfriend and I'm sorry that Alice did too. I can understand why that would be embarrassing for you. I don't want that. I don't want to embarrass you. Next time, I'll just wait in the car."

"Are you serious?"

Casey nodded, eyes fixed to the road ahead of them. Olivia felt an unexpected rush of affection for her.

"First of all, I'm glad your mom thought I was your girlfriend. I mean, how else would I have gotten her to show me those photographs and tell me all those stories." She turned in her seat so she was facing Casey. "Second of all, it wouldn't be embarrassing to me if you were my girlfriend." Olivia felt herself heat up internally as she said it. "Not at all. And I'm mystified as to why you would think it would be."

She waited for a response.

"I just thought…" Casey moved her hands in front of her, seeming to wave the thought away without completing it. "I'm just happy being the driver who waits in the car. That's all. Alice annoyed me. I didn't want my photograph taken and I didn't want any part of that 'Susie would totally bang her driver' crap either. And her questions were stupid and intrusive. I don't know how you put up with it."

"I don't know either."

Olivia meant it. After Casey had left, Alice had been bold enough to ask her more directly about the sex tape—and then a whole lot more questions about Billie and their onscreen, off-screen relationship. She was getting pretty sick of talking about her. Of talking about all of it. Why wouldn't they just let her act and ask her about the show? It was why she was there after all. It was funny, but the fans had a much better sense of what was appropriate than the media did.

"I don't have much choice. There's a lot of things I love about my job, but the constant questions, the constant intrusion and innuendo, not so much. But I have to put up with the bad bits to enjoy the good bits, so I just suck it up."

It wasn't easy. Lately, the endless PR—the way Susie permeated almost every aspect of her life—had been getting to her. At thirty-five, she wanted more for herself.

"I guess I'm just pretty private. I would find it hard."

"I find it hard too. Like I say, it's my job."

Casey didn't respond. She kept her eyes on the road, the tension back in her shoulders. Olivia didn't want it to be like this.

"I'm not surprised you said no to being photographed though." Olivia tried for something lighter. "Even in that pretty little Communion dress, you seemed grouchy about having your picture taken."

She was happy to see the corner of Casey's mouth turn up in a small smile.

"The lace on that thing itched like you wouldn't believe. It would make anyone scowl."

"You were scowling in a lot of those photos. It can't always have been the lace." Olivia meant to tease, but as she said the words, she realized that maybe Casey didn't have a lot to smile about when she was young. She wanted to take them back.

"I still do. Scowl a lot, I mean. Don't pretend you haven't noticed."

Olivia's phone rang.

"Oh, I noticed." She was happy to see Casey smile.

"*Are you nearly back at the hotel?*" It was Louise. "*We finished the run-through. Billie's gone upstairs to rest—though Liam says she's fucking rather than resting, but neither of us wants to think about that. They had that writer that everyone says Billie's involved with read Susie's lines, and when she got to the 'I want to undress you right now' part, it seemed to get Billie pretty worked up. Anyway, we're thinking of going out. We wondered if Casey might be able to drive us somewhere, to a bar, a museum—anywhere. We've got a couple of hours before we have to do tonight's interviews and we need to get out of this hotel. My boy here is climbing the walls.*" Louise finally stopped speaking. She was a force of nature.

"So you want Casey, but not me?" Olivia teased her.

"*Obviously. And I think we both know she's got no hope of resisting me. No one does.*"

Olivia put her thumb over the tiny speaker, muffling Louise, making sure Casey couldn't hear anything.

"You had better be joking." Olivia felt something close to panic. The idea of Louise and Casey was not something she wanted to dwell on.

"*I might be, I might not be. Though I have been wondering what magical transformation might happen if we got a few drinks inside her, got her to loosen up a bit. I bet she's a lot of fun when she's drunk.*"

Olivia wanted to say that Casey was fun even when she wasn't drunk. She had the urge to both defend her—and protect her—from Louise.

"You'll upset Liam if you keep carrying on like this." Olivia blurted it out without thinking. There were better things she could have said, but with Casey sitting beside her, she couldn't think of anything that wouldn't let Casey know that Louise was contemplating getting her drunk enough to seduce her—and that Olivia was absolutely never going to let that happen.

"*What's gonna upset Liam?*"

"Nothing, ignore me. Let me ask Casey our ETA. We're halfway home I think."

"We're ten minutes away if the traffic is kind to us." As Casey spoke, Olivia could hear Louise—away from the phone and luckily for her, completely missing the point—asking Liam if he had the hots for Casey.

"We don't know how long it'll take to get back. The traffic might slow us down. Casey said it might be another hour." Olivia told the white lie, ignoring Casey's sideways glance.

"*I'm not waiting an hour, Liv. We'll have to go exploring without you. You don't mind do you? We only have a couple of hours. We'll waste half that time if we have to wait for you.*"

Louise wasn't giving her the choice, but Olivia was relieved to be able to keep Casey to herself for a little while longer. And to keep Casey away from Louise. Louise had more of a game than even Susie did.

"Of course I don't mind, Lou. Have fun and stay out of trouble." Olivia said her good-byes and rang off just as they turned onto the main road that ran parallel to the river. She recognized the route. Casey was right, they were ten minutes from the hotel max.

Casey turned to her with a quizzical expression.

"They wanted you to take them somewhere. I just…" What could she say? "I wanted you to have some time to sort out stuff for your mom." She was shamed by the fact that it wasn't true, but Olivia couldn't exactly say that she wanted more time alone with Casey.

"I'm paid to drive for you. And I'm on duty. If they want to go somewhere, I should take them." Casey sounded a little annoyed.

"I know, it's just that I wanted…" Her mind was whirring. If she didn't stall them from going back, they were going to arrive just as Louise and Liam were departing. She realized where they were. "I wanted to go up there for a visit. And we won't have time if we go back to get them and they might not even want to do it anyway."

Olivia pointed at the Shard. London's tallest building. Casey had pointed it out to them on one of their drives past.

"I've got a couple of hours for a visit before I have to get ready for the interviews tonight. Have you?"

Casey looked at her watch. "I made plans to see someone. I was supposed to be off duty at five. But I probably have time for a visit if you don't stay too long. It's got parking. I could wait for you there."

"I thought we could both go up. It'd be nicer to have company, and it's better than you waiting in the car." Olivia hoped that was true.

Casey frowned, and Olivia wanted to take back her suggestion. It wasn't fair of her to ask, because Casey probably felt like she had to say yes. She was their driver and she was being paid to be nice to them. The sooner Olivia got her head wrapped around that dynamic, the less likely she'd be to make a complete fool of herself imagining that Casey spending time with her was anything else.

"I'm sorry. I shouldn't drop things on you outside of the schedule. You've got plans. Forget I asked. It's not a quick visit kind of place. There's a cocktail bar up there that the guidebooks say is a must-see. I don't want to rush it."

Olivia felt disappointed. It wasn't about missing seeing London from the top of the Shard, she didn't want to think of Casey having a date. But of course she did, she was gorgeous and London was full of women like Louise—like Olivia if she had the courage—who would happily take Casey out. And then take her home. Maybe even to the hotel room just two doors away from her own. She stopped herself from thinking about it.

Casey looked at her, her eyes looking dark in the dim light of the car. "Okay." She bit her lip. "But I'd like to do that with you, so maybe another time?" The way Casey said it made Olivia feel things—an intensity, a wanting, that she hadn't felt in years. "I definitely owe you a drink after this morning."

Olivia simply nodded. She didn't want to think this was Casey simply paying her back. She wanted instead to believe Casey when she said "I'd like to do that with you" with a look in her eyes that said she did.

"Okay, I'll consider it a rain check." Olivia smiled. "Now, put your foot on the gas and let's see if I can catch up with those friends of mine before they head out looking for trouble. Though I'm guessing Liam won't be happy to see me if he's hoping for some alone time with Louise."

Casey nodded, a pensive expression on her beautiful face. Olivia wanted to reach across and smooth the frown away with her thumb.

"You okay?" Olivia couldn't help but ask.

"Yeah, sorry, I was just thinking about my mom."

Olivia waited.

"I should be more patient with her. She's had a tough time. Not just this thing with Neil. Just generally. My dad, my stepdad. She hasn't been treated well."

Olivia could see the tension in Casey's arms as she gripped the steering wheel. They were crawling along in the traffic, barely moving.

"I can't stand to see her like this, but I'm pretty sure she can't stand it either. She needs more from me than I give her, more than maybe I can give her."

When she turned to face Olivia, Casey's face showed real upset, her eyes clouded with something painful. She couldn't stop herself from reaching out a hand and placing it on Casey's arm. She felt a shiver in her own body that was matched by a faint vibrating in the muscles in Casey's arm.

"You're here now. You don't have to be." It was all Olivia could think of. It didn't feel like enough.

The traffic began to move in front of them and Casey shifted the SUV into gear.

"We're moving. You might well catch up with them. Maybe there's still time to cramp Liam's style."

Casey was obviously forcing herself to seem more cheerful. Olivia wanted to tell her not to, to tell her that she could talk to her, whenever she wanted to, however she needed to. But she didn't. She simply nodded. They were practically strangers. Casey had friends, she had plans. She didn't need Olivia to intrude in her life.

She sank back in her seat as they entered the narrow cobbled street running next to the river that would eventually lead them to the hotel. She wasn't going to try to find Lou and Liam, she was going to let herself have a swim and half an hour in the sauna. And she was going to try not to spend that time thinking about how much Casey had come to matter to her in such a ridiculously short space of time.

CHAPTER ELEVEN

D on't." Olivia said the word without opening her mouth, keeping her body still, not wanting to attract attention. But her tone made it crystal clear that Billie should stop what she was doing.

"I know you don't mean that." Billie's voice was teasing, sensual as she let her fingertips graze the back of Olivia's neck.

Olivia reached behind her to lift Billie's hand away from its position on the back of her chair.

"I said don't. So don't, okay?" Olivia gave Billie a hard stare. If they hadn't been sitting side by side in a hotel room, a camera trained on them, waiting for the first of the morning's interviewers to come in and get them started, Olivia would have said and done a lot more to let Billie know how out of order she was.

What she wanted to do was walk. Walk out of the room, walk away from Billie's stupid flirtations and walk away from the day's obligations. Walk until she found the river and then get on one of the boats that drifted by. She'd call Casey and ask her to join her, and she'd leave Susie trapped in this hotel room with Billie and the succession of journalists who were going to be asking them the same questions over and over all morning. But Olivia couldn't walk out. As she'd explained to Casey, this was the price she paid for the privilege of being able to act for a living.

"We're supposed to have chemistry and this is supposed to be fun. I'm just getting us in the mood." She smiled at Olivia. "It's gonna be a long morning otherwise."

"It's gonna be a long morning anyway, and I don't like to be touched without permission, okay?" Olivia hoped that the microphones they were wearing weren't picking up any of their conversation.

"Don't be such a hard-ass, Olivia. I know you and I know this is your thing, playing a little hard to get. That's fine, but you should know that I haven't yet done a show where the person playing opposite me hasn't fallen for my charms, so you might as well stop fighting it." Billie's voice was light. She had to be joking, but her arrogance made it hard to tell.

Louise burst into the room. Liam trailed in behind her.

"Sorry we're late." Louise took the chair to Olivia's left, Liam the one next to that. "We had a little swim after breakfast and lost track of time. His fault." Louise jerked a thumb at Liam, as one of the production assistants moved in to mic them both. "He insisted on doing extra laps even after I told him we had to go. He's too obsessive about exercise." She sounded every kind of grouchy.

"How was it my fault? I spent like three minutes in makeup and you were in there for thirty. I could have done another twenty laps in that time." Liam sounded just as annoyed.

"Well, I missed you both. Billie filled the time by telling me all about the kind of personality I have." She gave Billie an icy look. "It was fascinating."

"Okay, we're good to go," the production assistant said as she moved behind the camera. "Are you guys ready?"

A man in a suit was ushered into the room and sat opposite them. They waited while a microphone was fixed to his tie. He coughed to clear his throat, consulted the pile of papers on his knee, and then looked up at them with a vacant smile.

"Charlie. BBC breakfast show, entertainment correspondent." He smiled at them nervously, looking like someone who would never willingly watch the show, not in a million years. This was going to be painful.

"So, um, you're here in the UK to promote *The West Side*? The Emmy-nominated LGBTQ show." He said the letters like they were new to him, clearly already out of his comfort zone.

"We are. And we're also shooting some scenes here, starting this weekend," Louise said. "And we've timed our visit perfectly so we can also be part of the huge Pride parade y'all are having. We brought our rainbow swimwear and our umbrellas. We came prepared for whatever your weather has to throw at us."

Louise was so good at this. She could effortlessly chat and charm, and she found none of it annoying or upsetting in the way that Olivia sometimes did. She still had so much to learn if she was ever going to get good at the game they were expected to play. But Olivia wasn't even sure she wanted to. She was losing herself in it somehow and it scared her.

She took a breath, made herself smile, and got herself ready to spend the morning fielding questions she didn't want to answer as graciously as she could. All the time remembering that she did this because the show's fans deserved it from her.

❖

"Do people often mistake you for the characters you play? Do they expect you to be as sexy or as confident and then get disappointed when you're not like that? Or do you feel a pressure to live up to them in real life? I guess that's one for Olivia. How much are you pursued by women who want you to be like Susie? To be like Susie is between the sheets. I mean, she is pretty hot and you do a pretty believable job with those sex scenes."

The rambling, excited woman in front of them was from an entertainment website. It was one of the ones that had gleefully run the story of Olivia's breakup and the subsequent release of the sex tape. She had no idea if this woman was involved then, but she didn't want to answer the question. It reminded her of Kristin, of the way she had compared her to Susie and absolutely found her lacking. It hurt. But she was hardly going to admit to that now.

The interviewer was looking at her with expectation, but Olivia couldn't find the words she needed to give an answer that wouldn't give away her feelings. Her silence was getting embarrassing.

"It's difficult for all of us. Not just Olivia." Liam spoke into the space she had left by not responding. "Sometimes the role, the story, calls for us to get naked, to kiss someone, to make love to someone. It's no better or worse than when we have to cry or shout or pretend to stub our toes. It's just acting. People would do well to remember that. We all understand it that way. And if people get confused and think we are the characters we play somehow—when we're obviously not—then we take that as a compliment that our performance is good and believable."

The answer was perfect and Olivia wanted to hug him. It was exactly what she would have said if she wasn't so madly inarticulate about the whole thing. Susie was everything she wasn't—confident, sexy, in charge—and being reminded of it on the daily was not good for her confidence, or her sense of self.

"I worry sometimes that it's possible to lose yourself in it all. I mean, I love walking around old neighborhoods and finding new places to eat. I love dogs. I love to read romances. And I'm painfully shy. Susie is none of those things. She's too busy kicking ass and sweeping women off their feet. I mean, it's amazing, but it's not me. I'm her, but she's not me. It's important to remind yourself of that sometimes and to not feel like too much of a disappointment in comparison."

The interviewer stared at her like she'd just admitted to something she absolutely shouldn't. She felt like she'd punctured a kid's favorite balloon. She meant to just agree with Liam, but the truth popped out, a truth no one expected to hear. But for some reason, she craved the need to be authentic, to say something truthful amongst this madness. She knew why. Casey. Casey was authentic. And Casey didn't even watch TV. She didn't know Susie at all. She would never compare them and find Olivia lacking. To Olivia, that felt great.

"She's not that shy." Billie spoke up, nudging Olivia with her elbow. "And anyway, you know what they say—it's always the quiet ones you have to watch."

The interviewer laughed. Billie had moved them all back into the realm of innuendo and lightness, far away from Olivia's somber truth about the struggles she had with the show and with herself.

"We're so happy to be in London. And we've been fortunate enough to be blessed with a driver who's also a tour guide, so we're seeing a lot of your beautiful city." That was Louise again. It wasn't true, but she was telling the interviewer exactly what she wanted to hear—and exactly what she'd told every one of the other five journalists who had so far sat in front of them.

Olivia looked at her watch. Only an hour had passed. It felt like six. She fixed a smile on her face and resolved not to say anything else authentic for the rest of the morning.

Casey put her phone on the desk. She'd spent the last half hour talking to Gina. She was in bed and unable to sleep and had made it clear that only the prospect of squeezing some juicy gossip out of Casey about *The West Side* cast was keeping her from hanging up. Casey didn't oblige, but Gina had fun trying.

Casey had had more than one opportunity to tell her about her developing feelings for Olivia but dodged every one. It wasn't just that she felt stupid, she didn't know how well she could articulate what she was feeling, and she didn't want Gina's inevitable go-for-it pep talk. Gina sent her to London with the instruction to get laid, to get back into the swing of things with a no-strings-attached holiday romance. And she was pretty sure Gina would say that Olivia was perfect for that.

Before Gina interrupted her, Casey had been online paying off several of her mom's debts. She started small, wanting to clean up as many of the outstanding bills as she could, but the credit cards and rent arrears hung over everything like a big black cloud.

She called her mom, wanting to update her, but also to see how she was doing. As the phone rang, she took in a breath, wanting her mom to be sober, to be okay.

"Casey, love, I was just going to call you." Her mom sounded breathless, excited even.

"What's up?"

"What do you mean, what's up? You know very well. It all arrived about an hour ago. I've been unpacking and getting everything put in its place. It looks amazing. I'm so grateful. I don't know how I'll ever be able to thank you. I promise I'll learn my lesson from all this and make a fresh start—"

"Mom, what are you talking about? What arrived an hour ago?"

"The microwave, the coffee maker, the TV, the radio—even a bread maker. I never had one of them before, but I'm definitely going to give it a try. I've always wanted to. Thanks, love."

Her mom said it like she was about to cry. Casey's head was spinning.

"Mom. It wasn't me. I didn't send anything."

"I don't understand. Who else would send me all this?"

"I don't know, maybe Jack." They were both silent on the call, knowing her brother would never do such a thing. Any money he had he spent on himself.

"Is there a card? Maybe a note in one of the boxes that says who the sender is."

"Let me look. I kept all the papers in case you needed them." Casey heard her mom rummaging around. "Here's something. Like a gift card or something. I missed it the first time around."

"What does it say?" It seemed unlikely, but Casey wondered if Neil might have been persuaded to replace everything as a result of the police confronting him with the audio she recorded.

"It says 'Sorry it's been so tough. I hope this helps a bit. Warm wishes, Olivia.' Aw, Casey, your Olivia sent me all this. Did she not even tell you? Oh, love, that's so nice of her. She's so lovely. You have to give me her number, so I can thank her myself."

As her mom gushed about Olivia, Casey began pacing. This was crazy. She couldn't let Olivia do this. They didn't need her charity. She felt a prickling under her skin that she recognized as shame. Olivia felt so sorry for her mom, for the way she was living, that she got someone to send her a load of stuff for the house. She could afford it of course, but that didn't make it right.

"I think you'll have to send it back—" She stopped herself. She couldn't make her mom do that. She needed that stuff. Casey had been meaning to buy it herself, but hadn't gotten around to it because she'd been focusing on the bills. She would pay Olivia back. She would sort it out. Her mom didn't need to be involved. Casey wanted her to have the new things, to be able to enjoy them arriving. "Don't worry, Mom. Olivia just didn't tell me she was doing it, that's all. I'll thank her for you."

"I can't believe she didn't tell you. That's funny. Are you two not speaking?" Her mom laughed. "Tell her they're beautiful and I love the red color. It really brightens the kitchen. I can't believe she remembered everything, remembered even that I was talking about being bored and wanting to take up baking bread to distract me from drinking. She's so sweet, Casey. A real keeper."

Casey rubbed her head, wanting to get her mom off the phone, wanting to find Olivia, to ask her what the hell she thought she was doing. She had spent most of her life not feeling good enough, watching other people do better than her. And now Olivia seemed determined to remind her of the gulf between them, at just the time she was starting to imagine that maybe they could connect on some level. She said a hurried good-bye to her mom and looked at her phone.

It was almost noon. At half past, she had to take Liam and Louise to the studios where they were starting filming. Maybe they'd all finished their interviews by now, maybe Olivia was already in her room. She got up, opened her door, and padded along the corridor. At Olivia's door, she knocked firmly.

"Who is it?"

"Me—Casey—do you have a minute?"

The door swung open and Olivia was standing in front of her, a hesitant smile on her face, looking stunning even in faded black jeans and a sage green T-shirt.

"Hi."

For a second, Casey forgot all about her reason for coming and they simply stared at each other.

"I just spoke to my mom. I—she asked me to say a big thank you. She was amazed by your generosity—" She stopped as a slow smile spread across Olivia's face

"She liked them?"

"She did. But obviously, I can't let you do that. It's a nice gesture, but it's not appropriate. I can't—I mean, I would get in trouble with my boss if I allowed a client to do that. Please let me know who you had buy them for you, and I'll figure out with them how much they cost and make sure you're paid back."

"You'll get in trouble? Even though I did it without you even knowing?" Olivia had a concerned look on her face. "I know I'm a 'client' to you," she emphasized the word sounding unhappy, "but to your mom I'm not. And this is something between your mom and me. So please let me—"

"Olivia, I can't let you do that. Please understand. I already feel—" Casey didn't want to admit to Olivia the feelings she had of never being good enough. A beat passed.

"Did she like the color?" Olivia asked. "The red."

"She did. Very much."

"I chose it. I thought it would look nice. She told me what he did, what he took, and I wanted to give her a pick-me-up. I'm sorry if it's made things awkward, but I just thought it would put a smile on her face."

"It did. A smile and then a few tears. It's an incredible thing to do for someone you hardly know and I just—" Casey decided to just say it. "I feel embarrassed. On her behalf, on my own behalf. I didn't want to get you involved in the first place, and I already felt bad about the whole thing, but now I feel like I'm this charity case." Casey willed the tension to disappear from her voice, her shoulders, her chest. Olivia had done nothing but try to help. She didn't deserve to be on the receiving end of Casey's defensiveness.

"I'm sorry, Olivia. I should be more grateful. I have a chip on my shoulder about growing up poor. We never asked for help, however bad it got. And we never expected any." She lifted her eyes to Olivia's expecting to see impatience, disgust even, but all she saw was understanding.

"I lay in the bath last night with my phone and had a lot of fun ordering that stuff. And I felt a lot of joy imagining your mom receiving the parcels and having a good day for a change. It wasn't charity, Casey. It was one woman understanding that another woman has had a tough time and wanting to reach out. It was all I could do in the circumstances. I thought you would say no if I asked for your mom's number so I could call and check in." She shrugged. "So this was my way of checking in."

"You were going to call and check in?" Casey asked.

"I'd have liked to."

"I'm sorry."

"You don't need to apologize. I mean, I know it's a British thing and it's charming and all, but there's no need to keep saying sorry. You haven't done anything. I'm the one who should apologize. I didn't think about this," she pointed into the space between them, "about this dynamic, about what it might feel like to you. I was just caught up in wanting to make Evelyn smile."

"Evelyn?" Casey raised an eyebrow. "First name terms already?"

"Yeah, of course. Moms love me, I already told you that."

"You did."

"So let me do this for her. No one needs to know and we don't need to mention it again. It's between me and Evelyn. And anyway," Olivia looked at her watch, "it's nearly time to go, so you probably need shoes or something."

Casey pushed herself away from the doorjamb. She would have leaned on it and chatted to Olivia for the whole day if she'd been able to. The woman was a wonder. She had just made this situation feel a hundred times better than Casey expected.

"Well, on Evelyn's behalf, thank you." Casey bowed slightly before heading back to her room. A few steps away from her door, she turned back. Olivia had stepped outside her room and was watching her walk away. Something about being watched like that by Olivia made her lose her train of thought for a second.

"How did you know her address?"

"I thought we might get in trouble there, so I noted down the address as we arrived and texted it to one of the assistants here with a note to say to send the police if I hadn't texted back within fifteen minutes." She smiled. "I watch a lot of 'woman in peril' shows. I'm always mystified as to why they never do that."

Casey shook her head. "You're something else."

"Thank you." Olivia waited a beat. "So are you."

Casey opened her door without looking back. Olivia really was something else.

Olivia closed the door and stepped back inside the room. From her position perched on the edge of one of the armchairs, Louise was looking at her like she had something to say.

"What?"

"What in the name of almighty Cate Blanchett was all that? You bought Casey's mom a load of stuff because she needed a pick-me-up? When did you meet Casey's mom? Why are you buying her stuff? What the hell is going on with you two?"

Olivia let Louise fire the questions at her back as she sat at the dressing table to apply the finishing touches to her makeup. She was glad to wipe away the heavy foundation they were always caked in when they did TV and replace it with something gentler and more natural.

She was buying time, deciding what she should say to Louise. Wondering what she'd say if she told her the truth about how she was already feeling about Casey.

"Liv, seriously, what's up?"

She turned on her stool.

"Nothing. We had a bit of spare time, so we visited her mom's house on the way to somewhere. She's having a crappy time and I felt a bit sorry for her, so I sent her a parcel of goodies to cheer her up. Ordered online, touch of a button. You know how I like shopping. It wasn't a lot of trouble."

She made it sound as casual as she could. Though the fact that she intended to tag along with Louise and Liam on the drive out to the studio so she could spend some more time with Casey was going to make Louise even more suspicious. It wasn't like she didn't have things she could do with her afternoon. She could stay in and read, explore the neighborhood, learn her lines. It was just that none of them compared with the chance to hang out with Evelyn's ever-so-gorgeous daughter.

"Number one, why was Casey here acting all like 'oh, you shouldn't have' if it was so low-key? Number two, when did you ever have spare time to swing by anyone's house? It takes three hours to get anywhere in this city. And number three, you hate shopping so don't give me all that."

They were good questions. Before *The West Side*, Louise played a down on her luck, addicted to opiates, trial lawyer in a miniseries. She was channeling all of that right now. Olivia was a good actress, but Louise had known her for more than ten years and she was pretty sure she would see right through her if she tried to lie.

"It's private, okay. But her mom has had some real shitty man trouble, and Casey has her hands full. She's been solid for us, for me—" Olivia had told Louise all about the way Casey stepped in and saved her. "And I wanted to help out a bit. That's all."

Louise looked at her. Olivia could tell she wasn't convinced.

"Yesterday? When you missed the run-through?"

"Yeah. Something came up. It was an emergency. Don't say anything, okay?"

Louise waved her words away.

"Look, I like her too, Liv. And I'm not talking about the way she makes me feel with that accent and the sleeves rolled up over those forearms." She smiled. "I mean, she seems pretty cool. But you know that you can sometimes be too generous. It's a great quality, absolutely. But don't let her take advantage of your good nature. She could have taken you to see her mom precisely because she wanted you to feel sorry enough to help out. Next she might tell you her brother is in jail and needs money for bail."

"It's not that. Not at all. You heard her. She wished I hadn't done it. It made her feel bad. Does that sound like someone who wants me to buy her mom stuff?" Olivia couldn't help but feel defensive. She didn't like Louise reminding her of the past. She had been far too generous with Kristin. She knew that. She bought her a car just two weeks before they split up. It had been humiliating. She didn't need to be reminded of it.

"I don't think she sounded happy about it, no. But, Liv, we don't know her. You don't know her, so just be careful. Not everyone has the best of intentions and not everyone is what they seem."

"I feel like—" Olivia didn't let herself finish the sentence. She was going to say that she felt like she did know Casey, that Casey somehow reminded her of home, of all the real things she had left behind when she moved to LA. But it sounded a little crazy even in her own mind. "I feel like I'm a better judge of character now. Maybe it's because of what Kristin put me through, or maybe just because I'm a little older. I think I'd know if she was playing me."

"Okay, okay." Louise stood. "I know that you always like to be the older sister, the wise and slightly disillusioned one. I'll get back in my fun-but-doesn't-know-much lane." The words could have been harsh, but

Louise said them with a smile and with arms outstretched offering her a hug. A hug that Olivia gratefully received.

"Are you okay?" Olivia meant to ask her this before Casey had knocked. Louise seemed subdued.

"I'm just anxious about today's shoot."

"Really?"

"Yeah. Ever since the read-through, Liam's been kind of distant with me. I know he's dreading it, and I don't want it to make things weird between us. We've been getting on well this trip. Really well."

Louise avoided her eyes as she spoke.

"And today we're going to kiss and touch each other, and I'm pretty sure that's gonna gross him out, but I don't feel like I can talk to him about any of it, because if I admit I need to, if I admit it's difficult for me, then he'll just give me that answer he gave earlier—we're all professionals, we're acting, we don't ever get our real feelings mixed up in it. I mean, it was a great answer but it's—"

She stopped speaking before finally lifting her eyes to Olivia's.

"Maybe it's just not what I wanted to hear. Maybe I want to think it's difficult for him, like it's going to be difficult for me. Because of the feelings, I mean."

"The feelings." Olivia couldn't quite believe what she was hearing. "Feelings for Liam?"

Louise nodded shyly before heading to the door. "We have to go. Casey will be waiting."

"No, you don't." Olivia moved to stop her from leaving, placing a hand on her arm.

"What is there to say, Liv? It's the biggest cliché there is, falling for a friend who doesn't feel the same way. It's just that normally you're not then put in a position where you have to strip each other's clothes off and pretend to have sex. I'm dreading this morning as much as he probably is, but for different reasons."

"Have you tried talking to him about it? Telling him how you feel. I mean, you never know." Olivia couldn't believe that Louise had the same kind of feelings that Liam had. Or that Casey had been right about that too. But she couldn't tell Louise how Liam felt, and she couldn't tell Liam either. She was caught in the middle.

"No way. I want to keep him as a friend. He matters too much for me to risk that. I'm not his type anyway. You've seen him—he's all fitness and discipline and improving his mind with serious books and subtitled films.

The only foreign TV I watch these days is the *Real Housewives of Atlanta*." She opened the door. "I better go get my stuff."

This time Olivia was the one who pulled Louise into a hug. "Don't despair, Lou. You are an absolute catch and if he has any sense, he'll realize that." She had said something similar to Liam. She had to hope they found a way to realize they both had the same kind of feelings. "And I'll see you downstairs in five."

"You're coming with us? I thought you had a free afternoon."

"I do. I thought I'd just tag along. It's a chance to see the studio setup." Olivia bit the inside of her cheek, willing Louise not to call her on it.

"To see the studio setup? That's very diligent." She turned back to Olivia from the open doorway. "Unusually and suspiciously diligent. Maybe later, we can have a proper chat about what's really going on with you and our insanely handsome driver."

"Maybe. Maybe not." Olivia blew Louise a playful kiss. "Now get going. Or you'll keep us waiting."

She quickly laced up her Converse, checked herself in the mirror one more time, and headed out. She wanted to get a head start on Louise simply because this afternoon, she was going to snag the front seat next to Casey. She'd checked her phone and the drive was going to take them the best part of an hour. That was time with Casey she wouldn't have if she stayed behind. And if Casey didn't have plans for all of the time that Liam and Louise would be on set, she was going to try to take her to lunch.

CHAPTER TWELVE

Casey was sitting in the car, considering her options. She had to be back here to collect them by five thirty, but until then, she was completely free. She decided to drive to the nearest stretch of river and take a long walk. The alone time would give her the chance to think. David's party was less than a week away, and she would have to see not just Hannah, but every one of the friends she had walked away from. In disgrace and in shame. She'd used the excuse of the job and her mom's situation to avoid facing up to things in the way she'd promised herself she'd try to, but the party would mean throwing herself in at the deep end.

She saw Olivia emerge from the studio hangar and walk toward the car. She looked every kind of beautiful. When she caught Casey looking in her direction, she smiled and gave her a little wave, and Casey felt the joy of seeing her in every part of her body.

On the drive over, Olivia sat up front with her and they had chatted easily. About the swinging sixties in London, about what happens on a studio shoot, about the best way to make bread using a bread maker. Olivia was cute, funny, and utterly engaging. And Casey had forgotten all about Liam and Louise in the back of the car, forgotten all about the fact they were client and driver. It felt good. But Olivia was a client and soon they were going their separate ways. Casey should have been more worried by just how good it felt.

"They kick you out for forgetting your lines?" Casey said as Olivia reached the car.

"Not this time. I was just checking it out. My studio scenes aren't until Thursday, so I don't really need to be here. I just came along for the ride."

Olivia was shuffling from one foot to the other, seeming nervous. It was adorable. She was adorable. Casey felt herself flush. This was her chance. She should ask Olivia if she had time for a walk by the river. Or lunch. Or something. Anything.

"I wondered if you wanted to have a coffee, or food, or something? I mean, if you have time." Olivia asked her the very question she'd been summoning the courage to ask.

"I'd love to." Casey didn't hesitate.

Olivia moved around to the passenger side of the car and got in.

Casey's mind was whirring as she tried to think of somewhere they could go. She didn't know this neighborhood at all.

"I tell you what." She took a breath. "We passed a tube station not even five minutes' walk from here, twenty minutes on the Jubilee Line and we'll be in London Bridge. If we go by car, I don't know how long it'll take. And I have to be back here by five thirty." Olivia was staring back at her in confusion. Casey made herself slow down. "Sorry, I'm not being clear. I'm trying to ask if you want to ditch the car, jump on the tube, and go to the Shard. To that cocktail bar that's on your list. I mean, yesterday we couldn't, we didn't have time. But today..." She lifted her hands as if to say today they had all the time they needed.

"I would love that." Olivia grinned. Her smile made Casey feel wonderful.

"I can walk you back to the hotel after and then catch a tube back here to get Liam, Louise, and the car. It's a perfect plan."

Olivia didn't respond. And when she turned her body toward Casey, Casey held her breath.

"It's an absolutely perfect plan."

And the way Olivia gazed at her made Casey think that maybe it was.

In the elevator, Olivia pressed the button marked fifty-two confidently. "It's the highest floor with a bar."

"I've never been up here." Casey had unexpected butterflies. They were nothing to do with how rapidly they were ascending and everything to do with getting to spend more time with Olivia.

"Me neither—obviously. Another first for me. Just like Estelle's steak pudding." Olivia offered Casey a shy smile.

The elevator doors opened, and they stepped out into a lavishly decorated reception area. Olivia introduced herself to the maître d' and explained that she'd called ahead and reserved a window table for two.

Through the open doors in front of them, Casey could see that the bar itself was just as sumptuous and ornate as the reception, with gold brocaded armchairs arranged in clusters around low tables, beneath elaborate chandeliers. The floor to ceiling windows—framed with beautifully colored heavy velvet curtains—provided incredible views of London on two sides of the room. There wasn't a table in there that didn't have a view. It was magical but intimidating, and about as far away from Café Brunest as it was possible to get. If she'd been looking for something to highlight the difference in the way they both lived their lives, this was exactly the right place to choose.

Casey let herself be led to a table in the far corner, hoping that the other people in the bar—like Alice yesterday—wouldn't realize that the shirt and pants she was wearing formed part of a uniform. But as soon as she sat alongside Olivia—both their chairs looking out onto the breathtakingly panoramic view of London directly in front of them—she forgot all about what she was wearing and let herself relax a little.

"Wow," Olivia said softly. "This view is amazing."

"Yeah, incredible. It almost makes me nostalgic for the city."

The waiter approached and they ordered cocktails. She wasn't really a cocktail kind of person—and she couldn't help but dread what they would cost—but Casey ordered one anyway. The days were ticking by, and she was determined to enjoy what little time with Olivia there was left.

Casey pointed out some of the more obvious landmarks and Olivia listened intently.

"You don't miss it at all?" Olivia asked when she'd finished.

"Not really. I could, but I don't let myself think that way because I don't live here anymore and missing it wouldn't help me."

"Yeah, I get that. I feel like that about Brooklyn. If I thought about it a lot, I'd miss it, so I don't." Olivia's tone was relaxed, confiding. "It's funny but being in London has made me miss Brooklyn more. There's something about this city that puts me in touch with my feelings about home. It seems 'real' in that way that Brooklyn is and LA definitely isn't. I feel—"

Olivia stopped when the waiter delivered their cocktails with a flourish. Casey was sorry for the interruption. She was enjoying hearing Olivia talk.

"Go on."

"Maybe it's stupid because I've only been here a week, but I feel like I could make real connections with people here. In LA, it's hard to know who's genuinely interested in me and who's looking to make a connection for the sake of their career. And I guess I mostly hang around with people in the industry, which makes it harder. In Brooklyn, I made good friends just from bumping into people and having everyday conversations. I met the couple who lived opposite me when we realized we were both feeding the same stray cat." Olivia became animated. "And I got friendly with the woman who ran the florist next to my parents' store because her son ran into me on his bike one day. And it was always good to know that we were friends because we had things in common. I didn't doubt for a minute that they liked me, Olivia, because I had absolutely nothing to offer them other than my friendship. Now, it seems like the main thing I have to offer, the main thing people like about me, is Susie. I can't get used to it, and it gets me down more than I like to admit."

"But you have so much to offer." Casey let the reassurance—the compliment—slip out. "I just mean, whether or not you're a big TV star, whether or not you're playing Susie, you seem like someone it would be very cool to be friends with. You're funny, you're smart, you're curious." She stopped herself from saying beautiful, though she wanted to. "That's a lot to offer." Casey hesitated. "I'm not surprised the florist liked you."

Olivia gave her a look she couldn't read before stirring her cocktail for longer than anyone could need to. Casey wondered if she'd said the wrong thing. She fished the orange peel out of her own glass for something to do and made herself look at the view. Looking at Olivia was causing her to say and think all the wrong things.

"That's very nice of you to say, but in a way, you illustrate my point."

"What do you mean?"

"I only know you because you've been hired to drive for me, and we're really only sitting here because of that. So I don't know if you're saying what you're saying because it's your job to be nice to your clients, because you want me to leave you a good review, or because you really mean it. Being like this, being 'famous,' or whatever you'd call it, means that I second-guess everyone and everything. It's tiring."

Casey put down her drink. She could have been offended by Olivia reminding her yet again that she was "just" the driver, but she knew that this time that wasn't what this was.

"I mean it. I'm your driver, yes. But I don't have to be sitting here with you. I chose to. I was the one who suggested we come here and I suggested it because I wanted to spend my afternoon off with you."

Casey was going out on a limb, but she didn't care. Despite all the adoration of the fans, despite the awards and the magazine covers, Olivia needed to hear that she meant something to someone who had nothing to gain from her. "And I already know I'm gonna get a great review because Louise thinks I'm cute." She smiled as she said it. "I'm here because I like you, because I like spending time with you. It's as simple as that. Maybe it's not as impossible as you think to meet people who don't want anything from you other than your company."

She held Olivia's gaze wanting her to feel it, to believe it. "And I don't know Susie—I've never met her, not even for a minute—but I already know that I like Olivia a whole lot more. I'm pretty sure Susie would annoy the hell out of me with all her bed-hopping and impossibly tight dresses."

"I had a feeling you quite liked the dress." Olivia's voice was low, teasing. Casey felt the impact of it in the tightening of the muscles low down in her core.

"Okay." Casey held up her hands with a smile. "I admit the dress was pretty damn hot, but I think you know what I mean. Whatever Susie might have going for her, Olivia has—you have—so much more."

Olivia looked down at her drink, then at the view. It seemed to Casey as if she was doing everything she could to avoid looking at her. She worried she'd gone too far and embarrassed them both. When Olivia eventually looked at Casey, her expression was serious.

"Thank you. For saying that, for coming here with me, and most especially, for never having known Susie."

Casey nodded.

"Well, thank you, again, for being so solid about my mom. It wasn't a very 'I'm a big TV superstar' thing to do. I was surprised, and it gave me a lot of other reasons to like you."

Olivia smiled.

"I have a confession to make. Three actually." Olivia leaned in closer and Casey felt the heat of her breath on her neck. She felt aroused by it despite everything she was telling herself about staying cool. "I've never bumped into Gerard Butler. He and I don't mix in the same circles. I've only been on a red carpet twice and he was nowhere to be seen. I just needed a good story to distract your mom with, and I read in a magazine once that he's popular with middle-aged women."

"That is a terrible lie to tell my dear old mom, but also completely inspired." Casey laughed.

"The second confession's nowhere near as bad, but I totally want to post a photo of myself up here to make Louise jealous. She's always telling me how weak my Instagram game is. I'm going to surprise her." Olivia held out her phone with a grin. "Will you?"

"Sure." Casey took the phone. She retreated a few steps so she could get the table, Olivia, and the amazing view in a single shot and snapped away. Olivia looked incredible. It wasn't that Casey hadn't noticed— she had. It was that seeing her through the lens of the camera somehow made her seem altogether more perfect. Her hair was tied back in a loose ponytail, the color of the T-shirt made her eyes seem a darker shade of hazel, and the arms showing beneath the capped sleeves were so smooth and perfectly formed that Casey wanted to run her hands along them, as if they were on a marble statue.

She watched with a smile as Olivia chose and then posted, one of the pictures. She showed Casey the post. She had tagged herself as being at the Shard and written about it being the high point of her trip, at the highest point in London. Given her own dislike of people showing off on social media, Casey found it surprisingly cute.

Olivia held up the phone again. "Now, a selfie with the two of us."

"No, it's okay." Casey's response was instant.

"Come on, it's a great view. It'll be a great photo." Olivia waggled the phone in her direction, an expectant look on her face.

"I'm just not into that. I'm pretty private." Casey felt churlish refusing, but she wasn't keen for Hannah, or any of their friends, to see her hanging out with Olivia Lang. And thanks to the numerous videos Hannah had posted that made Casey seem like some kind of monster, she doubted Olivia, if she knew any of that, would be that thrilled to be seen hanging out with her either.

"Okay, no problem. I'm sorry. I wasn't going to post it. It was just going to be a little memory of this trip for me. But I should know better than anyone not to force that kind of thing on people." Olivia put her phone on the table seeming embarrassed. She finished her martini.

"What's your third?"

Olivia looked at her with a confused expression.

"Your third confession. You said you had three."

"Oh, that. I just wanted to confess that your romance radar is a thousand times more powerful than mine." Olivia touched her empty glass to Casey's in a toast. "Louise and Liam. You were completely right about them. They both have the same kind of feelings for each other. But neither of them has said a word about it—apart from to tell me." She leaned a little closer, putting a hand lightly on Casey's arm. "But I'm telling you now, so we both get to be piggy in the middle."

She sat back. Casey felt the loss of her touch, her skin still warm where Olivia's fingers had been. She needed to get a grip. The way her body was reacting to Olivia, to her proximity, was not something she was used to.

"Wow. Well, I hope it works out for them. But that's kind of tough on you." Casey made herself say words.

"Yeah, a little. But mostly I fear for them. They're friends and they work together. It's going to be hard if things don't work out. It's one of the downsides of dating people in the industry. But I guess if you spend all your time working, then it's kind of hard to meet people who aren't in the industry." She shrugged, and Casey felt her heart sink a little in her chest, wondering if that was Olivia's way of letting her know that she and Billie had something going on. She wanted to ask but didn't have the nerve.

"We've got time for another." She kept her tone light. "At least you have, I'm driving so I better keep nursing this. If you like bourbon, give it a try. The menu said it was an old-fashioned old-fashioned—whatever that means. But it's pretty good."

Whatever this was between them, Casey liked being with Olivia and she didn't want them to leave yet.

Olivia looked at her phone. "I've got time if you have. I don't want to make you late to collect the lovebirds."

Casey signaled the waiter.

"And if you're free later...Forget it, sorry."

"What?" Casey was curious.

"Nothing."

"It was clearly something."

Olivia looked at her like she was appraising her, appraising the situation. And then she nodded ever so slightly as if she had decided on something.

"Can I be honest? Even if it means embarrassing myself."

"I'd hope you would be." Casey paused. "Be honest, I mean. Not embarrass yourself." She smiled what she hoped was a reassuring smile.

"I keep forgetting you're our driver, that we're not just hanging out as friends—or people who are getting to know each other, or whatever." She faltered. "And I was about to invite you to this awards show dinner thing tonight, forgetting you have a life and people to see here that aren't just us. Actual friends, I mean." She looked down, seeming embarrassed.

"Hey." Casey waited for Olivia to meet her gaze. "If it helps you not to feel embarrassed, then I should admit I feel the same. Sometimes I feel like I've known you a long time." Casey swallowed. She'd gone even further than Olivia and she was pretty sure she'd made Olivia blush.

"Come out with us then. I'm presenting an award and we're nominated for one too. We have a big table. There's room. You can watch me make a fool of myself reading the wrong name off the card while drinking the free champagne and eating the free food."

Olivia made the offer sound casual, but there was something in her eyes that made Casey feel like Olivia wanted her to say yes. Was she being delusional?

"You make it sound oddly compelling." Casey was pretty sure she would have watched Olivia paint a white wall at this point. She might even have braved feeling like a fish out of water at a fancy awards show for more time with her. "But I can't. I have dinner plans. Sorry."

"Of course you do. And having a date sounds better than watching us pretending to be delighted about not winning. Like I said, I keep forgetting you have a life." The words were a little bitter, even though Olivia's tone was gentle.

"It's not a date. My mom and my friend David. We're just catching up. We haven't seen much of each other, not since Hannah and I—since I left for Portland, I mean."

"Hannah is the one Estelle was hoping to see? The one your mom said thought she was too good for you. The ex you left London to avoid."

"You have a good memory."

"I do. When it matters." Olivia held her gaze, and something about the way she looked at Casey made her want to be honest. But she wasn't very good at talking about herself. It was just one of the ways she and Hannah were incompatible. Hannah's channel—her profile, her continued success—required her to keep talking about herself, to keep people interested. And for some reason Casey could never quite understand, people were interested in Hannah's life. What she wore, used, watched, ate. The kind of cats she had. And the kind of girlfriend she had. Hannah had tried hard to get Casey to appear in her videos. And Casey resisted. And eventually it became a problem for them. But she didn't feel like she wanted to explain any of that to Olivia.

"Yes, Hannah is the ex my mom doesn't like. The ex I wanted to get away from." She gave Olivia what she hoped was a rueful look that didn't invite further questioning. "But David is a really old friend. He and I grew up together, and I'm happy to be able to spend some time with him. I've been..." Casey hesitated, not sure whether Olivia was interested in her not-very-interesting life. "I've been avoiding catching up with people. Sometimes, after a breakup, it's awkward. Friends take sides and you don't know who's saying what to who. I went away rather than get involved in any of that. But coming back to sort things out for my mom means I can catch up with some of the people I left behind—and David is someone I miss and someone I know always had my back."

"That sounds awesome." Olivia checked herself. "Not the breakup, obviously. I mean having a friend like David."

"Yeah. Portland is cool, but it's not my home, and I haven't made a lot of friends there. My roommate keeps telling me loneliness isn't a good look on me, usually right before she tries to set me up with another blind date. She doesn't seem to get that, while I'd quite like more friends, I'm a bit meh about the whole dating thing." Casey tried to sound lighter than she felt, sitting up in her chair, feeling a little embarrassed. She hadn't meant to say as much as she had.

"So when you're in Portland, you're single?"

"Yes."

"And in London?" Olivia held her gaze.

"Yes, in London too. Between being at the beck and call of you lot and sorting out my mom, I don't know when you imagine I'm meeting women." Casey didn't feel any resentment. "I mean, I don't mind. I didn't come to London to meet anyone."

The waiter arrived.

"I'll have what she's having." Olivia pointed at the glass in front of Casey. "I'm very old-fashioned in my tastes." It was a joke, but there was something in the way Olivia said it, in the way she looked at Casey as she said it, that made Casey think she meant something more. And Casey realized she wanted to kiss her. Right there, right then. She let herself imagine how good Olivia's lips would taste, how soft her mouth would be.

She came back to her senses to see Olivia looking at her, her bottom lip trapped between her teeth and her head inclined toward her slightly. They both moved their attention back to the waiter at exactly the same time. Both of them seeming to find him utterly absorbing.

"Are you hungry? Want to get something to nibble on?" Olivia asked. "We kind of skipped the lunch eating part and went straight to cocktails."

As soon as Olivia said it, Casey realized she was starving. Olivia's company was completely distracting.

"Something with cheese?" Her stomach growled, happy she was finally paying it some attention.

"Good call." Olivia smiled at her.

The waiter found them a menu and they each ordered something.

"What about you? Maybe not single in LA and maybe not single in London either?" Casey finally had her chance to ask about Billie, and she wasn't going to let the waiter's terrible timing get in the way. She waited for Olivia's reply to ruin her mood, to spoil the imagined intimacy of the last hour.

"It's funny, but I get asked that a lot—whether I'm dating, I mean. I get asked about it more than the rest of them. It's weird. Maybe I give off a lonely vibe, or maybe it's because of Billie's constant hinting about the two of us—"

"I didn't mean to suggest that. I'm sorry, I thought we were just talking."

Casey felt a little thrown, like she'd overstepped the mark somehow. And she couldn't help but notice that Olivia avoided answering. She tried to think of something else to ask, something else to say, but she couldn't.

"I'm not seeing anyone. Here, or anywhere else." Olivia looked at her. "I've been single for a while. And while everyone at the studio—and probably half the fans of the show—would like it to be true that Billie and I are dating, we're not. I told you I don't do the whole mixing work and pleasure thing, but even if I did, Billie is absolutely not my type."

Casey wanted to be pleased because Olivia was way too good for Billie. But she and Olivia worked together. And as happy as she was at the news that Olivia was single, she guessed that anything she might want to develop between them would fall afoul of the whole work and pleasure rule.

The waiter deposited the plates—and Olivia's old-fashioned—in front of them with a flourish. They'd ordered the same thing—the large square platters containing less than Casey would have liked. But the presentation almost made up for the portion size. They let the waiter describe the different types of cheese and the small army of chutneys before they both tucked in, devouring the food with relish. Olivia making the kind of satisfied eating noises that Casey couldn't help but smile at.

"Oh, wow. Try this." Olivia held out her fork, a small piece of blue cheese on the end. "It's awesome." Her gaze was open and steady.

Casey had never been good at reading women's signals—unless they rammed her with a trolley—but yesterday and today, she felt something between them, felt that Olivia might even have been flirting. And now she was feeding her with her fork. While telling her that she didn't do workplace romances.

She took the cheese into her mouth, holding Olivia's gaze. Olivia's eyes widened and her cheeks reddened.

"Mmm. That's delicious." It was. And Casey was relieved to have the cheese to focus on. It was easier than being confused by Olivia's signals.

Olivia's phone made a beeping noise. She picked it up and frowned at it before unlocking it and scrolling through something.

"Damn."

"What's wrong?" Casey asked.

She handed the phone to Casey, then snatched up her drink and took a long, slow sip. Casey looked at the article that was open on the screen and felt her anger grow as she saw first the photo and then the headline.

It was a picture of her and Olivia in the hotel lobby. She had an arm threaded around Olivia's waist, and they were about to get into the elevator. The angle of the photo made it look a lot like Olivia had her head on Casey's shoulder, and the headline announced that Olivia had been drunk. She read the rest of the article and saw, with embarrassment, that they had implied Olivia had needed the help of a "mystery companion" to get her to her room.

She handed the phone back to Olivia.

"I'm really sorry."

"I'm obviously used to having my picture taken, but I still hate being photographed when I'm not aware of it. Especially like this, in a place where I'm staying. It's creepy and invasive."

Casey didn't know what to say. It was a crazy way to live. She couldn't do it.

"The story they've put with the picture is a complete fabrication. You weren't drunk and I only had my arm around you like that because those guys had shaken you up." Casey was surprised by how annoyed she was. "Why didn't whoever it was take photos of those guys harassing you? It would have made a much better story—and presumably they'd have made more money for that."

"Maybe they just caught the end of it and assumed I was drunk, or maybe those guys lied and told them I was." Olivia shook her head and took another gulp of the bourbon, staring again at the phone. "Or maybe they just wanted the chance to say something unpleasant about me. It happens."

Casey felt bad for Olivia.

"And I'm going to get a grilling from the studio about this when I get back."

"You didn't do anything wrong. Just tell them what really happened."

"I will. I'm sure they'll believe me. But they'll be mad I didn't tell them about it at the time. They're very protective of their brand." Olivia sounded weary. "They won't be happy, but they'll have my back. We've all coped with a lot worse things being said about me than this. Obviously. It's not as big a deal as that other thing."

Olivia looked at her. She seemed to be waiting for Casey to say something, to acknowledge something. But she couldn't, she didn't know what "other thing" Olivia was referring to.

After a few moments, Olivia pushed her plate away. "Maybe we should go. Maybe I should avoid being seen day drinking. They've probably got cameras on drones ready to catch me at it through the window."

It was a joke, but Olivia seemed upset. Casey obviously couldn't understand what it was like for Olivia, but she understood the upset of people telling lies about you. Hannah had done a lot of that when she was trying to make herself feel better about cheating on her. And all of it made her glad again for her ordinary life, for her complete anonymity in Portland.

When Olivia stood, she looked so sad that Casey had the urge to hug her, but she didn't dare. The bullshit story had completely killed what had been a nice afternoon.

"How about that selfie before we go?" Casey wanted to lighten things somehow. She held out her phone and stretched out her other arm, in an invitation for Olivia to come and stand by her side. The plate glass window giving out onto the view was immediately behind them. Olivia took the position next to her, and Casey felt an arm wrap around her waist. She leaned in to the touch, feeling the press of Olivia at her side.

She told herself the contact was innocent and platonic, but the beating of her heart and the tight, hot feeling low down in her core, told her a different story. She took a few pictures with her breath held, willing her body not to betray her by trembling.

"One last one for Evelyn." Olivia took Casey's phone, held it at arm's length, then leaned in to place a soft kiss on her cheek. Casey heard the click of the photo as it was taken. Olivia looked at the photo and smiled, handing the phone back to her. "You could probably sell that for a few hundred of your British pounds. Some of these websites will buy anything it seems."

Casey peered at the photo. Her face carried an expression of surprised happiness. If she'd ever had any kind of cool, Olivia was slowly obliterating it.

"Think she'll like it?"

"Who?" Casey had lost track of her thoughts.

"Your mom."

"Yeah, right, of course. She'll love it. It's a nice one of you—and you always were her favorite." She nudged Olivia and was rewarded with a smile.

Neither of them sat back down.

"Shall we go then?"

"Yeah, I'll walk you back to the hotel."

"I think I know the way."

"I've got time. And I want to. And not just because you clearly need a bodyguard."

"Bodyguard, huh? You're already my driver, my tour guide, and my imaginary girlfriend. Now you're adding bodyguard to the list. That's impressively versatile."

Casey was not good at this—she never had been—but she was pretty sure Olivia was flirting with her again.

"I also cook lasagna and play a mean game of poker. My talents are limitless."

As they got on the elevator, Olivia looked like someone who was deciding something.

"We're playing poker tomorrow night. It's a once-a-month-at-Louise's thing and she's refusing to miss it just because we're in London. You should get Louise to invite you, you could clean up."

"It might be too rich for my tastes. I don't have a lot of disposable income right now, and I'm pretty sure I'm rusty enough to get fleeced."

"Oh, we don't play for money. That's the wonderful pointlessness of it. Louise makes us play for pretzels. We each bring a bag and we play till they're gone. It's crazy, but it's always a good excuse to get loaded." She gazed at Casey, and Casey felt herself grow warm under Olivia's scrutiny.

"We probably have time to walk back along the river if you like." Maybe the breeze would give her back some of the cool she had lost amongst her now completely undeniable feelings for Olivia.

The elevator reached the ground floor and the doors opened.

"I'd like that a lot." Olivia smiled at her, and Casey's feelings were bittersweet. She was happy with this new connection between them but sad that they were running out of time. She shook the thought away. She would enjoy the here and now of the walk back to the hotel with Olivia and stop worrying about what their nonexistent future might hold.

CHAPTER THIRTEEN

Casey had arrived early at the restaurant. She sipped the wine she'd already ordered in the hope it would stop her mind from scratching at all the things she needed to think about but couldn't face. She hadn't heard back from the police about Neil, she hadn't reached out to any of her friends, and she hadn't even decided whether she was going to brave David's party. And on top of all that, she couldn't stop thinking about Olivia.

The whole week had been crazy. She'd started it guiltily admiring Olivia in the sauna and ended it feeling like Olivia was someone she really wanted to know better. And her bad mood was because they were about to say good-bye to each other for good. Casey was thirty-four. Too old to be having crushes. And definitely not the kind of woman who ever dreamed of holiday romances, but somehow, Olivia had gotten under her defenses and she didn't know what to do about it.

"Look who I bumped into on the way in." David approached the table with her mom beside him—her mom holding on to the crook of his elbow. He was smiling, but her mom seemed more wary. Casey got up to greet them.

"You look nice." She leaned over to peck her mom's cheek. She did look nice. She had on a pretty floral blouse and looked like she'd colored her hair since Casey last saw her.

"What about me?" David pulled her into a hug, and—like always— she let herself sink into his ample frame.

"Pretty fly for a white guy." It was their private joke. He was neither fly nor white. "Nice hoodie, David. Some of us dressed for dinner." Casey waved a hand down her body. She had made an effort. Of sorts. The shirt was new and she was wearing her best pair of jeans.

"I just told him that." Her mom smiled. "I called him a scruffy bugger."

"Right on both counts." David nudged her mom.

"Don't start." She slapped him.

"It's been too long, Evelyn." He kissed her cheek. "I've missed being slapped by you."

They settled themselves at the table and Casey felt her mood lift. They'd always had a good relationship and seeing them being playful together made her feel happy. Her mom was always easier to deal with when David was around.

"Did you find the restaurant okay, Mom?"

"Yes, the taxi dropped me off right outside."

"Taxi? I thought you were coming on the bus."

"I was running late." Her mom avoided her eyes. They both knew her mom didn't have money for taxis.

There was silence while Casey poured David some of the wine. She offered it to her mom, wanting her to say no.

"No thanks, love. I'll just have water. Going to try and stay on the wagon this time. And before you say it, I know I've said that before."

The lightness of a few moments ago had gone, and awkwardness hung in the air above the table. Casey felt annoyed with her mom. For trying and failing to stay sober so many times and for wasting money she didn't have on a taxi. And she was annoyed at herself for not being nicer about all of it.

"I told Mercy I was meeting up with you and she tried to invite herself along." David opened the menu as he spoke. "I wasn't sure how you'd feel about it, so I said no. But I guess you're going to have to face up to them at some point. Wasn't that at least part of the reason for coming back?"

"I guess." Casey didn't want to have this conversation in front of her mom. David's relationship with his own mom was very different—very functional and very open—and he forgot sometimes that hers wasn't the same. "It's just been so busy. I haven't had much time to think about it."

"Not that busy that you haven't been able to find time to shepherd drunken TV stars to their sleeping chamber. I saw you and the delectable Miss Lang in a clinch. I think half the gossip obsessed queers in the world did, but I was probably the only one who recognized her 'mystery companion' as you. I suppose I should say congrats and well played. Though I was surprised it was Olivia. You said she was a bit of a nightmare. And yet here you are, already enough of a showbiz couple to be getting papped."

"Olivia?" Her mom looked confused. "Your Olivia?"

"Your Olivia?" David asked, a matching look of confusion on his face.

"They've been dating a while. How do you not know that? I thought you two were thick as thieves." Her mom frowned at him. "Olivia said they met at some theater show they both went to. They got chatting in the bar after and decided they both liked each other, but Casey was too shy to make the first move, so Olivia had to."

"Your mom's met Olivia Lang?" David's surprise escalated into disbelief.

Casey flashed him a meaningful look. They'd known each other a long time. She had to hope he understood it was their "play along with me and don't say anything you shouldn't to my mother" look.

"We dropped in there a few days ago. Mom had some trouble with Neil and we were in the area, so I took some tea bags, had a chat with Neil, and Mom and Olivia looked at baby photos."

David was looking at her like she was insane. It did sound a little unlikely.

"She's nice, David. You'll like her a lot. She's very down-to-earth for an American. I mean, considering she's a big-time actress and all that." She leaned in. "And she encouraged me to try to stay sober and sent me all these lovely things for the house to replace the things that Neil stole. I told Casey she's a real keeper."

Casey was glad that the waiter chose that moment to come and take their order. But none of them were ready and David sent him away for a few minutes. They stopped talking and looked at the menus and she was happy to catch her breath, to lose herself in simply thinking about the food she wanted to eat.

So Olivia had told her mom a whole back story to how they'd gotten together. She couldn't help but smile. Olivia had a lot of talent and maybe screenwriting should be her next career.

David's insistence on paying the check had seen them all order desserts. Casey licked the spoon containing the remnants of her lemon cheesecake as, across the table, David did the same. Her mom had polished off a crème brûlée and was now fidgeting in her bag.

"Here." She handed Casey an envelope. "There's four ninety in there. It would have been five hundred, but I had to take a tenner for the taxi.

Sorry about that. I know it's not enough, that you've paid out more than that, but it's a start."

Casey opened the envelope to find a thick wedge of banknotes staring back at her.

"Where did this come from?"

"Neil. He said he was going to try and pay a bit more of it back when he could."

"Oh, come on. Really, Mom? You promised to stay the hell away from him." Casey couldn't help her anger.

"He pushed it through the letterbox and sent me a text. I haven't seen him, I promise." Her mom sounded convincing. "I don't even want to. Not any more. His message said something about the police and him being tricked into recording a confession and how he didn't want to go to jail. To be honest, I didn't understand it. But I was happy to have the money, to be able to give you some to help with all those bills you're paying off."

Casey looked again at the envelope. She couldn't believe that Olivia's plan had worked.

"He said he needed to stay out of jail for the sake of his nephews." Her mom scoffed. "He still thinks I don't know they're his kids—or that the bitch he spent my money on is his girlfriend. He must think I'm even stupider than I look."

"Which is saying something. Evelyn." David's teasing could have seemed unkind, but the hand he reached across the table and laid over her mom's made it clear that he cared.

"His girlfriend? Not his sister?" Casey couldn't quite believe it. The impulse to cause him physical harm bubbled up all over again.

Her mom nodded, meeting her eyes before looking away. Casey couldn't imagine how awful she must have felt about discovering that and still not daring to confront him.

"I turned a blind eye at first. I didn't know he'd end up leaving me for her. I obviously learned nothing from what happened with your stepdad." She turned to David, putting her hand over his. "I obviously am just as stupid as I look."

"Don't say that, Mom." Casey was upset but trying not to let it show.

"Well, I do have terrible judgment, especially where men are concerned." She took in a breath. "And it's cost me a lot more than the money Neil took from me. It cost me my relationship with you and I'll never forgive myself for that. I wish—"

"Don't, Mom."

"Let her say it, Casey." David spoke softly.

"I hated it when you went to America. I mean, I knew why you went, it must have been awful for you. And I was no help, no support. I'm self-obsessed when I'm drinking, but I should have been there for you. I'm sorry." She shook her head, tears in her eyes. It was almost unbearable for Casey to hear what she was saying, to see her like this. She had learned never to expect anything from her mom; she couldn't help but be moved by her apology. "And I know I can't do anything about any of it now and it probably doesn't help, but I miss you. And every day, I wish you weren't so far away."

"I miss her too, Evelyn," David said. "Casey is literally the only person I know who's happy to have a bowl of custard with me while we watch romcoms and argue about Jennifer Aniston's path to future happiness. I mean, who wouldn't miss that?"

It was the perfect way to lighten the mood and Casey was grateful. She loved David more than she would ever be willing to admit to him.

"I just said—once—that I think she'd be happier as a lesbian."

"You think everyone is happier as a lesbian." David smiled at her, and she could see the love he had for her in his eyes. It felt like something important.

"Maybe I should try it. It's not like loving men has ever worked out well for me." Her mom pulled a tissue out of her purse and began to blow her nose. "And I've always quite liked Jennifer Aniston. Maybe Olivia could introduce us and we could make each other happy." She got up as she spoke. "I'm just popping to the loo. But I'll have a coffee if you're not in a hurry to rush off." She headed toward the bathroom in the far corner of the restaurant.

Casey knew her mom, knew she needed some time to settle. And so did she. Her mom's regret—and her admission about missing Casey—had landed squarely in the center of her chest and now it lay there heavily.

She leaned over to grab her mom's bag from the chair next to her and stuffed the envelope full of cash into one of the inside pockets before zipping it shut.

"Two Irish coffees and a decaf filter, please?" David caught the waiter as he walked by the table.

"Good call." She was ready for a whiskey. "And thanks. For dinner and for being so great with Mom."

"It's my pleasure, you know that. Though I couldn't believe she waited this long to go for a pee. What kind of bladder does she have?"

Casey laughed.

"I've been bursting in a different way. You, your mom, and Olivia Lang. Spill all the details. Right now."

"It's a crazy story. I don't have time."

"Try."

"Don't be annoyed, okay? I was driving her to an appointment, my mom called, said Neil was in the house. I offered to take Olivia to her appointment and then have Tania pick her up after so I could go to my mom's, but Olivia insisted on coming with me. For some reason I'm not clear about, she told my mom she was my girlfriend. Told her a whole lot of things that weren't true. She's not psycho, don't worry. I think she was trying to distract and entertain my mom, while I dealt with Neil."

David shook his head in amazement.

"Dealt with Neil?"

"I didn't do anything violent, don't worry. I bloody well wanted to though. Olivia persuaded me to secretly record him with my phone. He kind of confessed. I sent it to the police. I suspect they've had a word with him and he thinks he needs to do something so my mom doesn't press charges. I guess that's why he left the money."

"And the photo of you and Olivia in each other's arms?"

"That was nothing. She was getting some grief off some guys in the bar and I stepped in. The picture makes it look like something it wasn't."

"So there's nothing going on? That's disappointing. That would have been quite the holiday romance."

Casey couldn't help the downward shift of her gaze. David caught it.

"Casey."

"Nothing going on, no. We get on well and I kind of like her, that's all. I mean, you've seen her. She's gorgeous. And she's smart and sweet and funny—all things that make me wish she lived in Portland and wasn't some big shot actress with this crazy life she has. But she doesn't and she is, so..." She felt embarrassed talking about Olivia that way. She was trying not to make their connection sound like more than it was, because of course it wasn't anything really.

"We had drinks this afternoon, in one of the bars in the Shard. It was nice."

David was looking at her with a curious expression on his face.

"And I suppose you being you, you still haven't googled her."

"No, I told you, I'm happy for her to just tell me what she wants to tell me."

"If you're saying you like her, maybe you should do a bit of searching for her name. You'll find what I found."

"I don't want to know."

"You do. You're just being avoidant."

"I'm not. It just seems intrusive. And I don't believe half the stuff they write anyway." Casey couldn't help feeling intrigued. David was making it sound like there was something she needed to know.

"I know that. Of course I do. I'm not saying it's all true, I'm just saying go and have a look. It's dramatic. Dating a costar, big public breakup, leaked sex tape. It sounded very scandalous, very Hollywood. I wouldn't have thought she was your type in that way. You couldn't even cope with Hannah's level of wannabe fame."

"I could cope with that. Just about. I couldn't cope with her cheating on me with one of our friends."

"I know, I know." David held up his hands. "Sorry. I know it's different. I didn't mean to say it wasn't. But you did hate the way Hannah worried about how everything looked, about her obsession with keeping her 'fans' happy. A TV star does seem an unlikely choice for you."

"I haven't chosen her. I haven't chosen anyone. I wish I hadn't said anything. Can we change the subject?"

Her mom returned to the table, and Casey couldn't help but wish she'd never left and she'd never had to hear any of what David had just told her about Olivia.

"Nice bathroom." Her mom sat down. "Thick white flannels to dry your hands."

"How many did you take?" David asked with a wink.

"How dare you?" Her mom slapped him on the arm. "I only took one of the small bottles of lotion. I've been doing a lot of cleaning and my hands are getting dry. And it said they were for customers' use."

"Let's see if there's anything worth pinching in the gents'." He headed off just as the waiter brought their coffees.

Casey was only half-listening to them as they bantered. Her skin prickled with what she figured was a mixture of shame and surprise. She was no prude, but hearing David talk about Olivia that way was shocking to her. She wanted to imagine it was because the Olivia she knew didn't seem like that sort of a person, but of course, that was the thing, there wasn't really an Olivia that she knew. She'd known her for a week. And Olivia was the star in a show that Casey had never even watched. It sounded like David knew her better than Casey did.

A sex tape. Damn. She hadn't imagined Olivia like that. She seemed too sensible somehow, too careful. Casey clearly wasn't the judge of character she thought she was. She felt a flush of heat in her cheeks as her sense of embarrassment grew. Olivia was an actress who happily took her clothes off for a living, so why wouldn't she be the kind of person who also made a sex tape? She wasn't the first and she wouldn't be the last. And just because Casey was feeling stupidly uncomfortable about it, didn't mean it was wrong.

Except to Casey, it was. She couldn't help feeling disappointed that Olivia was just another one of those people who wanted everyone to see them live every part of their lives.

"You okay, love?" Her mom was staring at her with concern. "You're doing that clenching of the jaw thing you do when you're stressed."

"Yeah, I was just thinking about that whole thing with Hannah." She wasn't, but she didn't want to tell her mom she was worrying about Olivia—her sweet fake girlfriend who seemingly thought making sex tapes was fun. "It still makes me angry."

"Me too."

"I don't think I realized until it happened just how wrong we were for each other. Or just how much I had misjudged her. I knew we were having problems, but I didn't think she would do that." Casey's voice stayed steady, but she could feel the shame and the anger inside at being reminded of it all. But none of the anger belonged here with her mom. She made herself calm down and took a slow sip of her coffee, feeling the heat of the whiskey in the back of her throat.

"I thought you'd come back, you know," her mom said. "I thought you'd have a few weeks away and then come back. I didn't know that was it, that I'd lose you."

"I thought I would too. I just meant to get away, to recover, to let things die down a bit and then I realized I had nothing to come back for. Not really."

"Casey, love." Her mom frowned.

"I don't mean that, sorry. Not in that way. I just mean I'd lost my job, I'd lost Hannah, and I'd behaved like an idiot. And the idea of starting over with everyone watching, everyone blaming me, or worse, pitying me, was just too much." She rolled her shoulders, feeling the tension. Not even the whiskey was helping. "It sounds a little dramatic now, but at the time running away just made sense. I figured that if I had to start over, I might as well do it in America where no one knew me or knew what a fool I'd been."

For Casey, the distance had been as much of a healer as time. She had repaired herself slowly in Portland. Maybe not completely, but enough.

"I'm sorry." Her mom leaned over and put a hand on her arm. Casey felt tears well up in her eyes that she blinked away.

"Whiskey doesn't usually make me maudlin."

"It used to make me horny." Her mom smiled at her, a soft smile, full of fondness. Casey couldn't remember the last time her mom had looked at her that way. "But since I'm not drinking, I'll have to rely on the thought of Gerard Butler in a towel in a steaming hot sauna."

"Ew, Mom." Casey couldn't help but laugh. But just like that, her thoughts were back on Olivia—the glistening sweat on her arms, the damp strands of hair stuck to her temples, the throatiness of her voice as she told Casey not to fall asleep.

The whiskey mixed with the wine and her mood to make her lust for Olivia confusing and shameful somehow. Maybe Olivia was nowhere near as sweet as Casey had been imagining and maybe it didn't matter. Even if Casey was stupid enough to still want something more from Olivia, there was no way that it could happen now. David had just reminded her of all the reasons why they were completely incompatible. And if Olivia was flirting with her because she wanted some kind of instantly forgettable holiday romance, then she had picked the wrong woman.

Chapter Fourteen

I'm surprised to see you here. I thought you said you had plans." Billie was standing next to Olivia's stool, a not very warm smile on her perfectly made-up face. She was dressed for a night out—low-cut dress, heels, immaculately accessorized. Olivia couldn't deny that she looked good, but even through the haze of the bourbon she'd been drinking, her every instinct told her Billie was someone to stay away from.

"How about I join you?" Billie put a well-manicured hand onto the seat of the stool next to Olivia's.

Olivia wanted to say no, to tell her she was waiting for someone. It wouldn't be a complete lie. She was waiting for Casey, hoping she might see her coming back from her dinner. Olivia was well brought up though, and saying no to Billie again, when she was so obviously alone at the bar, just seemed too rude.

"Sure." Olivia said without seeming too welcoming and looked back at her glass, swirling the ice cubes around before sipping at the drink. She didn't want to have to make small talk with Billie.

"We found this place in south London. Apparently, it's pretty inclusive of the Ls, Gs, Bs, and Ts, but also exclusive enough that you don't get bothered by people who aren't used to being cool around 'celebrities' like us." Billie had the good grace to put inverted commas around the word with her fingers. She smiled at Olivia before putting a lingering hand on her arm. "There's a few of us going. We're celebrating the big win. Why don't you come?"

"I'm not sure I'm in the right mood."

Billie knew why. She'd been there when Olivia was asked to explain to the studio's PR people about what had led up to the photo and then stood by as they scolded her for not telling them what had happened at the time. And when Olivia tried to brush it off, Billie butted in to claim the cast needed extra security, because "their driver couldn't be expected to be hanging around at exactly the right moment to rescue all of them." She'd made it into a much bigger deal than it needed to be, and the comment about Casey was obviously pointed.

"It's got to be better than sitting and drinking alone in the hotel bar. I mean, it's a mood, but it doesn't seem like a lot of fun. And I would have thought you'd be avoiding the being seen drinking alone thing after today. You never know who's watching."

Billie tried to sound playful, like she was teasing, but Olivia felt there was something underneath the words. She turned her head to look at Billie. Her gaze was expectant and her smile said she expected Olivia to jump at the chance of going out with her.

"I don't care who's watching. I haven't done anything wrong and I'm not going to hide in my room." Olivia sounded more defiant than she felt. She'd already had the same thoughts. But her desire to see Casey had made her take the risk.

"Well, come out with me then. I'm pretty sure Susie will thank you for letting her have a night off the leash." Billie offered Olivia a wink, clearly unaware that she'd just said the one thing that would absolutely guarantee Olivia would say no.

"No thanks, Billie. Thanks for asking. Sounds awesome. Have a nice time though." Olivia was being as polite as she could manage. "And Susie's fictional, y'know, so if you did want to go drinking with her, you might find that difficult." The last sentence came out a little sharp, and a small frown appeared between Billie's perfectly groomed eyebrows. For a second, she looked hurt, but then her expression hardened.

"Shame. Susie was the one I was anxious to go out with. Olivia seems like a bit of a tight-ass to be honest." She climbed off the stool.

Olivia wanted to tell her to fuck off, to stop bothering her, to understand that she wasn't the slightest bit interested. But it was going to be a long season if they couldn't find a way to get along.

"Look, I'm sorry. I'm just tired. And I'm not much of a clubber to be honest. Have fun though." Olivia reached out to offer a conciliatory pat on Billie's arm and she felt Billie's fingers close over her hand, making it impossible for her to withdraw it. Billie leaned in, speaking directly into Olivia's ear.

"Next time, don't be tired. I promise you we'll have a good time. But know that I'm not going to keep playing this game with you. It's getting boring. I know you think you're too good for me. But you're not." She pulled away and walked out of the bar before Olivia could react.

Olivia tracked her as she crossed the lobby, a little thrown by Billie's hostility. Almost immediately, Casey appeared in her field of vision, looking at her intently from a spot not too far away. Olivia held up a hand and Casey returned the gesture, a somber look on her face. Olivia lifted her glass and tilted her head toward the bar, hoping that Casey would join her.

When Casey finally walked slowly toward her, Olivia felt a pleasant tension in her body that she hadn't felt in a long while. She was wearing a tight black shirt over faded blue jeans. Jeans that hugged her muscles in all the right places and made it impossible for Olivia not to think back to the sight of her stretched out on a towel wearing just her shorts. She knew what Casey looked like under those clothes—her toned torso, her perfect breasts, those long muscular legs. She felt an ache between her legs and imagined just how wet the sight of Casey stripping out of that shirt would make her.

She'd had champagne at the awards dinner—on top of the cocktails she'd shared with Casey earlier—and now she was drinking bourbon. The combination had her feeling a little loaded and now, in Casey's presence, more than a little lustful.

"Sit down, have a drink with me." Olivia wanted Casey to stay, wanted her to take the stool that Billie had just vacated. She put a hand on it. "Billie's gone clubbing with some of the others." She felt like she had to explain. "She wanted me to go, but it's not really my thing."

Casey stayed standing.

"What is your thing?"

Olivia caught an undertone of something. It made her hesitate. Casey seemed unsure whether to stay or go.

"Moodily drinking whisky in a hotel bar, really hoping you're going to sit and have a drink with me." The alcohol, combined with her feelings for Casey, gave her a courage she didn't usually possess.

Casey's gaze was captivating. Her eyes were darker than usual in the low light of the bar and she seemed so serious. Olivia felt her stomach tighten. She liked being looked at like that by Casey.

"How about it? I might need a 'mystery companion' to help me up to my room after all this drinking."

It was supposed to be a joke, but Olivia couldn't help the edge to her voice. She was still annoyed by the story, but that wasn't Casey's problem. She rolled her shoulders, now fully expecting Casey to refuse to sit with her for fear of getting caught up in some more drama with her. Instead, she slid silently onto the stool next to Olivia and Olivia let out the breath she had been holding. She liked Casey—liked her in a way she hadn't liked anyone in a long time.

The bartender placed a paper circle in front of Casey, and she ordered an Irish malt.

"How was your dinner?" Olivia wanted to get Casey talking. There was a tension between them tonight that hadn't been there earlier, and she didn't know why.

"Okay, I guess. The food was good."

It was a start.

"And your mom?"

"She's good."

Olivia wasn't sure why this was going so badly, and she wanted a time-out to figure out what had gone wrong.

The bartender placed a glass of amber liquid in front of Casey. She took a slow taste.

"If you have the choice, Irish is always better than Scottish. Of course, I'm a little biased. My dad was from County Cork—my real dad, not my stepdad. And my great-aunt Annie would write me out of her will if she thought I was ever drinking Scottish when Irish was available." She traced the pattern of the crystal of her glass with a finger, then looked up at Olivia, her expression serious. "And I hope you know they spell it wrong too. The word 'whiskey' has an e in it. The Scots always forget."

"You're Irish? I didn't know that."

"There's a lot of things you don't know about me. And a lot of things I don't know about you. Maybe if we had more time, we could tell each other our secrets, but since we don't…" She waved her hand, as if waving the thought away. Casey sounded like she had also been drinking. Her gaze was steady, but underneath, she seemed upset about something.

Olivia couldn't stop staring at Casey's face, and when Casey touched her glass to her mouth to take another sip of her whiskey, Olivia felt the temptation, the yearning, to trace her fingertips across Casey's full lips, to lean in and then kiss her. She wanted to press herself against her and feel the tautness of the muscles in her body.

"Billie acts like she likes you."

Olivia blinked. She hadn't expected that.

"She doesn't. She's just playing at it. She's one of those people who only wants something to prove she can get it, to prove her own appeal."

The clarity of her thinking surprised her. "And I told you, I don't date inside the business. It's too…" She couldn't think of the right word. "It's too messy."

She wondered if Casey seeing her with Billie was why she was being like this. The jealousy—if that's what it was—was encouraging.

"But you dated an actress before?"

Olivia felt her stomach knot at the reminder.

"I did. It didn't go well. And that's why I won't do it again."

She waited for Casey to say more. She had expected this, expected that at some point Casey would have done the natural thing and searched for information about her. On some crazy level, she was glad—glad that Casey was curious enough about her to look and glad to be able to get it out into the open between them. If Casey was going to judge her for it, it was better to know now.

"My friend David loves celebrity gossip. He teased me about that story—the two of us, going into the elevator. And he told me tonight about you dating another actress, told me some stuff that I didn't know, stuff I didn't want to know. I'm sorry. It's none of my business."

"He told you 'stuff.' What kind of stuff?" Olivia could probably guess. It wasn't exactly a secret. She was amazed Casey didn't already know. But of course, the fact that Casey had no interest in the show and no idea who she was, was a huge part of her appeal.

"Like I say, none of my business. I'm sorry I brought it up."

"Casey?" Olivia put a hand on her arm. The skin was warm and soft. "What stuff?" She didn't want Casey to have been told things that weren't true.

"He just said about you dating an actress and having this big public breakup."

"And?" Olivia could tell that wasn't all.

"It's just me. I'm weird about privacy. I know you're naked a lot in the show. I mean, that Susie is…" Casey faltered.

"Yeah, unfortunately that's true. I was naive. No one told me you could say no to the nudity. Seems like I was the only one stupid enough not to sign that type of contract." Olivia couldn't help but sound bitter about it. "Anything else?"

"He said something about a sex tape that got leaked." Casey shifted in her seat, looking at Olivia more directly. Her eyes were almost black in the low light of the bar. "To be honest, I stopped him from telling me anything else. I didn't even want to know that much. I don't think it's for me to know things you don't want to tell me. And it's got nothing to do with me if that's your thing."

Casey's open, earnest expression shamed her. But the truth was she felt shame whenever she was reminded of it. And none of this was what she wanted to talk about when she asked Casey to come and sit with her. But since Casey had heard some of it, she wanted her to hear all of it. What had happened, not what people who had no fucking idea said had happened. She sipped the bourbon—wanting the comfort—and then pushed it away.

"I would have told you if I thought it was important, but it was a long time ago. And it's a pretty sorry story, one that doesn't reflect well on me."

"We all have sorry stories. But yours seems to end up with you being a big TV star who travels the world and has women throwing themselves at her feet. Doesn't look all that bad to me." Casey sounded a little quarrelsome.

"I don't know who you think is throwing themselves at me."

"Billie. For one."

Casey chewed her lip and a frown creased her forehead. Olivia wanted to kiss her right then. Her lips were so inviting, her eyes a deep dark brown. Olivia could only imagine the feeling of being in her arms, pressed close, those lips searching hers. Damn. She was losing her mind. It wasn't like her to do the falling hard thing. She was careful, cautious. She'd only just started to trust Kristin when she fucked her over.

And now she was going to tell Casey all about it. Maybe she'd pity her, or think she was stupid. Or maybe it would make her run a mile in the opposite direction.

"My last relationship ended in a very public kiss and tell." Olivia turned away from Casey as she spoke. If she was going to tell this story, she couldn't do it with Casey looking at her. And she didn't want to see her reaction, see the moment when she would decide Olivia was irretrievably stained by it all.

"I liked her, but she didn't feel the same way, so I ended up making a real fool of myself. Embarrassed my parents, the studio, the whole works." She looked across at Casey. "You really don't know any of this?"

Casey shook her head. The intensity of her gaze made Olivia shiver. It was wonderful and somehow completely terrifying.

"Maybe I'm not as famous as I think I am." Olivia tried to smile.

"I'm sure you are. I don't have a TV. I don't do social media. I guess I'm happier not knowing things."

"It sounds wonderful." Olivia remembered a time when her life was like that.

"And I know from experience that some things are better left in the past." Casey lifted her shoulders in a small shrug. "So you really don't have to tell me any of this. I'm sorry I even mentioned it."

"There was a sex tape." Olivia stared straight ahead. She took in a breath and let it out again. "We were in a relationship, and honestly, I thought it was going well. Maybe my romance radar was off even then. But while I was thinking about how well we were doing, she was building a little dossier on me. I was her passport to a fat check and gossip column glory. She made a video of us having sex—without me knowing—dumped me, and then sold it to a website, along with all the sexy messages we'd ever exchanged and an interview that said I could learn a thing or two from Susie in the bedroom." Olivia laughed bitterly. "And I don't know why I'm laughing because I was so badly hurt by it all that I haven't dated since." She swirled the liquid in her glass before taking a mouthful. "Maybe bourbon makes me giggle. Ha. You learn something new about yourself every day." The alcohol was giving her brain swirls where her thoughts needed to be.

Casey reached for her hand. The touch was gentle, reassuring, and probably platonic. But Olivia felt the pull of her attraction, her body craving more contact than Casey was offering.

"Turns out there's nothing you can do. I mean, you can spend a lot on injunctions to keep a video like that off the main sharing sites, but people think it's fun to send it to friends, and then the people they know share it and killing it becomes impossible. Like trying to catch the wind."

"That's awful."

"We'd been together for six months. Six months." Olivia took a breath. "Everyone told me to just ignore it, that people would soon forget about it, but I couldn't. I had absolutely no cool about it. I tried to have her arrested. It wasn't just that it was us having sex. It was that it was filmed without my consent, released without my consent. It violated my privacy, and as far as I was concerned, it was an assault—and a complete betrayal by someone I trusted. I felt so vengeful, so full of hate. Not my finest hour."

"I think most people would have felt like that." Casey cast her eyes down as she spoke and Olivia sensed, from her body language, that she seemed uncomfortable, but she needed to say it, to make sure—however bad it was—that she heard it from her.

"It turned out I was what they call an unsympathetic complainant." She wrapped the words in speech marks with her fingers. "The police came to the conclusion that someone who stripped naked and had sex with women on television as a job probably wasn't in a strong position to argue that their privacy had been violated by a sex tape." She measured out the words, feeling the weight of the awful memories press heavily on her chest.

"Are you serious?"

"Yeah."

Of all the things people had said to her, that had been the worst. Even in her darkest moment, people couldn't tell the difference between the pretending that Susie did and Olivia's actual life.

"She claimed the recording was consensual of course, and because of my 'lifestyle,' everyone said I wouldn't get any sympathy in court, so I was persuaded to drop it." Olivia couldn't stop her voice from breaking.

"Olivia, that's horrible. I'm so sorry."

"And exploiting me in that way, got her exactly the break she'd been wanting. Instead of a criminal record, she got a new career as a journalist for some shitty entertainment website. And I got bruised to the point of never trusting anyone's intentions—no matter how sweet and sincere they seem."

"Not everyone is—"

"What?"

"Nothing. I was going to give you some platitude about how not everyone is like that, but it's stupid. It doesn't take 'everyone' to do damage, just one person." Casey looked right at her. "But you can trust me. I hope you know that."

Olivia's mind had drifted into the past, but her body brought her back to the here and now. Casey still had hold of her hand and was grazing a thumb across the back of it. Their knees were touching. Olivia felt the effect of it low down in her belly. They were talking about things—sad, hurtful things. Things she had to accept she would never fully escape from. But in this bar, in the present, Casey was sitting beside her, looking like a cool drink on a hot and thirsty day, and the feel of Casey's hand on hers, of their bodies touching, was exactly what she needed. She did trust Casey and she liked her—a lot. And in that moment, she wanted her more than she'd ever wanted anyone.

She sipped at her drink—the sweet, smoky heat of it in her throat feeling wonderful.

"I loved that you had no idea who I was, no idea who Susie was. You just got to know me—plain old Olivia. And when you smiled at me, or laughed at my joke, I knew it was Olivia who was responsible. And when I annoyed you—and I know I did," she was gratified to see Casey smile, "I annoyed you because I was being Olivia. Maybe that's why I like spending time with you. I mean, apart from the fact that you're gorgeous and funny and have an accent that makes me go weak at the knees."

Casey's eyes widened in surprise. Olivia felt no embarrassment though. The drink was helping her to say it, but it was also the truth.

Casey leaned in. "I've had a few drinks. I'm not sure I'm going to be able to brush off you giving me compliments like that in the way I might when I'm sober."

Olivia felt Casey's breath against her cheek. She shivered before letting her hand drop to Casey's thigh, leaving it there for a moment before spreading her fingers possessively. Casey didn't move, but she swallowed, and the eyes looking back at Olivia had darkened. It was exactly the effect that Olivia had been hoping for.

"What would you do if you didn't know me and you came back from your dinner and saw me in the bar?" Olivia could feel the giddy intensity of the alcohol, letting her—making her—say what was on her mind, what she needed to say. It didn't seem to matter whether or not it was the right thing to say. She needed something from Casey, even if she didn't know exactly what it was.

"I'd offer to buy you a drink, I'd bore you about the kind of whiskey you should be drinking and then I'd pay you a lavish compliment or two, because…well, because you look amazing tonight. And I might try to slide onto this very stool and hope you'd let me spend some time getting to know you."

Hearing Casey speak to her that way was entrancing.

"Do it then. Pay me the compliment, buy me the drink. Act like you don't know me, but really want to." Even to her own ears, Olivia's voice sounded a little husky. It was part alcohol and part arousal. She felt so turned on by the idea of Casey coming on to her in a bar. The arousal shouldn't have been a surprise—Casey was attractive and charming—but they hadn't known each other for long, and Olivia wasn't someone who usually found this kind of thing easy.

"What's a beautiful woman like you doing sitting here drinking all alone?" Casey frowned before leaning in again, her mouth close to Olivia's ear. "I'm sorry. I should do better than that, but I've been drinking, and being this close to you is making me tongue-tied." The words—and Casey's hot breath—made Olivia feel weak with desire. She made herself concentrate. This was a game she wanted to play.

"I guess I'm partly drinking to forget." Olivia leaned closer. "And I'm partly drinking to make things seem more interesting." She brushed her lips across Casey's ear as she spoke. "And things just got a lot more interesting."

Olivia softly pressed down with the hand resting on Casey's thigh, feeling the hardness of the muscle through the fabric of her jeans and feeling overwhelmed by how much she wanted Casey.

Casey didn't move. She kept her attention focused on Olivia's face. Her eyes occasionally dropping to Olivia's lips. And when she didn't stop Olivia's hand from moving along her thigh, closer to her center, Olivia grew even bolder.

"Let's go upstairs." Olivia took Casey's hand and stood, weaving a little unsteadily on her feet. Casey snaked an arm around her waist to steady her in much the same way she had done days before at the elevator—except this time, aware of Casey's strength, feeling Casey's arm holding her tightly, there was no feeling of gratitude. Instead, every nerve in Olivia's body was vibrating with desire.

"Can you send two more of those up to my room please?" Olivia addressed the bartender, knowing she sounded a little slurry, but not caring. She waited for him to nod in her direction before turning and pulling Casey with her toward the elevator.

"We shouldn't do this." Casey was standing in the open doorway, her arms braced against the doorframe as Olivia—her arms threaded around her waist—tried to pull her into the room. Casey held firm, knowing that if she gave in, there would be no way she would be able to resist Olivia in the presence of a bed when she so obviously wanted exactly what Casey wanted—what Casey had to admit she wanted since the moment she first set eyes on her.

When Casey refused to budge, not allowing Olivia to pull her inside, Olivia leaned in, her eyes giving away what she was craving, as much as the hands that were now under Casey's shirt, the nails raking across her back. Olivia finally touched her lips to Casey's. They were warm and soft, but the kiss was hard and hot, and Casey felt the power of it in the heat, in the throb, between her legs. She couldn't stop herself from responding. She reached her hand into the hair at the nape of her neck and crushed her mouth against Olivia's. And when Olivia parted her lips, she deepened the kiss, dipping her tongue into Olivia's mouth. The warm wet softness of Olivia's tongue mixing with the taste of the bourbon caused the throbbing between her legs to grow stronger.

Casey pulled Olivia closer, wanting to feel her body, her breasts, pressed against her own. She bit down softly on Olivia's lower lip and was rewarded with a low moan and an even more demanding kiss. Olivia's hands were on her behind, pressing their bodies together at the waist, and Casey kissed Olivia again and again. Her tongue teasing Olivia, their kisses hard and wanting.

Not quite senseless, Casey heard a door open and close. She still hadn't crossed the threshold into Olivia's room, and she realized how reckless they were being, how visible they were to anyone using the corridor, or coming out of their room. She'd agreed to come upstairs with Olivia because she didn't want her to run into trouble or get photographed downstairs while she was drunk. But it would be much worse if someone caught them doing this.

The easiest thing would be to let Olivia pull her into the room, to lay Olivia down on the big bed and do everything they clearly both wanted. Instead, she heard herself speaking.

"Olivia, we can't do this." She pulled away from Olivia, taking a step back into the corridor.

"We can. You want to. I can see it in your eyes." Olivia stepped into the corridor to kiss Casey again. "I can feel it in your kisses." She ran a hand down Casey's abdomen, stopping halfway down the zip of her jeans. "I can feel it in your muscles."

Casey couldn't stop herself from tensing under her touch, proving Olivia right.

"It's not about how much I want to—that's not what matters." Casey moved Olivia's hand. "I'm still someone who works for you. And in the morning, sober and annoyed with yourself for getting drunk enough to fuck your driver, you're not going to want me around to remind you. And I need this job. You know how much I need this job."

Olivia stepped backward into the room. Casey could see the hurt on her face, see the slump of her shoulders. They looked at each other for a beat. Casey wanted to reassure Olivia somehow, but she didn't know what else to say, how to make the truth of their situation any different.

"I'm sorry, I'm just saying what we both need to hear." She was omitting the part about the feelings she had already caught for Olivia and how she didn't want to cheapen those feelings by letting herself do what she absolutely most definitely wanted to do to Olivia right then.

"It matters." Olivia spoke softly.

"What matters?"

"It matters that you want to. That you're only saying no because of the job and not because of me. Assuming that's the truth." Olivia backed farther into the room, putting more distance between them. Casey wanted to move forward and give her a hug. But hugging her would not be where things would stop.

She stepped into the doorway, forcing herself to relax, trying to chase away the arousal she was still feeling. She put her hands in her pockets, hoping it would stop her from reaching for Olivia, willing herself not to follow her into the room, as badly as she wanted to.

"I'm saying no because of the job. I'm also saying no because you're drunk and I don't take advantage of women who are drunk, no matter how attractive they are, how much I like them, and, yes, how much I might want to." She sighed and ran a hand down her stomach, realizing that her shirt had become untucked from her trousers. A flash of sense memory of Olivia pulling at the fabric and scratching her nails across Casey's bare back made her swallow. "And for what it's worth, I really, really want to. But I also want to be able to look you in the eye in the morning, and I don't want to get fired and I—"

"I wouldn't have you fired. Can you please stop saying that?" Olivia's eyes flashed with annoyance. Even annoyed, she was glorious.

"Okay, okay. I was just going to say that I want you hydrated and not too hungover to slay them at your TV thing in the morning."

Casey was trying to get them back to where they should be. She was trying to minimize the damage. Maybe in the morning, Olivia would view this as a missed opportunity—or even a bullet dodged—but for her, because of her feelings, this was so much more. And if she wasn't careful, she was going to get herself hurt.

"I'm trying to seduce you, and all you wanna do is hydrate me. Great." Olivia sat on the edge of the bed with a sigh. "Maybe Kristin was right and I do need to learn a thing or two from Susie. I'm pretty sure you wouldn't be saying no to her." She sounded petulant, but underneath Casey could hear the upset.

"Your ex is even more of a jerk than I figured if she thinks for a second that Susie has anything to teach you."

Olivia gave her a small, shy smile, followed by a huge yawn. She looked down at her shoes. She reached down to unstrap them, but her fingers fumbled with the tiny buckles.

Casey looked around the room as if assessing the danger to the both of them if she crossed the threshold. "Let me." She went inside, crouched down at Olivia's feet, and began to unbuckle her shoes. She'd had a lot to drink and the arousal was still thrumming through her body. Casey was showing a lot of trust in herself to be this close to Olivia and to resist kissing those lips. The lips that she now knew tasted as good as they looked.

"You don't even know Susie. How can you say that? Maybe if I was Susie…" Olivia's voice trailed off. Casey looked up at her. "I mean, if I had Susie's moves, I'd know how to make it impossible for you to say no. But," she sighed, "I'm clearly not Susie."

She sounded so defeated, so sad, that Casey couldn't stop herself from responding.

"Olivia." She looked up at her. "If you were Susie, I wouldn't even be here. I wouldn't have taken you to the Shard today. I wouldn't have been so happy to see you sitting there when I got back to the hotel, and I wouldn't be sitting here helping you take off your shoes while thinking about how cool and smart and sexy you are. And…" She waited for Olivia to properly meet her gaze. "If you were Susie, I wouldn't be contemplating pushing you back onto that bed to taste those damn lips of yours one more time, leaving myself unemployed and my mom homeless." She was taking a risk being so honest, but Olivia needed to hear it right then.

Olivia covered her face with her hands and moaned—and the sound of it, low in her throat, made Casey aroused all over again. She placed Olivia's shoes next to the bed side by side and got up, needing to be a little farther away. "I don't know Susie, but I know you. And I can't believe she's anywhere near as amazing as you are, Olivia."

She recognized her own voice but couldn't quite believe she was the one saying all of this to Olivia. What happened to that buttoned up English reserve she'd relied on to protect her heart for so long? She turned and walked to the door.

"Now, make sure you order up some water and coffee. We both have an early start tomorrow. And I don't suppose it's any consolation, but because of you—Olivia Lang—I'm going back to my room now for a very long, very cold, shower." Casey left the room, letting the door close behind her, not trusting herself to keep resisting Olivia.

"Fuck." She let the curse out softly as she leaned with her back to the corridor wall.

Falling for Olivia was ridiculous—and a total fucking cliché. She was the driver—the hired help—and even if she wasn't, Casey didn't feel ready for anything like this. Letting herself get used by an actress who was looking for comfort and reassurance about her sex appeal was the last thing her own self-esteem needed right now.

Gina would tell her to stop looking for love, to stop being so cautious and go back and simply enjoy what was on offer. To let herself have the pleasure of undressing Olivia, of putting her mouth on the soft skin and feeling that gorgeous body beneath her, without worrying about what tomorrow might bring. But that was Gina, not Casey. Casey had always loved with her heart first.

She pushed herself off the wall. A cold shower. She'd called it right. It was exactly what she needed.

CHAPTER FIFTEEN

Olivia lay sprawled on Liam's bed, scrolling through her phone. She was in a bad mood—capital B, capital M. It wasn't just the throbbing headache that the Tylenol hadn't shifted. It wasn't even the regret and embarrassment she felt about letting her feelings—and the alcohol—get the better of her and coming on to Casey like a bimbo in heat. Her mood was off because she'd wanted to see Casey this morning to apologize and to make sure everything was okay between them. But Casey had already gone, driving Billie and Louise to their morning appointments, instead of Olivia and Liam as had been the plan.

The change of schedule seemed deliberate. Olivia wasn't surprised. She had told Casey everything—every grubby detail of what had happened with Kristin—and then tried to drag her into bed. Shame coursed through her body, chased close behind by waves of nausea. Her hangover wasn't being gentle.

She had an afternoon of rehearsals after the morning's interviews and tonight was Louise's big poker game, so she wouldn't see Casey at all until tomorrow. She rubbed her temples and sighed deeply. Her attempt to get closer to Casey had backfired spectacularly, and she only had herself to blame.

Liam came into the room wrapped in a towel. "Are you gonna pout and sigh like that all day?" He hunted through the drawers in the dresser as he spoke. "You've got a face like a smacked arse."

Despite her mood, Olivia couldn't help but smile. They'd heard a woman say it to her child the day they arrived in London and they'd been using it ever since.

"I'm serious. You look fed up." Liam found a pair of shorts and slipped them on under the towel before dropping it and turning to her.

"That's because I am." Olivia responded grouchily. "I have a hangover and—" She waved at him to turn around. "I don't need a close-up of you in your underwear."

"Jeez, Liv, for someone who gets undressed and does unspeakably filthy things on camera, you're such a prude in real life." Liam picked up a pair of jeans from the chair and pulled them on. "Better?"

"Much, thank you." Olivia could have reminded him that it was Susie who did those things, not her, but constantly pointing it out was getting dull.

Liam sat on the edge of the bed. "I actually owe you a big thank you. I couldn't sleep last night because I was worrying about the big love scene Lou and I have to do today. And I came out of my room—" He cleared his throat. "I was going to go and see if Louise was up. I'd convinced myself I had to tell her how I felt and how difficult it all is for me." He picked at the bedcover. "But then I saw you and Casey and I went straight back inside." He smiled. "So you making out with Casey in the corridor saved me from making a fool of myself with Louise." He held out a fist for her to bump.

"You saw us?"

"I did. And I'm guessing that whatever happened with you two has got you feeling all weird and that's why you're sighing so much. I mean, I'm guessing, you can tell me I've got it all wrong, or that it's none of my business." His tone was kind. It always was. He was the sweetest of all of them.

"We kissed." Olivia let out a sigh of relief. She was so glad to talk about it with someone. "That was all."

That wasn't all. It wasn't even close to being all. She hadn't been able to stop thinking about it.

"It was incredible. And I wanted more, but she said no." Olivia put a hand over her face, glad this was Liam she was confessing to and not Louise. "And now I'm worried I've made things really fucking awkward and I wanted to talk to her about it, but she's not here."

"I can see why you feel awkward."

"You can? Why? I mean I do feel awkward, but why do you feel like I should?"

Liam went to the closet, riffling through the shirts before choosing one and slipping his arms into it. Olivia waited for him to come back to the bed and sit down.

"You're the beautiful actress in town on business and she's the impossibly handsome driver who's been hired to drive you around. It's kinda tropey. And if I were Casey, I'd have been worried about you waking up so full of embarrassment today that you'd fire me rather than face me. So I'd have said no too. And yeah, I'd probably be annoyed that you put me in that position when I'm just trying to do my job and be nice."

"Wow, you weren't tempted to sugarcoat it a little for me?"

"I could but I know you. I'm sure you're being twenty times harder on yourself than I am, so what's the point?" Liam buttoned up his shirt.

"I like her, Liam. A lot. We had this great afternoon together, and I decided to wait for her in the bar. But it wasn't because I was planning to come on to her." Olivia was careful to keep her voice neutral. "I just wanted to spend more time with her. But we had a bit to drink, and I realized I wanted to, you know, with her. I wasn't thinking about her being 'the driver' or how awkward that might make things, but maybe I should have. It's just that she's smart and sweet and gorgeous." She took in a breath. "And somehow she seems real and honest, when everything else in my life isn't." She tried to sound as casual as possible, but inside her chest, her heart was beating faster than usual. She knew what she was saying was crazy even as she was trying not to make it sound that way.

"Lou is gonna be so smug. She said the two of you were getting into something. I hate it when she's right about things." He smiled at Olivia kindly. "Are you going to do something about it? Do you know if she feels the same kind of feelings?"

Out of the three of them, Liam was the real romantic, the one who hadn't been bruised by love.

"I don't know." It was the truth, but she was also guarding herself, guarding this thing they had—whatever it was. "She kissed me back. She seemed as into it as I was for a while. And she said some really nice things to me last night, but we were both pretty drunk. My plan today was to apologize for coming on too strong, blame the drink, and see if she throws me any kind of a rope. I don't want things to be awkward. And I don't want to have to be in a car with Tania. Her driving terrifies me." She tried for a joke.

"Come on, Liv."

"What?"

"You can do better than that. Don't minimize it. It sounds like you like her. Don't write it off like that without finding out if she feels the same way."

"Are you giving me advice about speaking up when you've got feelings for someone, because…" She screwed up her face. "I'm not sure that you're exactly practicing what you preach."

"I know, but my situation is a little different. I want to stay in Louise's life, and if I come on too strong with these feelings, there's a chance I'll ruin the friendship. And that is the most precious thing for me in all this." He gave her a bashful smile. "It's different for you. If you take a shot and it doesn't work, you'll be out of here in a week. You can afford to take a chance with Casey."

"I know that rationally, but I don't think I'm wired that way. When I like someone, I need to know them, to trust them. I like to go slow. Usually. When I 'go' at all."

"Unless you're drunk, in which case you can be found making out with them in the corridor outside your room."

"Don't." Olivia covered her face with her hands before Liam pulled them away laughing.

"I'm kidding. And like I said, I'm grateful. I'm glad that I went back to bed without knocking on Lou's door. It was the wrong time to tell her. I was just freaking out because of today. But you don't have the time to go slow, Liv. If you're too careful, the opportunity will be gone. You've got to say something. Or do something. Take a chance."

Olivia didn't respond. He was right, but that didn't mean she wanted him to be.

"And what about you taking a chance?" She poked him. "Maybe you should tell her before you get started today."

"No. The moment's passed now. You saved me. Doing the scene with her knowing I'm pining for her would be the worst. I wasn't thinking straight last night."

"None of us were thinking straight last night."

Except Casey. She'd been thinking straight when she said no to Olivia and again when she had dodged her this morning.

Liam put on his socks and shoes. She had a flash of memory of Casey kneeling at her feet and unbuckling her shoes. It hadn't been what she'd have chosen to have Casey do if she was kneeling in front of her, but it was very sweet.

"I know it's ridiculous to get attached to someone in such a short span of time, but it's been nice to have someone new to spend time with." It was true, but it wasn't all Olivia could have said. It was nice to spend time with someone new who was also sweet, funny, and fascinating, someone who hadn't the faintest idea who Susie was, who didn't want a single thing from her. It was kind of fabulous. And the idea of leaving Casey behind in a week was tough. Tough enough that she'd already googled how far away Portland was from LA.

"Ouch."

"What?"

"Someone new? That's cold, Liv." He sat back down next to her, threw an arm around her shoulders and pulled her into a sideways hug. "Sometimes old and comfy is best—like your favorite hoodie or pair of sneakers."

"Old sneakers smell. Everyone knows that." Olivia stuck out her tongue before extricating herself from his hug and heading to the door. "See you downstairs in five?"

Liam nodded.

"Take mouthwash and your toothbrush."

Liam stared at her.

"You'll be drinking coffee all morning. Lunch might involve tuna or onion. You want Michael to make love to Jessie with stinky breath?"

He ran to the bathroom and Olivia couldn't help but smile. She thought she had problems, but she wasn't going to spend the afternoon making out with a best friend she'd fallen in love with, while a director told her exactly how far into her mouth she needed to push her tongue.

In two days' time, she was going to be doing exactly that with Billie, but the difference was that she didn't give a damn about Billie, or what she thought of Olivia's technique. And if Billie didn't stop being such a pain in the ass, she was going to brush her teeth in anchovy paste before every single one of their scenes together.

The idea of it made her smile. She walked to her room with a little more of a spring to her step than she had managed so far that day.

Maybe Casey avoiding her was a good thing. A day or two away from Casey—and all the things she was making Olivia feel—was probably just what she needed to get her thoughts straight.

Casey turned the corner. The corner she felt like she'd turned fifty times in the last ten days. They were on the home stretch back to the hotel, but the traffic—as ever—was crawling. As she saw the Shard up ahead, she couldn't help but think of Olivia. Not that she hadn't spent the best part of the day thinking about Olivia. About their kiss, about the schedule being switched so that Olivia could avoid being driven by her today.

Her mind was a confusing whirl of lust, regrets and surprise. Even drunk, she hadn't expected Olivia to make a move like that. But over the course of a mostly sleepless night, Casey had convinced herself that Olivia was entitled to a holiday romance, was entitled to want to have sex. Just as Casey was entitled to say no. It was okay and it didn't have to be awkward. When she eventually caught up with her, Casey would make sure Olivia knew that she was fine about it and they didn't have to avoid each other.

Except her heart was hurting. She was stupid enough to have wanted it to mean something. She had feelings for Olivia, but it seemed that Olivia just wanted a drunken fuck. Maybe she was more like Susie than Casey had ever imagined.

"Do we have time to go up real quick?" Louise asked from the back seat. "Take a quick Shard selfie."

"I don't think so, sorry. I was told you have to be back at the hotel to get changed and grab lunch and you're needed on set by one thirty. This traffic is already making us late."

"You found time to go with Olivia." Billie spoke up from the seat next to her.

"I did. That was an afternoon off for us both though."

Casey hadn't felt able to say no when Billie got in the front of the car, but she'd tried not to be drawn into conversation, keeping her responses to Billie's intrusive questions as short as she could manage. Billie seemed like someone who got attention whenever she demanded it, but Casey wasn't in the mood for her at all.

"So you and Olivia are spending your afternoons off together? That's sweet." Her tone suggested she thought it was anything but sweet.

"One afternoon," Casey corrected her.

"I can understand why you might want to hang out with Olivia. She's very appealing. She's rich, famous, attractive. But why she wants to spend time with you is a little more of a mystery."

Casey felt herself tense, felt her anger building.

"Billie, come on. Why are you going out of your way to be so obnoxious?"

Casey was grateful for Louise's intervention. Billie turned in her seat to address her.

"I'm not being obnoxious. I'm being honest. I think Olivia can do better. And I think it reflects badly on the show that it's our driver who's helping her into the elevator when she's drunk, rather than one of us."

"She wasn't drunk." Casey couldn't help but defend her. "You all know that."

"I'm just saying that's how it looks. That it reflects badly on all of us. These things don't have to be true."

"Like you've never been photographed when you're not at your best. It's happened to all of us, Billie."

"I'm photographed when I want to be and only when I've got something I want them to see. If you guys don't understand the power of controlling your own narrative at this point in your careers, then that's kind of sad."

They sat quietly for a few moments as the car inched along in the traffic. The atmosphere thick with all the things that weren't being said. Casey understood that Billie was jealous of her, but she couldn't understand why. She was no threat. If Olivia wasn't interested in Billie, it wasn't because of her. It was probably because Billie was an arrogant jerk.

"There's parking for the Shard up ahead on the left. Just pull in there please."

"I already told you, we don't have time. I'm supposed to keep you on schedule. I don't want you to be late getting back."

It was turning into a battle of wills.

"Forget it, Billie. Casey's right. You can't be late for rehearsals. I mean, I know you like to be, but it's kind of annoying for everyone when you are." She muttered the last sentence, but it was audible to both Casey and Billie. Casey couldn't help but smile.

Billie huffed and did a little sighing, but then a tense silence fell that Casey was grateful for.

"She won't always be the star of the show, you know? You'll see. I'm gonna get a lot more attention this season. And a lot more respect. And I know how to act like a star. I'm exactly what the show needs to liven things up."

Casey didn't need to look across at her to see the pout. She knew it was there.

"Did you really just say that out loud?" Louise laughed. "That Bond villain shtick is wonderful. We just need to get you a pussy to stroke. Oh, wait—"

Casey saw Louise's smirk in the rearview mirror and couldn't help but grin.

They were getting closer to the hotel, where she assumed Olivia would be waiting for them. If she was taking Billie to rehearsals, then Olivia must be going too. Despite everything, Casey felt her pulse quicken at the idea of seeing her.

"I don't think timekeeping is part of a driver's duties. And I think that if we want to stop somewhere, you should stop. It's up to us if we want to be late, not you." Billie sounded like she wanted a fight with someone and had decided Louise was too sassy to mess with.

"Understood." Casey couldn't afford to argue with her.

"Maybe Olivia has you feeling like you're important in some way, but the rest of us just need you to drive and do as you're told."

"Absolutely."

Casey couldn't stop her jaw from clenching. Billie was being a bitch, and they both knew that Casey could do nothing but tolerate it.

"I love that single word answer thing you keep doing," Louise said, a smile in her voice. "It's a bit James Bond in its own way. I feel like we have an entire movie going on in here. And I'm going to be Miss Moneypenny. It's a lifetime ambition. And it means that you," she poked Casey's seat, "have to flirt with me."

"I can't, sorry. I'm only allowed to drive. Flirting isn't in the contract." Casey was taking a chance by taking a dig back at Billie.

"Who even are you anyway?" Billie half spat out the words. "You're a nobody, but somehow you still manage to act like you're better than us. It can't be easy to drive with that stick up your ass."

"Billie." Louise said her name like a warning. "There's no need for that. We're just having a bit of fun."

"And I'm just reminding our driver of her place."

Casey was happy to turn onto the narrow street that led to the hotel. They traveled the rest of the way in silence. As soon as Casey pulled up, Billie jumped out and stalked into the hotel without a backward glance.

Casey got out and moved around the car to open the door for Louise, offering her a hand as she climbed out.

"I could get out by myself, but I like you doing it." Louise smiled at her warmly.

"All part of the not-very-good service, madam." She bowed.

"Don't listen to her. She's pissed because you wouldn't play with her."

"It felt more like an interrogation than playing."

"She's just curious. We're all a little intrigued by you. It's a compliment."

"Is it?"

"Kind of. Billie's jealous because she thinks you like Liv more than her."

"She's right about that," Casey muttered.

"And because she knows Liv likes you a lot more than her."

Casey couldn't help but react to Louise's statement. Had Olivia said something to her? She hated herself for thinking that way.

"It's like high school. And I'm far too old for it." She was chiding herself more than Louise.

Casey locked the car and walked side by side with Louise into the hotel. She wanted to see if Olivia was back from her interview. They needed to talk. She needed Olivia to know that the kisses—even now the memory of them made her warm—didn't mean they had to avoid each other.

"I'm curious about you too. Liv clearly thinks you're cool, but to be brutally honest, she's not always the best judge of character."

"I could get offended by that."

"Don't. I'm blunt. I find it's better that way. I know she sent a load of stuff to your mom and she said you were in some kind of financial difficulty. I just—"

"My mom, not me," Casey cut in, feeling a flush of shame. "And I didn't ask for that stuff. I wanted her to take it back. She wouldn't. She and my mom hit it off and she'd just had a load of stuff stolen—"

"It's okay. She explained it to me already. I'm just being protective of her. She's had tough times."

"I know."

Louise peered at her closely.

"Of course you do. It's not exactly a secret." She sounded disappointed. Casey felt like she'd said something wrong.

"She told me last night. I didn't know anything about any of it until she told me."

"Really?"

"I already told you, I've never watched the show and I don't do celebrity gossip. I didn't even know who any of you were until a week ago." Casey turned to her. "No offense."

"None taken. Look, I'm not saying you've done anything wrong. Just that any more gifts might look bad for you, that's all. She's got a big heart.

She trusts too easily, and I make it my business to look after her and to figure out who she's getting close to."

Now Louise was sounding like a Soprano.

"I'm glad she has you. But you don't need to worry about me and neither does Olivia. I'm one of those ridiculously proud people who grew up with nothing and ended up being pretty independent. I had no choice. And I'm not at all comfortable with people giving me stuff. So since we're being blunt, let me say that I'm not only someone she can trust, but I'm probably a safer bet than anyone else she's going to meet this trip." Casey couldn't help but feel annoyed, and she didn't try to hide it. She hadn't always behaved perfectly, but she shouldn't have to prove her character to anyone.

"You like her." It wasn't a question. Louise looked at her intently, and Casey couldn't stop the heat in her cheeks.

"I do. There's a lot about her to like."

"There certainly is." Louise took Casey's arm and steered them toward the hotel entrance. "Do you play poker?"

"Of course I do. But I've not played in a while, so I might be a little rusty."

"Rusty is good. I like to win." Louise smiled. "We have a game tonight. My room. Eight p.m."

Casey felt her heart lift at the idea of spending some time with Olivia. Even if that meant suffering more scrutiny from Louise. Olivia had mentioned the game in passing, but she hadn't invited her.

"Okay, sounds good. Can you do me a favor though?"

"Sure."

"Can you check with Olivia that it's okay for me to come?"

"Why would Olivia not want you to come?" Casey could hear the suspicion. Louise was living up to her promise of being protective.

"We just—" Casey stopped. "I don't know. Just because I'm the driver I guess and boundaries and all that stuff that Billie was saying about the show."

"Just that?"

Casey nodded.

Olivia obviously hadn't told Louise what had happened between them, and she certainly wasn't going to. Olivia could trust Casey not to say anything about their kiss, and she could trust her to stay away if that was what Olivia wanted.

"Just ask her and I won't be offended to get a text later disinviting me. I am just the driver."

"That's getting old." Louise headed for the elevators.

"Tell me about it."

Louise looked at her watch. "See you back here in an hour then. You've got plenty of time to go and buy the large bag of pretzels that will buy you access to tonight's game." Louise stepped into the elevator as Casey hung back.

"I thought I was driving Billie and Olivia to their rehearsal."

"Nope. You're taking me and Liam to the studio."

Another change that Casey hadn't been made aware of, another change that she assumed Olivia was responsible for. Her heart sank a little.

"Oh, okay. I hadn't realized there'd been a change. No worries." Casey put on a brave face, not wanting Louise to know she cared one way or the other. "I'm going upstairs for some food. I missed breakfast and now I'm starving." The hangover had been fairly mild; it had been her anxiety about seeing Olivia that kept her away from breakfast.

"Have some squeak and bubble for me."

"It's bubble and—"

"I know." Louise winked at her as the doors closed.

Chapter Sixteen

H e's a great kisser."

"Oh no, Lou. Don't tell me that. I don't want to know. And it's not fair to him for us to be talking like this."

"Well, I can't exactly say it to him, can I?" Louise replied as she laid out a large white tablecloth on the floor in the middle of the space she had cleared in her room.

"Maybe you should. Maybe the two of you should sit down and talk about exactly that. You can't be getting turned on when you're filming, it's against the code, you know that?"

"I'm not saying I was turned on…okay, maybe I was a tiny bit, but it wasn't like that. Lately I've been thinking a lot about what it would be like to kiss him and today—" She waved a hand as if to say she had finally found out.

"I can't believe I'm having to say this to you, because you're the one who's always telling me that it's easy because it's make-believe, but it was Michael kissing Jessie, not Liam kissing you."

"I know. I'm not stupid." She placed a linen napkin on each corner of the towel before opening a bag of pretzels out onto the napkin closest to her. "It's just hard to keep the feelings in check. I mean, I've seen his body before—you've seen him, he's always running around in shorts—but I've never tasted his lips, never felt his hand in my hair. It was hard to stay focused on what we were supposed to be doing."

"Damn, Lou. You have to try to not think that way when you're filming."

"I know. It's torture. And I know it'd be really bad for our friendship if he found out I was thinking any of this, but I can't help the feelings."

"Feelings?"

"Don't sound so surprised. I am capable of them, you know?"

"I didn't mean that. I thought maybe it was just lust, or a holiday romance, or something."

"You mean like you and Casey?" Louise stopped counting her pretzels. "When were you going to tell me about that, by the way?"

Olivia should have expected Liam to tell Louise. They were close—that was partly what had got the two of them into this mess. They liked each other. They spent a lot of time together.

"I was going to tell you myself. I just haven't had the chance."

"You've been here half an hour. I deliberately asked you to come earlier than Liam and Casey so you'd have time to tell me how you ended up making out with Casey in the corridor outside your room, with her refusing to let you drag her inside."

"I thought it was so you could swoon about Liam's kissing technique."

"That too." Louise smiled. She got up from the floor, sat on the edge of her bed, and sighed. "What the hell is going on? We're both falling for completely unsuitable people. Maybe London is the real city of lovers and Paris needs to hand over its plaque."

"I'm not falling—" Olivia couldn't even complete the denial. She was falling for Casey. She just wasn't ready to tell Louise that. "I think Casey's suitable." It was true. "And if I'd met her in LA, I'd probably be letting myself hope all sorts of things, but in a few days, we're going to be saying good-bye to each other so…" Olivia lifted her shoulders in a shrug.

"So what? She doesn't live on the moon. She's in the same country, the same side of the country even. You shouldn't give in so easily."

"It's not just geography. She was pretty clear last night she wasn't interested. It wasn't just that she turned me down when I was practically horizontal. I told her all about Kristin and she seemed bothered by it. I get the feeling she doesn't do that kind of drama. And she's not exactly interested in what we do." Perversely, it was one of the things Olivia liked about Casey. "It's going nowhere. I know that. I just hate the idea I might have made things awkward."

It was more than that. She was feeling things she hadn't felt before, and she was hurt that Casey didn't seem to feel the same way. The embarrassment about the drunken come-on was just an added extra.

"Well, I get the feeling she might like you. But maybe she needs a little encouragement. You are Olivia Lang after all. Best Ass in Hollywood. You can be intimidating to us mere mortals."

"Ha-ha, Lou."

"I'm serious. I think she likes you. And you obviously like her. And you've already kissed. I mean, I don't know what's stopping you."

Olivia didn't know how Casey really felt about her. They'd said things last night, but they'd both been drunk. And it was only as she lay back on her bed, after Casey had left, that she remembered that Casey had said she was cool and smart and sexy.

"I don't want to make a fool of myself. She's obviously been avoiding me."

"That's funny. She thinks you changed the schedule to avoid her." Louise smiled. "But she jumped at the chance to come tonight. Doesn't exactly suggest avoidance."

Olivia frowned.

"Well, maybe I'm just not sure yet. You're always telling me not to be so trusting."

She wanted to trust Casey. She had the best feeling when they were together. She loved kids, she was helping her mom, and she hadn't even taken advantage of a drunken Olivia throwing herself at her. But despite all that, they were practically strangers. And Kristin had left Olivia feeling like her instincts were unreliable. She sighed deeply. Her thoughts had been spooling like this all day.

"Anyway, Liam's not unsuitable. He's a catch." Olivia wanted to change the subject.

"He's one of my best friends and he doesn't like me that way. I think that makes him pretty unsuitable."

"Maybe he does." Olivia said it without thinking and instantly wanted to take the words back. It was frustrating watching them torment each other, but that didn't mean she had a right to wade in. "I just mean, you don't know that he isn't interested, because you guys have never talked about it. Maybe you should."

Louise was looking at her suspiciously.

"Do you know something?"

"No." She found it impossible to lie to Louise. "Maybe." She put her head in her hands and groaned. Liam was her friend, but she'd known Louise for much longer.

"Did he say something to you? Don't hold out on me, Liv. I'm suffering here. I haven't told you because I felt so fucking stupid, but I've been feeling like this about him for months."

"I can't say. It's private." Olivia relented. "But just give it a try with him. Make a play. See what happens. You know what they say: fortune favors the brave."

"He likes me." Louise stood up and whirled around, a huge smile on her face.

"I didn't say that." Olivia offered a half-hearted denial.

"You didn't have to. Why didn't he say anything?"

"If he liked you—and I'm not saying he does—then he's probably as worried about ruining the friendship as you are. And maybe he thinks you don't like guys, or wouldn't date a trans guy. It happens." Olivia was saying more than she should. No amount of "maybe" or "probably" was going to stop him from being mad at her if things didn't work out. "But please don't tell him I said anything."

"I won't." Louise pulled her into a hug before heading off in the direction of the closet. "Now I have five minutes to find something to wear that's going to make him notice that I'm the one he's been waiting for all his life."

Olivia couldn't help but laugh, but Louise's confidence, her willingness to take a chance, was something that Olivia had always admired. Next to her, she always felt timid.

"And you should be doing the same," Louise said from inside the closet.

"What's wrong with what I'm wearing?" Olivia had dressed to impress Casey. The idea that she might not have succeeded sent her confidence nosediving.

"I don't mean the outfit, stupid. It's gorgeous. I mean, you should give it a try with Casey. The fact that Billie doesn't like her is probably all the recommendation you need." Louise emerged from the closet. She stripped off the checked shirt she was wearing and replaced it with another. Something tighter and much more low-cut. Olivia gave her the thumbs-up. Liam didn't stand a chance.

"Thinking about it, Billie was being super weird again today. She got in Casey's face about the two of you hanging out, saying you're disgracing the show by being seen drunk and being seen with someone who wasn't—I'm paraphrasing—your celebrity equal."

"I wasn't drunk."

"That's what Casey said." Louise sat at the dressing table and started to apply a little more makeup. She turned to Olivia. "Billie seemed pissed at her, obviously jealous as hell. Seems like everyone but you is aware of the fact that you and Casey have something going on."

"I don't know, Lou. I have a feeling she's worth more than I can give her. She's a real person, with friends and a real life. Sometimes I don't even know who I am anymore. She doesn't need me butting in and turning things upside down. She already told me how private she is. Even if she did like me and even if we had more time, I don't think she'll want to be sucked into the madness of this life we lead." Olivia took a breath finally. "It's different for you and Liam, you're already both in the middle of it."

The hopelessness of the situation had dawned on her early that morning, when she'd woken up with a raging thirst and a thumping headache. She was beyond grateful that Casey had stopped them from acting on their desire when they were drunk. It would have felt cheap. And she wasn't the kind of person who needed that kind of playmate. When she fell for someone, it was a heart and soul thing. But she couldn't lay that at Casey's feet so soon and expect her not to run a mile.

She trailed her fingers across the bottles of beer lined up on the cart that Louise had ordered up from room service. Poker night was always more fun with alcohol—and seeing Casey would be easier with a little liquid courage—but she grabbed a soda, not able to face the beer after last night.

Louise turned on her chair to face her.

"You look great. He won't stand a chance." Olivia smiled.

"And you, my sweet, look gorgeous. Let's slay." She offered out a fist and Olivia bumped it. Not sure she was the slaying type, but happy that Louise thought she was.

At the sound of a knock on the door, Louise got up to answer it. Olivia felt herself tense, knowing this time it had to be Casey. Liam was already sitting beside her on the floor, his pretzels laid out in neat rows of ten on the napkin in front of him. His mood seemed off and he was already at the bottom of a bottle of beer.

Louise swung open the door to let Casey into the room.

From Olivia's position on the floor, Casey looked about seven feet tall. She looked up at her and was met with an earnest gaze. And the small smile that came with it made Olivia heat up inside. Her reaction wasn't visible, but it didn't help her hold on to that sense of cool she had promised herself she was aiming for tonight.

Casey was wearing a faded gray T-shirt. The jeans were the same dark blue denim she'd worn yesterday, and they stretched as tight across her thighs as Olivia remembered.

Olivia's throat went dry. *Jeez.* She closed her eyes, willing herself to calm down. When she opened them, Casey was still looking at her.

"Where should I sit?" Casey asked.

Olivia indicated the space next to her. "The room doesn't have enough chairs, so Louise decided to improvise the poker table."

"I guess it works." Casey offered a small wave to Liam and settled herself down—her crossed legs mirroring Olivia's.

"How many do I need?" She held up one of the bags of pretzels she had brought with her.

"Count out a hundred. We'll eat the rest," Louise replied, pushing the cart toward Casey. "And grab yourself a drink." She grabbed a cushion from the couch and joined them on the floor.

Casey leaned across and took a soda from the cart. She was obviously planning to stay sober enough to fight Olivia off tonight should the need arise. Olivia felt a sliver of shame at the idea it might be true. She had to let it go. All she'd done was come on to someone she found attractive after she'd had a few drinks. It wasn't a felony. Especially since that someone had kissed her back with just as much passion. She was single and so was Casey. The only complication was them working together, knowing each other for little more than a week, and living wildly different lives. She squeezed her eyes shut before rubbing them vigorously. She was not going to get upset about it. Not tonight. Not with Casey sitting two feet away.

"You okay?" Liam asked quietly, putting a hand on her knee.

"Just about. You?"

"Peachy." The set of his jaw suggested that maybe that wasn't true.

Louise dealt the cards and everyone threw in their pretzels.

"Texas Hold'em rules. No limits." Louise offered the explanation to Casey. "If you run out of pretzels, you'll have to start stripping." She turned to Liam. "You too, sweet cheeks."

Liam blushed before taking a long pull on his beer. Louise smiled at him with what Olivia could now see was more than just her usual fondness. How on earth had she missed the two of them falling for each other?

"No Billie?" Casey asked.

"She doesn't play. She wanted to come and watch, but then I told her you were coming and she got all snarky and decided to go and have a swim instead," Liam replied.

"I have that effect on women all the time," Casey said with a wry smile.

"She's just jealous. She wants to get her hands on Olivia, and she thinks you being here is going to cramp her style."

"I'm not sure she's that keen on me after today," Olivia said, not wanting Louise to say any more. "I lost my temper during rehearsals. Billie kept asking for line rewrites for Susie. You know what she's like. Absolutely everything has to be said. And Susie's just not like that. She lets her actions speak more than her words. But Billie wanted her to spell everything out and I had to put my foot down."

"Sometimes having things spelled out can be helpful." Louise looked at Olivia, but it was obvious she was speaking to Liam. "Some of us need things to be said out loud, really plainly."

"Yeah, some of us do." Olivia couldn't help but agree. "But not Susie. I think Billie just wanted to make it awkward for me by having me say all these over-the-top loving things to her. She's so fucking weird."

"I think she's annoyed you won't succumb to her charms and she's paying you back. Her hating on Casey is the same. She spent the whole day trying to get Casey to be charmed by her, failed miserably, and then got into super bitch mode. It wasn't pretty." Louise turned over a card and they resumed their betting in silence.

Across from her, Casey seemed thoughtful, and Olivia couldn't help but feel bad. She probably just wanted to do her job, earn her money, and say good-bye to the whole circus, but first Olivia and now Billie were giving her attention she clearly didn't want.

"Do you remember that guy I dated back home? Nathan. The guy who used to set up the stage at the theater school."

Louise changed the subject and Olivia was grateful.

"Of course I do. He was cute. You tried to set me up with his brother. You couldn't believe I wasn't interested in double-dating. I think you had difficulties understanding the concept of lesbianism back then."

"I still do. Why would you limit yourself so narrowly? I like to think I'm someone who believes in equal opportunities. I give everyone the equal opportunity to be loved by me, to love me. I think that makes me generous." She said it with a smile.

"Or possibly a little slutty." Olivia couldn't help the cheap shot. She knew Louise's speech was meant for Liam. To let him know that she had dated guys.

"I've known you for three years and you've only ever dated women," Liam said as he cleared the "table" of the pot of pretzels he had just won.

"I only ever have women show an interest in me these days. Maybe it's because of the show. Maybe other folks assume I wouldn't be interested, because of Jessie I mean. Michael is the first man they've let her sleep with and we've had to wait till season four." Louise waited a beat. "Till today."

It felt like everyone was waiting for Liam to speak. But he looked down at his pretzels, silently sorting them into small piles.

"So you're looking forward to capitalizing on the new storyline with lots of male attention and new boyfriends?" Olivia threw a soft pitch in Louise's direction.

"No, I'm not. I'm sick of meaningless hookups with people who don't even know me. I want something more meaningful, with someone I like, someone I love, someone I can imagine buying a pet with one day."

"What kind of pet?" Liam asked the question without taking his eyes off Louise.

Olivia couldn't stop herself from reaching out a hand and prodding Casey's thigh. Casey looked across at her and widened her eyes. They both knew that this was important.

"A dog, maybe two." Louise's eye contact with Liam was just as intense.

Liam looked away first, seeming to find his beer bottle fascinating.

Casey leaned across and stole one of Olivia's pretzels, popping it into her mouth before Olivia could object.

"Hey."

"What?" Casey smiled and lifted her shoulders as if to protest her innocence.

From the other side, Liam slipped one onto her pile and she rewarded him with a kiss on the cheek. But Casey messing around with the pretzels was exactly what was needed to lower the tension, and her timing was one more thing for Olivia to admire about her.

Louise dealt the next hand and Olivia realized her pile of pretzels was a lot smaller than when she'd started. She wasn't the best at poker when she was concentrating, but tonight, with Casey on her mind, she was barely paying attention to the game.

"What about you?" Louise addressed Casey. "You dodged all Billie's questions about your love life today like you'd been learning interview avoidance skills from this one." She jerked a thumb in Olivia's direction. "We're all sad singles. What about you? Single? Married with six kids? Sharing a dog with someone special?" Louise asked. "I mean, I'm gonna find it hard to believe there isn't someone. I imagine you get a lot of offers."

Louise's tone was a little flirtatious, but that was just Louise being Louise. Olivia guessed she was trying to help her out, but Casey had already told her she was single. She waited for Casey to avoid answering. She wasn't someone who seemed to like talking about herself.

"My building doesn't allow dogs."

Olivia smiled. It was a good answer.

"But I'm guessing the building allows girlfriends. I mean, I'm assuming you don't live in a convent." Louise persisted. Olivia loved her best friend, but right then, she wanted to strangle her. She wasn't exactly being subtle.

"It allows girlfriends." Casey picked up her cards, clearly wanting to get back to the game. "And my roommate would definitely approve. She spends half her time trying to find me one."

Olivia couldn't help the jealousy that bubbled up.

"But I've been taking a well-earned break. I decided I'm happier to Netflix and chill on my own, and not just because it means I never have to share the popcorn."

Olivia got up to grab another soda. On the way to the cart, she deliberately stubbed her toe against Louise's knee, wanting to let her know that her grilling Casey was not what Olivia needed—or wanted. Louise looked in her direction and Olivia shook her head in warning.

"Liv said you're only visiting. Does it feel weird to be back, or good to be home?" Liam asked. "I know whenever I go back home to Milwaukee, I miss it. It's a place that reminds me who I am. It doesn't matter if I've been away a month or a year."

It was a good question, and Olivia wanted to hear Casey's response.

"I miss London, because it's London, you know. The culture, the history, the ridiculous buzz of the place. Here you can be anything—anyone—you want. But you've seen it…it's also crowded, noisy, polluted, and expensive." She smiled. "But I sometimes think that whatever's wrong with it, it's mine. This was where I was born and it's always been my city, my place, my home."

She sipped her soda. Olivia watched her lips caress the edge of the can and felt her reaction in the unmistakable pulsing between her legs. She knew she was holding her breath, her memories of Casey's mouth on hers running riot.

They'd stopped playing and were all listening to Casey.

"So why did you leave then?" Liam seemed genuinely interested.

"A well-earned break, like I said."

"That sounds glib. Like the kind of answer you'd give Billie." The challenge came from Louise, and Olivia was grateful. She should take the toe-poke back.

"You're a tough crowd." Casey placed her bet, tossing three pretzels onto the pile.

"You're forgetting we avoid answering awkward questions for a living. We know glib when we hear it." Louise made a rolling motion with her hands as if to tell Casey to stop stalling.

"I had a breakup here. One of those girlfriend cheats on you with someone in your friendship group type of dramas. I'm sure that happens all the time in your world, so maybe it's not very shocking, but for me..." She seemed to search for the right words. "For me, it was hard to get past. And it kind of ruined the way I felt about the place."

Olivia knew some of this, knew that Casey had left to escape a difficult situation with an ex. But the rest of it was a surprise.

"After we broke up, she had a lot to say about the whole thing. She had a platform. She was active in social media, on YouTube. She said a lot about it that I didn't want people to know. Things that should have stayed between us. When I left it all behind, it meant I didn't have to face people who knew what had happened and I felt a thousand times better."

Olivia's heart ached for her. She wanted to reach across and comfort her. The strength of the feeling surprised her.

"And being back—is it hard?" Olivia didn't want Casey to feel pressured by the questions, but this was as much as she had told her all week, and she was grateful to understand her a little better.

"A little, but not as much as I expected. I'd like to think it's because I've done a lot of moving on, but it might just be that you guys have kept me so busy I haven't had time to dwell on the past."

Olivia sat back down on the floor next to Casey.

"Do you ever think about coming back? I bet your mom would love it if you did."

"I considered it in the beginning. The adjustment was hard. I missed people, missed my job, missed the city." Casey looked at her as she spoke, and Olivia had the feeling they were the only two people in the room. "But there were more reasons for staying away than coming home."

"What did you do before you left?" Liam asked as he cleared the table of his winnings. His pile of pretzels was twice as big as everyone else's.

"I was a youth worker. Not all that far from here. I worked with troubled kids—those that were on the verge of running away, or not doing well at home. It was great, I loved it. And I miss it a lot."

"It's a shame you had to leave that behind as well." Olivia meant it. But she caught the downward shift of Casey's eyes, the slight tension in her shoulders. She'd somehow said the wrong thing. She felt bad. She didn't want Casey to be upset, to be reminded of tough times.

"Do you miss Brooklyn? You made it sound like you had a good thing going on there." Casey returned her gaze to Olivia, and Olivia felt captured by it.

"I do." She wanted to give Casey an honest answer. "I liked having seasons, walking the dog, and I had a lot of fun being on stage—New York has so many cool theaters—and I sometimes miss that."

"I don't. Sometimes the ones we performed at had more rats than people in the audience," Louise said. "It was bleak sometimes, and I'm pretty sure I'd miss the adoration. There was never anyone waiting for us at the stage door."

"I'm not sure I'd care." Olivia meant it. She loved acting, she loved Susie, and she was proud of what they'd done with the show, but the rest of it was a grind. "The being photographed, talked about, intruded upon. I hate it. You take it in stride, but I'm not sure I'll ever get used to it."

Maybe, like Casey, she was just a private person who'd ended up in the wrong career.

"And I don't know how I'll ever get tough enough to cope with the industry, the people like Kristin—and Billie. People who don't care what they do, who they step on, to advance their careers." Olivia looked at Casey. Her face carried a small frown, and Olivia wanted to know what she was thinking.

"Wow." Louise's voice rang out, disturbing the intensity of her connection with Casey. "How did things get so serious? Poker night is usually all about gossip and beer."

"You always do that," Liam said. "Make a joke whenever things get too emotionally honest. It's a form of deflection. It's like you're scared of feeling your own feelings about things."

Olivia saw Louise blink and then blink again. It was the closest thing to a double-take she'd seen in real life.

"That's not true," Louise replied, sounding a little hurt. "Maybe it's precisely because I'm feeling my own feelings that I change the subject. And maybe you should be grateful that I'm deflecting and not expressing them."

"What's that supposed to mean?" Liam asked with a frown.

"Nothing." Louise backed down. "Just that poker night is supposed to be a bit of light relief, not full of our collective angst. When did we all get so angsty anyway?"

"Actually, she's right. Louise promised me lots of laughs, a mountain of pretzels, and juicy industry gossip about people I'm certain I've never even heard of." Casey took Louise's side. She and Louise seemed as different as chalk and cheese, but Olivia could tell they liked each other.

"I've got a good one," Louise cut in, speaking in a low conspiratorial tone. "I saw Kristin a few months ago. Inside the Honda Plaza."

"You already told me." Olivia tried to close Louise down. She didn't want Casey reminded of the car crash that was her relationship with Kristin.

"But what I didn't tell you—because I thought you'd get pissed at me—was that after I saw her, I put on my best Southern-lady-from-out-of-town accent and told the mall cop I saw her shoplifting. It was lame, but it was all the revenge I could think of taking that wouldn't see me put in prison. Though," she smiled, "maybe that wouldn't be so bad, especially since I can't seem to find love on the outside."

Liam laughed.

They all looked at him.

"I think that might be the first time I've heard you laugh in two days," Louise said with a smile.

Liam lifted his shoulders in a half shrug. "Well, I'm sorry, but tonight hasn't exactly been a barrel of laughs. And I've had a very weird few days at work." He looked at Louise as he said it. The tension cranked up a notch. "So forgive me if the idea of you and some Big Boo prison daddy dyke seems like light relief."

"I think she was probably imagining Ruby Rose. But it's good to remind her of Big Boo. It might help keep her on the straight and narrow," Casey joined in, smiling.

It was a smile that made Olivia weak at the knees. She was happy she was already sitting down.

"I don't think she's ever been on the straight and anything." Liam continued the teasing, and Louise play-punched his thigh. He grabbed her hand and Olivia couldn't help but notice the shift in the atmosphere as the two of them wrestled with their hands, neither seeming to want to let go. She looked at Casey, who was also watching the two of them with interest.

"I need some air." Casey got up and Olivia couldn't help but feel disappointed. She still hadn't had the chance to apologize for her drunken behavior, or—if she could find the courage—to talk about what was going on between them.

"Want to come?" Casey spoke directly to her. "Maybe we could walk along the river down to Tower Bridge. It's beautiful at night. And it's not that far."

"That sounds great." Olivia jumped to her feet.

For a second, there was silence. Louise looked at Olivia and then at Liam. He looked from Olivia to Casey and back to Louise.

"I think I'll stay here and eat this huge pile of pretzels I seem to have won. Drink another one of these beers Lou sprung for."

"I'm not sure we were invited." Louise gave Liam a nudge with her foot. "Your superhero name should totally be Captain Oblivious."

Liam blushed.

"Go and have your walk." Louise smiled at her. Though, truthfully, it was closer to a smirk. "Go on." Louise waved them away.

"I think we've been dismissed." Olivia tried to sound more casual than she felt. A twilight walk with Casey along the river was not going to help her get her feelings in check. Was Casey as oblivious as Liam, or did she know how many butterflies Olivia was feeling right then?

The loud knock on the door startled her. Louise got up to answer it. It was Billie. She stepped into the room without waiting to be asked and walked straight over to Olivia.

"Thought you should see this." She handed her an iPad.

At the center of the screen was a close-up photograph of her asleep in the back of a car. In the back of Casey's car. Covered in Casey's jacket. She scanned the text that accompanied the picture. It was the same crap as before. Suggesting Olivia had been drinking and was sleeping it off in the back of the "official car," while studio executives tried to figure out what to do about the fact that her drinking had become a problem for them.

Olivia couldn't believe it. Her brain tried to process everything at once. The website was the same one that had run the story the day before. They'd said she was drunk then too. But none of it was true. It was crazy.

The photo was a surprise. It was from the first day, the afternoon Casey took her to eat pie. She handed the tablet to Louise.

"I don't understand what the hell is going on."

"Someone's clearly got it in for you." Billie said what was obvious.

"Or someone is looking to make a bit of money." Louise looked up from the screen before passing it to Liam.

Olivia couldn't see past the photo. Casey told her she'd been asleep for maybe half an hour. It was mid-afternoon and the parking lot had been almost empty. She didn't remember seeing another soul.

"Did you see anyone that day?" she asked Casey.

"What day?" Casey frowned at her.

Olivia signaled for Liam to pass Casey the iPad. She looked at it for a moment and then lifted her eyes to Olivia's.

"I don't remember seeing anyone. But I went to get coffees, remember?" Casey's brow furrowed. "But I was gone for less than five minutes. I didn't want to leave you out there sleeping on your own."

"Olivia was sleeping in the back of your car?" The question was Billie's. Her tone was accusing.

"She had jet lag. She fell asleep on the way home. I let her nap for a while. I nipped out to get coffees for when she woke up. I didn't know there were any photographers around. I didn't see them, or I wouldn't have left her—obviously."

"You expect us to believe that in the five minutes you left Olivia alone, someone that wasn't you happened upon Olivia sleeping in the car, took her photo, and then decided a week later to sell it to a website?"

There was a moment of silence.

"I don't 'expect' you to believe anything, Billie, I'm just telling you what happened. I was gone for five minutes and I didn't take the photo, so someone else must have."

Casey turned to look at Olivia. Olivia could see the anxiety, the tension, in her face, even as her words sounded defiant. She wanted to say something comforting, but she didn't know what to say. She couldn't conceive of Casey taking her photo and selling it, but the idea of some random paparazzi happening upon her in the car seemed so unlikely. And—she hated herself for even having the thought—Casey did need the money. For her mom. Things were desperate, she understood that much. She felt a sinking feeling in her stomach. Could she really be that wrong about the kind of person she thought Casey was?

Olivia shook the thought away, ashamed for even thinking it. There had to be another explanation.

"It could be someone from the hotel maybe."

Casey looked at her with a mixture of hurt and disappointment and then her expression closed. The hurt replaced with a blankness that made clear Olivia's defense of her had come a moment too late.

"I think I'm going to go and have that walk." Casey moved toward the door. "I'm sorry someone did that. That someone has enough animosity toward you to not just sell the photo, but to make up the lies that went with it." Without waiting for a response from Olivia, she left.

Olivia fought the urge to go after her.

"It's obvious that she did this." Billie moved to Olivia's side. "We should report her in the morning. Ask for another driver. I knew there was something off about her. I don't know why you let her get so close. I would have thought you'd learned your lesson last time."

"Shut up, Billie. You don't know anything about her." The defense of Casey was automatic, but maybe Olivia was the one who didn't know her. Her instincts had let her down before.

"Thanks for bringing it to our attention, but you can go now, Billie. We'll take it from here." Louise sat down and started to gather up her pretzels.

"Well, I'm going to talk to the studio people and see if they can do a cease and desist thing with this website. They can't say these things about Olivia without evidence. I mean, this isn't just about you getting photographed. The studio will be annoyed about this. Another story about you drinking on the job. And all of it reflects pretty badly on the show."

"I wasn't drinking. I wasn't even on the job, Billie. It was my day off. Can you stop being so fucking dramatic?" All of Olivia's frustrations were boiling over. "Maybe you should just leave like Louise asked you to and stop interfering. I can deal with this on my own, Billie. Like you kindly pointed out, it's not like I haven't had plenty of experience." This time, Olivia didn't hide her anger.

Billie didn't even flinch.

"Of course you have. You've been very unlucky. The studio's shown a lot of patience clearing up these situations for you." Her words were sympathetic, her tone sounded anything but. She was reminding Olivia of what she already knew—the studio would be annoyed by this and they might start to question whether she was unlucky, or just showing poor judgment. There was even a chance they might start to lose patience with her.

Billie left the room and Olivia sat on the floor. She put her head in her hands. Liam slid along the floor till he was next to her, pulling her into a sideways hug.

"It's okay, Liv. No one's going to care. This website is trash anyway. No one believes a word they print."

"I just can't believe Casey would do this." Olivia's brain was scrambling to make sense of it all. She was finding it hard to imagine Casey wanting to hurt her.

Louise joined them on the floor. "Me neither. I mean, I know she needs the money, but I had a good feeling about her. And I thought you two had something good brewing. It seemed like she really liked you. I'm surprised."

"I don't think it's Casey," Liam said.

"Why?" Olivia let herself hope.

"The first photo they ran had Casey in it, so she obviously didn't take that one. And whoever sent that photo to the website was the one who started with this whole 'Olivia is drunk on the job' thing. And if it was Casey, why go with that story? Why not tell them that Olivia had been assaulted? It's a much better story." He waited a beat. "Then today, there's another photo, another suggestion that Olivia's drunk, on the same website. It only makes sense if the same person sent both photos and pitched the same story, and since Casey couldn't have taken the first one, it would be a massive coincidence if she took and sold the second one to the same website."

They sat quietly for a moment.

"They're remaking *Columbo*. You have to audition," Louise said. "That makes perfect sense and you are awesome."

"And I agree with Lou. Casey seems pretty smitten with you. That much is obvious even to me."

"Like you'd know if someone was smitten with you," Louise muttered. "And who even says 'smitten' any more. Hey, Liam, the nineteenth century called, it wants its word back."

Olivia waved a hand at Louise, wanting her to be quiet.

"So someone else is taking photos, selling them, and making it look like I'm drunk? But why? Who?"

"At first I thought it could be a hotel employee. They could have gotten the first shot easily enough. And they have CCTV, so they could have seen you in the parking lot and taken a quick photo. It's taken through the side window, not with the door open."

"Because that would make it too obvious it was Casey," Louise chipped in and Olivia shushed her.

"I'm just playing devil's advocate. It doesn't mean I think she did it."

This time, Liam shushed her.

"I told you it's not Casey. But it could well be Billie." Without giving them time to react, Liam continued. "Number one, she's mad at you because you keep saying no to her. Number two, you're the star of the show, and we all know she hates playing second fiddle to anyone. Causing trouble for you like this will see your crown get tarnished and maybe that gives her an opening. And number three, she's much more likely to understand that websites are interested in this kind of stuff than Casey is. She's always getting herself deliberately 'caught off guard' by photographers. It's how she keeps herself in the spotlight. She said as much."

"Do you really think Billie would do this? It's kinda dark, even for her." Louise said what Olivia was thinking. It was hard to believe.

"It's Billie." Liam sounded emphatic. "There's no other plausible explanation. And her coming in here to show you the article is just the icing on the cake for her. She gets to glory in your discomfort and try to lay the blame on Casey." Liam drained the beer in his hand and put it down. "It's a win-win."

"What a nasty little bitch." Louise reacted before Olivia. "I mean, she was acting all Bond villain about you in the car earlier today, but I had no idea she meant it, that she was capable of this."

"I need to go and talk to Casey."

She had to. She had so much to apologize for. And Casey had every right to be mad at her. Because Olivia had doubted her. It was an instant, but it was there. And while she was at it, she should apologize for kissing her, for making Billie jealous, and for putting her in the middle of all this. And then she should obviously stay as far away from Casey as possible. Casey didn't deserve to be caught up in all of Olivia's crap. It could cost her the job.

"I need to let her know that none of us think she's guilty of this."

"Yeah, I think you do." Liam reached for another beer. Louise handed him one.

"You deserve that, Columbo. And you deserve a pizza to go with it. How about we order one up?"

He nodded enthusiastically.

Olivia gave Liam a kiss on the cheek before standing to leave. She had the thirty seconds it was going to take her to reach Casey's room to figure out exactly how she was going to salvage something meaningful from the wreckage of the last twenty-four hours. If she couldn't, then she would have helped Billie to achieve at least one of her objectives—driving a wedge between her and Casey.

The walk to Casey's room took her past Billie's. She had a lot she wanted to say to her too, but that could wait.

She stopped outside Casey's door and took in a deep breath before knocking tentatively. When she received no answer, she knocked again more loudly and waited. She still had no idea what she was going to say.

Damn. Too late, Olivia realized that Casey had gone out for the walk she had promised herself. She headed back to her own room. It would all have to wait till tomorrow.

❖

Casey leaned against the railings and let the night air cool her down. She was wearing only a shirt, and she welcomed the breeze on her arms and her neck. She focused on the glimmering lights on the water in the hope they would soothe and calm her.

The churning feeling was mostly Olivia related. She was mad at Billie of course. If she'd stayed in the room any longer, she would have said a lot of things to Billie that would have been hard to take back. But Olivia doubting her, Olivia believing that she was the kind of person who would have taken a photo of her while she was asleep and then sell it for money, was a kick in the stomach. She hadn't said it out loud, but she didn't need to. Her hesitation said everything.

Casey had let Olivia see her life up close, and Olivia had formed a view of her because of it. It clearly wasn't a good one. And if Olivia knew all the things Casey hadn't yet told her—the kind of things that Olivia had even admitted she would feel vengeful about—her judgment would be even harsher.

She took in a couple of deep breaths. The cold air in her lungs felt good. Right then, she couldn't feel anything but sadness about the way things had gone, but tomorrow, she was going to make herself feel grateful to have had this wakeup call. She had found it impossible to deal with the nonsense that came with Hannah's "career," but Olivia's was much worse. She didn't want—or need—the drama.

"Hey."

Casey turned and found herself face-to-face with Olivia. She looked a little flushed—and very beautiful. It would all be a lot easier if Casey's pulse didn't quicken quite so much at the sight of her.

"I hope you don't mind me coming after you. I wanted the walk. You made it sound as if Tower Bridge at night was worth the effort." Olivia sounded hesitant and a little out of breath. "And you asked me to come with you—before Billie came and crashed the evening."

"I wasn't expecting you to come after all that." It was true. "I just wanted to clear my head." She couldn't send Olivia away, but she was no longer in the mood for a moonlit stroll with her.

"I had to leave. I was worried Louise and Liam were going to start making out. I figured making an escape was the safest option." Olivia made the joke, but the cheerfulness was forced.

Casey leaned back against the railing.

"You can see Tower Bridge up ahead." She angled her head. "It's probably no more than a five-minute walk from here." She didn't move. She wanted Olivia to go without her. "You can't get lost."

Olivia looked down at her feet, but not before Casey caught the look of hurt. She felt bad for hurting her feelings. But she was embarrassed and angry at being suspected by Olivia.

"Casey, please. Can we talk?" Olivia lifted her head and fixed her gaze on Casey.

Casey could talk. She could tell Olivia how confused she felt, about the feelings she had for her and how surprised she was by their intensity. And she could ask Olivia if she had any of the same feelings. But Billie's jealousy, the leaked photos, and the humiliation of Olivia believing Casey was the kind of person who would do that to her, had reminded her of just how crazy Olivia's life was, and suddenly talking seemed pointless.

"We don't need to. In Britain we like to say 'some things are better left unsaid.' And it's true. Maybe right now there are things we both could say that we'd be better off not saying."

Casey was finding it hard to look at Olivia. The unhappy expression on her face, the tension in her body. Despite everything, Casey had the impulse to comfort her.

"Well, I'm not from Britain, I'm from Brooklyn. And in Brooklyn, we say what needs to be said and we hope that—if it comes from a good place but isn't said perfectly—people will cut us some slack."

Casey didn't respond. She was torn between wanting to walk away and wanting to hear what Olivia had to say.

"Look, Casey, I'm sorry, okay. I'm sorry for coming on to you in the bar. I'm sorry for being drunk enough to let myself kiss you and try to drag you into my room. I don't know why you'd believe me, but I'm honestly not the kind of person who does that kind of thing. I'm not." Olivia held her gaze steadily. "And I'm sorry that I made things awkward between us. I didn't want that. I was really enjoying getting to know you, spending time with you. And I'm sorry if I've ruined that. I really am."

Olivia sounded sincere. Casey should accept the apology and let them move past it all. But somehow, hearing her regret the kiss and blame the drink was hurtful. She realized she had hoped it had meant more to her than that.

"That's what you're sorry about? Well, okay, I'm sorry too. I'm sorry I didn't maintain the 'boundaries' that I should have when I let you kiss me, when I kissed you back. It was naive of me, for a lot of reasons." Casey took a breath. "But I'm more sorry you thought I was someone who would take advantage of you, of your celebrity, to make a quick buck. It shouldn't need me to say it again, but I would never—"

"Don't, Casey. You don't need to say it."

"It seems like I do. You know, if I'd wanted to make some money, I could have got a great photo of you and Billie cozying up in the bar. Or maybe one of you drunk, in your room, on your bed, begging me for it. I mean, I don't know the going rate, but maybe that one would have earned me enough to pay a couple of months' rent for my mom. Isn't that what you all think? Isn't that what you think?" Casey couldn't keep the anger from her voice. She was so disappointed in Olivia. And in herself for daring to imagine that Olivia was different, that she wouldn't judge her and find her wanting, like Hannah had.

"No one thinks that." Olivia stepped closer and put a hand on Casey's arm. "Not even Billie. Not really. It just suits her to try to blame you because she can see that we have..." Olivia faltered. "That we've become close, that we have something she wishes she could have."

Olivia shrugged, but the intense way she looked at Casey suggested the words were anything but casual and Casey couldn't look away. Seeing Olivia standing there in the fading twilight, Casey felt the pull of her attraction, felt her good intentions slipping away. She moved her arm, breaking the contact between them. She needed to get a grip on this.

"We have become close, probably a little too close in the circumstances. But let's not make a big deal of it. I'm single, you're single. You're entitled to get a little drunk and do something you regret. And I'm entitled to want a life that's simple enough not to see me fired for sleeping with a client, however much I might want to." She couldn't stop herself from admitting it. "And I shouldn't even blame you for suspecting me—"

"Casey," Olivia said with annoyance. Casey held up a hand, asking Olivia to let her finish.

"I just mean, in your position, I might suspect me too. I had motive, means, and opportunity. But whatever you might think about me and my life, I would never do that to you. I would never stoop that low." Something poked at her from the past, telling her she was wrong. She pushed the thought away. The situation with Olivia was completely different. "And tomorrow I'm going to ask David to find you another driver. It's easier on everyone, me included."

"Casey, please."

"What, Olivia? It's the best thing to do. You know that, really." Casey desperately needed Olivia to help her make this situation easier.

"I don't want you to do that. I really don't. And please believe me when I say that I don't think you would exploit me like that. It's not at all who I think you are, and that's not just because I don't think for a minute that you've heard of any of the entertainment websites that would be willing to pay cash for a photo of me. Though we both know you haven't." She tried for a smile, but she couldn't quite make it reach her eyes, and Casey couldn't help but be moved by it.

"But you not knowing those websites, not knowing Susie, and being completely unimpressed by me and this weird life I live, are things that I really appreciate about you." She lifted an eyebrow. "And since we're clearing the air, I should probably admit there are a lot of things I appreciate about you."

Casey felt her body react to the comment in precisely the way it shouldn't. She willed herself to just walk away, but the hope that she and Olivia could salvage something from the mess of the last twenty-four hours kept her rooted to the spot.

"Well, if we're being honest, I should apologize too. For letting things get out of hand, for kissing you back and then having second thoughts."

"You're sorry for having second thoughts?" Olivia sounded surprised.

"No." Casey stopped herself, testing the truthfulness of her denial. "Yes, in one way. But no in another. I just mean that you can't take all the blame for that. I was drunk too and I wanted to kiss you. There are a lot of things I appreciate about you too." Casey couldn't help but smile.

They looked at each other for a long beat.

"So we're going to spend the next week 'appreciating' each other, say good-bye and then become Instagram buddies?" Olivia spoke first. She kept her voice even, and Casey couldn't tell if she was as upset as she was. She was an actress after all.

"I guess so. Except..." Casey paused. "I don't do Instagram."

"Of course you don't."

That time, Casey caught something under the words. She didn't want Olivia to be upset, but she didn't like to think she was unaffected either.

"Shall we walk?"

"Okay."

They headed off slowly and after a few paces, got into step with each other. Casey felt Olivia's hand in the crook of her arm. The touch of her fingers against her skin was a surprise. She looked at Olivia. She was staring out across the river. Casey made herself relax. She could do this. She could manage her feelings, be friendly, and keep things simple.

They kept the river on their right and walked slowly along the path. The warehouses—long since converted into luxury apartments—loomed over them on the left.

"Things have gotten pretty intense between Lou and Liam." Casey chanced the remark, wanting them to talk about harmless things.

"They spent the afternoon undressed and in bed together. I imagine it's made them face up to a few things about how they're both feeling."

"It's just all so weird to me. All those people watching you make out with someone you have a thing for. It seems so exposing somehow. I can't imagine wanting people to watch me kiss my girlfriend. It was bad enough Hannah wanted to broadcast the rest of our life."

Olivia stopped walking.

"I don't want people to watch me kiss my girlfriend either. I'm private too. Believe it or not. I don't want people photographing me when I'm sleeping, or videoing me without my consent. Just because I'm an actress it doesn't mean I don't want privacy." Olivia sounded annoyed.

"I'm sorry."

"Stop apologizing." Olivia's tone was brusque.

"No, I was judgmental. I didn't mean to be."

They kept walking. They were closer to the bridge. It was lighting up the river barely fifty yards away. It looked golden in the yellow of the spotlights that lit it up across its length. The iconic structure was one that everyone recognized as belonging to London. Casey had forgotten just how beautiful it was.

"This might be a good spot for a photo." Casey stepped closer to the railing on the riverside. "And you can't see it because the bridge is so brightly lit, but behind it is the Tower of London, resting place of your favorite anointing spoon." Casey tried to lighten the mood.

"It's so beautiful." Olivia was by her side, and she pulled out her phone to take a few photos of the bridge. "I can't imagine you could get a better view of it than this. The light is perfect."

And Casey couldn't imagine a better person to share it with. The reality of the depth of her feelings for Olivia made her feel sad, not happy. In a few days, Olivia would move on to Paris and these feelings—of lust, of love, of possibility—would be completely redundant. And Casey would be back to the cold hard reality of dealing with her mom's mess and getting back to her life in Portland. In theory, Portland would make her close enough to Olivia to chance staying in touch, but even thinking that seemed too hopeful after today. Their lives were just too different, and if Hannah had taught her anything, it was that those differences never stopped being a problem.

Casey stepped away from the railing and put out her hand to take the phone. "Want me to take one? Your fans will love it."

Olivia looked at her and shook her head. Instead, she reached for Casey's hand and used it to pull her back to her side.

"I know how much you hate selfies." Olivia straightened her arm, with the phone out in front of them. "But I also know you can't say no, because you know as well as I do that we don't have a lot of time together, and I think we're going to be happy to have some memories of this trip. Something for us, not for Instagram."

Casey heard the catch in Olivia's voice. And couldn't help but be glad that she was finding this as hard as she was. She slipped an arm around Olivia's waist, pulling her closer. And when Olivia leaned her head against her cheek, Casey let herself relax for the first time that day. Olivia took a couple of photos while they posed and tried to smile like they meant it.

And when Olivia finally put her phone down, neither of them moved. They were standing together, their backs to the river, their hips touching, Casey's arm still looped around Olivia's waist.

"This is crazy."

"It is." Casey understood exactly what Olivia meant.

Olivia turned to her. They were inches apart. It would have been so easy for Casey to just kiss her. She wanted to. She knew now that Olivia would welcome it. But it wouldn't help. It wouldn't stop the clock, and it wouldn't do anything to make the differences between them feel less like a chasm.

"Shall we head back?" Casey spoke first.

"In a minute." Olivia slipped her hand into Casey's and held it tightly. "The quiet is nice. The darkness is nice. Being close to you is nice."

Without giving any warning, Olivia leaned into the space between them and kissed her. The kiss was much more tentative than the night before, but it still sparked something in her body and Casey couldn't help but respond to the feel of Olivia's lips on hers—soft, warm, and wanting. She pulled Olivia closer, feeling the press of her breasts against her own, deepening their kiss. She cupped Olivia's cheek as they kissed, her skin soft under Casey's fingertips. And when Olivia dipped her tongue between Casey's lips, Casey felt her arousal like an electric current running down her spine and landing between her legs. She opened her mouth, inviting Olivia to be bolder, her own tongue meeting Olivia's, their kisses hungry and desperate, until finally Olivia broke away, breathless, her eyes wide, her lips full and red.

"I'm sorry. I didn't mean to do that. It was kind of a Susie move." She looked up, as if gathering her thoughts. "I meant to do it, obviously. I just know it wasn't smart—in the circumstances."

"I guess it wasn't all that smart—in the circumstances." Casey turned them so that Olivia had her back to the railings. She had one arm on either side of her. And resisting the impulse to kiss her was impossible. She grazed her lips against Olivia's softly and slowly, her kisses gentle and then not so gentle. Her mouth claiming Olivia's hungrily. She dipped her head to feather kisses across the smooth skin of Olivia's neck, letting herself taste the skin with her tongue and then with her teeth. Olivia moaned at the contact, pushing herself harder against Casey, her kisses more urgent and wanting and her hands on Casey's ass. Her desire was intoxicating, and Casey found it hard to stop. But from somewhere, Casey registered the fact that she was supposed to be steering them into safer waters, not swimming in the deep end. She pulled her mouth away from Olivia's and pushed herself off the railings with a sigh.

"I'm sorry. I shouldn't, we said—" Casey was mad at herself for her lack of self-control.

"Maybe it's okay, maybe it matters somehow that we can't stop kissing each other."

Casey made herself stand a little straighter, made herself think a little straighter. The kissing didn't matter. What mattered was someone like Casey would always feel like an outsider in Olivia's world—the one who got accused, the one who didn't measure up and got cheated on. It wasn't self-pity; it was her experience. And suddenly everything about her feelings for Olivia seemed absurd.

"The kissing doesn't matter. You have your life and I have mine. And being thrown into a situation where we coexist for a couple of weeks, doesn't mean a thing. None of this matters, and if we stop now, no harm done, we can go our separate ways without any regrets." Casey felt ashamed of herself for the lie. But it was for the best. She needed to put some distance between Olivia and her feelings.

"You think that none of this matters?" Olivia sounded hurt, but Casey couldn't afford to care. She already felt embarrassed enough.

"When I suggested we go for a walk, it was so we could say exactly these things, so we could clear the air. We kissed. We might even want to keep kissing. But it doesn't matter. In less than a week, I'll be driving someone else around London and you'll be flirting with your new French driver."

Olivia looked at her intently before shaking her head. "I don't believe you think that."

Casey couldn't repeat the lie. Her heart was aching in her chest.

"Maybe we should head back." She turned away from Olivia, indicating the path they had just walked down. She tried to sound casual, willing her face not to give her away. She looked at her watch. "I forgot that I said I'd call Gina." Casey was no actress and it probably sounded as fake an excuse as it was.

Olivia seemed to get the message. She set off, walking next to Casey, but staying silent, as they walked back to the hotel.

In the lobby, Casey feigned a need to talk to Reception, not wanting an awkward elevator ride. After Olivia had gone, she went to the bar, ordered a whiskey, and downed it in one gulp. She pushed herself off the bar and took in a deep breath.

They had feelings for each other. They hadn't defined them, but they both knew they were there. But Casey was right. The feelings didn't matter. The feelings didn't get them anywhere.

They'd agreed to be friendly. Casey could do that. She was going to get a good night's sleep and trust herself enough to hope that tomorrow, when she saw Billie, she would be able to hold her tongue, keep her job, and see out the week until they all boarded that Eurostar train that was going to take them to Paris and out of her life.

CHAPTER SEVENTEEN

Olivia picked up her phone and typed out a text to Casey.
    Hey. Want to grab a drink? I'm downstairs.

She sighed before deleting the text without sending it, in the same way she'd done three times before. She knew Casey was upstairs. She'd seen her bring Louise and Liam back to the hotel half an hour ago. But Olivia hadn't been quick enough to intercept her, so now she'd stationed herself in the bar with a glass of wine and a script in front of her, hoping that if Casey did come down, she might catch her.

The strength of her need to see Casey surprised and slightly scared her. She had often wondered if she'd been so bruised by what Kristin had done to her that she wouldn't ever be able to trust again. But somehow Casey had her feeling not only that she might have found someone she could trust, but—she let herself admit it—someone she could love.

Except Casey had decided that whatever else was good about the two of them, there were too many obstacles to make taking a chance worthwhile. Olivia was having a hard time accepting it, and she missed Casey more than she had expected.

Her phone dinged. She looked down at it hopefully. It was Louise.

Where are you? Want to drink with me and hear me pine about Liam?

She didn't, but she was a good friend.

Sure. I'm downstairs in the bar.

Olivia forced herself to look back at the script. Susie was telling Phoebe to forget all about her, to stop pretending that they could ever have anything that would be worth Phoebe leaving her life of comfort and safety for. It was a good scene. It would have been better still if Susie didn't relent and then fuck Phoebe in the front seat of her car. It was very Susie, and she normally didn't care, but with all that was going on, the idea of working with Billie on the scene was disturbing. She read the lines over and over, willing them to sink in, not sure if the wine was helping or hindering.

"Hey, babe." Louise settled into the chair opposite. "Not exactly the best place to learn your lines." She pointed up at the speaker, now playing what sounded like Dua Lipa.

"Yeah, I know. I just wanted to get out of my room for a while."

Louise caught the waiter's attention and ordered a glass of wine.

"Well, that's not entirely true." Olivia felt a small stab of embarrassment. "I was kind of hoping Casey might pass by."

"You still haven't seen her?"

Olivia shook her head.

"Have you tried calling?"

"I'm not doing that. She obviously doesn't want me to."

"A text?"

"No, it's okay. I'm just doing the silent pining thing, and if it's meant to be, the universe will throw her into my path somehow. I'm just helping by watching the elevators, while totally pretending not to."

"Why not ask them to switch up the schedule? We'd be happy to have Tania." Louise gripped the edge of the table comically.

"I did think of that, but Casey driving me would also mean driving Billie. And I think that whole situation with Billie is part of what's freaked her out."

"She's a monster. I still can't quite believe she leaked those stories about you."

The waiter put Louise's wine on the table, and she took a sip and sighed.

"We don't know that for sure."

"We do. It's one of the things I wanted to tell you. Liam is so fucking awesome. He called up the journalist who ran the two stories, said he was Billie's manager and the payment hadn't come through. You should have seen him. I was falling off the chair with all the swooning I was doing. He was wearing his blue checked shirt and his glasses, and he's so talented at acting that he even started to look like someone who would totally be Billie's manager. A very sexy manager—"

"Lou." Olivia waved a hand in front of her face. "Is there a point to this story? Apart from to illustrate your raging thirst for Liam."

"Oh yeah, sorry. Anyway, this woman is so dumb that she just says. 'But we didn't agree to a payment. We were offered the stories for free,' and then she suggests he go and check with Billie, as there's obviously been a mix-up. I think she skipped the 'protect your sources' class in whatever sleaze journalism school she went to."

"Are you serious?" Olivia couldn't quite believe that Billie would want to hurt her like that.

"Yeah. Turns out Liam was right with his theory."

"But why?"

"You'd have to ask her. My theory—and Columbo agrees with me— is that she's just jealous. All that stuff she said about wanting to become the star of the show. She's not happy you get all the attention. And I'm guessing her offering herself on a plate to you so many times and you giving it the 'hell no,' hasn't helped. I imagine her ego is not used to people saying no."

Olivia's brain was scrambling to process what Louise was telling her. Billie was annoying, but Olivia had always thought she was harmless.

"That's crazy. Do you think I should be telling someone? To protect myself, I mean. What if she does it again and tomorrow's story is worse?"

"Up to you. But I'm pretty sure she'll deny it, so Liam would have to get involved as a witness. And then the studio will want to know why we didn't tell them before. It seems like a lot of trouble. Why not just talk to her? Tell her you know, tell her to back off. Threaten to tell the studio if there's any more stories. It might work."

"Knowing she's done this makes shooting scenes with her even more impossible. It's bad enough anyway, but now—" Olivia couldn't keep from panicking. "Fuck, Lou, she could get anyone to get a picture of me on set. I'm close to naked for half the scenes we're shooting together. I can't go through that again." She pressed her fingers to her temples, willing herself to calm down. What was it about her that attracted these kinds of people?

"She won't do that. She's got it in her head to blame Casey, and Casey isn't anywhere near the set." Louise put a hand over hers. "Talk to her. Warn her off. And remember that it's Susie naked on set, not you. Susie and Phoebe. Not Billie. It's just acting. Trust me, I've been telling myself this like a damn mantra every time I've been on set with Liam. The tension between us is off the charts, and shooting those kinds of scenes together is making it worse. It's so fucking confusing."

Olivia willed her brain to process what Louise was telling her. Billie had done this to hurt her, because of professional jealousy. It was absolutely insane. It felt like the last straw.

"You've got to say something to him."

Olivia made herself focus on Louise and on Liam and not on her panic about being exposed against her wishes yet again.

"I will. I'm building up to it. I think I kind of wanted him to go first, but there's no sign of it. All we're doing is sitting close and gazing at each other. Yesterday, we were holding hands without realizing it. And when we did, we both pulled away, horrified."

"Lou, come on. You know Liam. He's going to need you to make the first move. You're intimidating because he knows you're a lot more experienced than he is."

"Cheers, buddy." Louise laughed. "I'll take that the way I hope it was intended."

Olivia held up her hands. "You know what I mean."

"We have Friday night off. I was going to ask him to take me out to dinner or something. Get him a little drunk. And then try and make it obvious."

"Good idea. Take him to that restaurant Casey mentioned, the one that's on the riverside next to Tower Bridge. It's a very romantic setting."

Olivia felt herself flush at the memory of being there with Casey. They had shared a wonderful kiss, and then Casey had pulled back. Olivia had almost heard the shutters come down. She couldn't stop thinking that it was her fault—for suspecting Casey, for not managing Billie better, for having this life that no normal person like Casey would want.

"Hey, are you okay?" Louise's voice brought her back into the here and now.

"Yeah, sorry. I was just thinking about Casey." She had told Louise about the kisses, about what might well turn out to be their last conversation. "Is it crazy to feel this way after knowing someone for such a short time?"

"I don't think so. Love is weird. Sometimes you fall for a complete stranger and sometimes for one of your best friends. Who decides what's crazy and what's sane? I mean, I'd have told you that there was no way in a trillion years that little fitness fanatic and I would—"

Olivia let her thoughts drift away from what Louise was saying. She was running out of time. Casey had managed to avoid her for three whole days. Tonight was Thursday, and on Sunday morning they left for Paris. If Olivia didn't do something, she'd never know whether or not these feelings she had were enough to create something that was more than just a few holiday kisses. She'd never forgive herself.

❖

"Hey, babe." It was Gina.

"Hey. You just caught me. I was on my way out the door."

"Without your phone?"

"Sauna."

"I think I'd still take my phone. I'm not good at the whole switching off and sweating thing. Well, apart from the obvious." She laughed. "Do you have five minutes for me?"

"I do, of course." Casey sat back down on her bed.

"How's things? Feeling any better?"

Casey had told her all about Olivia—being kissed, accused, and kissed again—and Gina had been surprisingly gentle. No anger, no entreaties about getting laid. She just listened as Casey got it all off her chest—and made the odd comment about how hot Olivia was. And now she was calling again. Casey must have sounded more out of sorts than she'd realized when she laid out the whole sorry story.

"I'm good, I think. I'm staying busy."

"Busy is good."

"Yeah, and thanks for letting me have another week. I'm nearly there with my mom's stuff. We had a good meeting with her landlords yesterday and they seemed sympathetic. It's just that, although she's doing well, I feel like I should stick around a little longer till it gets properly sorted."

"Hey, no problem. I was calling to tell you I've figured out a way for you to work remotely. It means I can justify paying you when your vacation ends. And that means you won't have to resort to releasing any more of those compromising photos of Olivia."

"Real funny, Gina, thanks."

Gina was Gina. She couldn't take things seriously for long.

"How's she doing? I've been keeping an eye out for pictures of her looking haggard and heartbroken because of you, but nothing yet. Though I did see some stunning photos of her in a tight red dress in a glossy magazine, looking a whole lot like someone you wouldn't be able to cope with."

"Oh, I didn't realize it was out already." Casey made a mental note to look for the magazine, even as she told herself it wasn't anything she should care about. "I was there that day. She looked awesome. And for the record and only because you're making me say it, I could cope."

Gina laughed. "Atta girl."

"We haven't seen much of each other, but when I have seen her, she's been looking as beautiful as ever. So maybe she's not suffering at all. I've been mostly driving Louise and Liam. I think it's deliberate. She probably asked for things to be scheduled that way to make it less awkward."

It was what Casey needed and she should be thankful, but she wasn't. Not at all. She missed Olivia. More than she should.

"I don't know why you just didn't go there. I mean, I do, because you're you and you were stupid enough to catch feelings, but a holiday romance with Olivia Lang is a pretty amazing memory to come back to Portland with."

Casey had asked herself the same question. She and Olivia could have had a good time, made some nice memories, and said good-bye.

"She deserves more than that. I deserve more than that. I'm not you, Gina. Opening my heart up to Olivia would mean getting hurt when she walks out of my life in just the way we both know she's going to. Our lives are just too different. It's hard, but maybe it wasn't meant to be. What can I do?"

"Eat too much. Drink too much. Watch romcoms and cry. On the very rare occasions that I let myself fall for someone, and obviously that's usually someone unsuitable, that's where I end up."

"Well, I decided to sweat rather than eat. The gym, the sauna, running along the river. I occasionally let myself stop to stare moodily at the water. I'm a different kind of cliché."

"But it sounds like you're still suffering."

"Maybe a little."

"Okay, go and sweat some more. I love you. I wish you weren't quite so stubborn and risk averse, but I love you."

"Thanks…I think. I love you too."

Casey plugged her phone back into the charger and headed to the sauna. It was a little after four, and even with Gina's interruption she was hopeful that she'd have the place to herself.

Olivia had only managed to visit the sauna three times over the entire trip, so it was kind of ridiculous to have a favorite spot. But as she entered the room, she could see through the steam, a figure stretched out on the bench she'd been hoping to occupy. There was no one else in the sauna and there were plenty of other benches for her to choose from, but somehow she still felt disappointed.

As she settled herself on one of the other benches and her eyes adjusted to the steam, Olivia realized that the person occupying "her spot" was Casey—stretched out in her shorts and bra, with a towel laid out beneath her. Olivia felt a mixture of anxiety and hope. She hadn't mustered the courage to reach out to her, yet here she was, in the sauna where Olivia would no doubt have spent some of her time thinking about how much she was missing her.

"I hope you're just resting your eyes. I told you before that sleeping in the sauna is dangerous."

Casey slowly turned her head in Olivia's direction. A beat passed with them just looking at each other.

"I didn't know it was you. I was closing my eyes in the hope of avoiding having to make small talk. Yesterday I got stuck with a very talkative woman from one of the Dakotas. It wasn't good."

Olivia wasn't sure if Casey was telling her that she had no interest in talking to her, or if she was just being Casey.

"I'm sorry. I didn't mean to disturb your peace. I was hoping for a bit of quiet time myself." Olivia settled herself back onto the bench, leaning against the wall, not yet ready to lie down. Knowing that Casey being so close had already made relaxation impossible.

"I didn't mean you. I just meant I didn't want to talk to random strangers." Casey pushed herself up onto one elbow on the bench. It meant that Olivia had a very good view of the length of her body, the muscles coated in a film of sweat, curves where she wanted curves to be. She couldn't help but swallow. Casey in her sauna outfit looked even better than she remembered.

"I'm not sure if I qualify as a random stranger or not. I mean, we haven't exactly seen much of each other lately."

Casey bit her lip, obviously deciding whether to say something.

"It's true. I've seen a lot more of the lovebirds than you. I get the feeling that they got over their poker night awkwardness. They seem pretty cozy."

Olivia didn't want to be reminded of poker night. She swallowed down the embarrassment.

"I've hardly seen them. I've been in the studio with Billie most of the last two days, and last night I stayed in learning lines while they went to see a movie." Olivia felt Casey's eyes on her. The same intensity, but also the same feeling that she was holding herself back.

"And was it worth it? Did you remember your lines today?"

"Today wasn't hard. I said about three sentences. We shot a scene in a car—a car that had been cut in half so that the cameramen could get multiple close ups of me straddling Billie while she put her hands and mouth all over me. I don't normally care because it's acting. But this time—with Billie—after everything I know she's done and gotten away with—" She stopped herself. "I'm sorry. I don't know why I'm telling you all this. But I had an urge to scream and run away. And then when I got back here, I had this real need to steam it all away."

"So it was Billie?"

"Seems so. She'll deny it of course. And the studio won't do anything. She has them wrapped around her little finger. They sent a threatening letter to the website for me. And there's been no more photos, so maybe she's had enough fun."

"I'm sure Billie would say it's because I haven't been around you to take any—"

"Don't, Casey." Olivia interrupted. "Please don't." She didn't want to be reminded of it. She felt ashamed for doubting Casey. "No one thinks that."

It wasn't exactly true. Billie had almost persuaded the studio to ask for a replacement driver. Olivia had been forced to step in and demand that Casey be allowed to stay.

"How's your mom?" Olivia wanted to change the subject.

"She's doing well. She keeps asking me to bring you round for dinner. She's been baking bread—not always successfully judging by some of the photos—but I think she wanted to show you she was making good use of the bread maker."

Olivia wasn't sure if there was an invitation there or if it was just conversation. She decided to play it safe.

"So I guess that means you haven't told her yet?"

"That you never met Gerard Butler? Why would I burst that balloon?"

"Funny. You know what I mean. That I'm not really your girlfriend."

"I was waiting to see. I had hopes of wearing you down." Casey looked away, seeming awkward. "I'm sorry. It was a joke and not a very funny one I know. I joke when I'm nervous."

"I make you nervous?"

"Well, you are Olivia Lang. And you are almost naked and sitting three yards away."

This time Casey held her gaze and Olivia felt like maybe she was flirting. It was so hard to tell. The last time they'd seen each other, they had kissed and Olivia had dared to hope the kisses meant as much to Casey as they had to her. But Casey had pulled back and then avoided her and Olivia didn't know where they stood now. And her heart hurt because of it. It was something that people said, but she had never experienced. But thinking about Casey, about how good they might have been together if the circumstances were different, gave her an actual ache in her chest where her heart was.

"Well, since that means I'm technically still your girlfriend, don't you think you should stop avoiding me and take me out somewhere?" It took courage for Olivia to say it, but they didn't have time to mess around. In three days' time, she was leaving for Paris and she might never see Casey again.

"You want to go out with me?" Casey frowned and Olivia couldn't help but find the furrowing of her brow cute. There was too much about Casey that she found cute. Though, given the insistent throbbing between her legs, maybe cute wasn't really the right word.

"I do. If that's okay. If you're free, if you want to." Olivia swallowed. She needed to stop talking.

Casey sat up, swinging her long legs off the bench and shuffling a little closer. Now Olivia could see her in all her glory. The damp had caused her hair to stick to her forehead and temples in unexpected short curls. It was sexy and Olivia had to stop herself from reaching out to run her fingers through it.

"Okay." Casey's expression was serious. "Where would you like to go?"

"I honestly don't care. It would just be great to spend some time with you." Olivia felt her heart lift. Casey wanted to see her. It was impossible not to smile. "I've missed you."

Even in the low light of the sauna, Olivia saw Casey react. Her eyes darkened and she seemed to sit a little straighter. She couldn't tell if she'd said the right thing or the wrong thing.

"When could you be free tomorrow? How early?"

Olivia was pretty sure that they only had a half day of filming left. By the time Tania got them back to the hotel and she had a long shower to scrub all trace of Billie from her skin, it would be around four.

"Is four too early?"

A slow smile spread across Casey's face. It was a smile that had Olivia feeling all sorts of feelings. She couldn't pretend this didn't mean as much as it obviously meant to her. This thing with Casey was not casual.

"That's perfect. I have an early finish too and the place I'm thinking about needs us to have a bit more time."

"Where are we going?"

"I'm not telling you. You'll just have to trust me."

The choice of words didn't seem deliberate, but Casey's gaze was intense.

"Meet me in the lobby at four." Casey picked up her towel. "And bring a warm jacket. I'm not bringing my mom. It's just you and me, sorry." The steam had made her voice low and wonderfully husky. "And in case you were wondering, I've missed you too." The way she looked at Olivia as she said the words left even Olivia in no doubt that she meant them to have exactly the effect they were having. Olivia felt her blood heat and it had absolutely nothing to do with the sauna.

Olivia cleared her throat. "I'll look forward to it."

Casey nodded, pulled open the door, and left. The momentary cold draft was a welcome distraction. Olivia moved her towel to where Casey had been lying, lay back on the bench, and smiled. It was the first real smile she'd managed in days. Casey was taking her out on a date. She might have suggested it, but Casey had willingly agreed.

Olivia closed her eyes and let herself remember the taste of Casey's lips. The memory was bumped to one side by the recollection of just how delectable Casey had looked stretched out in front of her three minutes ago. She was going to enjoy this sauna more than she had imagined.

Chapter Eighteen

Given how hard she was trying, Casey wondered if she would be able to pull off the look of nonchalance she was aiming for. Her body language was supposed to be saying that she could take or leave this date, that she hadn't even noticed that Olivia was now twenty minutes late. But she was pretty sure her face was giving away all of her feelings. Her desperate desire to spend some time with Olivia, her worry that she might have had second thoughts, and her anxiety that even if she got today absolutely right, she was going to lose Olivia anyway.

Casey had chosen an armchair with a clear view of the elevators, and her glance reflex was hard at work. Every time a door opened, she looked, and every time it wasn't Olivia, the feeling in her chest got heavier.

Her phone beeped and she fished it out of her pocket. It was Gina. She put it away without responding. As she looked up, the middle elevator door opened and Olivia stepped out. Casey didn't even pretend not to look at her. She looked stunning. She was wearing a pretty floral shirt over the Capri pants she'd worn that first day, that disastrously bittersweet day of sightseeing they'd shared.

Olivia offered up an apologetic wave and hurried in her direction. Casey took a breath, got up, and waved back. Olivia reached her in a moment.

"I am so sorry I'm late," Olivia said softly.

Olivia looked to the ceiling momentarily, as if to compose herself and then gazed intently at Casey. Her hazel eyes showing concern.

"They insisted on a reshoot. There was nothing I could do. And I thought I'd get ready quicker than I did. I couldn't find anything that I wanted to wear, and," she took in a breath, "I am so happy you waited. I had this fear that you wouldn't."

Casey had the urge to reach out and touch her, to gently run her thumb along Olivia's furrowed brow, to kiss those worried lips and tell her it was all okay. But of course she didn't move. She was going to let herself have this time with Olivia. She'd decided that she'd never forgive herself if she let Olivia just leave, but that didn't mean she was going to lay herself on the line.

"At least you remembered your jacket." Casey kept her tone light.

In a few days, when Olivia had gone, Casey would have plenty of time to regret her timidity. But now was the time for lightening the mood, for pretending none of it mattered as much as it did, and luckily, Casey was in the advanced class as far as this was concerned.

"There's a cab waiting outside, if you're ready."

"We're not walking?" Olivia lifted an eyebrow.

"It's a bit far—even for me."

"You're still not going to tell me where we're going?"

"I'm still not going to tell you where we're going."

Olivia smiled at her and then reached out to put both hands on Casey's arms, turning her in the direction of the exit. "Come on then. I'm impatient when it comes to surprises."

As the train rumbled along the tracks, Olivia watched the open green fields of Sussex roll by. The view out the window was what she had always imagined England looked like. There were sheep dotting the fields and fluffy white clouds that contrasted beautifully with the blue sky. Olivia was beyond happy that they were leaving London. She had always wanted to go to Brighton, and Casey choosing it as a destination for their surprise "date" was a sign of something good.

In the sauna, Olivia had almost suggested they go to the little theater they passed days before. The play was one she liked and she would have been happy to sit next to Casey in the dark, maybe have a glass of wine at the intermission. But this was better. Doing this meant they could see each other, talk to each other. She wanted them to make the most of every remaining minute they had together. And if that was at an English seaside town, with the fish and chips and hot donuts Casey had promised her were absolutely mandatory, then that was even better.

What she mainly wanted was for them to keep talking, to keep getting to know each other, and—who was she kidding—to kiss on the beach as the sun went down. She'd spent the last ten minutes listening to Casey tell her about Brighton's history, and it had been fascinating. But she couldn't stop staring at Casey's mouth as she talked. And sometimes, if she was being honest, her thoughts had not been about English monarchs and health spas.

"After London, it's got England's biggest LGBTQ population. We offer a weekend tour here called Piers and Queers. It was a lot of fun to put together the itinerary for Gina. We won't have time to see much of it, but I'll try and pick out a couple of highlights near the center of town." Casey smiled at her, and Olivia felt a little skip in her heart.

"I feel privileged to have an actual tour guide for a date." Olivia regretted the word as soon as she said it. Neither of them had called it a date. Even though she'd spent all day thinking about it that way.

Casey looked at her with a serious expression, and Olivia waited to be corrected, to have her fantasy about this being something special brought crashing down. Casey probably took people to Brighton all the time. She certainly sounded pretty practiced talking about it.

"I'm offended." Casey frowned. "Last week, I was tour guide, driver, girlfriend, and bodyguard. Now I've been relegated to just tour guide. I knew I should have driven. You're only impressed by me when I'm driving, fighting off unwanted admirers," she hesitated, raising her eyebrows, "and wearing my uniform."

Olivia silently let out the breath she'd been holding. Casey was teasing. And when she bent to lean her head a little closer, Olivia took in another breath.

"I feel privileged to be taking you on a date. And I'll apologize in advance if I'm not very good at it. It's been a while. I mean, I even forgot to tell you how great you look. And you do. Look wonderful I mean." Casey bit her lower lip. Olivia had come to understand it was something she did when she was nervous. It was very sexy.

"I don't really date either." Something about the two of them sitting so close, their hips and thighs touching—the intimacy forced by the narrow train seats—made Olivia want to tell Casey things about herself. She spoke quietly, not wanting the others in the packed train car to hear.

"Why not?" Casey's voice was low and her gaze earnest.

"Just, y'know, the show. It makes things unreal. Look at Kristin. Hell, look at Billie. Acting like she likes me and then leaking stories to cause me trouble. It's hard to trust people, to trust their intentions." She tilted her head toward Casey, speaking in almost a whisper. "It's not that I don't meet women. I do—all the time. Sometimes I even meet women I like. It's just that the job and Susie always get in the way."

They pulled into a station. They both looked out the window to see which one it was.

"I met a woman on set a few months ago. She was one of the showrunners. She reminds me of you." She held Casey's gaze for a beat and then looked down at her hands. "She seemed so unfazed about working on the show. Plainspoken, treated everyone the same. We'd spent a bit of time talking. She seemed like she had a great approach to life and I decided I liked her. I was trying to work up the courage to ask her for a drink." Olivia chanced another look at Casey, finding nothing but interest. "Anyway, the day I decided to do it was the day I heard her boasting in the cafeteria to one of the makeup girls about how she was being chatted up by 'Susie' and couldn't wait to tell all her friends." Olivia sat back in her chair, annoyed by the memory even now. "Even she couldn't tell me apart from Susie and she worked on the show."

"That must be tough."

"There are so many worse problems to have—I know that—but sometimes I think that if I keep going like this, I'll lose my own sense of who I am, of what I'm worth. And too much will pass me by."

"Could you stop?" Casey's eyes held Olivia. The intensity of her gaze made Olivia feel seen in a way she never had. It was unsettling, but also wonderful. "Could you quit and do something else? Something that makes you feel less lost." Casey moved her hands as she spoke, and Olivia was mesmerized by them. The long fingers, the strong arms. Her pulse quickened.

"I signed a contract for five seasons. They can fire me, but I can't quit—not without a very good reason." She shook her head. "And it's been good for me, I should be more grateful."

"But you hate it."

"Not all of it. I hate the attention, the backbiting, the endless PR. I hadn't expected that to be so tough. But I love the acting part. I always did." Olivia tested the truth of it in her mind and realized that Billie was ruining even that for her. The idea of spending the next six months working alongside Billie on the show made her feel miserable.

"But the not-acting part of your job seems to be something you spend a lot of time doing."

"It is. But I just know there are a million things I could be doing that are much worse. It's a great show, a great part, and even with Billie doing her best to ruin it for me, I should still be grateful."

"I remember being grateful that someone as smart and successful as Hannah was willing to love me. I'm pretty sure I even told myself I could do a lot worse. And for a long time I let myself mistake that feeling of gratitude for happiness." Casey took her hand. "Don't sell yourself short. It never ends well. And I think happiness is more than feeling grateful."

Casey's words and the feel of her touch made things shift a little. Olivia knew she was right, knew she needed to find the courage to take more of what she needed for herself.

"Did you ever come here with Hannah?"

Casey looked surprised by the question. Olivia was too.

"Yes." Casey paused. "Her family live close by and we came to see them sometimes. We had some nice times here."

Olivia wanted Casey to be honest, but it wasn't the answer she wanted. She didn't want Casey to be thinking about Hannah while they were here. She thought that she wasn't curious about Hannah, but of course she was. Casey had had a serious relationship with her, been damaged by it enough to move to another country, but they had never talked about it.

"You guys had fish and chips and hot donuts on the pier?"

"God no, never that. She wouldn't eat fried food. She was a health fanatic. She promoted health and beauty products on her channel. She took it very seriously. I guess world domination requires a certain level of commitment. She couldn't pimp vitamins and then be seen eating fatty fried foods. Bad for the brand."

"So that's why she'd never had one of Estelle's pies."

"Not just that."

Casey seemed to hesitate, and Olivia wondered if she was looking for a way to deflect her questions.

"I only went to the café when I was working, and since Hannah didn't ever approve of me 'wasting my life' doing youth work, she never came to my office. It wasn't just that it was youth work—though she did think those kids, those families, were beyond helping—I think she resented the energy, the focus I gave it. She wanted me to put that energy into making videos with her for her channel, to turn us into this celebrity YouTube couple who catalogued every aspect of their lives. She told me it would be lucrative for us both, that I wouldn't have to work. But I wanted to. I loved my job more than anything. She never understood that."

Casey rolled her shoulders. Olivia could see the tension in her body, feel it in the grip of her hand. Olivia stroked the hand with her thumb. She was happy that Casey was finally trusting her enough to talk about Hannah.

"I can't imagine you making lifestyle videos," Olivia said gently.

"I did try in the beginning. I did a couple of videos with her. But I was hopeless. And I was never comfortable with the way that she wanted to share everything about our life. I mean, it was up to Hannah what she told people about herself, but I didn't like the intrusion into our life together. And when the sponsorships started to happen, I absolutely didn't want to pretend to like or use the things she'd been sent to promote. It just seemed so dishonest. I was bad-tempered and judgmental about it. But I shouldn't have been, because a lot of people do it and it's probably what cost me Hannah. She got sick of me not playing my part, not wanting the things she wanted, so after a while, she replaced me with someone more willing, someone who loved making the videos with her, someone who could fake all the enthusiasm I couldn't. She just forgot to tell me that she wasn't just replacing me on screen, she was replacing me full stop."

Casey sat up straighter, releasing Olivia's hand to run her hands through her hair anxiously. Olivia could see she was fighting not to get upset.

"It's okay."

"Yeah. It is. It was a long time ago, but it's still hard to stomach. Of course, now I understand that us splitting was better for both of us." Casey turned to her. "It's just that sometimes I still feel humiliated by it. That she had the nerve to choose one of our friends to cheat with, that it went on for weeks without me knowing, and that I had been naive enough to believe they were just making videos together. I felt like such an idiot when I found out. And while I was busy grieving, she was busy rewriting the story of what had happened, not wanting to get blamed for the cheating. She told all our friends I was impossible to live with, that I'd driven her to seek comfort with Zoey because of my 'unreasonable behavior.'"

Casey stopped speaking, seeming as if she was remembering something painful.

"I didn't handle myself well when I found out about it, that's true. I was angry and I was vengeful, but everything I did came after I found out about Hannah and Zoey. Not before, like she claimed. And the worst of it was that I felt like the only way I could defend myself—and let our friends know that Hannah was lying—was to tell them all the truth about how long she'd been cheating on me. And that was too embarrassing to admit to. So I let her tell her stories, have our friends, and I just left."

Casey couldn't meet Olivia's eyes. She was finding the back of her hand fascinating.

"That's awful, Casey. I'm sorry." Olivia didn't know what else to say.

"Don't be. It's all water under the pier." Casey tried to joke, but Olivia could see from the set of her jaw that talking about it was difficult. "I figure that coming here again is a good way of reminding myself that old memories are exactly that—old. And coming here with you is a chance to create some new, much better memories to replace the old ones." Casey held her gaze, taking her hand again.

Coming from anyone else, that would have sounded far too smooth, but from Casey it just sounded heartfelt. And Olivia couldn't help feeling happy at the idea that they were making memories. Two people bruised by love and thrown together in the most unlikely of circumstances. She just had to make sure that the memories weren't all she was left with when she departed for Paris.

"It's nothing special. I mean, compared to the beautiful beaches you have in California, but I like it. And at night, it's kind of magical." Casey felt stupid for expecting Olivia to be impressed by the narrow stony beach, the quaint beachside cafés, and the old piers and bandstands. To her, Brighton was a romantic place, full of history and life. And it was a place she'd sought out whenever London was too much. But to Olivia it probably just seemed a little shabby.

"Hey." Olivia said the word like a gentle admonishment. "Don't be like that. It's wonderful." She nudged Casey with her knee. "The Royal Pavilion was amazing, the fish and chips were awesome, and not just because we didn't get attacked by seagulls, like you said we would. And right now, it's special because we're here." Olivia offered her a sweet smile, and Casey wondered if she had any idea the effect those words had on her.

They were sitting side by side on the beach, looking out at the dark silhouette of the old, ruined West Pier. The waves were breaking on the stones just a few meters away, and the sun was setting. Casey couldn't have imagined a better way to end the evening.

They had rushed around the Royal Pavilion just before it closed, then hit the amusement arcades on Palace Pier. And the fact that Olivia had a small stuffed dolphin sticking out of her bag—won by Casey on the Dolphin Derby—made her prouder than it should.

But all evening—all week actually—she'd felt the clock ticking, and she knew she needed to say something. Olivia was going to leave in a couple of days, and if Casey was the only one feeling the depth of these feelings, she needed to know, so she could say a nice good-bye and go back to being the person she was before she came back to London, before she fell for Olivia.

"This trip has been crazy." Olivia broke the silence first.

"They have worked you guys pretty hard."

"That wasn't what I meant."

"What did you mean?" Casey pulled her knees up next to her chest and rested her head on them.

"I meant," Olivia mirrored Casey's position, leaning her cheek on her knee, "that I didn't expect to come to London and meet someone who would introduce me to steak pudding, save me from being harassed, stop me from making a fool of myself when I was drunk, kiss me in the shadow of Tower Bridge, and encourage me to quit my hugely popular TV show because it's not making me happy. That kind of crazy. And I'm pretty sure I'd never have predicted that the last Friday night of my trip would be spent wandering along a Victorian pier, eating fish and chips with you by my side." Olivia gazed at her and the look in her eyes made Casey feel captured and ridiculously aroused.

"That does sound kind of crazy," Casey said. "But my trip to London has been even more insane. I met this actress who I thought was going to be a real pain in the ass. Turns out that as well as being drop-dead gorgeous, she's funny, smart, and easy to talk to. My mom—who hated every one of my actual girlfriends—has fallen in love with her. And insanely, this very same actress seems completely unaware of how wonderful she is."

Casey had never been bold, never good at taking what she wanted, but right now she wanted to lean over and kiss Olivia before it was too late and she regretted not doing it for the rest of her life.

"Thank you." Olivia responded so quietly that Casey almost missed it.

They sat silently for a few moments, just looking at each other. And Casey felt like this was her chance. To do something, to say something that told Olivia how she felt. She reached across and took Olivia's hand, holding it as if it was something precious. Olivia covered it with her own and gently stroked it with her thumb. Casey felt the muscles low down in her stomach tighten at her touch.

"I'm glad you invited me. And I'm happy—really happy—that, in amongst all the madness of this trip, we got the chance to get to know each other." Olivia smiled, but Casey could see something behind the smile. She watched Olivia take in a breath and let it out again.

"And I like you, Casey. A lot. And maybe it's a little much to say that because we've known each other such a short time, but if I'm honest, I don't often feel this way, and if I don't let you know that I've wanted you to kiss me for every minute of the last three hours, I'm going to kick myself all the way back to London."

Casey wanted to say something to reassure Olivia that it wasn't crazy, that she felt absolutely the same way, but of course, words failed her. All she could think about was the idea of kissing Olivia and the fact that Olivia wanted her to.

She leaned closer, tentatively brushing her lips against Olivia's. It was the softest of kisses, but it was electrifying. She kissed Olivia again, less gently, and Olivia responded. Casey pulled Olivia to her, kissing her again, even harder, the softness, the taste of her lips, causing Casey to ache with desire. She deepened the kiss and Olivia moaned softly, reaching her own hand up into Casey's hair, kissing her back with just as much wanting. Casey's whole body responded and when Olivia parted her lips, murmuring her name into their kiss, Casey dipped her tongue inside, needing to taste her. The warm wetness of Olivia's mouth, the feel of their tongues touching, made Casey feel like she was on fire.

Casey turned her body and pulled Olivia between her legs. She wanted her closer, wanted their bodies to be in contact, not just their mouths. She kissed Olivia hungrily, without holding back, using the hand on her back to press their bodies together. They kissed like people who had wanted to kiss for a long time, their lips crushing against each other, their hands in each other's hair, the kisses making them breathless. And when Casey felt Olivia's tongue inside her own mouth, she opened herself up to it, glorying in the feel and the taste of her. She was already wet, already wanting more.

Casey gently lowered Olivia to the ground, needing to feel her beneath her. She grazed her lips with soft kisses, taking care not to press her too hard into the stones. But when Olivia reached up for her, clasping both her hands around her neck and pulling her down into a passionate kiss, Casey let herself do what they both wanted. She kissed Olivia hard, parting her lips and tasting her again. Then she moved her mouth from Olivia's lips to her neck, trailing kisses from below her ear to her collarbone and back again before biting down softly on the soft skin of her neck. Olivia moaned beneath her, letting out a soft curse and digging her nails into Casey's back, pulling her even closer. Casey kissed her and grazed her hands across Olivia's breasts, feeling Olivia arch her body toward the touch. Casey kissed her again with all the passion she was feeling, her body hot, the throbbing between her legs almost unbearable—both of them breathless and wanting.

Olivia shifted beneath her and Casey broke their kiss.

"Did I hurt you?"

"No, don't stop," Olivia said without taking her eyes off Casey. "I'm enjoying having you on top of me." Her voice sounded thick with arousal, and Casey couldn't help but dip her head back down to press her lips to Olivia's. Olivia grabbed at Casey's jacket, pulling her closer. She kissed Casey hard, her tongue again inside her mouth, her hands now inside Casey's shirt, and Casey knew that she was almost past the point of no return.

"Olivia, wait." The words came out low and hoarse. She pulled herself away and up into a seated position. Her body still pulsing with her arousal. She didn't want to stop. She wanted them to keep kissing, to do whatever the stones would allow them to do. But they had to. They were both a little too old to be fucking on the beach.

"What time do you start work in the morning?"

Olivia blinked at her, obviously not expecting the abrupt change of conversation.

"I have to be on that Pride parade float thing at noon. Why?"

Olivia leaned up and kissed her, pulling Casey down on top of her again. Her mouth was impossible to resist and Casey lost herself again in the feel of Olivia's soft lips, in the press of Olivia's breasts against hers. She made herself stop, rolling off Olivia and onto her side.

"We're going to get arrested if we carry on. And it's getting late, so we either have to stop and get the train home—" Casey faltered. She saw the look of disappointment in Olivia's eyes and felt encouraged. She was pretty sure Olivia wanted this as much as she did. "Or we could see if any of the hotels," she pointed to the promenade lit up fifty yards behind them, "could put us up for the night."

Casey hadn't ever been good at this kind of thing. But her feelings for Olivia made her brave. "I would really like us to carry this on." She leaned across and placed a soft kiss on Olivia's lips. "Somewhere without stones." She kissed her again, harder this time. "And with a bed."

"Oh God, I would like that too." Olivia ran her hands down Casey's back before moving them inside her jacket, inside her shirt, grazing her fingertips against the skin of her back. "But only if you promise me we're going to pick up exactly where we left off."

Casey couldn't have said no even if she'd wanted to. And she didn't want to. The idea of a bed, of Olivia underneath her on a bed, with Olivia looking at her just like she was looking at her right then, was the best idea she'd ever had.

Casey was standing with her back against the door, looking at the room. It was fancy by Brighton standards, but nowhere near as fancy as their London hotel. But she didn't care and she hoped Olivia felt the same. It had everything they needed—a large bed, a twenty-four-hour laundry service, and a balcony with a sea view. A balcony onto which Olivia had now disappeared. There was probably a lot to like about the room, but Casey couldn't see past the bed, and she desperately wanted Olivia to save the sea view for the morning.

They had headed into the nearest of the large hotels on the promenade, walking hand in hand, in a way that felt as natural as if they'd been doing it for years. At the crossing, waiting for the lights to stop the flow of traffic so they could cross, Olivia leaned over and kissed Casey. Seeming not to care who could see them. It wasn't a chaste kiss. She tangled her fingers possessively in Casey's hair and pushed her tongue inside Casey's mouth, making her knees go weak with desire at just about the same time as the lights went green. As they crossed the road, Olivia gave her a sweet shy smile, a smile that suggested she had no idea just how damn sexy she was.

"It's got an amazing view." Olivia stepped back into the room, leaving the balcony door open. "It's very romantic." She smiled but seemed a little less confident than she had been when they were outside.

"I wanted it to be romantic. I wanted us…" Casey had so much she wanted to say to Olivia about how she was feeling, but the words wouldn't come. She took a breath and decided it didn't matter that Olivia made her tongue-tied. She could show Olivia how much she wanted her with her actions, not her words.

"Come here." Casey was still standing with her back to the door.

Olivia held her gaze, while slowly moving toward her, and her beauty, the sound of her breathing, the look in her eyes, made Casey want her even more.

"You are so beautiful." Casey tried to damp down her desire so she could speak. "And so incredibly sexy." She reached out for Olivia as she got closer. "And I've spent every single minute since we got up off those stones, imagining myself undressing you."

"Oh, Casey." Olivia's eyes widened as she said her name, in a way that was part moan and part plea. The sound of it was intoxicating. Casey took her by the hands and turned them so that Olivia had her back against the door. She slipped her hands inside Olivia's jacket to lift it from her shoulders, allowing it to fall to the floor behind her.

Casey bent to touch her lips to Olivia's, and this time, there was none of the hesitancy of earlier. They kissed hungrily, their lips crushed together, Olivia's back against the door and their bodies pressed against each other. Casey darted her tongue inside Olivia's mouth, their tongues touching in a way that she already knew drove Olivia wild. Olivia pushed herself even harder against Casey—her kisses deep and searching, her hands grabbing at Casey's ass.

Casey broke off from kissing Olivia to slowly unbutton her shirt, making her fingers go faster when the shirt was open enough to reveal Olivia's bra. It was lacy, low-cut, and exactly the same blood red as the dress she had worn all those days before. Casey swallowed, her mouth dry. Olivia's breasts filled the bra perfectly, and Casey badly wanted to taste them. She let the shirt drop to the floor on top of the jacket.

She dipped her head to kiss Olivia's neck, to trail kisses along the newly exposed skin of her shoulders before biting down gently on the soft smooth skin just above Olivia's collarbone. Olivia took in a breath, and Casey worried she had been too rough. But the feel of Olivia's hands roughly pulling Casey's shirt from out of her jeans, the fingertips trailing across Casey's skin—caressing her back, her stomach, and her breasts— said different. Casey looked down and watched Olivia fumble with the buttons of her own shirt until it was open. She reached behind Olivia as they kissed, moving her lips down to kiss the skin between her breasts as she unclasped Olivia's bra and tossed it to the floor. She stood back to look at Olivia.

"I never let myself imagine you would be this beautiful," Casey said, brushing the back of her hand across Olivia's shoulders, across her breasts, feeling Olivia's intake of breath as her eyes closed. And Casey gloried in the heated look in Olivia's eyes when she opened them again and leaned in to kiss her possessively.

"Well, you look and feel every bit as good as I knew you would. I spent an insane amount of time trying to push that image of you stretched out in the sauna out of my mind." As Olivia spoke, she moved her hands inside Casey's shirt, playing with the edge of Casey's bra with her fingers, grazing Casey's breasts with her palms,. Casey felt the throbbing between her legs, already knowing how wet she was.

She stopped Olivia with a kiss before running her hands across Olivia's breasts once more. Olivia's eyes darkened with desire. Casey reached down to unzip Olivia's pants, but Olivia got there first, sliding them off her hips and adding them to the pile of clothes. The sight of Olivia in just her panties was more than Casey could bear. She took off her shirt and threw it on the floor before kissing Olivia hard, her arm around her waist, steering them toward the bed, every fiber of her body wanting Olivia underneath her.

Casey lay Olivia down onto the bed before unbuttoning and kicking off her own jeans. As she allowed herself a moment to take in the sight of her, Olivia reached up and pulled Casey onto her, opening her legs so that Casey could slide her thigh between them.

Casey kissed her gently and then less gently, trailing her lips along Olivia's neck and shoulders, Olivia's moaning telling her that she was doing the right thing. Casey drifted lower with her kisses until her mouth closed over one of Olivia's nipples. She sucked it gently, flicking her tongue across the tip. Olivia writhed in pleasure beneath her, her center grinding against Casey's thigh.

Casey continued to taste Olivia's breasts, moving her mouth from one nipple to the other, Olivia's soft whimpers telling her she was doing the right thing. When Casey teased her fingers along the edge of Olivia's panties, Olivia grabbed Casey's hand and pushed it inside, between her legs.

"Please, Casey." Olivia pulled Casey into a kiss at the same time she pulled her own panties down as far as she could reach, leaving Casey in no doubt what she wanted. She pushed them past Olivia's knees and shifted position so Olivia could kick them off.

The sight of Olivia naked beneath her, the feel of her thigh already wet with Olivia's arousal and the wanting look on Olivia's face, made Casey's desire to fuck her even more desperate. She stroked Olivia in long sweeping movements, gliding her fingers through the wetness. On each upward stroke, she gently brushed Olivia's clitoris with her fingertip, the touches making Olivia moan loudly with pleasure.

She kissed Olivia hard, her tongue inside her mouth, squeezing Olivia's breast with her free hand, and Olivia lifted her hips off the bed, pushing herself against Casey's fingers, seeming to want exactly what Casey did.

"I want to fuck you." Casey wanted—needed—to be inside Olivia.

"Please." Olivia said the word like a growl, and Casey didn't hesitate. She pushed her fingers gently inside Olivia and then, as Olivia opened herself up farther, buried them deeper, and began the gentle, insistent thrusting that had Olivia gasping her name and arching her back, wanting just as much as Casey could give her.

With her other hand, Casey was still caressing Olivia's breast, tweaking her nipple, and when she dipped her head to taste it again, Olivia let out a soft elongated curse, grabbing for Casey wildly. Scratching her back, touching her breasts, then pulling Casey tightly to her in a rocking embrace, the movement matching Casey's thrusts inside her. Casey could feel Olivia losing control, her breathing becoming more ragged, her cursing getting louder. She increased the speed and intensity of her fucking, brushing her thumb across Olivia's clitoris with every thrust. The panting and grinding from Olivia telling her that she was close.

"Don't stop…don't stop that, Casey. Please. I'm coming. Oh fuck." The words came out with difficulty, every one swallowed as soon as it was said. Then Olivia wrapped her arms around Casey and came, crying out noisily, her whole body shuddering as the orgasm hit.

Casey was so close to coming herself that one touch from Olivia would have sent her over the edge into her own climax. But she didn't care about that. Olivia clinging on to her, silently allowing the waves to wash over her, was wondrous and something that Casey wanted to simply drink in. As she felt Olivia's shudders subside, felt Olivia's muscles finally relax their grip on her fingers, Casey withdrew them.

Olivia nestled in her arms, murmuring her name, and Casey felt like every cell in her body was vibrating. She was aroused, she was overwhelmed, and she was shocked to realize that all she could imagine was a future in which they were together and Olivia always made her feel this way.

"That was amazing." Olivia took Casey's hand and ran it along her thigh. "Goose bumps." She looked up at Casey and the shy way she did this, coupled with the way she bit her lower lip, gave Casey goose bumps all of her own.

"You are amazing." Casey tilted her head down to kiss Olivia softly. She felt completely alive.

"I want to say things, complimentary things, thankful things, but I don't have the words. I'm not sure if I ever have the words, or if it's a symptom of what you just did to me that my brain is so swirly, but..." Olivia pushed herself up on one elbow so she was face-to-face with Casey. "I'm pretty sure of one thing right now, and that's how much I want to taste you."

Casey felt the power of the words—the words Olivia claimed not to have—land like a jolt between her legs. She was already wet, already throbbing with her desire. The pleading look Olivia gave her, her eyes heavy, her lips full and red was entrancing and all she could do was nod.

Olivia pushed Casey onto her back before kissing her possessively, at first slow and gentle and then hard and demanding, her tongue in Casey's mouth. She reached around to remove her bra before tracing her fingers down Casey's chest and across her breasts. Casey couldn't stop herself from shivering under the touch. Olivia dipped her head to close her mouth over one nipple and then the other, caressing them with her tongue, sucking them greedily. Casey closed her eyes, tipping her head back in pleasure. Olivia moved her mouth down Casey's torso, tracing her tongue across her ribs, along her abs and down to the edge of her shorts. Casey took in a breath, her arms spread out, her hands flat on the bed as if to steady her. Olivia looked up at her and Casey could see nothing in Olivia's eyes but desire.

"These need to go." Olivia slowly pulled Casey's shorts down her thighs, past her knees, and then cast them onto the floor. She moved off the bed and pulled herself upright, looking down at Casey.

"You are an absolute dream," Olivia said almost to herself before kneeling down on the floor at the edge of the bed. She pulled at Casey's legs until Casey inched herself down the bed. Olivia knelt between her legs, a hand on either thigh, and every fiber, every nerve in Casey's body was vibrating in anticipation.

Olivia pushed Casey's knees farther apart, trailing kisses along the inside of her thigh. When she reached Casey's center, she brushed the lightest of lingering kisses against it before pulling away and continuing dotting kisses down her other thigh. Casey's insides contracted, and she felt the heat of her arousal like a fire in her core.

"Please, Olivia." Casey didn't even try to hide how desperate she was. She wanted Olivia's mouth on her more than she'd ever wanted anything else in the world.

Olivia lifted her eyes and looked at Casey for a long beat, and Casey took in a breath. And then she felt the pressure and the warmth of Olivia's tongue as she ran it across her swollen center, and Casey couldn't stop herself from crying out. Olivia stroked her tongue up and down her length, flicking her tongue across the swollen bud of her clitoris. Olivia's tongue teased and probed, and Casey could only grab at the bedclothes, her eyes clamped shut, the pleasure almost too intense. She didn't want to come but wasn't sure she could hold on. She wanted to lose herself in Olivia, in how Olivia was making her feel.

Olivia used her thumbs to open Casey up to her, to allow her tongue to probe even deeper, gently sucking on her clitoris, and Casey's moans became louder. Her breathing was rapid now, her body grinding into the bed to the rhythm of Olivia's tongue. When Olivia increased the speed and pressure of her tongue, it was enough to push Casey over the edge, and her orgasm came full force, crashing in with what seemed like a vivid burst of color and light, her whole body bucking as wave after wave of pleasure coursed through her body. She reached down a hand to tangle her fingers in Olivia's hair, wanting to touch her somehow. Olivia still had her mouth closed over Casey's center and Casey rode out her orgasm that way. As she came back to herself, Casey looked down at Olivia, now gazing up at her with what she dared to imagine was something more than arousal, something more than the satisfaction of the sex.

"Wow." Casey smiled at her. "That was—" She didn't finish. "I'm not sure there's even a word for what that was."

"That's good, right? I mean, it's a good word you're searching for." Olivia looked unbelievably shy for someone who had just left Casey unable to feel the lower half of her body. It was adorable.

"Come here." Casey shuffled herself back up the bed, holding out her hands for Olivia to join her. "It was better than good, better than amazing." Olivia lay down next to her, and Casey put her arms around her. Olivia laid her head on Casey's chest and Casey reached an arm around her waist, stroking her back softly. "It was everything I hoped and imagined it would be. And…" The feelings Casey had been trying to put away for days were lodged in the back of her throat. She shook her head slightly, trying to regain her composure. "And I need you to know that I think you're wonderful."

Olivia shifted in her arms, lifting her head so that she was looking at Casey. Casey tried to maintain the eye contact that Olivia was seeking, but she feared her eyes would give away what she was feeling. And that the intensity of her feelings would spook Olivia. She looked away, not able to keep the tension out of her body, feeling embarrassed and overwhelmed, wishing she hadn't said what she'd said.

"Casey, don't pull back. Please. Not after this."

Olivia moved so she was on her side, her head now level with Casey's. She pulled Casey's arm around her body, bringing her closer. Their faces were inches apart. It was impossible for Casey not to kiss her. Olivia responded, and they kissed each other slowly, tenderly, with a different kind of passion. But Casey felt her blood heat again, and when she pulled Olivia in for a deeper kiss, her body wanting more, Olivia broke the kiss before reaching down and taking hold of Casey's hand.

"Thirteen hours by car." Olivia smiled at her shyly. "Two hours twenty minutes by plane."

Casey frowned. She was missing a key piece of information somewhere.

"The time it takes to get from LA to Portland. I should be embarrassed by the fact that I looked up the travel times, but I'm not." She stroked Casey's hand with her thumb. "I decided somewhere between your mom's kitchen and that stony ass beach that I like you, Casey. I really like you. And this," Olivia swallowed, sounding unsure, "is not something casual for me. I'm not Susie. I'm not at all the kind of woman who does this without it meaning something."

Casey felt her heart expand in her chest.

"Me neither."

Olivia was looking at her intently, clearing expecting more. She had every right to.

"I think you're incredible. Every time you've said Susie is the one with all the appeal, the one everyone falls in love with, it's been so hard for me not to take you into my arms and tell you…show you…how wrong you are."

"I think I might have quite liked that. Your arms are a thing of wonder."

Olivia stroked a hand down Casey's arm. It made her shiver and froze her thoughts for an instant.

"And I'm sorry if that's a bit full-on, but—" Casey stopped. She didn't know what else to say that wouldn't scare Olivia away.

"It's very full-on." Olivia smiled. "But it's what I need to hear. It might seem strange to you, given what I do for a living, but I don't have a lot of confidence. And for the obvious reason, I find it hard to trust. But you," she kissed Casey, "have gotten under my defenses. Even after I knew I'd fallen for you, I tried to keep you at arm's length, but I couldn't."

"You've fallen for me?" Casey couldn't stop herself from asking. It was everything she hadn't dared to hope for.

"I have." Olivia had a serious look on her face. "I know you hate my life, find it ridiculous, whatever, but if you didn't, if you could find a way to come to terms with it, I would love it if we could keep going with this. See where it takes us. I mean thirteen hours is nothing, right? Unlike you, I quite like driving."

"I think I might fly." Casey smiled and was rewarded with a lingering kiss. It was a kiss that turned into another and another. And when Olivia pulled away, Casey felt breathless and unbelievably turned on. She let Olivia's kisses quell her anxiety and she tried to let herself imagine it could work, but even with Olivia lying next to her, gazing at her like she meant all of it, Casey felt doubt poking at her from somewhere.

"My life is small. But I like it that way. It's missing a dog and the kids I'd like to have, and yes, it's missing a beautiful, talented girlfriend that my mom would approve of, but it's never going to be able to offer you the things you're used to. I like long walks and Sunday roasts, and my ideal Saturday night would be playing board games with those kids I don't yet have. I'm kind of boring."

"Casey, you are not boring. And I don't know what it is you think I want that you don't have. All of that sounds pretty wonderful to me."

"I'm not saying it's not what you want, but it's not your life. Your life is awards dinners, red carpets, jealous costars, being followed by photographers. It's an LA kind of life and I'm sure you've gotten used to it. I just wonder if you..." Casey hesitated, feeling panic rising in her chest that she fought to tamp down. "I just think that you'll realize at some point that you need someone who's a lot more comfortable with that life than I am. Even Hannah thought I wasn't...you know?" Casey didn't let herself finish. She didn't want to sound self-pitying. She just didn't want Olivia to wake up one day and be disappointed by who Casey was. She couldn't stand the idea of that.

"Number one, Casey, I'm not Hannah. And number two. You think I don't know that you think my life is crazy? You've made it clear. You think I don't know my life is crazy? I've told you it is. I've told you how much I hate the whole 'LA kind of life.'" Olivia sat up and moved away from her. "So if this is you deciding this isn't what you want, that I'm not what you want, then please just say it rather than making excuses. I'll wish you told me an hour ago, before I made such a fool of myself, but I'd rather know now." Olivia sounded upset, and Casey reached for her, pulling her back down next to her.

"Olivia, that's not what I mean, not at all. I want us to do this. I want you in my life. I guess I'm just imagining being in LA with you and what that might feel like. And how full of people like Billie your world might be—confident, beautiful, happy to do anything to get what they want. I don't even have you yet and I'm already thinking I'll lose you to someone like her."

"If I wanted Billie, I could have her. I'm not being arrogant, Casey, just honest. And I have women 'like Billie' throwing themselves at me all the damn time. I don't want them, any of them. I haven't been interested in anyone in a long time. Until you came along and swept me off my feet." She took in a breath. "I like you, Casey—a lot—but I don't want to get hurt and I know I'm not exactly in a position to ask you for any kind of commitment, but I need to know that you're in, that you're going to give us a chance. That you're not going to let this crazy job I have get in the way for us. And in case you need to hear it, Hannah was a fool to let you go and her judgment is not something you should waste a single minute thinking about."

Casey had fallen in love with Olivia somewhere along the way, and wherever that was going to lead her she had no choice but to go. And if their differences made it impossible, then she would get herself hurt. But there was no way she wasn't going to give it a try.

"I'm in." She leaned across and kissed Olivia, trying to transmit her intention with the kiss as much as her words. "I'm all in. The way I feel about you, I don't have a choice."

Olivia smiled and Casey kissed her again, running her hands along her beautiful body, glorying in her smile, letting herself hope. She moved closer to Olivia, easing herself into a position where their legs were straddling each other, needing the closeness, wanting to feel the length of Olivia's body pressed against her.

Olivia began to move, grinding her wet center against Casey's thigh, and Casey couldn't help but react. She kissed Olivia hard, crushing her lips with her own. She slid down Olivia's body, taking her nipple gently into her mouth, feeling the hard bud against her tongue, swirling her tongue around it, while Olivia roughly caressed Casey's breasts, pinching and squeezing her nipples in a way that made Casey moan with desire.

"Don't." She moved her head back up Olivia's body to press a soft kiss to Olivia's mouth. "Or I'm going to lose concentration."

Olivia laughed and pushed Casey's head back down to where it had been before and Casey kept peppering soft wet kisses down her body, feeling Olivia grow taut and tense beneath her, hearing her soft moans of pleasure. She ran her tongue across Olivia's stomach, past her navel—the skin soft and slightly salty—and down between her thighs, longing to taste her. Olivia opened her legs wide, and Casey slid her hands underneath her butt to lift Olivia to her mouth, running her tongue along the swollen flesh. She moved her tongue in circles, flicking it across Olivia's clitoris, turned on by the noises Olivia was making that said she was enjoying it as much as Casey was.

She felt Olivia's fingers in her hair, urging her on, and when Casey took all of her into her mouth, sucking greedily, Olivia whimpered with pleasure. Her head was tilted back against the bed and her hands were in Casey's hair.

"More." Olivia's voice was low and hoarse, and Casey knew what she wanted. She pulled her hand from beneath Olivia's butt and grazed her fingertips along the inside of Olivia's thigh, wanting to let her know that she had understood. All the time, she stroked Olivia with her tongue, stopping only when her fingers were where Olivia wanted them to be, where Casey wanted them to be. She closed her mouth over Olivia's clitoris and began sucking at the same time that she filled Olivia with her fingers.

Olivia lifted herself from the bed, pushing herself onto Casey's hand, wanting her deeper, seeming hungry for more. Casey kept up her rhythm, sliding her fingers in and out before curling them slightly. Olivia let out a long loud curse as Casey found the right spot. Casey continued, increasing the speed of her thrusts, sucking and licking greedily, knowing Olivia was on the edge of coming. With a cry of pleasure, Olivia let go and gave in to a shuddering climax, her breathing rapid, one hand in Casey's hair and the other grabbing for Casey's wrist to hold her inside, to stop her from withdrawing. Casey watched Olivia ride out the wave of her orgasm, her eyes clamped shut, her muscles juddering against Casey's fingers. Eventually, she opened her eyes and shifted position, allowing Casey to withdraw.

"Casey, I can't even..." Olivia put a hand on either side of Casey's head to guide her up along her torso, until she could lean down and kiss her. "That was unbelievable. I feel like I'm made of liquid."

Olivia's voice sounded throatier and Casey loved the sound of it. Her hair was mussed, her face was flushed, and her lips were plump and red. And all of it was beautiful to Casey.

"Or maybe I feel like a rag doll. Something floppy anyway."

Casey shuffled them to one side of the bed and pulled the duvet across them, settling Olivia's head on her chest. Her own center was aching and wet, but all she wanted was Olivia in her arms.

Olivia yawned. Casey stroked her hair, enjoying the closeness almost as much as what had gone before. "We should have some of that champagne they left for us. I think there's a lot we can celebrate. And you've made me thirsty. And a little hungry. And floppy. I think you've finished me off." Olivia yawned again, and Casey felt her breathing deepen. "But I'm talking too much. Am I talking too much? I think I am." The words came out like a murmur.

Casey didn't answer, nor did she move a muscle. She continued to gently stroke Olivia's hair with her fingertips as Olivia's eyes fluttered and then closed. She looked down and couldn't help but smile. The last time she'd watched Olivia sleep had been very different. How was it possible that over the two weeks since then, she had fallen in love with her?

"I'm still waiting for you to open the champagne, you know?" Olivia shifted in her arms as she spoke, looking up at Casey with an earnest gaze.

"I thought you were sleeping."

"Me too. But it turns out being this close to you has given my body other ideas."

Casey placed a tender kiss on Olivia's forehead before rolling out of the duvet and onto her feet. The champagne was on the table, in an ice bucket, two glasses sitting in front of it. She began to open it, watching as Olivia shuffled under the covers and into a seated position, a smile playing on her face.

"What?"

"This view is even better than the one from the balcony." She picked up a pillow and hugged it to her chest. "Even better than the one from the fifty-second floor of the Shard."

"Did you make me get up for the champagne just so you could fulfill some depraved naked sommelier fantasy?" Casey narrowed her eyes, pointing the bottle in Olivia's direction.

"I did. And I'm not even sorry."

"I see." Casey nodded as she popped the cork and poured them each a glass. She draped the white square of linen that had come with the bottle across her arm and walked slowly toward the bed. "Well, I don't want you to feel too guilty, but it's very bad to objectify people in that way, especially naked sommeliers. I mean, we're only here to serve you good quality alcoholic beverages. We deserve a little better."

Casey put the glasses down next to the bed, her eyes not leaving Olivia's. The throbbing between her legs telling her that there were a lot of things she wanted right then more than the champagne.

"I'm sorry. You're right, you deserve better from me. Let me apologize properly." Olivia pulled back the covers with a smile, inviting Casey to join her. She didn't hesitate. The clock that was counting down the time they had left together was ticking as loud as the beating of her heart. And she didn't want to waste a single minute of their time together by sleeping, drinking champagne, or looking at the view.

Chapter Nineteen

"So, the wanderer returns," Mercy called out to Casey as she got close before pulling her into a big hug. "It's been too long."

They were standing outside the café where they always congregated to watch the parade. It was half café, half bakery, and one hundred percent queer. And happily for David, just two doors away from his office.

"It has. Where's the missus?" Casey felt bad for hoping Naomi wasn't coming.

"She's on her way. She's buying face paints. She's promised to paint rainbows on us all. Be very afraid."

Casey smiled. Despite everything, she was happy to see Mercy. They were good friends once. Really good friends. With Hannah and Naomi in tow, they'd taken trips, spent holidays together, and even had a short-lived spell of playing foursomes at badminton. But as things disintegrated between Casey and Hannah, Naomi took sides and Casey's relationship with Mercy became collateral damage.

"How are you?" Casey asked.

"Week from hell. Ready to cut loose, so yay for Pride. Yesterday I had a fourteen-year-old run away from her foster home. Finally tracked her down at her grandma's but not before I got a few more gray hairs. One of those days where I dream of jacking it all in for something else."

There was a silence between them.

"Tactless, I'm sorry," Mercy said.

"It's okay. It's not like I envy you the chance to deal with a runaway. But yeah, I still miss it."

"You know we'd have you back in a heartbeat."

Casey and Mercy had worked in the same office. They'd been a pretty formidable team.

"I live in Portland. The commute might be a little tough," Casey said. Deflection was her superpower.

"You don't have to though. You could come home. David said you're not completely happy there."

"Nice to know I'm a conversation piece."

"Hey, come on. He misses you. I miss you. We talk about it sometimes, about how good it would be if you came back. I'm not going to apologize for that."

"I'm sorry. I'm a little on edge today. That wasn't fair."

"It wasn't." Mercy nudged her. "But I forgive you."

"Good."

"I'm pretty sure your desk is still the way you left it. Not exactly a shrine, more like we've been too busy to clean it." She smiled. "And I've still got half your old cases. I'm pretty sure the kids would love to have you back almost as much as the managers would."

"I'm not sure I'd be all that welcome." Casey shrugged.

"You walked out, they didn't fire you. And the arrest isn't a deal breaker. It's not like you were charged with anything. Trust me, they're so desperate for qualified staff that they'd welcome you with open arms."

"Cheers."

"I don't mean that. I just mean you love the work, you're qualified, and we're always short-staffed. And I never got why you felt you needed to leave in the first place. You had a good reputation. You should have just explained. They would have understood—"

"Understood that my girlfriend had me arrested for 'smashing up her studio,' or understood that I was so 'dangerous' she tried to take out an injunction to keep me out of my own house?" Casey felt a tightness in her chest every time she thought about it. "I'm not sure they'd have been all that understanding about me being arrested. I saved everyone a lot of time and paperwork by walking out."

"A lot of things happen in the heat of a relationship breaking down. They might have understood. And anyway, everyone knew it didn't happen the way Hannah said it happened—"

"That's not true," Casey interrupted. "You knew it wasn't true because you knew me and because you knew she'd been cheating, but to the hundreds of thousands of people who watched her tearful 'breakup' videos, she was the victim and I was the monster."

"She just wanted to create a bit of drama. Drama is what gets the views and the views are what brings in the money. You know that. She was playing that game long before you guys broke up."

Because it was Pride and because Mercy was once a good friend, Casey swallowed what she could have said. It wasn't a bit of drama. It was real life. Her life. And between her own stupidity and Hannah's need to vindicate herself for cheating on Casey, she had been damaged by the whole thing. It was impossible for her to simply shrug it off the way Mercy seemed to want her to.

"Can we change the subject?" Casey asked quietly.

"Sure, sure. Sorry. I didn't mean to get into all that either. Let me start again." Mercy paused for dramatic effect. "How the hell are you, Casey Byrne? I've missed you."

"I've missed you too, Mercedes Martin." Casey exhaled, willing the tension away. "And I'm fine. I've been busy. Sorting out some house things for my mom, working all the time. I haven't had a lot of spare time."

"I'll let that one slide. We both know you've been avoiding me." Mercy's tone was kind. "But promise me we can have a proper catch-up before you go back? I'll even leave the wife at home." Mercy's dark eyes were serious and Casey felt bad. Mercy hadn't done anything wrong. Naomi had been the one who had known Hannah was cheating, the one who had chosen not to tell her.

"Definitely. It's a promise."

They faced each other awkwardly for a moment.

"I don't know if David told you, but I'm moonlighting as a driver to the stars. And I'm doing better than you because I haven't had a single one of them run away from me yet." Casey lifted her eyebrows to signal the joke and that she was changing the subject.

"Yeah, he said you're driving half the cast of *The West Side* around town. That's a pretty great gig. I love that show."

"It's been a lot of fun. Mostly. Some unexpected moments."

Spending time with Olivia had been fun. And falling in love with her had been completely unexpected. But it was something she intended to keep to herself for as long as possible.

"Hey." Naomi appeared next to them unexpectedly. "Good to see you, Casey."

The hug she gave Casey was tentative.

"Thanks. You too."

"How's Portland? How's life?"

Casey guessed that every single thing she told Naomi would get back to Hannah—and Zoey. And she hated the idea of them looking at her life and finding it lacking. It was something Hannah had always needed to do, to measure her life against other people's and feel like she was doing better.

"It's good, thanks."

They stood in silence.

"I'm going inside to get a coffee," Naomi said. "Nice to see you again, Casey." She gave Casey a small nod and disappeared into the café.

"Well, that wasn't awkward at all." Mercy let out a nervous laugh. "She's sorry, you know."

"She should be." Casey had told Olivia all this was water under the pier. She had to make sure it was true. "But it was all a long time ago, so tell her she doesn't need to be awkward around me. Things worked out for the best. Zoey is a much better match for Hannah than I ever was."

And I'm moving on with Olivia Lang. Casey wondered how loudly Mercy would scream if she told her the truth.

"Well, that sounds healthy. And it'll make it less tense for everyone at the party later if you guys can get along."

"Yeah, I guess so."

Casey hadn't yet told David she was going to miss the party. She'd told herself a hundred times it was right to want to spend Olivia's last night in London with her, and she was pretty sure he'd understand, but she couldn't deny the relief she felt at being able to dodge Hannah too.

Casey's phone dinged as Mercy headed inside to find Naomi. She fished it out of her pocket. It was Louise.

We just turned onto your street.

Finally. Casey let out a breath and smiled.

Olivia gave in and snagged one of the beers kept on ice in a cooler at the back of the float. It was a hot day and there was nowhere to shelter from the sun. The parade was moving at the pace of those walking—and singing, chanting, and dancing—meaning they hadn't moved more than three miles in the last thirty minutes.

"I can't believe we're doing London Pride, Liv. Look at the crowds. These beautiful people are our people, and they are ready to party with us." Louise pulled her into a hug before spinning her around in some form of dance move that Olivia was pretty sure breached all the health and safety guidance they'd been given before they got on board.

Louise was in a party mood. There wasn't an inch of her that wasn't covered in rainbows. And she made Olivia—with her rainbow garland and cute little rainbow earrings—look like she hadn't made an effort.

"Leave her alone, Lou," Liam said with a smile. "She's had a rough night."

Louise had even cajoled Liam into wearing a rainbow vest over his otherwise naked torso. And she hadn't stopped touching him since they'd climbed on board. His arms, his back, his neck, his chest—anywhere there was bare skin. Old Liam would have found it overwhelming, but new Liam seemed to be reveling in her attention. It seemed that Michael making love to Jessie on screen had lowered both their real-life inhibitions.

"Does that smile she can't keep off her face suggest a rough night to you?" Louise laughed. "She looks exactly like someone who's spent the night in bed with our gorgeous driver."

"Don't, Lou." They knew she'd spent the night with Casey in Brighton, but Olivia hadn't been ready to tell them she'd fallen for her. And she didn't want them making it sound casual. It wasn't. Not to her.

"Don't tell me you're regretting it? Come on, Liv, you're entitled to a bit of fun. And from what I saw this morning, it looked like you were having a lot of it."

Olivia and Casey had said a lingering good-bye in the doorway to Casey's room. Casey refusing to allow her inside, seeming to understand that Olivia had intentions that would have made them both late. But as they kissed one last time, Louise came out of her room and caught them red-handed. Casey blushed adorably and disappeared inside. And Olivia was left to face Louise's inquisition. An inquisition that lasted as long as it took Olivia to change her clothes, dab on some makeup, and gratefully escape downstairs to Tania's waiting car.

"I'm not regretting it. I just don't like you making it sound like I'm fucking 'the driver.' I'm not Susie." She hesitated. "And Casey is much more than that to me." She caught the look that passed between Liam and Louise.

Louise held up her hands. "Okay, I'll stop. But that look on your face that says you keep remembering all the delicious things you did to each other last night needs to go too. It's not fair to those of us who aren't getting any."

The look Louise gave Liam wasn't subtle. Nothing about her was subtle. It was one of the things Olivia loved most about her. She needed honesty and straightforwardness from the people in her life. They were qualities that had attracted her to Casey. Along with all the other more obvious ones.

"That one, that look." Louise pointed at her but addressed the comment to Liam. "It says she's feeling all gooey inside, but she's not giving us any of the details. No fair."

"We're supposed to be working the crowd, not standing around and gossiping," Billie shouted across to them.

For once, Olivia was glad of the interruption, glad to escape Louise and her prying. Billie had a handful of T-shirts. Every few yards, she was throwing one down to people watching the parade, while smiling and waving and occasionally posing for a photograph. They'd all been doing the same, but now Olivia wanted a sit-down and a beer. She didn't want to be a party pooper. She was just tired.

She smiled as she took a swig of the beer. She wasn't "just" tired, she was exhausted. Mentally and physically. And it was wonderful. The sore muscles in her back, calves, and thighs a testament to the night—and morning—that she and Casey had enjoyed before reluctantly leaving their love nest and getting the train back to London.

"Susie, can I have a selfie?" a young woman shouted up at her, walking alongside the float, easily keeping pace with it.

"The name's Olivia."

She could have gotten annoyed with her, but what was the point.

"Yeah, of course, sorry." The woman waved her identity crisis away just like that.

Olivia knelt down close to the edge of the float—a well-decorated flatbed truck with open sides, which she'd been nervous about falling off ever since they got on board. The woman held her phone out at arm's length and took a few shots, impressing Olivia with her ability to walk, pose, and keep them both in the frame.

As soon as she had what she wanted, the woman shouted for Phoebe, moving to the rear of the vehicle in the hope of attracting Billie's attention. Olivia watched as Billie jumped down from the float, posed for a selfie in the arms of the grateful fan, and climbed back on board with the help of one of the assistants. It was kind of impressive. She pulled her gaze away and sat on the edge of the truck, her legs dangling over the side.

She held out her phone and took a selfie. The decorations were visible and bright behind her, the show's logo bright purple against a silvery background. She deleted it and took another. And then another. Eventually, she decided that the one on her screen made her look cute and she sent it to Casey with a message that said: *Happy Pride, I miss you.*

Olivia was trying not to overthink things, trying not to hold back. It was Pride and she was missing Casey. And she was pretty sure, after everything they'd said and done last night, that she had a right to say it.

Her phone dinged.

Happy Pride. Anyone throw any underwear at you yet?

And then again.

I miss you too x

Olivia smiled. It was exactly what she needed to hear. Arriving back at the hotel had been strange. It felt a little like the bubble they had created for themselves, away from the reality of their situation, had burst. And worse, tonight was her last night in London. Olivia couldn't help but let the doubts creep back in. They had a lot to do to make sure this wasn't just some intense and crazy holiday romance.

"Olivia." The voice was Billie's. "Are you sure you want to be drinking that in full view of everyone? It's a temptation for whoever's got it in for you to take a photo of you holding that beer and looking—if you don't mind me saying it—pretty rough around the edges."

When Olivia looked up at her, she had a condescending smile on her face. One small shove would be all it would take to topple Billie off the truck. She didn't want to kill her—not yet anyway. A small fracture that would take her out of action would be enough. Olivia wasn't proud of the impulse, but Billie's nerve in talking about whoever had it in for Olivia was breathtaking. Billie was still denying it—even when the three of them had confronted her with Liam's "evidence," but they all knew she was the one who had been planting the stories. And she knew they knew.

"Louise said I should stay out of your way. And I've tried, but honestly, Olivia, you do seem kind of out of control and I'm worried about you."

"Are you serious?"

"Of course, I'm always serious where you're concerned."

When they confronted Billie, her denials had been worthy of an Emmy. Billie got angry, upset, and then doubled down on blaming Casey. Even going so far as to suggest that Casey could have given the stories to the website while pretending to be Billie. When Olivia pointed out how little sense that made—the website offered no payment, Casey had no reason to harm her—Billie simply glared at her and walked out.

"You're insane." Olivia couldn't think of a better word. She took a deliberately long pull on her beer and turned away.

Billie got next to her on the edge of the truck. "We have to clear the air, Olivia. You can't keep ignoring me. We have a whole season of shooting to get through." Billie tilted her head as she spoke. Olivia recognized it as her sincerity pose.

"I don't have anything to say to you, Billie. And there's no one else here so you don't have to keep pretending. We both know what you did. I'm just struggling with the why part. I've never caused you any harm, never been anything but professional, so your desire to try to ruin my reputation is mystifying. And trying to blame Casey—someone else who has done nothing to hurt you—is just pathetic."

Billie's expression hardened. "I did it because of that look on your face right there. The one that says that you think you're so much better than me. But guess what? You're not. You being the star of the show doesn't mean a thing. It just means you got lucky playing Susie. But I'm younger and I know how to play this game. Phoebe is already popular and you—with your stupid hang-ups and your determination to make a fool of yourself—are in my way."

For the first time since she'd known Billie, she sounded like she was speaking from the heart.

"In the beginning, I genuinely liked you. I thought you were shy and needed a little encouragement from me. Then I thought maybe you were playing hard to get and wanted me to be the one to seduce you. Turns out I was pretty wrong about that." Billie sneered as she spoke. "You're more like Susie than I realized. Fucking around with Casey is such a Susie move. I mean, she's hot, but where's it going to get you? Apart from another bad news story, a story that I will happily pass on to one of the many journalists that I've cultivated. Because that's how this business works, whether you like it or not. You should thank me. Maybe you being a drunk and fucking 'the help,' will make you seem more interesting. Though I seriously doubt it. You're a fool to think that what matters is how good you are at acting."

Billie shook her head. Her dismissal of Olivia was as clear as the threat she was making, but all the time her face carried a sweet smile and her tone suggested she wouldn't hurt a fly. She was a much better actress than Olivia had ever given her credit for.

"For the record, I never thought I was better than you—or better than anyone—that's your insecurity speaking. And honestly, Billie, if you're that desperate for it, you can have it. The adoration, the star billing, the cover shoots. I never wanted that anyway. You didn't need to fight me for it. I would have willingly given it to you."

Olivia should have been angry, but she wasn't. The games, the frustration, just made her weary and sad.

"I only ever wanted to act. But you're ruining even that for me now. And I'm so damn tired of your bullshit, Billie. You need to leave me alone and leave Casey alone too. And if you don't, I promise you that I will make sure that every studio, every journalist, every website I come across, hears the story of how you were so pathetically insecure and attention-seeking that you paid people to take photos of me and then made up a load of lies to try to ruin my reputation."

"Who's going to believe you?" Billie shot her a condescending look. "My lawyers would take you to the cleaners if you so much as suggested any of that was true."

Olivia pulled her phone out from her pocket and waved it at Billie.

"That would be true unless I had a recording of you confessing it all to back up what I was saying. Honestly, Billie, it's the oldest trick in the book. Recording it when your nemesis confesses. Maybe you're not as switched on as you think you are. It's my lawyers you need to be worrying about, not your own."

Olivia gave Billie a cold, hard stare and got up before she could respond. She had no wish to spend a minute more with Billie than she had to. And of course, if Billie called her bluff and asked to hear the recording, she was in trouble. Because there wasn't one. She hadn't been prepared—or switched on enough. Not this time around.

Olivia moved to the back of the float where Louise and Liam were posing arm in arm for a photo. She grabbed a handful of T-shirts from the huge barrel behind her and began to toss them into the crowd.

Olivia felt a spark inside. It wasn't anger, it was the beginnings of a crazy idea. Maybe she could use this mess with Billie to get out of her contract. She could claim harassment and the need for a break. And get them to send Susie away somewhere for a while, give Billie—give Phoebe—the star billing she was craving. She wasn't bluffing when she said she didn't want any of it. Maybe this was a chance to escape the madness. To get back to doing something that made her happier.

Her phone dinged in her hand. The message was from Casey.

I'm not sure if donuts are allowed while you're representing that healthy West Hollywood brand of lesbian of yours, but if you stick your hand out in about thirty yards, I could make your sweet Brooklyn self very happy xx

Olivia read the message again, not understanding it the first time around. Then she lifted her gaze and scanned the sidewalk ahead of them.

As promised—and looking like every fantasy Olivia had ever had—Casey was standing at the roadside half a block away, holding a rectangular cardboard box. Olivia waved excitedly and her breath caught as Casey began to walk slowly toward the truck. She was wearing a tight white T-shirt and bright pink shorts, and Olivia didn't know where to stare first.

The float was barely moving, so Olivia had plenty of time to register the arousal coursing through her body at the sight of Casey. It wasn't a surprise. She had always wanted Casey like that. She'd wanted her since the moment they'd first met. But now she knew exactly what Casey tasted like, how it felt to have Casey on top of her, inside her—

She made herself stop. The day was hot enough.

The real surprise, as she watched Casey getting closer, was the way her heart lifted in just the way the romance books said it should. And she couldn't keep from smiling, knowing that despite her worries that she'd never let herself trust anyone enough to fall in love again, in two weeks, Casey already had her heart.

Casey got into step next to the truck. She held out the box, seeming a lot shyer than when they'd said good-bye three hours ago. "I got some for Liam and Louise too. I figured they wouldn't let you not share. They're good. From David's favorite bakery." She pointed ahead to where she'd walked from. "It's one of his many Pride traditions that we have lunch there and watch the parade go by. I was kind of hoping we might see you."

Olivia took the donuts and sat down, putting them next to her on the edge of the truck.

"It's a miracle you did."

"Not quite a miracle." Casey looked sheepish. "Louise was keeping me posted on where you were. I thought the float had broken down or something. I've been waiting with those donuts a lot longer than I expected."

Olivia wanted to jump down and hug her. But she didn't dare. There were too many people. They stared at each other for a beat.

"Nice shorts. Not sure I've seen you in pink before." Olivia widened her eyes.

"Yeah, David won't let me wear them when I'm working for some reason." Casey smiled. "He also just told me I'm letting the side down today because of my absence of rainbows. He'll be glad to see you're doing your bit." Casey looked her up and down slowly and Olivia got turned on all over again.

Olivia willed the universe to keep the truck moving at a snail's pace so Casey could keep walking alongside, so they could keep talking and wouldn't have to say another good-bye so soon after the last one.

"I'm heading back after this—"

"I've got the rest of the day off—"

They spoke at the same time.

"After you," Olivia said.

"I'm heading back after this. I'm wiped out. I thought maybe I'd skip out on David's afternoon plans and take a nap."

The truck put on a spurt, and Casey had to jog slightly to keep up with Olivia.

"That's us." Casey pointed at a café a few doors away. Outside it, the small seating area was decorated with balloons and garlands and packed with people. As they drew almost level, the truck once again slowed to a halt.

"Well, after this I'm completely free and I'm definitely going to need to sleep, so maybe I'll see you at the hotel later. We could share a nap space." Olivia tried to make the suggestion sound light, but it was anything but. Her body craved Casey, and she couldn't stop her heart from counting down the minutes they had left.

"A nap space, huh?" Casey said. "I'm pretty sure sharing isn't going to help either of us nap. And I say that with the wisdom of my last experience of sharing a space with you where napping was supposed to happen." The look that flashed across Casey's face told Olivia they were having the same memories. "But the answer is still yes. Though at some point I need an actual nap, I'm not sure I'll last the night otherwise. You might as well know what you're getting into with me—"

Casey stopped speaking, seeming embarrassed.

"I'm not saying you're necessarily getting into something with me. I just mean…I was making a joke, about not being able to do two nights without sleep."

"I get the joke. And I totally get the need to sleep. But—" Olivia stopped herself. She wanted to tell Casey that she hoped like hell they were getting into something, but Casey seemed in a strange mood. And Olivia couldn't stop thinking about the fact that Casey hadn't yet invited her to David's party. It was her last night and she wanted to spend it with Casey. Surely Casey felt the same.

Heads began to turn in their direction, and Olivia guessed some of the people outside the café had recognized her. She heard her name, heard Susie's name. There were phones pointing in her direction. Casey looked behind her and visibly tensed. Olivia's heart sank a little. Of course Casey didn't want her at the party. Her presence would be disruptive, just like this. Olivia might feel just like a woman wanting her new lover to want to spend time with her, but things were a lot more complicated than that.

"Well, it was nice to bump into you. And thanks for the donuts." Olivia jumped down from the truck, lifted off her rainbow garland and placed it around Casey's neck. She wanted to hug her, to kiss her, but that would have created even more of a scene and Casey wouldn't thank her for that. So instead Olivia patted her arms platonically before stepping back reluctantly. "Now you look a little more festive."

"Thanks, I think." Casey smiled.

"And I'll see you later for that nap. Maybe we could grab a drink before your party. Or if that's not possible, I'd like to book you for breakfast tomorrow." Olivia didn't want to sound desperate, but leaving without some more time with Casey was a horrible thought. "We leave at lunchtime."

"I know." Casey looked at her with an expression that said she was trying to figure something out. The truck rolled forward a few feet, but Olivia didn't move.

"What are you doing later?"

"We're going to try to find somewhere to go out. Lou wants to celebrate our last night. I think she was hoping you might be able to recommend a bar or a club."

Casey gazed at her.

"Can I take you out to dinner first? I was thinking I'd give the party a miss, and I thought we could—"

"Yes." Olivia felt all her anxiety drain away.

"I didn't tell you what I was planning." Casey grinned.

"I don't care, the answer is still yes."

The look in Casey's eyes made Olivia want to wrap herself around her.

"So you're Olivia Lang." A tall, bear of a man offered Olivia a hand to shake. He had a smile on his face. "I have heard so much about you from this one. You wouldn't believe it to look at her, but she can gush when she wants to. And you, my dear, have had her gushing this past couple of weeks." He arched an eyebrow. The double meaning was clear. Olivia couldn't help the laugh that escaped. Casey looked like she wanted to strangle him.

"This is David. My employer. Used to be one of my best friends, until about fifteen seconds ago." Casey pulled a face and David laughed.

Olivia shook his hand, happy to meet him.

"Come on, Liv. Peel yourself away from her. I know you don't want to, but you're gonna get left behind." Louise's voice was clear, even amongst the noise of the parade, and Olivia turned to see Louise and Liam peering down at her. The truck inched forward as if to make a point.

"Hi, Casey." They both gave Casey a wave.

"She's right. I should go." Olivia could leave Casey happily now that she knew they had plans to be together. "I'll see you later. I can't wait."

"Oh, you're coming to the party? That's fantastic." David sounded genuinely excited. "We can get properly acquainted. And you won't be sorry. My Pride parties are legendary—though of course I would say that. There's an amazing DJ, amazing food, amazing decorations, and amazing guests. And it'll be amazing to have you. Bring your friends too." David gestured in Louise and Liam's direction. "I think people might lose their shit a little bit when you arrive, but then they'll be cool. It's a London thing to act unimpressed by everything, even when it's big TV stars drinking my fabulous Pride mojitos."

"They were thinking of going clubbing," Casey cut in, seeming tense all of a sudden.

"Nonsense. Everywhere will be ticketed. They won't get in anywhere decent." He turned to Olivia. "And this is about as authentic as you can get. A Pride party with actual homegrown London queers."

"Sounds better than anything we would have come up with," Louise said from behind them. "I think it'll be fun."

Olivia turned to Liam, who simply lifted his shoulders as if to say he didn't mind either way.

"Casey?" Olivia wasn't sure she wanted Casey to agree. A party meant they wouldn't be alone. Though they would be able to go home together, and she did feel bad for keeping Casey away from her friends and making her miss David's party.

"Okay." Casey reached down and gently squeezed her hand, and Olivia felt a rush of happiness. But the expression on Casey's face seemed troubled and Olivia wanted to ask why. "You'll enjoy the party a lot. It's a great way to say good-bye to London. And I just want to be where you want to be, so why not?"

Olivia couldn't not react to the words, or the shy half smile that Casey offered her. She pulled Casey in for a hug.

"Hey, you two. Get a room." The shout was from Louise.

Olivia looked up to see everyone on the truck staring down at them, including Billie.

"I should go."

"Me too."

"I'll see you later then?"

"Yes, you will...for a nap." Casey smiled.

Olivia looked at the stationary truck, not quite sure how she was going to manage to climb back on board without injuring herself. She was pretty sure, like Billie, she'd need one of the assistants to help. Before she could ask, Casey stepped closer. They were face-to-face, inches apart, and Olivia could feel her heart beating in her chest. Casey's eyes were almost black and she had her bottom lip trapped between her teeth. It took every bit of control Olivia had not to lean in and kiss her.

Olivia felt Casey's hands on her hips, slowly moving her a step or two backward till her back was resting against the edge of the truck. Then, in one movement, Casey lifted her at the waist, until Olivia could lay her hands flat on the truck bed behind her and boost herself so she was once again sitting on the edge of the truck.

Olivia wasn't exactly one of those fainting Southern belles, but being lifted like that by Casey had her feeling a little giddy, and a lot aroused.

Casey stepped back as the truck began to inch forward.

"Later then."

Olivia nodded.

"I'll be counting the minutes." If Olivia hadn't been staring at Casey's beautiful face, she might have missed the words. She wasn't even sure that Casey had meant her to hear them. But she had and Olivia felt a thousand rainbows had just rained down all their sparkles upon her.

Olivia watched Casey walk back into the café with David before slowly getting to her feet.

"Do you think if I climb down, she'll help me get back on board like that?" Louise fanned herself with her fingers.

"Hey. I'm standing right here. You don't need Casey," Liam replied, flexing his biceps and smiling.

Olivia was gratified to see Louise turn a shade of pink, glad she wasn't the only one disgracing herself by swooning.

"You have to admit," Louise nudged her, "that was damn cute. And I'm pretty sure that a few dozen people got the money shot, so we can't blame Billie when that one appears online." She shook her head. "I hope Casey knows what she's getting into."

She was pretty sure Louise hadn't meant to crash her mood. But she had. Casey had made it clear time and again that she wasn't interested in the limelight, and Olivia could only hope the three of them crashing David's party wasn't going to make Casey have another set of second thoughts.

CHAPTER TWENTY

You've invited us to a house full of queer people to drink and dance and you're worrying we might not enjoy it?" Louise was standing in front of Casey, her hands on her hips, a big smile on her face. "Have you even met me? I'm gonna have a blast. And so is my dance partner." She tried to make Liam salsa with her. His face—and his hips—suggested he wasn't sure.

They were in the wine section of the supermarket closest to David's house and Louise's voice—never quiet at the best of times—rang out loudly.

"Lou, she's not saying that we won't enjoy it. Just that people will recognize us and might decide to be freaked out about us being there, take photos, whatever." Liam looked at Olivia for help, shaking his head.

"Just watch out for people taking photos when you're shit-faced and making out with Liam in the kitchen." After a day watching them do everything but kiss, Olivia had decided Louise and Liam needed some help getting over the line.

They both turned to look at her, their faces carrying matching expressions of surprise.

"What?" Olivia lifted her hands. "I'm just using a hypothetical example."

Louise narrowed her eyes. "Well, same goes for you and Casey. I think if anyone's going to get photographed tonight, it'll be you and that 'handsome mystery companion' of yours everyone's so curious about. Especially after this afternoon's display."

"Let's just choose some wine and go," Casey said, sounding tense, and Olivia worried all over again. She'd been that way since they'd set off for the party.

Louise handed two bottles of prosecco to Liam. And then picked up two more.

"We're good to go," Louise said. "But do you need me to grab you a bottle of vodka to help you face up to your ex?"

"I might need more than one."

Olivia was happy to see Casey joke about it. She didn't know Hannah, but she couldn't imagine that facing her after all this time was going to be easy for Casey.

"C'mon, Casey," Louise said. "You're turning up at a party with three of TV's 'hottest' queers, that has to feel like the best 'fuck you' to a celebrity-obsessed ex ever."

"Not to me. I mean, maybe someone like Hannah would see it that way—and I'm pretty sure partying with the three of you will be irresistible content for her next video—but I don't care. It was too long ago for me to still feel vindictive."

"Well, you're a better person than me, because my vindictiveness would have no expiration date. And I'd be delighted to rub her face in how well I was doing by turning up with Liv on my arm."

"Yeah, well, like I say, I'm not made that way. I'm only putting myself through this at all because I know David really wants us there and you guys deserve to party. If I had my way, it would just be me and Olivia having a nice quiet dinner somewhere." Casey leaned across and kissed her on the forehead, and the love Olivia felt for her bubbled up in her chest once again. She had been right to trust her, right to allow herself this chance.

"Gee, thanks. We could be offended that you'd like to ditch us. But luckily, this prosecco and the imminent disco dancing means we're too excited to care." Louise turned Liam in the direction of the cashiers with a flourish.

"She and David are going to get on like a house on fire. Same energy, same attitude toward life." Casey smiled at her before picking up and examining a bottle of red wine.

"I want that too." Olivia had to say it.

"For David and Louise to get on?"

"No." Olivia pulled on Casey's hand, wanting her closer. "For us to have more time together—just the two of us. No friends, no Billie, no exes. I know this is our last night, and I can't help but feel sad about it."

"Our last London night," Casey corrected her, and Olivia was happy to hear it.

She looked up and down the aisle and then pulled Casey into a kiss—a hungry, wanting, passionate kind of kiss. Someone turned the corner to join them scanning the wine shelves and Casey pulled away, but she kept hold of Olivia's hand.

"Shall we try something French?" Casey asked, holding up a bottle. "Or do you want to play it safe and go for something Californian?"

"Come to Paris next weekend and we can try something French then."

Olivia had been trying to find the right time to ask. She wasn't sure that the supermarket was the most romantic of settings, but she couldn't be cool around Casey and she couldn't bear the idea of not seeing her for the three weeks it would take them to finish their European tour and get back to the States.

"They've given us next weekend off. Maybe you can visit. The Eurostar only takes two hours and you won't have to drive anywhere. We can see Paris. They have boat trips. I already checked. And they include dinner sometimes. My hotel has a sauna." She couldn't stop talking. Casey was looking at her like she was crazy.

"I'm sorry, I thought—" Olivia felt like she'd said the wrong thing. Was it crazy? To want something more for them? She didn't see why.

"You had me at 'come to Paris' actually." Casey took both her hands. "I know I'm in a strange mood today, but it's not because I have any doubts about us, not at all. It's because I've spent half the day hanging out with people I haven't seen in a long time, people who remind me of a not very happy time in my life." She hesitated and gave Olivia a tight smile. "And now we're going to see the person who chased me out of my hometown, ruining a lot of good things I had going on in my life." Casey swallowed, seeming a little upset.

Olivia waited, sensing she had more to say.

"And she's got a lot of things she could tell you about me. I'd like to think she's past it all, but she might not be. Maybe after tonight you won't want me to come to Paris."

Olivia felt a creeping unease at Casey's words.

"Are you guys coming?" Louise hollered at them from across the store.

"Sure, sorry. Two minutes," Olivia shouted back at them. When she turned back to Casey, she was studying the shelves again.

"I'm taking this Bordeaux. And that bottle of gin for David."

Casey had talked about Hannah cheating on her and feeling humiliated enough to leave town. But now Casey seemed to be suggesting—for the first time—that Hannah had things she could say about Casey that Olivia might not want to hear.

"What kind of things?"

Olivia wanted Casey to stop looking at the wine and to look at her.

"Do you want white or red?"

"Casey? What kind of things?"

Casey turned to face her. Her expression serious, her face tense.

"I don't know. But I know Hannah. She lies. She's always lied. And she especially lied about what happened between us. I guess she didn't want the cheating thing to look bad for her. To cost her subscribers. She rewrote everything that happened, made me seem like the bad guy. She denied cheating. She told everyone she got with Zoey after we broke up because I treated her so badly and that she was lucky to have Zoey there to 'save' her. She had a platform, a way of telling her story. And I didn't. So her version was what people believed. It was horrible. And tonight you're going to meet her and I have no idea what she'll say. She's actually very relatable, believable. It makes her good at what she does. You'll see that if you meet her. David says she's past all of it, that she was saying how nice it would be to see me, but I can't trust that. And anyway, I absolutely don't feel the same way."

Olivia could see that talking about it wasn't easy for Casey. But she was glad that she was getting some of it off her chest. No wonder Casey had been weird all evening. After everything, she didn't want to see Hannah at all. Let alone with Olivia in tow.

"I've met a lot of people like that, Casey. A lot of people who lie and who lie well. I was easy to fool once, but not anymore. And I'm not going to be fooled by her. Don't worry." Olivia lifted Casey's hand to her lips and kissed it.

"One thing." Casey took in a breath before shifting a little closer, holding Olivia's hand more tightly.

"I broke one of her cameras. We were arguing and I knocked over the tripod. But it was a complete accident, just me being clumsy. She knew that, but she took her chance. Me breaking her camera made her the victim and me guilty of 'smashing up her studio.' And it gave her the chance to have me arrested. And being arrested cost me my job. You can't work with kids with a criminal record." Casey ran an anxious hand through her hair before she fixed Olivia with a defiant look. "I'd like to tell you I was sorry, but I wasn't. It was an accident, I promise you, but sometimes I wish I'd smashed them all, that I'd done what she pretended I'd done. I felt so humiliated and angry about everything."

Olivia could understand the impulse, even if she was finding it hard to imagine Casey angry like that. She seemed so controlled, so careful.

"You have a criminal record?" Olivia couldn't help but be shocked.

"I don't. They dropped the charges pretty quickly. But the arrest was enough to cause me trouble at work. They were obliged to investigate, and I couldn't bear the shame so I resigned. And then I ran away. It's ancient history now, all of it, but—" Casey stopped mid-sentence. "We should go. They're waiting for us."

"They can wait. This is important."

"I just think there's a chance she might say something, to make trouble for me, for us, somehow. I should be completely irrelevant to her. She got everything. The girl she wanted, our friends, the chance to make some dramatic content at my expense. Fuck, she even got London."

Olivia could see Casey fighting to keep her composure.

"But I'm going to walk in there in ten minutes with you, Louise, and Liam and it's going to drive her crazy. And I can't help but think she's destructive enough to still want to ruin things for me."

"She sounds like a monster."

"She's just very insecure and driven and needs to be the center of attention."

"But otherwise a real sweetie, huh?"

"I guess so." Casey shrugged. "I'm sorry."

"And now I understand why you've been so on edge all evening."

"I'm sorry."

"Stop apologizing."

"It was part of why I wanted to skip it. I don't need to be reminded of it all."

"But David is your friend. And this is his big night." Olivia put her hands on Casey's waist, pulling her a little closer. "So fuck Hannah and her toxic self-centeredness. We're going to turn up loud and proud and you're going to dance with me to Bruno Mars just like you promised."

Casey rolled her shoulders before taking in a breath. Olivia could tell she was trying to work the tension out of her body.

"I feel like the dance was a promise exacted from me under torture." Casey widened her eyes playfully, and Olivia understood she was trying to lighten the mood.

"It was still a promise."

That afternoon, neither of them had napped. And with Olivia's mouth on her, Casey had been so close to coming that Olivia knew she could have gotten her to agree to anything. The memory made her flush.

Casey picked up the bottles she wanted. Olivia grabbed a couple of bottles of red without really choosing.

"Next time, no secrets. Trust that I'm going to understand. I've been there, you know that."

The eyes that stared back at her were dark, beautiful, and still a little fearful.

"Just promise me that you'll stay away from her."

"Okay." Olivia tucked one of the bottles under her arm and took hold of Casey's hand. They walked side by side to the cashier.

"I can't believe Lou hasn't come inside to chase us out. She's not known for her patience." Olivia said the words at the same time that Casey pointed toward the window at the front of the store.

Louise had her back flat against the glass. In front of her, one hand in her hair and the other around her waist, was Liam. They were making out like teenagers. Under enough light to give everyone a pretty good view, not that anyone seemed to care.

"I guess they found something to do while they were waiting for us," Casey said.

"Hallelujah." Olivia couldn't help but grin. "About time."

She put the bottles down in front of the cashier.

"And if they're going to be that discreet about it, you and I dancing to Bruno Mars won't even register with the party people."

She was happy to see Casey smile. This was their last night—their last London night—and she wasn't going to let some vindictive ex of Casey's crash the mood. She'd coped with every shitty thing Kristin had done and said about her, and now that Casey had finally trusted her with the truth, she was going to help Casey do the same.

Casey didn't want to leave Olivia's side. It was partly because this was going to be their last night together for a while and partly because— even if it wasn't—she didn't feel at all inclined to share Olivia with anyone else. Their arrival caused the kind of commotion that Casey feared it would, but people soon settled down. In fact, her friends, David's friends, all seemed perfectly unfazed by Casey turning up with Olivia Lang on her arm and with Louise Garland and Liam Morris in tow. Mercedes had squealed, but only a little bit. And now, people were drinking, dancing, laughing, and mostly ignoring them. And blissfully, there was absolutely no sign of Hannah and Zoey.

"I think we should go back inside. We're being very antisocial."

Casey nodded but silenced Olivia with another kiss. She wanted to pull Olivia into her lap, but the garden was well lit—thanks to David's obsession with fairy lights—and they were not well hidden. She contented herself with pulling Olivia close and turning her body so that they could press themselves against each other. She deepened the kiss, and when Olivia parted her lips in a soft moan, Casey couldn't stop herself from tasting her. Their tongues touched and Olivia brushed her hands across Casey's breasts, and Casey felt herself heat with arousal once again. When they stopped kissing, they were both wide-eyed and breathless.

"I think we're being very sociable," Casey said as she placed a kiss on Olivia's forehead. "But I guess you mean with other people." She shrugged. "You're probably right, maybe it looks rude, impolite, whatever. And I don't want that. You shouldn't want that either. I'm sure it's bad for your image to be hiding out with me in the garden for the whole party."

"I think somewhere on this trip—thanks to Billie—I decided I'm going to care a lot less about my image. Caring about it doesn't make me happy, it makes me confused and worried and inauthentic. I think I need to do a lot more of what makes me happy and stop worrying about who's watching. And you," Olivia kissed her again, "are making me happy." The kiss was a lot less chaste than Casey's, and within a few seconds, they were lost in each other again. Olivia pulled away, a hand on Casey's chest. "But while this bench is currently my favorite place in London, you came here to reconnect with friends you left behind, and I feel bad about monopolizing your attention."

"Don't. I'd rather be out here with you. I can catch up with them after you've gone to Paris."

"But will you?"

"I will. David has already promised to bring my mom to come and see me in Portland. And I agreed to have dinner with Mercy, and a couple of the other women I used to work with, next week. I even said Mercy could bring Naomi if she wanted to. I'm trying. Being here tonight was for David's sake because he invited you all and it's his big party, but it doesn't mean everything has to be said and sorted while we're here."

"Okay. But we should still stop hiding. If nothing else, we should go and see if Louise and Liam are behaving themselves."

Olivia was right. Casey didn't want to hide. What she really wanted was for them to get out of there as quickly as possible. It was partly a desire to leave before Hannah showed up and partly a desire to get Olivia in a room with a bed. With a sinking feeling in her stomach, Casey realized that Hannah might even have arrived while they'd been outside.

"Let's go in, say good-bye to David, and slip away. We have two empty hotel rooms to choose from. We can leave Lou and Liam here as our dancing ambassadors. I'm pretty sure David will understand."

Olivia turned to her, a serious expression on her face.

"I want nothing more than to go back to the hotel with you, but I figure that's me being selfish. These are your friends, we're supposed to be celebrating Pride together, and anyway, you promised me a dance." Olivia touched the back of her hand to Casey's cheek. "And if it's Hannah you're trying to avoid, don't worry. She's the one who behaved like a monster, not you. You don't have to hide. Say a polite hello and then ignore her. She'll hopefully get the message that you've moved on to better things." Olivia squeezed her hand. "Now let's spend some time with some of those cool friends of yours."

Casey felt the same small stab of guilt that had been bothering her since they left the supermarket. She hadn't told Olivia everything. She had left out the part about uploading the videos that made Hannah so mad with her. She knew why. She was worried that Olivia wouldn't understand. But she shouldn't have kept it from her. And as soon as they got back to the hotel, Casey was going to tell her and explain why she'd done it. And she was going to trust that Olivia would understand why it was completely different from what Kristin had done to her.

"Okay. I'll do you a deal." Casey got off the bench and offered her hand to Olivia. "Let's go and say hello, have our dance, and then leave."

Olivia used the hand to pull Casey into an embrace. "Two dances, some more cheese. And then we leave."

"Deal." They shook hands and then turned toward the house. "What are the chances that Louise and Liam are dirty dancing?"

"Pretty strong. They even snogged on the doorstep while we were waiting for David to let us in."

"Say it again," Casey asked Olivia with a smile.

"Snogged. Snogging. Snog."

"I love it. It's my favorite of your new British-isms. You speaking British is very sexy."

"I should bloody well hope so, mate." Olivia winked. Her Cockney was coming along nicely. And it made Casey want to snog her.

They entered via the veranda. The room was even more crowded now. Casey scanned the partygoers, looking for Louise and Liam, but also looking for Hannah and Zoey. They were nowhere to be seen. Casey felt a wave of relief.

They threaded their way through the partygoers toward the dance floor set up by David at one end of his cavernous living room/dining area. In the corner, Louise was dancing with Mercy and David, while Liam was standing against the wall, beer in hand, chatting with Naomi.

"Doesn't look like anyone missed us much." Olivia laughed.

As they got closer, David spotted them and waved enthusiastically.

"I was going to come look for you, but I figured you hadn't gone out to the garden to look at the roses, and I didn't want to be traumatized by the sight of you two making out under my new arbor." He pointed a thumb at Louise. "These two have been bad enough. I had to tell the DJ no more slow dances until they agreed to stop with the tonsil tennis." He laughed.

"Here you are. Come on, I've been waiting for you." Louise grabbed for Olivia's hand. "Dance with me." With her other hand, she pulled Casey into the circle. "You too." Casey couldn't help but laugh. Louise drunk was even more of a tour de force. "No more hiding in the garden. It's Pride, take pride in your love." She gyrated to what Casey thought might be Lady Gaga, not letting go of either of their hands.

Casey was a slow-dancing-in-the-dark kind of dancer, but the wine she'd drunk, Olivia's arm around her waist, and Hannah's continued absence, conspired to make her feel more relaxed than she expected. After a few minutes, she was bumping hips with Mercy and Olivia, watching David and Louise attempt something that looked like it belonged on TikTok, and cringing as Mercy told them all the story of how Casey had broken her wrist by crashing into a speaker while drunk dancing at Naomi's thirtieth birthday party.

"This is fun." Olivia leaned in and said the words into her ear. "I'm glad we came." Casey let herself place a soft kiss on Olivia's lips. She was having fun. And she was happy to be there, with David and Mercy and with the new friends she had unexpectedly made while driving a bunch of pretty amazing and unexpectedly down-to-earth TV stars around London. And of course, it was fun because she was with Olivia, the woman she'd ended up falling in love with.

When the music slowed, Casey pulled Olivia to her, not caring that they were in company. She let herself enjoy the feeling of having Olivia in her arms, their bodies pressed gently together, swaying in time to the rhythm of the song.

"I'm glad to have found you," Casey murmured into Olivia's ear and was rewarded with the feel of Olivia's hand in the small of her back, pushing them together even closer.

Across the room, in the entrance to the hallway, she became aware of a commotion as people arrived and were warmly greeted by those nearer to the doorway. Casey tensed—waiting, expecting—and Olivia pulled away to look at her quizzically. She gestured toward the door with an incline of her head at just the moment Hannah and Zoey entered, carrying several rainbow-covered bags in each hand.

"Goodies from the sponsors of our Pride video. Help yourselves. And happy Pride." Hannah addressed the room loudly, confidently. Her voice sounded just as Casey remembered it. "Sorry we're so late, but it was totally worth it. We got to interview some amazing people. The video is going to be lit."

Hannah assumed that the whole room would be interested. Of course she did. And maybe they were, maybe it was just Casey who didn't give a fuck about that sort of thing. Zoey handed Hannah a glass of white wine, and Hannah gave her a peck on the cheek before turning her attention to the group of women in front of her.

"I guess that's her," Olivia said quietly.

Casey just nodded. Her mood crashed through the floor.

"That was quite an entrance. I especially like the implication that she left all the amazing people behind to grace us with her presence. I mean, we should be grateful, right?" Olivia slid an arm around Casey's waist and squeezed it.

Casey watched as Hannah scanned the room and saw the surprise that she tried and failed to hide as she caught sight of Casey standing arm in arm with Olivia Lang. Casey couldn't believe no one told Hannah about Olivia. She assumed Naomi—who had seen Casey with Olivia at the parade—or even David would have passed on the gossip. Not that they were lovers, but that Casey was bringing them to the party, the very kind of "amazing" people—famous, rich, influential—that Hannah loved. Perhaps she'd have graced the party with her presence a little sooner had she known.

Looking at her, Casey felt a mixture of shame and anxiety. For once, it wasn't the shame of having been cheated on, it was the shame that she had ever thought that Hannah—with her obsessive desire for fame—was what she needed or wanted in life. The anxiety was easier to understand. And it was linked to the idea of Hannah and Olivia meeting. It was hard to imagine that Hannah would see Olivia or Louise or Liam and not try to make a connection. And Casey's primary instinct was to take Olivia far away from everything Hannah might say or do.

Across the room, Hannah lifted a hand in her direction. Casey nodded before turning away, turning back to Olivia—an Olivia who was looking at her with concern in her eyes. She didn't want to see it there. She didn't want Olivia's pity.

"It's okay," Olivia said as she reached down to take Casey's hand.

"I know it is." Casey tried for a smile. "I was ready to leave anyway. Maybe we can finish this dance and leave."

"Of course. I just need a few minutes to speak to Kate again."

Casey frowned.

"She's a theater director. We spoke earlier. I promised I'd give her some of my contacts in New York. A tiny bit of shop talk. We can go after that. Trust me, my only desire right now is a room, a bed, and you." Olivia tilted her head to kiss Casey, but Casey felt awkward now. Like the PDA was something that Hannah would take as a provocation. "Hey, come on." Olivia chided her. "You don't have any reason to hide, or any reason not to kiss me."

"I know, I'm sorry." Casey gave in to the kiss, and it restored her. "Go do your networking. I'll wait in the kitchen—with the cheese."

"Five minutes. I'm popping to the loo as well to have a wee." Olivia exaggerated the Britishness of the statement, kissing Casey's cheek with a smile before leaving her side. And Casey felt her heart swell. For a second, she imagined them living happily together in London. Close to her mom, to her friends, in the city she loved. She shook the thought away. It was a pipe dream.

In the kitchen, Casey sat at the breakfast bar and pulled one of the delicious cheese platters closer to her. She challenged herself to see how many kinds she could try in the five minutes she had. She piled some crackers onto the plate in front of her and set to work.

"You never could resist cheese."

Casey willed herself to just keep eating, to ignore her. She had nothing to say to Hannah. And nothing good was going to come of them reconnecting. But whatever else was wrong with her childhood, she had been raised to be polite.

"Hello." Casey pushed the plate away before finally turning on the stool to look at Hannah. "You look well." She managed a smile, but inside her instincts were screaming at her to get up, find Olivia, and leave.

Hannah walked slowly around the counter and climbed onto the stool opposite her. She took a small plate and cut herself a slice of Stilton. They sat in silence as Hannah loaded the cheese onto a cracker, took a small bite, and made a satisfied noise. Casey had no choice but to wait and Hannah knew it.

"I just came to say hi, so things weren't awkward for you." Hannah's gaze was open, neutral. "But it seems I don't have to worry about that. You've surprised me. I mean, it's a little on the obvious side, but it's quite a statement. Turning up with half the cast of *The West Side*. It's a great way of proving to everyone that moving to the States has been good for you. Even if it does upstage David a bit." Hannah paused, but Casey could tell she hadn't finished. "And I guess from that display out there, you especially want us all to know that your bit-of-London-rough shtick still has enough appeal to get someone like Susie to fall for your charms. I guess I should say well played."

"Her name's Olivia, not Susie."

"Of course it is." The smile Hannah offered her wasn't a warm one. "Either way, you two look surprisingly good together. I just hope you're going to be okay when she moves on to cozy up with her next driver. I mean, you don't always cope well with breakups."

Casey couldn't understand why Hannah was bothered enough to even try to push her buttons. She surely couldn't care less about Casey, not after all this time. Hannah didn't care much about anyone but herself. But maybe not being the most important, the most famous person at the party annoyed her. Casey corrected herself mentally. There was no maybe about it. Of course it did.

"Not that it matters, but David invited them, not me. It's Pride. They don't know anyone in London and they wanted to party. And he didn't seem to worry about being upstaged by them. He's enjoying having them here. Maybe not everyone thinks the way you do."

"Well, Olivia Lang clearly 'knows' you. And I can't pretend I'm not surprised. I didn't think celebrity was your thing. You must have told me a thousand different ways how it wasn't." Hannah tried to keep her tone friendly, but Casey could hear the hostility underneath.

Casey stood. She could have told Hannah that Olivia was appealing to her because, although she was famous, she didn't want to be. And it didn't define her, it didn't represent everything Olivia wanted from life. She was nothing like Hannah in that way. But Casey had no intention of staying and talking to Hannah. She had nothing to say to her. Hannah was unpleasant, irrelevant, and in her past. She had Olivia. And she could have David, Mercy, even Naomi in her life, without having to give a toss about Hannah. She'd been stupid not to realize that sooner.

"I'm heading out. I'm glad the channel's going well. Enjoy the rest of your evening." Casey pushed her stool back under the breakfast bar.

"I will. And I'm super happy you seem so well." She didn't sound happy. "You left and just ducked out of sight and no one knew how you were doing. We were all so worried about you, concerned about how you were coping. It was a lot for you to lose—me, your job, your friends. It's good to see that you're mostly okay, even if you did feel the need to turn up here and try and show off a little."

Every one of Hannah's words had been chosen to rile Casey, to remind her that they "all" talked about her after she left, to remind her that, thanks to Hannah, she had lost everything, even to suggest maybe she wasn't quite over it. And Hannah needing to remind her of it all so spitefully was what? To pay her back for daring to turn up, with Olivia and the others, looking like she was enjoying herself.

"You were worried about me?" Casey felt herself heat up. It was anger, but she was determined to control it. She took in a breath and let it out again. "Of course you were. I imagine the guilt was hard to bear. Getting me arrested, making all those videos about our breakup, full of lies, the stories you told to turn everyone against me, to make it easier to hide all the bad things you did. Are they still up on the channel making you money? I hope so. At least my misery and the destruction of my reputation was lucrative for you." Casey kept her voice calm. It took a lot of effort. "But do you know what? I don't care about any of it anymore. And I'm surprised you do."

"I don't. I'd be happy to let it all go. But it's impossible. I come and say a friendly hello and here you are still talking about it, still blaming me for what happened to you. And you never think about your part in it. You were impossible to live with, you wouldn't support me with the channel—"

"I was busy. I had a proper fucking job." Casey couldn't help but interrupt. Hannah's version was bullshit.

"And you got yourself into trouble, not me. I didn't have you arrested for nothing. You forget that. Even now, look…" She hesitated. It was as if even Hannah couldn't believe the nerve she had. "You're getting all angry again for no reason."

Casey turned to leave and then stopped. Olivia was in the doorway, looking at her with an expression full of worry. She stepped into the kitchen, and Casey had no idea just how much of the exchange with Hannah she'd heard.

"I just came to say I'm ready to go now." Olivia looked from Casey to Hannah. And Casey fought the urge to tell her to leave. She didn't want Olivia anywhere near her past, anywhere near Hannah or her poison.

"You're leaving already? That's a shame, I was hoping we might have a chance to get acquainted." Hannah got up from her stool and offered Olivia a hand to shake. "I'm Hannah Wilson. From the Rainbow Endeavors channel. Maybe you've heard of it. We're closing in on half a million subscribers. The podcast is kind of new, but the audience is growing fast."

Casey watched in amazement. Minutes ago, Hannah had been digging up the past, digging at her, accusing her of using Olivia and the others to get back at her somehow. It was ridiculous and unpleasant. But now she was all business. A convincing smile on her face and a lightness in her tone. This ability to pretend, to play both sides, was why she never belonged in Hannah's world.

Olivia ignored the outstretched hand, and Casey wanted to hug her for it. But it didn't seem to faze Hannah at all. She dropped her hand to her side and kept talking.

"We reached out to your people. We were hoping for an interview while you were in town. You, Billie, any of the cast really. But no response…" She lifted her shoulders in a shrug. "But we made this great Pride video today. It's still to be edited, so we could absolutely include a segment from tonight if you were up for it. The three of you, enjoying an authentic Pride party in queer old Clapham Town. It would be fun and really good publicity."

"For who?"

Olivia moved to Casey's side. The feel of her close by was settling to Casey somehow.

"For both of us."

"You think I'm going to gain from being on your channel?" Olivia's tone was even, but Casey could tell how annoyed she was. "*The West Side* has an audience of three million, and every one of us has over a million followers on Instagram. The studio has one of the best PR teams in the business, and in the past two weeks, we've done every queer-themed radio, TV, and web-based channel in London that's worth doing. If they didn't respond to Rainbow Endeavors' request for an interview, there's a good reason for that."

Hannah looked at Olivia like she'd just been slapped.

"But even if it was worth doing, asking me now, here, at a party when I'm clearly off-duty and enjoying myself…" Olivia looked at Casey as she said the last part. "Well, I don't mean to be rude, Hannah, but it's kind of crass." She reached down for Casey's hand and squeezed it. "Shall we go?"

Casey looked at Olivia and nodded. It was all she could manage. In front of them, Hannah opened and closed her mouth like a fish. A moment, however brief, of her being affected by Olivia's brutal dismissal of her. But Casey saw the way she quickly composed herself, the stiffening of her posture, the fixing of her expression.

"It's all the same to me." Hannah sat back down on the stool. "I mean, I've got a story to tell either way. The mighty Olivia Lang—with none of Susie's street smarts—letting herself fall for yet another unsuitable woman, seemingly learning no lessons from her past."

Casey felt the anxiety start in her feet and creep slowly up her body. She should have turned and ran, gotten Olivia as far away from Hannah as she could. But for some reason, she couldn't move. It was like knowing you were going to crash but not knowing how to stop it.

"You don't know a thing about me."

"I know enough. I mean, it's hard to keep secrets in your business." Hannah looked at Olivia neutrally, seeming completely unbothered by the way the conversation had gone. But Casey's heart was beating its way out of her chest. "It's why I'm surprised that you'd let yourself get involved with someone like Casey. Broken home, arrest record, anger management problems. I mean, I can't imagine your PR team would think that's good for your brand."

Casey pulled at Olivia's hand, wanting to leave. It wasn't true that she couldn't control her anger, not in the way that Hannah meant, but she could feel her temper rising and she didn't want to have an argument with Hannah at the party. To ruin things for David or to spoil her last night with Olivia.

"If you're talking about getting Casey arrested for breaking your camera and hoping to shock me with it, then try a bit harder. I already know and I don't care. And not that it's any of your fucking business, but Casey makes me happy and happy is the only 'brand' I'm interested in. Feel free to make one of your story videos about that. I think most people would understand. Unlike you, they might even be happy for us."

Olivia turned her back on Hannah, and Olivia's defense of her gave Casey the strength to do the same. They walked hand in hand toward the hallway.

"Fair enough," Hannah said as they reached the door, raising her voice so they had no choice but to hear her. "But when you have your first bit of trouble in paradise and she's angry and jealous enough to want to cause you some harm, don't say I didn't warn you." She laughed bitterly. "You think I had her arrested because I cared about a camera? I had loads of them. I had her arrested to stop her from uploading private videos to my channel, videos that the two of us had recorded on her phone years before. And maybe she didn't do it for money like that ex of yours, but it was done to harm me, to harm my reputation." Hannah smiled a sly smile. "But if that's the kind of person who makes you happy, Olivia, go for it."

Hannah's words caused a tightness in Casey's chest. In two sentences, Hannah had laid bare everything she had dreaded telling Olivia, everything she knew she should have explained as they stood in the supermarket hours before. For a few seconds, Olivia didn't react. They kept walking hand in hand, and Casey had a ridiculous hope that maybe she hadn't heard. But Olivia released her hand, opened the front door, and stepped outside, and when she finally turned to Casey, the look in her eyes was fearful.

"Tell me it's not true."

The panic was coursing through Casey's body. Everything she dreaded about the party had come true. She leaned back against the front door to steady herself.

"They weren't sexual. Not at all. Nothing like that. I promise. It was just Hannah complaining about sponsors—"

Olivia took a step away from her.

"It's true?" The expression on her face was one of disbelief and then upset. "You put private videos of her online. What—why the hell would you do that?"

"She cheated on me, she humiliated me. She made all these videos about me, about us breaking up, about why it was my fault. And it wasn't fair…they were full of lies. I didn't know what to do. How to make her stop. I thought—"

At the time, Casey hadn't made herself stop and think. That was the problem. She was hurting and she wanted to hurt Hannah in return, so she'd used the only thing she had.

"There were just two of them, they were so short. Little video clips we recorded on my phone when we were messing about. I forgot all about them, and then when she did all that to me—" Casey couldn't get the words out quick enough, and when she did, she knew they weren't enough. The expression of dismay on Olivia's face was awful to see. "I was drunk, feeling mad at her. It was the middle of the night, hardly anyone saw them. I woke up. I knew it was the wrong thing to do, so I took them down."

"You want credit for taking them down? It doesn't matter that you took them down, you put them up in the first place. You had no right. It's a—" Olivia seemed to be struggling to speak. "It's a complete breach of trust. It doesn't matter if you're drunk, or angry. You have no right to publish private videos without consent."

"I know what happened to you with Kristin was terrible, hurtful, but this isn't the same—"

"You knew what happened to me and that's why you didn't tell me," Olivia said, her face flushed with upset. "Telling me the half of the story of what happened with Hannah that would make me feel sorry for you. But not telling me the part that made you look bad. And if Hannah hadn't been so vindictive, I wouldn't ever have known. Not until the first time you got mad at me for something and decided to do the same to me." Olivia was struggling not to cry, and Casey wanted to go to her, to hold her. But she didn't dare.

"I would never do that to you. Because it's you, because I don't believe you would ever hurt me the way Hannah hurt me, and—" Casey was finding it hard to speak, her own fear and upset had the words sticking in her throat. "And because I do know it was wrong."

Olivia began pacing along the path that crisscrossed David's small front yard. Casey didn't know what to say or do. She had tried to leave what happened with Hannah in the past, but now it was screwing up the future she'd hoped to have with Olivia. Casey tried to calm herself, to find a way to explain better.

"I'm sorry I didn't tell you. I know I should have. I just didn't want to admit to it, to explain how low I'd had to go to get her to stop telling people things about me that weren't true. And I hoped it wouldn't matter to you because it was so long ago and I'm a different person now."

"It matters, Casey, of course it does. She might have treated you badly, but that didn't give you the right to use what she obviously imagined were private moments to try to ruin her reputation, her career. I know better than anyone how much that stuff sticks to you when you're in the public eye. There's no excusing it."

"What about my reputation and my career?" Casey couldn't help raising her voice. She couldn't believe Olivia was taking Hannah's side and her frustration boiled over. "Hannah cost me my job. A job I loved, a job I was good at. A job which, if we're being honest, was a lot more important than making lifestyle videos or being on TV. But maybe me losing my job doesn't count, maybe it's only you famous people who get to worry and whine about having their reputations destroyed. I should probably be thankful to Hannah too—for showing me the total fucking double standards you operate under."

As soon as she said it, Casey realized she'd gone too far. Yards away, Olivia was now standing, stiff as a board, staring at her. The hurt was visible. Her eyes were full of tears she was fighting not to shed. And then Olivia turned, walked out of the yard, and along the street, away from her.

Casey hurried out onto the sidewalk and called after her.

"Olivia, wait. I'm sorry. I—" She stopped, her frustration, her sorrow, overtaking her. She doubled over, hands on her knees, fighting for composure. What could Casey say? Nothing that could change the past and nothing that would change the way Olivia felt about it. Olivia was right. She had chosen not to tell her about the videos because she was worried about her reaction. But she hadn't expected Olivia to be so disgusted by it, to so rapidly identify with Hannah and to not let Casey explain. For the past two weeks, Casey had been worrying about how hard it might be to overcome the differences between the lives they led, and in three long minutes, Olivia had shown her why she'd been right to worry.

Casey let the night air wash over her, taking deep breaths until the large fist that felt like it was pressing against her heart shrunk to a size that allowed her to breathe again. She felt paralyzed. There was no way she was going back inside, but following Olivia back to the hotel didn't seem like a good idea either. Olivia had made her feelings plain.

She pulled her phone from her pocket and dialed.

"Sorry, did I wake you?"

Her mom sounded sleepy.

"Can I stay at yours tonight? No, it's okay, honestly, Mom. I just need somewhere to sleep that isn't the hotel."

Her mom was full of questions Casey didn't want to answer.

"We just had an argument, that's all." Casey knew that wasn't all it was. The argument had exposed everything that was wrong between them. And the realization caused unexpected tears in her eyes and a heaviness in her chest.

She ended the call and set off toward the tube station that would carry her to her mom's. She couldn't believe their last night had ended like this. Casey stopped walking.

"Our last London night."

She made herself say it out loud. Surely it couldn't end like this. With Hannah ruining her life for a second time. But then she remembered how Olivia had been so quick to judge her, not caring about what had driven her to it. And she was hurt by it all over again. Maybe this was a wakeup call, a bullet dodged. She took in another deep breath and willed herself to just keep walking.

CHAPTER TWENTY-ONE

Merci, monsieur. Je t'aime. Voulez vous coucher avec moi, ce soir? I'm remembering more than I expected, Liv. It's bon. Tres bon. I'm going to drive Liam wild whispering to him in French when we're making the amour."

Louise was sitting on the edge of Olivia's bed. Her French was hurting Olivia's ears, but she didn't have the energy to protest. This was their third day in Paris, and she hadn't had a decent night's sleep since leaving London. Or more accurately, since leaving Casey in David's front yard. They had just finished yet another round of TV interviews and she had gone to her room, hoping for a nap. But Louise followed, claiming to have something important to talk about.

"Are you even listening, ma cherie?" Louise lay down next to her.

"I'm listening. But I'm tired and I'm not in the mood for hearing about you seducing Liam with your bad French. Sorry." Olivia didn't even try to hide her bad mood. Why should she? Everything had gone wrong on this trip to Europe. Not just Casey—falling in love with her and then being stupid enough to lose her—but the show, Billie, her feelings about all of it. Everything had changed. And she was tired. Tired of playing the argument with Casey over and over in her mind, tired of crying, tired of being Susie, and tired of not sleeping. And right then, all she wanted was a nap. A nap Louise seemed unwilling to let her have.

"Did you really want to talk to me about something?"

"I do." Louise pulled herself up into a sitting position, resting her back against the headboard. "But only if you promise to stay awake and pay attention."

"Okay, okay. Get on with it." Olivia sat up, mirroring Louise's position.

Louise turned to her and took her hand. The pause was long and dramatic. And Olivia could already feel herself losing patience.

"What are you going to do about Casey?"

Olivia sighed. She didn't want to have this conversation again.

"What do you mean, what am I going to do? There's nothing to do. I'm going to hurt like this for a long while. I'm going to be angry with myself for being dumb enough to fuck things up with her, and then I guess, eventually, I'll recover."

"That's not what I meant. And you know it. Honestly, Liv, you're such a cliché. And I say that while loving you like the annoying older sister I never had." Louise smiled at her and shook her head.

"How am I a cliché? And more to the point, why am I listening to you talk about Casey again? I don't need it." Olivia rubbed her temples. She could feel a headache starting.

"You're a cliché because you're totally living up to the 'inexplicably refusing to communicate with the woman of your dreams' trope. I've seen that storyline a dozen times, and it always leaves me shouting in frustration. Just call her and have the conversation you two need to have before you lose each other for good out of sheer stubbornness. Tell her you watched some of the videos Hannah made about her and explain how sorry you are for the way you reacted at the party and for all the things you said. And see if she'll forgive you."

Louise squeezed her hand, and Olivia felt the upset building all over again.

"And please tell her what you said to me. That you understood why she did what she did after you'd seen what Hannah said about her, that you would have done worse if Hannah had said those things about you. For fuck's sake, Liv, just call and tell her all that. I can't believe she doesn't want to hear it, that she's not as heartbroken as you are."

Olivia cried for hours after watching Hannah's videos. Hannah made sure to keep blaming Casey, to find new ways of making herself seem the victim. She'd said Casey was aggressive and vindictive and impossible to live with. She even talked about Casey losing her job "with children" as if she was somehow not safe to have around kids, while not mentioning that her own lies were the only reason Casey had lost that job. It made Olivia sick to her stomach. And honestly—as she'd admitted to Louise—she would have done anything she could to make Hannah stop. But instead of being understanding and letting Casey explain, she had blamed her, judged her, letting her own history with Kristin cloud that judgment. And she had ruined everything. Olivia had never felt so heartsick.

"I can't."

"Why can't you?"

Olivia wasn't sure she could explain.

"This is going to sound weird, especially after what we argued about, but I think she's too good for me. I can't give her what she needs, what she wants. And my life, right now, represents everything she doesn't like. She made that clear. Even changing my life, making it less crazy," Louise didn't know that Olivia was taking steps to do just that, "I'm not sure that it wouldn't still be a problem for us. Being with me would upend that quiet life she's carved out for herself in Portland."

"Maybe she wants it to be upended," Louise said. "Do you never think of it that way? She told you Portland was kind of lonely for her, that she missed London, her friends. Maybe she wants a bit of upheaval."

"You're wrong. I know her better than you. She doesn't love Portland, but that doesn't mean she's ready to embrace all the craziness that comes with this life. Being around Billie would be a problem, and she'd hate being photographed all the time. And the media would scratch at her, trying to find out things about her, about her family, her life. I can't do that to her. It's bad enough when they do it to me."

"I hate to break it to you, Liv, but you're not that famous. Or that interesting. They'll scratch for a while, but then they'll stop. She'll cope. Look at what she coped with from Hannah. And you said yourself that Billie's behaving herself now that she thinks you have a recording of her incriminating herself. I think you're making excuses. I think you're the one who's scared of having their life upended." Louise sounded serious. "It isn't my business to say this, Liv, but you've got to let yourself love someone one day. And whatever's happened, I think Casey might be the one. Jeez, you even like her mom. How perfect do you want it to be?"

"I know." Olivia felt the frustration all over again. "But I messed it all up. I told you, I tried to reach out. She isn't interested. I showed her who I was and she's run a mile."

"You texted a twelve-word apology the morning we left. That's not trying. And it's not opening a door. You know Casey. She's going to need that door to be wide open before she even moves an inch toward it. You sided with Hannah and you were willing to believe the worst about her. You need to give her more than twelve words."

It was all true, but that didn't mean Olivia knew what to do about it. She was in Paris and Casey was getting ready to go back to Portland. She'd blown it. And even a novella of an apology from her wasn't going to fix things.

"There's no point. You didn't see the way she looked at me, Lou. It was like she understood that I was just like Hannah. I think it was what she feared all along, and when push came to shove, I lived up to her worst fears about me and about the world I live in. And the horrible irony of it all is that I don't even want to live in that world anymore. I'm probably more tired of it than Casey is."

Olivia wasn't going to tell Lou until they got back to LA. They were in each other's pockets here in a way that they weren't at home, and if Louise reacted badly, it was going to make the trip even tougher. But keeping it from her—and from Liam—was close to impossible. It had been a hard decision and it was another reason why she hadn't been sleeping.

"I'm leaving the show." Olivia made herself say it. "Just for a bit. I'm taking a break. I realized this past couple of weeks that I'm burned out with it."

"What?"

"That whole thing with Billie, seeing my life the way Casey sees it, it just isn't what I want to be doing at thirty-five. I want something more. Something just for me, not for Susie, not for the studio, not even for the fans."

"When did you...how come you didn't tell me?" Louise's voice quavered slightly, the shock turning to upset. Olivia knew her well enough to know she was trying not to cry.

"I'm telling you now, Lou. I only decided a couple of days ago."

"Because of Casey?"

"Yes and no. Me leaving the show doesn't help one way or the other with Casey. Brooklyn is even farther away from Portland than LA is. And I fucked that up regardless of geography. But meeting Casey, loving Casey, made me realize I want different things. A home I get to live in, kids, time with my parents before they get old, maybe even a dog."

Saying it out loud to Louise moved her. Olivia was ready for something else. It had taken Casey to help her see that.

"Somehow that whole thing with Billie—her going as far as she did to fight for 'star billing'—made me realize I've never cared enough to want any of it that badly. And maybe I should spend some time doing something I enjoy enough to fight for."

"But how did you get them to agree. The show without Susie is nothing."

"That's not true. I hate to say it, but Billie has turned Phoebe into a popular character. Jessie and Michael's romance has everybody all worked up and excited. And some of Susie's storylines could easily be rewritten to give Jessie or Phoebe more of a role. I told them about Billie and the web stories and that I'd go public if they didn't release me. I channeled Susie and acted all badass, so they didn't have a choice."

"I can't believe it. I'm gonna miss you like crazy." Louise was crying softly. Olivia reached over to give her a hug.

"I'll miss you too. But it's only for six months. And I'm planning on visiting. I mean, I'll miss your PDA with Liam too much to stay away." Olivia tried to lighten the mood, to make Louise smile. "Because it's not awkward at all for me watching my best friends snogging."

As soon as she said the word, Olivia was reminded of Casey, of them in the garden at David's, of all the things that had felt possible and wonderful and hopeful. Was she stupid not to try harder to rescue something with Casey?

Louise's sniffling grew quieter and she pulled away from Olivia.

"It sounds like you need it, so I'm happy for you. Sad for me, but happy for you."

"At least you have Liam."

Louise nodded and they sat quietly for a beat.

"But it's weird how you can be so decisive about that and so hopeless about Casey. I think you should channel a bit of Susie to try to figure out what to do about Casey. I don't think Susie would let one stupid argument get in the way of potential happiness with a tall, dark, handsome tour guide. Especially once she'd experienced being held in those incredible arms of hers."

"Lou—" Olivia had tried not to torment herself with her memories of Casey kissing her, being held by her, the two of them lost in each other's pleasure.

"I'm serious. You need to do something. And it needs to be decisive. Try to get her back. Send a message, call, do something. Don't just sit there and let her go. I just don't think that's really what you want. And if you're taking time off, you can spend all the time you like in Portland." Louise got up from the bed and walked to the door. "And now I'm going to let you have your old lady nap."

She stopped.

"And I'm going to make Liam comfort me about you leaving."

The way she said the word "comfort" left Olivia in no doubt about what she meant. She couldn't help but smile.

Louise let the door close behind her, and Olivia lay back on the bed and closed her eyes, making herself breathe in and out slowly. She tried clearing her mind of everything, willing the sleep to come. But she couldn't. She had one thought and only one thought.

She couldn't lose Casey.

Olivia hated to admit it, but Louise was right. Casey might not be perfect—Olivia certainly wasn't—but she was amazing, and together they could have something special. What was the point of taking a break, making space to be happier and not having Casey to share it with somehow? Olivia sat up, suddenly wide-awake. She needed to find a way to apologize properly, ask Casey to forgive her, and beg her for another chance.

"I was thinking of redecorating the living room with some of that money Neil has given me. Maybe some nice green wallpaper there." Her mom pointed at the far wall. "And then paint the rest something neutral. Be nice to freshen things up a bit."

Casey pulled her attention away from her phone. She was expecting David, but he was late.

"Sounds like a great idea."

"They always say you need a man about the house for that sort of thing, but I was talking to Jenny next door and she said she does all her own wallpapering. She even offered to help. And Neil was hopeless at that kind of thing anyway. I mean, how hard can it be? If I mess it up, I can always ask Jack to help redo it...not that he's got much patience for that sort of thing."

Her mom's chatter used to drive Casey crazy when she was younger, but now there was something oddly comforting about it. These last few days, she seemed so bright, so full of plans, that Casey enjoyed being around her. And she certainly looked a lot healthier than when Casey had walked into her kitchen barely three weeks ago. It wasn't just that she'd stopped drinking, she was eating better—a lot better, if the massive dinners she'd been sharing with Casey were anything to go by. And she seemed a lot lighter in her mood. Getting away from Neil was clearly more of a relief than either of them expected.

"Maybe I could help."

"Thanks, love, but you don't have time. It'll take me a week just to choose the wallpaper and you'll be gone by then." Her mom tried to sound okay about it, but Casey caught the tremor in her words. "It'll be nice to take my time with it anyway."

Casey had surprised herself by choosing to spend the week at her mom's rather than with David. It made the multiple appointments they'd had to attend to sort out the last of her debts a lot easier, but it wasn't just that. David's house—his garden, his kitchen, his living room—was a three-dimensional reminder of everything that had gone wrong with Olivia, and it was far too raw for her to revisit that.

"Are you sure you don't want to come and have some breakfast with us?" Casey wouldn't have minded at all. Her flight back to Portland was Tuesday and after that, she wouldn't see her mom for months. The thought had been bothering her more than she expected, and more than once she'd been tempted to bump her departure date.

"No, no thanks. You go and spend some time with David. He'll miss you when you're gone. It's such a long way, it's not like he can pop over and see you for the weekend."

Casey knew her mom well. She had the same difficulties that Casey did when it came to expressing her emotions. And that was her way of telling Casey she'd miss her.

A car horn beeped, and her mom moved to the window before pulling back the curtain and waving.

"That's him. In another one of his big fancy cars." She laughed. "The neighbors will think he's a drug dealer."

Casey crossed the room and gave her mom a hug. Hugging wasn't something they normally did, but if loving Olivia had taught Casey anything, it was that every day—every minute—counted, and she didn't have a lot of time left with her mom. Her mom received the hug stiffly before relaxing and putting her own arms around Casey, squeezing her tightly.

"Go and enjoy your breakfast." She pulled away, hiding a sniffle. "And tell him next time, you expect to be picked up in an actual limo."

Casey picked up her phone, wallet, and jacket and headed for the front door.

"Mom?" She turned back.

Her mom looked at her.

"Thanks. For having me here, for feeding me, for not asking too many questions. I'm sorry—" Casey felt an unexpected welling up of emotion. She wanted to apologize to her mom for not having Olivia anymore, for not being able to watch them bake bread together. For losing the "girlfriend" her mom still thought she'd had for much longer than she had. It was silly. Her mom had other things to worry about, but somehow Casey felt like she'd let her down.

"Sorry for what, love?"

"Nothing. I was just thinking about the decorating, about not being here to help." Casey avoided saying what she'd been about to say.

"I've got Jenny to help. She's like you, you know. Part of the rainbow family." Her mom widened her eyes. "And we're getting on really well."

"No way." Casey shook her head and smiled.

"Her full name is Jennifer. You know, like Jennifer Aniston. It's got to be a sign."

Casey laughed and her mom joined in. She had no idea if her mom was teasing, or if she and rainbow neighbor Jenny were getting close, but either way, seeing her mom laugh was a real tonic.

"I'd better go. I'll see you later and we will definitely talk more about Jenny and her DIY skills," Casey said with a smile as she left the house. Heading down the path to the car, she lifted a hand to say sorry to David for keeping him waiting.

"I just know that extra time was not spent on hair and makeup." He rolled his eyes at Casey as she climbed inside. "So I hope to hell it wasn't because you were crying in your bedroom again."

Five days ago, Casey wouldn't have been able to take the joke. Even now, it was tough. But the teasing was the way they showed each other love. David had checked in with her every day and this—the offer to go out for breakfast—was part of that same care he'd been showing her since the party.

"Actually, my mom was telling me she and the next-door neighbor have been getting close. They're planning to wallpaper together."

"Oh, Lord. I hope you've checked him out thoroughly."

"She."

David thumped the steering wheel in delight. "Go Evelyn. Finally dipping her toes into the Sapphic stream." He turned to Casey. "She's probably gonna be better at it than you are."

"It wouldn't be hard. I set a pretty low bar." Casey waited while he found a gap and joined the traffic on the main road.

"Talking of which, have you seen sense yet?" David meant well and that made it hard for Casey to get annoyed with him, but the constant prodding about Olivia wasn't helping.

"If you're asking me if I've called Olivia, the answer is no."

"You could text."

"I haven't done that either."

"You should. I don't want to keep saying it, but she apologized, she reached out. And you're sitting on your stubborn ass doing nothing to sort things out, to get her back. You owe her a conversation, Casey. I can't believe you don't want to, that you don't miss her."

"I thought today was about us having breakfast, not about this."

Casey was sad rather than angry. She wanted to call Olivia, of course she did. She missed her like crazy and her heart was hurting. But what was the point?

"No law that says we can't chew some fat while chewing the fat about this." He turned to her again. "See what I did there?"

"I did. Very good."

"And I have some news. I mean, I'm guessing you haven't been near any entertainment websites today."

He cursed at a driver who pulled out of a side road without waiting.

"No, I haven't. I've been too busy crying in my room." Casey lifted an eyebrow in his direction.

"She's leaving the show."

"Sorry?" Casey heard him. She just couldn't quite believe what he was saying.

"Olivia. A six-month break. They're not saying why, so there's a lot of speculation online, but Louise said she's just had enough of the craziness, said she wants 'something else' from life."

"You've been in touch with Louise?" Casey couldn't believe it. "When did you two get so close?"

"Hello. Did you forget the time you and Olivia walked out of my party and left me and Louise wondering what the hell had happened?" His tone was gentler than the words he was saying. "We've formed a support group. Or maybe it's more of an action committee, I don't really know." He lifted his hands from the wheel in a half-shrug.

"Seriously, David. What the hell?"

"What do you want me to say? We both think the two of you are being stubborn, stupid, and…" He searched for a word. "Well, mostly stubborn. And you both seem so unhappy about not being together."

"I don't like it. I don't like the idea of you talking about me, about how unhappy I might or might not be with Louise. With anyone. I had dinner with Mercy last night and we managed a whole night without her feeling the need to ask me about it. We managed to find a lot of other things to talk about. And it was just what I needed. Maybe you and your new friend, Louise, should try that—talking about other things."

Casey felt as annoyed as she sounded. But she also couldn't help but react to the news that Olivia was unhappy. She didn't want her to be. But the fact that she was gave Casey a little sliver of hope.

"I'm sorry. We just hit it off. And I guess we both want our best friends to be happy, and somehow we both seem to think we know what's best for our best friends." David at least had the good grace to look sheepish.

"Sounds like Olivia knows what's best for Olivia. She's taking a break and, presumably, going home to Brooklyn. Good for her."

Casey meant it, but she was surprised. Olivia had seemed kind of burned out with everything surrounding the show, but she'd never sounded like she was willing to give it all up. Not even for six months.

"I know Brooklyn is even farther away from Portland than LA is, but it doesn't make it impossible. Louise said that she's promised to head west for regular visits."

"David," Casey said. "Don't. I'm serious. I know you mean well, but it's not helping."

David turned into a side street, and Casey realized that they were heading for Café Brunest. She hadn't thought to ask him where they were going. And she couldn't exactly tell him that she wanted to go somewhere else. He pulled into one of the spaces opposite the café and turned off the engine. When he turned to look at her, he seemed serious.

"Please just call her then. She apologized and you owe her a call. A chance to explain. I know she's as sorry as you are. I can't stand the idea that she might be your person and you're letting her get away. There's got to be something my romantic ass can do about it."

Casey felt an inexplicable urge to hug him. He was going about this all the wrong way, but he was doing it with love. And she loved him for it.

"I'm staying here in London." Casey hadn't completely decided until she said the words out loud. And she didn't want to face up to the fact that Olivia no longer being within reach of Portland helped her make up her mind.

"Are you serious?" David was looking at her in shock.

"I am. I miss you. I miss London. I even miss my mom. I should never have let Hannah chase me away last time." Casey hadn't given it anywhere near enough thought, but her gut told her it was the right thing. She was killing time in Portland and she wanted more than that for herself.

"Gina has already figured out a way for me to work remotely while I'm here, so I'm sure I could keep doing that for a while."

David's face broke into a wide grin. "Well, damn, that's fantastic. So bloody fantastic. For a thousand and one different reasons." He tried to hug her but got caught by his seat belt. They laughed. "You have made my day. And I suspect you've made Evelyn's year. Does she know?"

Casey shook her head. "No one knows. I just decided."

"Well, let's go and celebrate. No champagne, but I'll toast you with some toast."

"Sounds good."

"Go get us a table. I've just got a quick call to make." David waggled his phone at her. "Two minutes I promise. I just need to sort out this job for tomorrow."

Casey frowned at him before getting out.

"Oh, Casey," he said and she leaned back in.

"I don't suppose you're free tomorrow, are you? One last job before you leave me? I've got a VIP coming in from France for the tennis. Wants a woman driver. All a bit last minute."

It was the last thing she wanted to do. But she owed David for everything he'd done for her this trip. And then some.

"Of course."

David looked relieved and oddly, very pleased with himself.

Casey walked into the café and instinctively sat at the table she had shared with Olivia. She let the grief of everything that had happened between them wash over her again. And then she tormented herself with the regret she felt at not responding to Olivia's message. At the time, hurt and confused by Olivia's reaction, she ignored it. It was too little and far too late. But now, the regret poked at her. If she had responded, they might have worked things out and she might have been happier—really happy— at the news that Olivia was taking a break from the show because she wanted more from life. She would have felt encouraged and excited. Now, it just felt like a cruel reminder of how badly she had fucked things up.

Estelle came into the room at the same time that David barreled in through the front door. He seemed even happier than when she had left him two minutes ago. He reached Estelle in three steps and bent down to kiss her on both cheeks.

"Two Full Montys with tea, please, E. And I hope Bruno's got some black pudding back there, I'm starving." David took the seat opposite her, and Estelle headed back to the kitchen at her usual snail's pace.

Casey was having a hard time thinking about anything that wasn't Olivia.

"I love her, you know. I know it sounds soppy, but I didn't expect to fall in love. And I think, as mad as it sounds, that it started right where you're sitting now. With me watching her eat steak pudding with this amazed, delighted look on her face." Casey stopped speaking, embarrassed that she'd said what was on her mind.

"I don't think it's soppy, it's wonderful. And you know what else? You love her. You used the present tense." He smiled at her sweetly. "It's important."

Casey waited for him to tell her again all the reasons why she should call Olivia, why she should try and save them. But he didn't. He sat serenely, looking at her with a satisfied look on his face.

"I guess it is important." Casey let herself feel the sadness. At least being in London would mean she had people who could help her get over the heartache. And it would mean a lot more of Estelle's cooking. It wasn't much but it was something.

Chapter Twenty-two

The line of drivers waiting outside the arrivals hall at St. Pancras was a lot smaller than the one at Heathrow. Casey took a spot at one end and held up the sign that David had provided for her. She was meeting some big-shot French banker—a woman—in London for a few days to "do" Wimbledon. It was the middle of the day on a Saturday, and the drive was going to be horrendous. Casey kept telling herself it was one last job for David before hanging up her chauffeur's uniform for good, but it wasn't doing much to improve her mood.

It had now been exactly a week since Olivia had left—passing through this very same Eurostar terminal—and in the shower that morning, Casey had promised herself she was going to stop tormenting herself with all the things she should have done differently and get out of the fug she was stuck in. Mercy had tipped her off about a house share in Kennington—a neighborhood she liked—and the remote working for Gina was set up to go full-time starting Monday. Things were moving in the right direction, and she was grateful.

She watched as a woman came out of the arrivals hall and ran into the arms of her girlfriend. They hugged and kissed and spun each other around. It would have been something she once found sweet. But now, her heart bruised by Olivia, the feeling of loss still heavy in her chest, Casey turned away. This weekend was one she had promised to spend with Olivia in Paris. If she had trusted Olivia with the truth, maybe they would have survived what Casey had done in the past and she'd have been getting off a train in Paris, with Olivia there to greet her like that.

Casey might have wished that Olivia had shown a little more faith in her, had given her the chance to try to explain, but what would she have said? She'd done the wrong thing. And Olivia was too good for her. She had always known that really. And she guessed that, deep down, Olivia had always known it too.

The doors to the arrivals hall slid open again, and a steadier trickle of people starting coming out. Casey cursed as someone jostled her, trying to force themselves into a better position at the railings where people were lining up and waiting. She dropped her sign and bent to pick it up.

"Casey."

She jumped into an upright position, not expecting the woman to know her name. She was ready to apologize, but the word got stuck in her throat. Standing in front of her, a small rucksack over her shoulder, an uncertain expression on her beautiful face, was Olivia. Casey felt everything slow down and then speed up again—and that included her heartbeat.

"Olivia, what are you doing here? I thought you'd gone."

Casey regretted the choice of words. Olivia hadn't gone, not really. She was gone from Casey's life, but she had every right to come back to London, to be in whatever city she chose.

"I have the weekend off." Olivia was still gazing at her, and Casey felt herself unable to look away. Every day since Olivia had walked away from her, Casey had wished for the chance to see her again, to have a chance to explain, and with Olivia standing in front of her now, all she could do was stare.

"I figured London was only a couple of hours away and I…" Olivia hesitated, her voice breaking slightly. "I missed seeing a lot of the things I wanted to see when I was here before I left, I mean." Olivia looked down, seeming upset about something. Casey felt the urge to go to her, to hold her. But after everything that had happened between them, she understood that it probably wouldn't have been welcome.

"Paris is pretty cool. It has a lot of great things you could see." Casey tried to make herself seem unaffected by Olivia's presence. She was doing it for her own sake, but also for Olivia's. She wanted to make them running into each other easy on Olivia, less awkward.

"Casey, please." Olivia looked up at her, her expression hurt. "I was hoping we could have a coffee or something. Is that possible? I hoped at the very least that you'd hear me out."

"I can't, I'm sorry. I'm not saying I don't want to." Casey wanted to. The strength of her longing to go with Olivia, to hear what she had to say, was surprising even to her. "But I'm working. I'm expecting someone any minute now, someone I have to drive to Wimbledon. It'll take me half the day to get back here."

"Christine Lagarde?" Olivia said the name on Casey's card with a smile that Casey didn't understand. "Don't be mad, okay. It was all David and Louise's idea. I didn't want to go along with it at first, but I just couldn't find the courage to call you, and I realized how desperately I missed you, how stupid I'd been. And we'd said we were going to spend this weekend together. I—" Olivia seemed like she ran out of words.

"Christine Lagarde is not getting off this train?" The penny slowly dropped.

"She might. She's a real person I think. But if she does get off the train, you don't have to drive her anywhere. David sent you here to meet me. And Louise sent me here to meet you. I think they both think we have things we need to talk about."

Casey couldn't decide if she wanted to strangle David or hug him. She looked at Olivia—at the beautiful, fascinating, wonderful woman that the universe had tossed in her path three weeks ago—and hope crept up inside of her. How could she say no?

"I would love to have a coffee with you."

Regents Canal was nowhere near as impressive as the River Thames, but the towpath was quiet and Casey was grateful for that. They walked about half a mile before Olivia spotted a bench and asked if they could sit. Now they were sitting and watching the ducks, both of them seeming stuck for words.

Having Olivia this close and not being able to reach for her, to kiss her, to even hold her hand, was something close to impossible. Casey had her hands in her pockets in the hope it would help.

Olivia had come back to her. She was giving them a chance, but Casey felt terrified at the idea that she wouldn't be able to explain, that she wouldn't be able to say the right things, to make things better. She took in and let out a deep breath and turned to Olivia.

"I think everything I say next is going to sound like I'm making excuses. But I'm not. Honestly I'm not. I didn't behave in a way that I'm proud of. And obviously I wish I'd done it differently. Not just with Hannah, but with you. I should have just told you all of it, explained properly, asked for your understanding and hoped..." Casey hesitated, not sure what she had expected.

"Hoped that I didn't react as horribly as I did, hoped that I didn't judge you without even knowing what had happened." Olivia held her gaze. "I'm the one who should be sorry. I was too quick to judge. Maybe you won't believe me, but it's not like me to be like that. I just couldn't stop thinking of what Kristin did, and I let it get in the way of listening to you, believing in you. And I've spent a week wishing it had gone differently, worrying that I'd lost you."

Olivia's voice was thick with emotion, and when she stopped to compose herself, Casey couldn't help but reach for her hand. And when Olivia let her take it, turning it, so they could entwine their fingers, Casey felt like someone had just lifted a weight from her chest. She let herself enjoy the feel of Olivia's hand, let herself breathe.

"Well, I want you to know it's not at all the kind of thing I would do again. And I should have tried harder, for us. I should've gone after you. I told myself that forcing you to listen to my excuses wouldn't work. I think deep down," Casey took in a breath, "I thought maybe you wanted a way out, that you knew that the two of us weren't going to make it."

"That's absolutely not true." Olivia's denial was quick, and it gave Casey the encouragement to continue. If they were going to have a chance, they needed to say what needed to be said and put everything behind them.

"When I found out about Hannah and Zoey, I was devastated. Things hadn't been great between us, but I wasn't expecting her to do that. I saw them, I heard them—" Casey stopped. She'd never told anyone this. "I came back early. They were recording a video. I don't know what made me listen in, but I did. They were talking about how and when to tell me, how they might introduce their relationship to their audience. They were worried. Not about me, but about whether it might turn people against them and cost them sponsors. It was so casual, so callous. I didn't burst in on them or anything dramatic like that. I just went out. And I got drunk. I don't know if I was drowning my sorrows or drinking for the courage to confront her."

"You don't have to tell me all this." Olivia's voice was gentle. She stroked Casey's hand with her thumb.

"I think I do. Whatever else happens, I don't want there to be any more secrets between us." She rolled her shoulders, willing the tension out of her body. She made herself focus on the feel of Olivia's soft stroking.

"That night was when I stumbled and broke the camera. I think it was a light bulb moment for Hannah. She wasn't bothered about me finding out about her sleeping with Zoey—I think it was a relief actually—but me breaking the camera gave her the chance to play the victim online and to have me arrested. You know all this. They suspended me at work. They started an investigation. She started making videos about how awful I'd been to her, about how much she'd suffered with me, and I couldn't stand it. If it was true, that would have been one thing, but it wasn't, none of it. I just—"

Casey couldn't bear to carry on. She rubbed a hand across her forehead. The feelings were no longer fresh, nowhere near as hurtful, but telling all this to Olivia was hard.

"I just wanted her to stop. To be left alone. So...well, the rest you know."

Olivia stared at her in silence, and Casey had no idea if what she said had helped or made things worse.

"I'm sorry I didn't show more understanding. I was so stupid, Casey." Olivia took in a breath. "And I've missed you so much." She said the words so softly, but the power of them and the intensity of Olivia's gaze, caused Casey to shiver.

"I'm sorry I almost ruined things."

"No more apologies." Olivia placed a finger on Casey's lips as if to silence her, and Casey felt like all the blood in her body rushed to the spot where Olivia's finger was. And when Olivia moved her finger, softly tracing it across Casey's bottom lip, Casey grew hot, aware of the throbbing that had started low down in her center. "Nothing's ruined. We came back from the brink."

Olivia's eyes were wide and when she dropped her gaze to Casey's mouth, Casey didn't hesitate. She snaked an arm around Olivia's waist and pulled her closer, her lips seeking Olivia's. When she felt the soft warmth of them pressed against her own, Casey moaned.

"I've missed you too," she whispered into Olivia's ear before returning her mouth to Olivia's. They kissed like people who had missed each other—desperately, searchingly, breathlessly. Casey's hand in Olivia's hair and both of Olivia's hands in the small of Casey's back, under her shirt, on her skin. And when their tongues touched, Olivia moaned and pushed herself closer to Casey.

"I want more." Olivia broke their embrace first. "I need more." The look in her eyes made it clear what she meant.

"So do I. But—" Casey waved a hand around them. She felt exactly the same, but they were sitting on a bench in the early afternoon and the towpath was pretty busy. "I don't want you arrested for public indecency.

And…" Casey had been dreading this part. "There's probably a lot more to talk about."

"About you staying in London?" Olivia held her gaze steadily.

Casey frowned. "How did you—"

"David. Via Louise. Of course." She smiled. "I guess you heard about me leaving the show the same way."

"Yeah." Casey nodded. "Our very own news service."

Olivia's eyes contained a sparkle that Casey didn't understand.

"I love London. It's not perfect, but it's mine. And apart from you, most of the people I want to be close to are here. It makes no sense to be anywhere else." She hesitated, not sure after everything that had happened that she had a right to say it. "And with you being in Brooklyn, not LA, Portland doesn't even have the advantage of being close to you. It's probably easier to get from London to New York, than New York to Portland."

"I guess that's true." Olivia leaned across and kissed her. Slowly, deeply, sexily. And Casey felt her senses flood with arousal. When Olivia pulled away, it took Casey a moment to come back. "I haven't bothered to check the distances."

Casey was confused. Olivia was acting like she wanted them to have something, but she seemed completely unaffected by the fact that they would be an ocean apart in one week's time. Maybe she had this wrong. Maybe Olivia wasn't coming back to her.

"I guess you're happy about having the break. I was surprised. I mean, I know you were sick of the PR stuff and Billie, but you love acting. What will you do for the six months they've given you?" Casey was rambling, trying to cover up her confusion. Not wanting Olivia to think she'd been expecting them to pick up where they'd left off—making plans to see each other after they'd left London.

"I'm not really taking a break." Olivia took Casey's hands in hers. "Something I begged the 'news service' not to tell you until we'd met, because I wasn't sure you'd still want…" Olivia stumbled over her words. "Want this, want me. After everything. So I begged Louise not to tell David, but of course she did. So I got her to beg David not to tell you, and thankfully, he agreed."

"Olivia, I have no idea what you're talking about and it's driving me crazy."

"I know. I'm sorry. I always think Lou is the drama queen, but maybe a bit of it has rubbed off on me."

"Olivia." Casey made herself sound stern.

"I'm not taking a break and I'm not going to be in Brooklyn, because I got a new job." Olivia paused to place a tender kiss on Casey's lips. "A theater job. When I told your friend Kate that I was free to work, she offered me something. Straight away. It was awesome. It doesn't start for a couple of months, but when it does, it's in London."

Casey couldn't do anything but stare.

Olivia laughed. And the sound of it was delightful to Casey.

"You're going to be in London?" Casey felt her heart swell.

"I am. For at least six months. And I'm going to need a tour guide. And maybe a bodyguard. And most importantly of all, Casey, I'm going to need a girlfriend. One who makes my heart flutter, my knees weak, and my body feel like it's feeling right now. Alive, aroused, and horny enough to go and get a room in that fantastic St. Pancras hotel that I only ever saw the outside of, but which I'm sure has vacant rooms and almost certainly a spa."

Casey grinned. She didn't know what to celebrate first. She got up and pulled Olivia to her feet. "I love you, Olivia, so fucking much. And I'd be happy to fill the role of girlfriend, especially now that I know it's a full-time position." She kissed Olivia, pressing herself as close to her as she could while turning them around in a kind of happiness-induced spin.

"This has been the craziest three weeks of my life." Olivia put her hands on either side of Casey's face. "And I know things will never be the same again. But that's a good thing. And it's all because of you. I love you too, Casey."

For a few seconds, they just gazed into each other's eyes. And then Olivia smiled.

"Now, I need you to tour guide me to that hotel before I do things to you out here that will get us both arrested."

"Yes, ma'am."

Casey took Olivia by the hand and they walked slowly back toward King's Cross. This time there was no need to rush. The clock had stopped ticking on their love. And everything felt possible.

EPILOGUE

Olivia tied the string around the pudding bowl, checked that the foil was properly positioned, and then managed to balance it on an upturned plate in a saucepan half full of water. Now she just had to wait five hours—five incredible hours—for it to cook. When Estelle gave her the recipe, she thought she was joking. She couldn't believe the amount of trouble that was involved. I mean, it was good, but not that good.

She took off her apron and tossed it onto a chair, hoping that Casey would be happy that on their special day she was getting a steak pudding that would hopefully—possibly—be just as good as one of Estelle's.

The living room was suspiciously quiet, and when Olivia reached it, she could see that Casey and the twins had gone out to the garden. She tried not to worry that each of them was crouched over a plant pot, holding a trowel, with a huge bag of compost, split wide open, sitting between them. She looked at the recently cleaned rug—one of the many ways they'd been getting ready for Louise and Liam's visit—and then looked back at the soil they were all covered in. What could possibly go wrong?

"Hi." Olivia stepped outside. "I'm not even going to ask you what you're doing."

It was a hot day, and Casey was wearing running shorts and a tank top. Olivia let herself drink in the sight of her, feeling herself flush at the memory of them making love that morning, grateful that the boys had decided to sleep in for once.

"You're just in time." Casey gazed up at her with a smile. "We're going to grow some apple trees." As she said it, Olivia realized that both Teddy and Nick were holding apples.

"Is that how you grow apple trees? From apples?"

"We'll find out." Casey winked.

"Mine's a red one." Nick held out his apple. "Teddy's is green." Olivia crouched down next to him, stroking his head before leaning over to plant a soft kiss on Teddy's cheek. He was ignoring her, concentrating on shoveling soil into his pot. Most of it ending up on his feet. She leaned against Casey, letting her arm drape across her legs. The long muscular legs that were on show in the running shorts that she was super happy Casey had decided to wear today.

"I forgot to tell you, but Louise said Liam has finally persuaded her to start running."

"Wow. Sounds like the kind of crazy thing you do for the person you love." Casey raised an eyebrow in her direction and smiled.

"Hey, I told you, I can't run. I'm a 'watch TV while I'm on the elliptical' kind of woman. And anyway, I made you a steak pudding. Five hours and counting. That's the kind of crazy thing you do for the person you love." She leaned in and planted a soft kiss on Casey's lips, deepening it more than she intended to when Casey parted her lips and reached a hand up into her hair. "It's an anniversary gift. To match the one you very generously gave me this morning."

Olivia enjoyed seeing how dark Casey's eyes grew, happy she had the power to make her aroused like that.

"It's not our anniversary. I told you you can't count the fact that we went to Estelle's two years ago today as our anniversary."

"It's the day we first met."

"Yeah, and we spent the day grouching at each other. And anyway, we met the day before. In the sauna. And I'm offended that you don't remember that because I most definitely do." Casey looked her up and down and then smiled. Olivia felt the power of her gaze in the pulsing between her legs. "But I'll take the anniversary gift because I'm happy to have you cook me steak pudding on any day of the year."

Olivia pressed her lips to Casey's once more before standing up. "I'm glad you feel that way about the pudding because I'm going to rehearsals in about fifteen minutes and you need to make sure that the water in the saucepan doesn't boil dry. Otherwise, no steam, and that means no steamed pudding."

Olivia and Casey both watched as Nick buried a miniature toy soldier in the pot in front of Casey. Laying it down and then covering it carefully with soil.

"What are you doing, buddy?" Casey asked.

"He died in battle this morning, so I'm burying him."

"Yeah, your pot is for the dead soldiers," Teddy chipped in. "And our pots are for the apple trees."

"That sounds like a very good plan." Casey lifted her eyes to Olivia's and shrugged before walking with her to the threshold of the living room.

"I spoke to the social worker by the way. She said no problem on taking them on a trip to the seaside. They even offered some money to help pay for it. It's what they do when kids are still in the foster system. I said no, of course. I know how stretched those budgets are." She frowned. "She also said that now that we're only a couple of weeks away from the six-month point, she'll send in the adoption paperwork and start the ball rolling on that. I just hope they can see past the fact that we're both kind of self-employed."

Olivia could hear the tension in her voice. She knew how much Casey wanted the adoption to work. She felt the same way. They'd talked about children from the outset, but taking on the twins had been unexpected. Something Mercy had engineered that had worked out well for everyone. But being without them would be heart-wrenching.

"They will." Olivia pulled Casey into another hug. "They know the boys deserve a stable home with lots of love, and that's exactly what we can offer them. You have driving as well as a well-paying job, and I have a ton of savings and a growing theater career. We're a dream team." She kissed Casey's forehead. "Don't worry so much."

Casey broke the hug and held Olivia out at arm's length. "The seaside trip is as much for us as them. They've never seen the sea and I want them to. But that weekend is also our real anniversary, the anniversary of the time we stayed in Brighton without meaning to. When I first realized I had completely fallen in love with you and didn't want to live my life without you." Casey's voice was quiet but certain. She had gotten better at expressing her feelings. And Olivia felt her heart swell with the love she felt for her. "I even managed to get a room at the same hotel. It's a family room. So I guess we might end up spending the night a little differently this time." She pulled a face. "Parenting is its own reward."

"You are wonderful." Olivia kissed Casey again before reluctantly stepping away from her.

"Have a good rehearsal."

"I will."

"And don't forget to get those tickets for me, Liam, and Lou for Saturday. Mom has already agreed to watch the boys, so you'll have three of your biggest fans cheering wildly for you. I am planning to bring flowers to throw on stage."

"I hope you're joking. That was the kind of thing my dad used to do."

"At least I'm not throwing panties," Casey teased her. "I think you've forgotten how to enjoy the attention of your fans."

"That's not true. Twice this week, when we left the theater, there were people waiting for me to sign programs at the stage door."

"Doesn't that often happen?" Casey looked at her with confusion.

"Yeah, it did in the beginning, but it was mostly people who remembered me from *The West Side*. This week, I had people who had just seen the show and thought it was great and decided to wait to get their program signed. Not people who already knew me as Susie. One of them didn't even realize I was American." Olivia couldn't keep the pride from her voice.

"Baby." Casey came to her, taking her hands. "I'm so proud of you." The look she gave her was so full of love that Olivia couldn't help the tears that pricked the back of her eyes.

"Sometimes I can't believe this is my life." Olivia leaned into Casey, resting her head on Casey's chest, enjoying the feel of Casey's arms wrapped tight around her body. "Living in London, back on stage, mommy to that pair of beautiful soil-spreading monsters." She lifted her head from Casey's chest and looked up at her. "And being loved by you—like I dreamed I might be—every day for the rest of my life."

"I love you too." When Casey bent her head to kiss her, Olivia closed her eyes, letting her senses get flooded with everything that Casey's kisses had always made her feel—alive, safe, loved, and impossibly aroused.

Olivia finally pulled herself away.

"Maybe after you've vacuumed up all that dirt," she pointed at the soil Casey had tracked into the house, "you can vacuum the boys before you let them back inside." She blew Casey a kiss and headed for the hall to grab her bag and coat. She wasn't going to be late because the little theater that had given her the chance to get back on the stage—the Ovalhouse—was a ten-minute walk from their Kennington house. She smiled to herself as she opened the front door. She'd found Casey in London. She'd found herself in London. And now she wouldn't swap this life for anything.

THE END

About the Author

MA Binfield is stranded on that little island off the coast of France known as the United Kingdom. It's a magical place, with endless mugs of tea and lots of the kind of weather that makes you stay home to read and write. A passionate public servant, with a perennially bad back, MA is tall and hopelessly romantic. She is fond of the ocean and boiled eggs, and loves writing about women loving women. This is MA's third novel.

https://www.boldstrokesbooks.com/authors/ma-binfield-306
mabinfield@yahoo.com

Books Available from Bold Strokes Books

Busy Ain't the Half of It by Frederick Smith and Chaz Lamar Cruz. Elijah and Justin seek happily-ever-afters in LA, but are they too busy to notice happiness when it's there? (978-1-63555-944-6)

Calumet by Ali Vali. Jaxon Lavigne and Iris Long had a forbidden small-town romance that didn't last, and the consequences of that love will be uncovered fifteen years later at their high school reunion. (978-1-63555-900-2)

Her Countess to Cherish by Jane Walsh. London Society's material girl realizes there is more to life than diamonds when she falls in love with a non-binary bluestocking. (978-1-63555-902-6)

Hot Days, Heated Nights by Renee Roman. When Cole and Lee meet, instant attraction quickly flares into uncontrollable passion, but their connection might be short lived as Lee's identity is tied to her life in the city. (978-1-63555-888-3)

Never Be the Same by MA Binfield. Casey meets Olivia and sparks fly in this opposites attract romance that proves love can be found in the unlikeliest places. (978-1-63555-938-5)

Quiet Village by Eden Darry. Something not quite human is stalking Collie and her niece, and she'll be forced to work with undercover reporter Emily Lassiter if they want to get out of Hyam alive. (978-1-63555-898-2)

Shaken or Stirred by Georgia Beers. Bar owner Julia Martini and home health aide Savannah McNally attempt to weather the storms brought on by a mysterious blogger trashing the bar, family feuds they knew nothing about, and way too much advice from way too many relatives. (978-1-63555-928-6)

The Fiend in the Fog by Jess Faraday. Can four people on different trajectories work together to save the vulnerable residents of East London from the terrifying fiend in the fog before it's too late? (978-1-63555-514-1)

The Marriage Masquerade by Toni Logan. A no strings attached marriage scheme to inherit a Maui B&B uncovers unexpected attractions and a dark family secret. (978-1-63555-914-9)

Flight SQA016 by Amanda Radley. Fastidious airline passenger Olivia Lewis is used to things being a certain way. When her routine is changed by a new, attractive member of the staff, sparks fly. (978-1-63679-045-9)

Home Is Where the Heart Is by Jenny Frame. Can Archie make the countryside her home and give Ash the fairytale romance she desires? Or will the countryside and small village life all be too much for her? (978-1-63555-922-4)

Moving Forward by PJ Trebelhorn. The last person Shelby Ryan expects to be attracted to is Iris Calhoun, the sister of the man who killed her wife four years and three thousand miles ago. (978-1-63555-953-8)

Poison Pen by Jean Copeland. Debut author Kendra Blake is finally living her best life until a nasty book review and exposed secrets threaten her promising new romance with aspiring journalist Alison Chatterley. (978-1-63555-849-4)

Seasons for Change by KC Richardson. Love, laughter, and trust develop for Shawn and Morgan throughout the changing seasons of Lake Tahoe. (978-1-63555-882-1)

Summer Lovin' by Julie Cannon. Three different women, three exotic locations, one unforgettable summer. What do you think will happen? (978-1-63555-920-0)

Unbridled by D. Jackson Leigh. A visit to a local stable turns into more than riding lessons between a novel writer and an equestrian with a taste for power play. (978-1-63555-847-0)

VIP by Jackie D. In a town where relationships are forged and shattered by perception, sometimes even love can't change who you really are. (978-1-63555-908-8)

Yearning by Gun Brooke. The sleepy town of Dennamore has an irresistible pull on those who've moved away. The mystery Darian Benson and Samantha Pike uncover will change them forever, but the love they find along the way just might be the key to saving themselves. (978-1-63555-757-2)

A Turn of Fate by Ronica Black. Will Nev and Kinsley finally face their painful past and relent to their powerful, forbidden attraction? Or will facing their past be too much to fight through? (978-1-63555-930-9)

Desires After Dark by MJ Williamz. When her human lover falls deathly ill, Alex, a vampire, must decide which is worse, letting her go or condemning her to everlasting life. (978-1-63555-940-8)

Her Consigliere by Carsen Taite. FBI agent Royal Scott swore an oath to uphold the law, and criminal defense attorney Siobhan Collins pledged her loyalty to the only family she's ever known, but will their love be stronger than the bonds they've vowed to others, or will their competing allegiances tear them apart? (978-1-63555-924-8)

In Our Words: Queer Stories from Black, Indigenous, and People of Color Writers. Stories selected by Anne Shade and Edited by Victoria Villaseñor. Comprising both the renowned and emerging voices of Black, Indigenous, and People of Color authors, this thoughtfully curated collection of short stories explores the intersection of racial and queer identity. (978-1-63555-936-1)

Measure of Devotion by CF Frizzell. Disguised as her late twin brother, Catherine Samson enters the Civil War to defend the Constitution as a Union soldier, never expecting her life to be altered by a Gettysburg farmer's daughter. (978-1-63555-951-4)

Not Guilty by Brit Ryder. Claire Weaver and Emery Pearson's day jobs clash, even as their desire for each other burns, and a discreet sex-only arrangement is the only option. (978-1-63555-896-8)

Opposites Attract: Butch/Femme Romances by Meghan O'Brien, Aurora Rey, Angie Williams. Sometimes opposites really do attract. Fall in love with these butch/femme romance novellas. (978-1-63555-784-8)

Swift Vengeance by Jean Copeland, Jackie D, Erin Zak. A journalist becomes the subject of her own investigation when sudden strange, violent visions summon her to a summer retreat and into the arms of a killer's possible next victim. (978-1-63555-880-7)

Under Her Influence by Amanda Radley. On their path to #truelove, will Beth and Jemma discover that reality is even better than illusion? (978-1-63555-963-7)

Wasteland by Kristin Keppler & Allisa Bahney. Danielle Clark is fighting against the National Armed Forces and finds peace as a scavenger, until the NAF general's daughter, Katelyn Turner, shows up on her doorstep and brings the fight right back to her. (978-1-63555-935-4)

When in Doubt by VK Powell. Police officer Jeri Wylder thinks she committed a crime in the line of duty but can't remember, until details emerge pointing to a cover-up by those close to her. (978-1-63555-955-2)

A Woman to Treasure by Ali Vali. An ancient scroll isn't the only treasure Levi Montbard finds as she starts her hunt for the truth—all she has to do is prove to Yasmine Hassani that there's more to her than an adventurous soul. (978-1-63555-890-6)

Before. After. Always. by Morgan Lee Miller. Still reeling from her tragic past, Eliza Walsh has sworn off taking risks, until Blake Navarro turns her world right-side up, making her question if falling in love again is worth it. (978-1-63555-845-6)

Bet the Farm by Fiona Riley. Lauren Calloway's luxury real estate sale of the century comes to a screeching halt when dairy farm heiress, and one-night stand, Thea Boudreaux calls her bluff. (978-1-63555-731-2)

Cowgirl by Nance Sparks. The last thing Aren expects is to fall for Carol. Sharing her home is one thing, but sharing her heart means sharing the demons in her past and risking everything to keep Carol safe. (978-1-63555-877-7)

Give In to Me by Elle Spencer. Gabriela Talbot never expected to sleep with her favorite author—certainly not after the scathing review she'd given Whitney Ainsworth's latest book. (978-1-63555-910-1)

Hidden Dreams by Shelley Thrasher. A lethal virus and its resulting vision send Texan Barbara Allan and her lovely guide, Dara, on a journey up Cambodia's Mekong River in search of Barbara's mother's mystifying past. (978-1-63555-856-2)

In the Spotlight by Lesley Davis. For actresses Cole Calder and Eris Whyte, their chance at love runs out fast when a fan's adoration turns to obsession. (978-1-63555-926-2)

Origins by Jen Jensen. Jamis Bachman is pulled into a dangerous mystery that becomes personal when she learns the truth of her origins as a ghost hunter. (978-1-63555-837-1)

Pursuit: A Victorian Entertainment by Felice Picano. An intelligent, handsome, ruthlessly ambitious young man who rose from the slums to become the right-hand man of the Lord Exchequer of England will stop at nothing as he pursues his Lord's vanished wife across Continental Europe. (978-1-63555-870-8)

Unrivaled by Radclyffe. Zoey Cohen will never accept second place in matters of the heart, even when her rival is a career, and Declan Black has nothing left to give of herself or her heart. (978-1-63679-013-8)

A Fae Tale by Genevieve McCluer. Dovana comes to terms with her changing feelings for her lifelong best friend and fae, Roze. (978-1-63555-918-7)

Accidental Desperados by Lee Lynch. Life is clobbering Berry, Jaudon, and their long romance. The arrival of directionless baby dyke MJ doesn't help. Can they find their passion again—and keep it? (978-1-63555-482-3)

Always Believe by Aimée. Greyson Walsden is pursuing ordination as an Anglican priest. Angela Arlingham doesn't believe in God. Do they follow their vocation or their hearts? (978-1-63555-912-5)

Best of the Wrong Reasons by Sander Santiago. For Fin Ness and Orion Starr, it takes a funeral to remind them that love is worth living for. (978-1-63555-867-8)

Courage by Jesse J. Thoma. No matter how often Natasha Parsons and Tommy Finch clash on the job, an undeniable attraction simmers just beneath the surface. Can they find the courage to change so love has room to grow? (978-1-63555-802-9)

I Am Chris by R Kent. There's one saving grace to losing everything and moving away. Nobody knows her as Chrissy Taylor. Now Chris can live who he truly is. (978-1-63555-904-0)

The Princess and the Odium by Sam Ledel. Jastyn and Princess Aurelia return to Venostes and join their families in a battle against the dark force to take back their homeland for a chance at a better tomorrow. (978-1-63555-894-4)

The Queen Has a Cold by Jane Kolven. What happens when the heir to the throne isn't a prince or a princess? (978-1-63555-878-4)

The Secret Poet by Georgia Beers. Agreeing to help her brother woo Zoe Blake seemed like a good idea to Morgan Thompson at first...until she realizes she's actually wooing Zoe for herself... (978-1-63555-858-6)

You Again by Aurora Rey. For high school sweethearts Kate Cormier and Sutton Guidry, the second chance might be the only one that matters. (978-1-63555-791-6)